The shining splendor of our Zebra Lovegram logo on the cover of this book reflects the glittering excellence of the story inside. Look for the Zebra Lovegram whenever you buy a historical romance. It's a trademark that guarantees the very best in quality and reading entertainment.

IRRESISTIBLE PASSION

"You beast! You're—you're no gentleman!" Maud cried, as she struggled to dig herself out of the yielding hay.

Alan laughed again and climbed into the bin, dropping on one knee beside her. Catching her hands, he forced her down on her back and imprisoned her hands above her head. His face was very close.

"It's not caning you need, it's kissing. Aye, that and more, much more. You've held yourself back too long." His voice was husky with his swelling need for her.

"Let me go!" Maud cried, writhing in his grip. Instead, he lowered his body over hers, pressing her deeper into the fragrant hay. His lips poised above hers, then slowly, languidly, covered her cries.

Maud fought to resist him, until the soft murmuring of his kiss gradually overcame her, turning her resentment to waves of warm desire. Her body slackened and her hands, released now, slid over his shoulders and caught his silky hair between her fingers. His lips held her prisoner as her body flamed and her arms sought him, drawing him down against her.

PUT SOME PASSION INTO YOUR LIFE... WITH THIS STEAMY SELECTION OF ZEBRA *LOVEGRAMS!*

SEA FIRES   (3899, $4.50/$5.50)
by Christine Dorsey
Spirited, impetuous Miranda Chadwick arrives in the untamed New World prepared for any peril. But when the notorious pirate Gentleman Jack Blackstone kidnaps her in order to fulfill his secret plans, she can't help but surrender — to the shameless desires and raging hunger that his bronzed, lean body and demanding caresses ignite within her!

TEXAS MAGIC   (3898, $4.50/$5.50)
by Wanda Owen
After being ambushed by bandits and saved by a ranchhand, headstrong Texas belle Bianca Moreno hires her gorgeous rescuer as a protective escort. But Rick Larkin does more than guard her body — he kisses away her maidenly inhibitions, and teaches her the secrets of wild, reckless love!

SEDUCTIVE CARESS   (3767, $4.50/$5.50)
by Carla Simpson
Determined to find her missing sister, brave beauty Jessamyn Forsythe disguises herself as a simple working girl and follows her only clues to Whitechapel's darkest alleys... and the disturbingly handsome Inspector Devlin Burke. Burke, on the trail of a killer, becomes intrigued with the ebon-haired lass and discovers the secrets of her silken lips and the hidden promise of her sweet flesh.

SILVER SURRENDER   (3769, $4.50/$5.50)
by Vivian Vaughan
When Mexican beauty Aurelia Mazón saves a handsome stranger from death, she finds herself on the run from the Federales with the most dangerous man she's ever met. And when Texas Ranger Carson Jarrett steals her heart with his intimate kisses and seductive caresses, she yields to an all-consuming passion from which she hopes to never escape!

ENDLESS SEDUCTION   (3793, $4.50/$5.50)
by Rosalyn Alsobrook
Caught in the middle of a dangerous shoot-out, lovely Leona Stegall falls unconscious and awakens to the gentle touch of a handsome doctor. When her rescuer's caresses turn passionate, Leona surrenders to his fiery embrace and savors a night of soaring ecstasy!

Available wherever paperbacks are sold, or order direct from the Publisher. Send cover price plus 50¢ per copy for mailing and handling to Zebra Books, Dept. 4155, 475 Park Avenue South, New York, N.Y. 10016. Residents of New York and Tennessee must include sales tax. DO NOT SEND CASH. For a free Zebra/ Pinnacle catalog please write to the above address.

ASHLEY SNOW

WILD WANTON LOVE

ZEBRA BOOKS
KENSINGTON PUBLISHING CORP.

ZEBRA BOOKS

are published by

Kensington Publishing Corp.
475 Park Avenue South
New York, NY 10016

Copyright © 1993 by Ashley Snow

All rights reserved. No part of this book may be reproduced in any form or by any means without the prior written consent of the Publisher, excepting brief quotes used in reviews.

Zebra, the Z logo, and the Lovegram logo are trademarks of Kensington Publishing Corp.

If you purchased this book without a cover you should be aware that this book is stolen property. It was reported as "unsold and destroyed" to the Publisher and neither the Author nor the Publisher has received any payment for this "stripped book."

First Printing: May, 1993

Printed in the United States of America

*This book is affectionately dedicated to
Pauline, Erin, and Frances.
My sisters and my dearest friends.*

Suffolk, England
1756

Chapter One

"Maud! Come quick. It's the players' coach!"

Maud Mellingham looked up to see her friend, Hetty, smiling at her over the bottom half of the buttery door, her large white mobcap bobbing up and down.

Sitting back on her heels, Maud strained to hear the rattle of the wagon out on the road, and the noisy clamor of the people running alongside as they laughed and called to one another. With a thrill of excitement she scrambled to her knees, then hesitated as she remembered. "But Lady Julia . . ."

Lifting the latch, Hetty threw open the bottom half of the door. "Bother Lady Julia. Besides, I just saw her go inside the house. Come along. If we reach the gate first, we can watch them ride past."

Maud needed no further encouragement. She threw aside her scrub brush and jumped to her feet, not even bothering to smooth her damp skirts. Hetty was already halfway across the courtyard, and Maud had to hurry to catch up with her at the wooden fence, where they both jumped up to stand on the bottom row of slats and lean their arms on the top of the gate, peering down the road. They were a study in contrasts: Hetty, dark-haired and thin, with a long, narrow face already old beyond its years, and Maud, full-figured for her seventeen summers, red-gold hair peeking from beneath her mobcap, her large, vividly blue eyes shining with excitement.

The wagon with its enthusiastic crowd had almost reached the entrance to Squire Bexley's manor house, the horses tossing their gaily colored plumes in nervous response to the loud, cheerful clamour of the apprentices, field hands, serving wenches, and assorted children who scampered along beside the coach.

"Faith, Hetty, isn't it exciting! They're coming here to Thornwood. They're actually going to put on a play in our barn!"

As the painted vehicle drew abreast, Maud's eyes widened with amazement. She had occasionally seen the stages that stopped at the Running Man Inn on their way to and from London, but never had she seen anything as gorgeous as this. With its white and gold paint, it looked like a gypsy wagon. It had its own little house, and the roof was piled high with boxes and barrels and crates. And sitting on top of the whole thing were the players—women with bold eyes who laughed and called down jokes at the apprentices, several lean men in shabby coats with their noses in the air, as though the rabble was beneath their concern. The driver was a thin man with a black hat pulled far down on his face, who looked neither to the left or the right but concentrated on his horses. Sitting beside him was a handsome fellow in a velvet cloak, who waved his plumed hat and smiled down at the crowd. As the wagon slowed to make the turn inside the gate, his eyes caught Maud's and, for an instant, lingered in surprise. He gave her a wide grin and swept his hat in a bow that surely was meant expressly for her.

Maud quickly looked away, blushing with embarrassment. Yet her blue eyes glinted with eager anticipation, as she jumped down to join the crowd swarming around the coach as it made a wide swing onto the path leading into Squire Bexley's courtyard.

Hetty jumped down beside her. "Oh, la, there's Lady Julia coming out of the house. We'd better get back before she sees us."

"But maybe she'll ask us to help."

"You know better than that. If you haven't finished that buttery floor, you won't be allowed to do anything else. Come on. We'll have a chance to slip out to the barn later and look around."

Much as she hated to admit it, Maud knew Hetty was right. If only Squire Bexley had been here to greet the players, things might have been different. The Squire was good-natured about occasionally allowing his servants a little freedom, though never when his dour-faced wife was around.

"After the floor is dry, I've got to scour the shelves. But I'll come and get you once I've finished," Maud said, and ducked behind the stone root cellar to take a path which led to the buttery by a back way.

"I'll be in the kitchen," Hetty called back.

By this time Lady Julia had made her way through the crowd to speak to the handsome fellow in the plumed hat, and Maud was able to slip past the courtyard and back to her drudgery without being noticed. As she dropped to her knees and sloshed the water on the stones, her mind wandered deliciously over the thrilling sight of the beautiful coach, and the wonderful people who rode on it. She had heard Cook and several of the older servants speak scathingly of such people, saying that actors were no better than they ought to be. Yet to her they seemed touched by magic. How wonderful to put on beautiful clothes and pretend to be someone you were not. To speak lines of poetry that moved others to tears. And best of all, to ride atop that beautiful wagon, visiting all kinds of exciting places. To see the world and experience all its wonders!

Yet she had long ago learned to keep such thoughts to herself. "Don't know why anyone 'd want to bother," Cook had remarked scathingly, when Maud expressed her desire to see more of the world than Thornwood. "Oi lived fifty year in this village, forty of 'em 'ere in this kitchen workin' for Squoire. Oi never been no further than the Running Man Tavern on t'edge of the village. Nor do Oi ever want to be."

Maud had been appalled at the casual way Cook made such an admission, which to her was little better than a sentence of death. And yet she knew very well that most of the servants in Squire Bexley's household had never been farther into the world than the fields at the edge of the village. Most of them took it for granted that she, too, would go no further.

Her hand paused over the brush as she recalled the rest of Cook's advice. "Marry young Robbie and raise a family, lass. That's wha' God intended for a sweet-faced young thing loike ye'self. And stay away from the Squoire. He's a good enough man, but he's got the busiest hands in England!"

She backed up, washing the floor up to the open doorway, where she dumped the brushes in the pail and lifted it by the handle. Outside the sun was warm on her hands, red and raw from the strong lye soap. She paused at the well and rinsed them, resting against the stones briefly to look longingly across the yard toward the barn, where the wagon had pulled up. People were moving in and out, carting the crates and barrels off the wagon.

The truth was, Squire had always been rather decent to her, smiling genially when he passed through the yard, pinching her cheek playfully at the Christmas fetes, and allowing her, one memorable May, half a day off to visit the fair in the village. Not like his sour-faced wife, who went around with a holier-than-everybody attitude and was forever looking for some reason to scold the servants. Lady Julia had even once taken a cane to Hetty, though never to Maud. She was proud, was Lady Julia. Hetty had explained that their mistress was a daughter to Lord Bambridge, who owned nearby Denton Hall, a much larger and more elegant manor house than Thornwood. Lady Julia thus had a right to be proud.

"Well, young lady. Enjoying the warm day, are you?"

She was so absorbed in her thoughts, she hadn't heard the horse ambling by until the man spoke. Glancing up quickly, she recognized Lord Bambridge smiling down at her. Speak of the devil!

"Oh! Good morning, sir," she said, as she began hurriedly drying her hands on her apron. She felt a red flush climbing her cheeks.

"It's Maud Mellingham, isn't it?" his Lordship inquired kindly. "How are you, young Maud? Is the Squire at home?"

Lord Bambridge sat easily on his white horse, the long tails of his gold-laced, blue coat spilling over the saddle, one ringed hand resting casually on his hip. The bright sunlight turned the white wig he wore to spun silver. Yet, for all his grandeur, his manner was courteous, even to a kitchen maid.

"I don't think so, sir, but Lady Julia is inside. Shall I go and tell her you're here?"

"No, no. Don't bother. I'll tell her myself. You have enough to do, I'm sure." His eyes strayed down the pathway to the commotion near the barn. "Wonderful things happening here, aren't they? I suppose you'll be attending the play tonight."

"Oh, yes, sir. Squire Bexley has said we all may go. It's truly quite exciting, sir. We're all looking forward to it."

"Ramsey," Bambridge called to the man who had ridden up behind him. Looking around, Maud recognized the thin, pale face of Lawyer Samuel Ramsey, a man she knew well since he frequently visited Squire at the Manor House. With his narrow face, pursed lips, ever-present black suit and grizzled wig, he often seemed comical until she remembered his profession. He had a way of looking through her as though she wasn't there, but that could have been because he was so frequently absorbed with a nagging cold. Even now he held a very large cambric handkerchief to his long nose.

"Do you hear this young maid?" Bambridge went on.

"She speaks very well for a servant, doesn't she? Your parents must have raised you well, Maud."

"Yes, sir, they did. They were good people, but they died in the plague ten years ago. That's when I came here to Thornwood."

"Yes, I recall. Well, Maud, I hope you enjoy the play tonight, for you're not likely to see another any time soon. Traveling players don't come to this part of the country very often. Come along, Ramsey."

Bambridge rode away on his big white horse with the lawyer following, sitting awkwardly on his skinny brown mare. Maud looked longingly after them, wondering if she dared slip off to the barn and watch the fun. Not yet, she decided. It might be better to wait until things quieted down a bit.

Lord Bambridge found his daughter in the summer parlor, standing as far away as possible from the light that streamed through the twelve-paned window. One of the young maids was busily polishing a silver tea set, while Julia, hovering like a predator, watched for the slightest indication that it was not being done right. It was one of Julia's traits that he liked the least.

"Good morning, daughter," he said, throwing his hat on a nearby chair. "That's quite a commotion in your yard. Half the countryside is agog with excitement over tonight's performance."

Julia reluctantly turned from supervising Hetty to give her father a perfunctory kiss on his cheek. "Good morning, Father. I didn't expect you to come gawking. All this to-do over a decadent troupe of actors!"

"Actually I came to see your good husband, but was told he's not here. And don't be too hard on the gawkers. It's little enough excitement they get in their hard lives."

Julia sat primly on the edge of a straight-backed cane chair. "As always, you are too kind, Father. I've never seen a shabbier bunch of gypsies than that so-called troupe. If I had my way, they'd be sent packing within the hour. But nothing would do Squire Bexley, but that they use our house and our barn, and half the countryside be invited to watch. It's disgusting!"

Lord Bambridge shook his head. He had long ago resigned himself to the fact that his eldest daughter had inherited all the coldness and stiffness of his dead wife, while receiving almost nothing of his own more moderate temper. Lifting the tails of his coat, he settled into a chair opposite Julia. "Well, Squire always did like a bit of fun, and you can't blame a man for that. Perhaps I'll just wait here for him. How long will he be, do you think?"

Julia turned her face away to avoid revealing the scowl this news brought on. How like her father to drop in unannounced and settle himself down in the parlor for an hour or two, where he would effectively prevent her from completing her daily list of chores.

"He should be back within the hour," she said grudgingly. "Would you like something while you wait? Tea, perhaps, or ale?"

"A little port would be nice. Ramsey, give me those papers and have a seat on the settee. Bring a glass for Ramsey, too, Julia."

"Hetty, fetch the port and two glasses for my father. Hurry there, you lazy girl."

"But, Miss Julia, the silver . . ."

"Carry the silver to the pantry and finish it there. And make sure you do it right, or it will have to be done all over again." She watched as Hetty bobbed a curtsey and picked up the heavily laden tray to leave the room. "Servants! You have to be at them all the time, and even then they don't do half their work. They are my most severe affliction."

"Perhaps if you were a little less hard on them, my dear, your life and theirs would be easier. I have always felt a little kindness goes farther than a harsh word or blow."

Julia looked down her sharp nose at her father.

"Their lives are not hard. They are cared for, fed, housed and clothed by their betters. In return they give slovenly work and decadent behavior, and it gets worse every year. But how would you understand? It was Mama who always kept things running smoothly at Denton Hall. Because of her strictness, you could afford to be soft with the servants."

Lord Bambridge picked up a clay pipe from the side table, and stroked the long stem carefully with his fingers. "Dear Julia. I can always count on a lecture from you. But this is such a pleasant day, I shall not allow it to bother me. Come now, tell me the latest gossip. You always have an ear to the ground. Who's having an affair with whom? How much did the Squire lose at the horse race last week? When are you going down to London?"

"Really, Father," Julia sniffed disdainfully. "You do go on about the most foolish things."

Half an hour later Squire Bexley rode into the courtyard of his rambling country house on the broad back of his favorite mare. He had been in the saddle since early that morning, and every muscle and joint was loudly complaining. With a grunt, he heaved himself down just as Maud came around the corner from the buttery, carrying a bucket filled with damp brushes.

"Here, girl," Squire called. "Where's that groom, Jody? He knows he's supposed to collect my horse when I ride up."

Maud set the bucket on the cobbles and wiped at her brow with her sleeve. "He's probably still at the barn watching the actors unload their wagon, sir. I'll be happy to take the horse down myself, if you want."

Squire Bexley straightened his coat and hitched up his belly. Though he was only of middle years, his excess weight and fondness for hard drink made him look nearly as old as his father-in-law. "And what do you know about horses, eh? Aren't you afraid of them?

Most serving girls are."

"Oh no, sir," Maud said, smiling as she reached for the mare's bridle. "I grew up around horses. Of course, they were working ones, not grand creatures for riding. But I've often seen your mare in the barn and often petted her." Gently she stroked the mare's soft nose. "See, sir, she knows me. She's very gentle with me."

Squire Bexley stepped back, watching the horse nuzzling the girl's arm. "That's more than I can say for myself," he said half-jokingly. "Let's see, you're . . . Maud! That's right, isn't it?"

Maud gave him a warm smile. "That's right, sir. Maud Mellingham."

"But last I remember, you were just a child. You've grown up while I wasn't looking."

"I've been here at Thornwood for ten years, sir. Since my parents died in the last plague."

"Of course. Now I remember." Squire Bexley put a pudgy finger under Maud's chin and lifted her face. His tongue went suddenly dry, and he licked his lips. "What are you doing scrubbing floors, Maud, my girl. You ought to be in the house. You're old enough now, and . . . well built." Extremely well built, he added to himself. What an enticing morsel, with her firm breasts bulging above her scanty shift, and her rounded hips evident beneath the layers of her skirts. Her young skin was like poured cream, emphasizing the deep blue of her large eyes and the pink of her deliciously curved lips. Tendrils of red-gold hair peeked from beneath her wide cap and lay damp on her white forehead. The Squire found himself suddenly filled with a familiar, growing excitement in his lower parts. "Yes, I shall speak to Mistress Julia at once. We must have you in the house, my girl."

Maud began to grow uncomfortable. Squire Bexley didn't yell or curse at his servants, or raise his hand to them. Yet his manner toward her had always been casual and offhand, as though he was not really aware that she existed. Now his intense gaze and glinting eyes were enough to bring all of Cook's warnings rushing back to her mind.

"I'll just take the mare down to the barn," she said, leading the horse away.

"Yes, do that," Squire Bexley answered, and stood watching as Maud led the horse down the hill toward the outbuildings behind the house. He was going to have to work out a plan, he mused. Julia knew of his weakness for young serving girls, and it was going to be difficult to find Maud a place inside the house without arousing his wife's suspicion. Perhaps the girl had escaped his wife's attention as she had his own, growing up overnight from a gawky, skinny child into this luscious, rounded, delectable delight. Well, he would find a way to have her. He always did, and Julia be damned!

The horses had been turned out to pasture to allow the troupe to store their paraphernalia in the barn until that evening's performance. As Maud led the Squire's mare toward the stables, she saw the actors walking by another path up to the house, where she knew Cook was waiting to serve them refreshments in the kitchen. The groom, Jody, was one of the stragglers who followed them, but he broke away when he recognized the mare, and ran to take the reins from Maud.

"Oh, Lor'," he cried. "I never saw Squire ride in. It'll be the switch for my back for this, as ever God spoke! Give her over. I'll put her out in the lower field."

Maud was disappointed, for she had set her hopes on getting inside the barn. "Can I help you unsaddle her?"

"No. I'll put up the tack. Thanks, Maud, for bringin' 'er down."

He pulled the mare around and headed for the tack room near the barn, while Maud stood watching. It seemed strange that there were none of the other stablehands about, until she remembered that they had all gone to gawk at the actors. She knew she ought to hurry back to the courtyard, but the barn was so enticingly near, she could not bear to go. She stood rooted to the path, while Jody pulled off the saddle gear and led the mare away toward the fields. Glancing around to make certain no one was watching, Maud ran toward the wide, open doors of the barn.

It was dark inside and she stood for a moment, waiting for her eyes to become accustomed to the gloom. Like a metamorphosis transforming before her, the customary order of the barn took on a magical hue. Maud stepped forward into the enormous clutter that had been deposited haphazardly around. There were tubs and barrels overflowing with gauzy, glittering clothes. Scattered among them lay plumed helmets, shields, and spears. She gave a small gasp as she recognized a full chariot, or what seemed to be a chariot until she stepped closer and saw it was only a wooden cutout. Propped among the stalls were more wondrous concoctions — a mermaid's tail, enormous gilded wings, and painted silhouettes of trees and columns. At the back of the building, ropes had been strung and hung with clothes, to shake out the wrinkles from traveling. And in the rafters, a dragon perched among huge cutouts of clouds.

Staring up at the dragon, Maud turned a full circle, her mouth gaping and her eyes wide with wonder. She had never seen anything so marvelous, or so beautiful. Then she heard a bird chirping.

The singing was very near. Looking around, she saw the small, colorful creature hopping about in a tall wire cage sitting on the floor.

"What a pretty thing," Maud cried and stepped closer to the cage. She was about to kneel and stick her finger through the bars to attract the bird, when the frenzied trilling suddenly took on the form of human speech.

"Chirp, chirp, chirp . . . good morrow, miss, chirp, chirp . . ."

Maud gasped and stepped back, staring at the little

creature hopping about inside the cage. When the chirping grew louder and more animated, she began to think she had imagined the words.

"Chirp, chirp . . . you're a pretty thing, too, chirp, chirp . . ."

All at once the magical barn was transformed into a sombre, threatening place. Maud turned and headed for the door.

"Chirrp, chirrip, don't run away, pretty miss. I won't hurt you . . ."

The hairs on the back of her neck came alive. Keeping close to the open door, Maud turned, intrigued in spite of herself. "What kind of bird are you?"

"Chirp, chirp . . . just a fellow, chirp, chirp, who makes words and songs. Please, chirp, chirp, come talk to me . . ."

"I never heard a bird who could speak words," she said, and took a few steps closer to the cage. The little bird kept hopping about but—after all, Maud reasoned—it was very small and could not possibly be a threat. And it was wonderful the way it could speak. She inched closer.

"Chirrrip . . . what's your name, chirrip . . ."

"Maud. Maud Mellingham." She leaned down closer to the cage.

"Chirp, chirp. Maud. Pretty name, pretty name, chirp, chirp. My name is Everarde. Everarde, chir . . . r . . . rup!"

Maud knelt beside the cage and stared in astonishment. "Why, you're not a real bird at all," she cried. "You're a painted toy. What is this?"

"Oh my. We have been found out," said a man's voice behind her. She jumped to her feet, and turned around to see a tall figure unbend from the shadows and step into the light. His voice dropped to a normal register. "But you were fooled for a few moments there. Admit it."

Maud took a few steps back, keeping her eyes on the man whom she recognized at once as the fellow with the plumed hat from the coach. Seeing him so close, he was even more handsome than from a distance: tall, broad-shouldered, graceful in his motions, with dark hair that fell to his shoulders, smiling green eyes deeply set in his long lean face, a firm jaw, and a wide, shapely mouth that was as strong as it was inviting.

"Did . . . did you make those sounds?" she asked in a strangled voice.

The man laughed. "Allow me to present myself," he said, giving her a graceful bow. "Alan Desmond, mistress, at your service. And alas, no, it was not I who created those magical sounds, but that slovenly fellow over there behind Apollo's chariot. I only wish I was able to make that little bird perform so wonderfully, but, as of yet, I have not mastered the art. However," he added archly, "I have mastered many others."

Maud turned to see another gentleman step from the shadows behind the wire cage. He was smaller than Alan Desmond, and slimmer, and he wore a neatly tied, gray bagwig. His hands were as delicate and graceful as a woman's, as he waved them while giving her a formal bow. When he raised his head, she caught the merry twinkle in a pair of faded gray eyes. "Jeremy Oaks, mistress. Your servant."

"You both played a trick on me," she said, trying to sound offended when actually she felt relieved and delighted. "That was not gentlemanly of you."

"On the contrary," Alan Desmond said, perching one hip on a nearby barrel, "we merely gave you a preview of the wonders you will see later this evening. You will see them, won't you? You are coming to the performance?"

"Oh yes. We've all been given permission to attend. But how did you do it? What is the trick?"

"Oh, we never reveal the secrets of our magic," Alan said, eyeing Maud. "Do we, Jeremy?"

The smaller man chuckled. "Well, let us just say that a magician can do wonders imitating birdcalls with a little talent and a piece of onionskin."

"And Jeremy here is the most talented imitator in

the whole of England."

Jeremy bobbed Desmond a bow. "You're too kind, sir."

"Yes, I am. And in return you can do me the kindness of leaving Mistress Maud here with me, while you go up to the house for your refreshment. I'm certain anyone who appreciates the paraphernalia of the actor's craft the way Maud does, would like to hear what all these things are for. I'll stay and explain them to her."

Jeremy looked from Maud to Alan and back to Maud. Then he shrugged. "Very well, Mister Alan. But don't forget, we've yet to get the stage ready."

"I know."

Jeremy slipped out of the shadows and toward the open door while Maud, still peering upward, walked around the cluttered floor of the barn. "What are those funny-looking things?" she asked, pointing to two long, round, metal cylinders with handles at each end, that were propped against the wall.

"Those are the rollers with which we make the sea toss and foam," Alan answered, making motions of the waves with his hands. "It's quite effective."

"And that?" she asked, pointing to the outline of the chariot.

"That is Cupid's noble flying machine. His noble steed is in front of it — the dragon complete with clouds. It doesn't look like much close up, but it's very believable when seen from the pit. Here, try this on."

He reached out to set a helmet festoned with several huge red plumes on top of her mobcap. Maud gave him a delighted smile and pulled it down over her forehead.

"How do I look?"

"Absolutely enchanting," he breathed.

"But not like a Roman general?"

"No. More like a perfectly lovely young maiden. You're quite pretty, you know. Have you ever thought of going on the stage?"

Maud felt her cheeks growing warm and reached up

to remove the helmet, which was much lighter than she had expected. "Of course not. Actresses are wantons with no reputation to speak of. Oh," she cried, looking up suddenly and blushing even deeper, "I didn't mean to insult you . . ."

To her relief he threw back his head and laughed. "You've been listening to too many sermons, my girl. They say the same thing of many a serving wench."

"It wasn't a sermon. It was Cook who warned me."

Alan reached out and lightly twirled his finger around the end of a long curl that fell over her breast. "Oh, Cook. And I'll wager she's an old hag who never had a man in all her fifty years."

Suddenly self-conscious, Maud lowered her eyes and stepped back from him. "Perhaps. But she's wise, and she's always been a good friend to me."

Casually she moved to an upended barrel standing by itself and perched on it. Alan didn't follow her. He was beginning to realize that this girl was younger and more naive than he had thought when he first saw her. And what a beauty she was! A perfect oval face, skin like fine porcelain, huge sapphire eyes filled with a childlike wonder. What possibilities she offered, he thought. Her freshness and loveliness would grace any stage in England. Keeping a distance between them, he leaned against a cluttered stack of musical instruments and folded his arms across his chest. He was pleased to see Maud relax a little.

"Since you travel around with the players, I suppose you must visit many wonderful places," she said shyly.

"Oh yes, all the grand cities. York, Bristol, London . . ."

"London! How wonderful," she cried, her eyes shining. "Tell me what it's like."

"What would you like to know?"

"Are the streets really made of gold? Are there lots of fine palaces, and are they as large and as beautiful as they say? Do the women all wear gorgeous frocks, and wigs as tall as a butter churn?"

Alan laughed at her enthusiasm. "No, the streets are definitely *not* made of gold! They are cobbled, and dirtier than any yard here at Thornwood. But the palaces are very large and grander than any others in the world. And the ladies in their frocks quite take your breath away. Some of their wigs are even taller than a butter churn."

"Taller!"

"Yes. As tall as two of these drums on top of one another."

"But how do they keep them from toppling over?"

"It takes careful maneuvering, especially with those wooden pattens they are fond of wearing. Of course, most of them don't try to walk—they're carried."

"Carried! How? In the arms of a footman?"

"No. They ride in fancy sedan chairs supported on two poles, which are carried by two stout men. They clutter up the streets something fierce."

"Why, I never heard of anything so silly. Why don't they ride a horse, if they don't want to walk?"

Alan laughed. "That would be rather difficult because of the huge side hoops on their dresses. In fact, I don't think they could manage it at all. There are other wonderful things in London, you know. There is a garden where everyone goes to walk in the evening amid marble statues, with orchestras playing music deep in the ground, and where you can drink tea in the little temples set along the walks. And there are illuminations in the evenings more spectacular than anything you've ever seen at Thornwood. There is the opera where everything is sung, not spoken, and cathedrals big enough to put the whole of Thornwood House inside. And much, much more. You shall have to come to London someday, and see all these wonders for yourself."

"Oh, I should like that more than anything in the world." Her face fell as she remembered how seldom a servant would ever have the chance to leave her village for any reason. "But I don't see how it can happen. None of Squire's servants leave Thornwood."

Alan glanced toward the open door when he heard the other actors laughing and talking, as they walked down the path from the house. He reached for Maud's hand and pulled her from her perch, slipping an arm around her waist. Maud gave a start of surprise. She was uncomfortable and self-conscious standing so close to this attractive man, yet at the same time her body tingled with a delicious warmth that was as delightful as it was unfamiliar. His face was so near hers, she could clearly see the thick lashes that fringed his eyes and the tiny laugh lines that creased the corners.

Alan leaned closer. She felt the warmth of his breath on her cheek. "I must go back to the house," she said, not daring to look directly into his eyes.

He was encouraged by the small shiver he felt go through her body. "You are coming to the play tonight, aren't you?"

"Oh, yes. I wouldn't miss it for anything."

"And the frolic afterward?"

Maud tried to move, but his arm pinned her close to his hard body. "Yes. Squire has said we may all attend."

"Good. He leaned forward and kissed her luscious lips, soft as down and sweet to his taste. "We will have more time to talk tonight. I have many more wonders of London to describe to you."

Lightly his fingers coursed up her laced bodice to softly touch her breast. Her body shivered, and beneath the thin fabric of her shirt, her nipples stood erect and firm. She felt herself blushing down to her toes. "You mean there's more?"

"Oh, much more." His arm slackened, and she slipped from him and ran to the door just as several people entered from outside. She was dimly conscious of two women in tawdry gowns and three men behind them. One of the women stopped and stared, first at her, then, swiftly, back at Alan. When she turned to Maud again, there was blatant hostility in her hard black eyes.

More self-conscious than ever, Maud ran from the barn and down the path back to the house, not stopping at all until she reached the privacy of the buttery. She closed both halves of the door and leaned against the splintered wood.

She was gasping for breath from her run, but her heart was singing within her. Unexpectedly she had enjoyed a great adventure. She had been given an astonishing look at what lay behind the stage of a playhouse, and heard wonderful descriptions of a great city like London. And best of all, she had been kissed by the most beautiful man she ever met.

What a glorious day it had turned out to be!

Chapter Two

That evening when Maud stepped into the barn, she had to blink her eyes to believe the transformation that had taken place. The far end of the building was bare and open, and separated from the rest by a large rectangular, towering frame that marked off the stage. Several chairs were placed just in front for Squire, Lady Julia, Lord Bambridge, and any other gentry who might turn up. Behind them several rows of benches waited for the better townsfolk and the house servants. The rest of the audience, including Maud, crowded the rear and filled up the empty stalls.

But the most amazing part of the transformation was the light. Never had Maud seen the old utilitarian barn so brightly illuminated. A row of lamps burned in front of the rectangular frame that marked the stage, while suspended from the rafters was a large tin chandelier ablaze with light. The effect was so magical, that she didn't even mind the smoke or the oppressive odor of burning tallow.

Even the actors seemed transformed. Maud barely recognized the face of Diana, the goddess of chastity, as the hard woman who had stared at her so belligerently that morning. And the portly man in the long coat with the plumed helmet atop his wig, seemed the very picture of majesty, though she remembered him looking quite shabby earlier.

Alan Desmond, looking more handsome than ever, stepped out to give the prologue; watching him, Maud's heart fluttered so wildly with excitement that she did not comprehend much of what he said. After the play began, she watched for him with every new entrance, but he did not appear again, and soon she was so caught up in the roll of the waves, Cupid flying among the clouds drawn by a fire-breathing dragon, the rumbling of thunder, and even the flash of lightning, she forgot everything else. Most of the long speeches went right over her head, but she didn't mind. A magical world had come suddenly to life before her eyes, and she was enchanted.

During the second act, when the little bird in its big wire cage suddenly began spouting words among its songs, she looked around smugly, wondering if anyone else knew it was done by a clever little man with a piece of onionskin. Everyone else was either openmouthed with wonder or laughing delightedly, and for the first time in her life, she felt a little superior. It was a pleasant sensation.

By the time the story came to a close, the clapping and cheering shook the rafters. Everyone except Lady Julia was delighted with the fantasy of the play, and admired the effects the machinery had produced. During the short commotion that followed the last bow, everything was cleared away from the main section of the barn, and tables groaning under all sorts of good foods were set near the door. Kegs of ale were broken open, and the fiddlers Squire had hired from the village took their places. Some of the lamps had to be put out to prevent an accidental fire from starting during the vigorous dancing, but that only made the barn more cozy. Maud noticed that many of the servants were already pairing off and heading for the shadowy corners.

She spotted Alan standing near the stage talking to the Squire and his wife, and inched her way closer.

"That was clever writing, young man," she heard Lady Julia say, "but your effects need far more thought. It was too easy to see how they work."

Maud took a closer look at Alan as it dawned on her that he had written this wonderful play. So he was not just an actor, he was a playwright as well. What a talented, intelligent, beautiful man!

"Speak for yourself, Julia," Squire boomed. "I couldn't see how it was being done. And I didn't care, either, I was so swept along by the story."

"You are very kind, sir," Alan said, giving the Squire a short bow.

Lord Bambridge fingered the ribbon of his fob and gave Alan a searching look. "I have seen the players at Drury Lane and the Haymarket many times. Your plays can stand against theirs, I feel, even to the great Cibber. Your actors, of course, are nowhere near so accomplished as the London players."

"It is not easy, my lord, to convince actors to leave London."

"No, I suppose not. As to the content of your play, I suspect you are flirting with danger just a little. Am I right?"

Alan gave him a sardonic smile. "Your lordship is too clever."

"I would caution you to make your references a trifle more oblique. Of course, out here in the country it does not matter so much. But this play on a London stage might well earn you a room in the tower. Just a friendly warning, you understand. You're a talented fellow, and I should hate to see your gifts go to waste."

Alan bowed again. "You are kind to say so, my lord, and I shall certainly heed your warning."

Glancing up he spotted Maud standing just behind the group. "And now, if you will excuse me," he said, backing away from them to go to her.

"What did Lord Bambridge mean?" Maud asked as he took her arm.

"Oh, nothing important. He was just showing off."

The music struck up its tinny refrain, while around them couples began forming lines for a reel. There was so much laughter and noise, Maud had barely been able to hear Alan's answer. "Do you want to dance?" he shouted down at her.

"Do you?" she started to say, before her arm was grabbed from behind. Turning she saw Squire Bexley grinning at her.

"Maud, you lovely little creature. You must give your generous employer a turn on the floor tonight! Come along."

Maud looked frantically at Alan, who stepped up to her. "I had already asked, sir, but since it is your frolic, if you insist, you shall have the honor."

"Oh, indeed, I do insist," the Squire said, yanking Maud toward the middle of the floor. She looked back at Alan and was reassured by his smile. After all, it *was* the Squire's party, and she did owe him at least one turn on the floor. Everyone knew his proud wife would never lower herself so far as to dance a reel, and by the night's end Squire would have partnered every girl there.

It turned out to be not so bad after all. There was much stomping and laughing, not the least of it from Squire himself. Everyone, servants and gentry alike, threw themselves into the merriment, intent on making the most of the opportunity for a little fun. Even Alan got drawn in, pulled in to the reel by one of the actresses from the play. He ended up in the same set with Maud, and made the most of the times they were thrown together, especially when the men had to try for a kiss. She received a light peck on the cheek and a meaningful glance that promised more later from Alan, and a very moist, demanding smack from the Squire.

The steps had barely ended before Alan had her hand, and was pulling her outside.

"That's very warm work," he said, as he slipped an arm around her waist and drew her down one of the paths that led toward the pastures.

"Is that why you wanted to go outside?" Maud said archly.

"No. You know it isn't." At the first hayrick he fell down into the straw and pulled her down with him. Maud was glad to stop and rest, until she heard a giggle from the other side of the haystack and saw two dark shadows detach themselves from it. As she recognized her friend, Hetty, and one of the stableboys, she began to feel uncomfortable. Deliberately she settled in the hay with some distance between herself and Alan. To her surprise, he let her.

She lay on her back, looking up into the brilliantly starred night, and sighed. "I don't think I've ever been so happy."

"It becomes you," Alan said thoughtfully, leaning on one elbow to look down at her. In truth, she was even more beautiful in the moonlight than inside the brightly lit barn. He was surprised by a strange sense of awe. He had long ago decided that life had made him too jaded to ever be moved by a woman's innocence again, yet here he was, barely able to breathe. The sweet smell of the hay was refreshing after the heavy, sweaty odors of the barn. In the distance the fiddle could be heard playing, its melodies now and then obscured by the laughter of the dancers. As Hetty and her stableboy moved away, a quiet settled around them that made the night even more delicious.

"And are you not happy living here at Thornwood?" he asked, turning on his back to look up at the sky.

"Oh, it's not so bad. I've worked in the kitchens since I was seven, so I'm used to it. Squire is good to his servants. It's only his wife that makes our lives miserable. I guess that's because she's so miserable herself."

Alan put his hands behind his head and stared up at the stars. He was beginning to feel relaxed himself after the rigors of the day. "In truth, she looks like she would lead a husband a merry life. She's a veritable Katherina Minola."

"Who is Katherina Minola?"

"A character in a play. If you saw more of them you'd certainly know of Katherina, for she's a famous shrew."

"Squire says he may have me moved into the house, which would be easier work. I think I'd like that."

"Humph. I'd watch out for that Squire, if I were you. He looks at you as though he would like to eat you."

"Now that's strange. Cook is always warning me about him, too, yet for most of my life, he has barely noticed me." Until recently, she thought, remembering the strange looks he had given her by the well.

"Another of Cook's famous warnings. But this time she's right. Really, Maud, you are the most innocent thing I've met in many a day. Don't you know what the Squire is after?"

Maud sat up suddenly. "I don't know what you mean."

"Have you ever known a man? Been kissed? Thrown into the hay?"

Smoothing her skirts, Maud tried to think how to answer. The truth was, she *had* never known a man, at least not in the sense she suspected Alan meant. And the few quick kisses she had received from the stableboys or potboys were more annoying than enjoyable. Certainly they were not like the one Alan had given her earlier, which she had felt down to her toes.

Alan sat up, clasping his hands around his knees. "No, I don't think you have, though how you managed to stay so innocent while growing up as a servant on a farm is more than I can fathom."

"Well, the truth is . . . no, it sounds too silly."

"Go on, please."

"The truth is, I've always wanted more than to be pulled down behind the door, or forced into a hastily arranged wedding to a poor farmer. I suppose it sounds arrogant, but I always felt different from the others, even from my friend, Hetty. To take that path and throw my hat over the windmill that way, would make me like them, with no future and no hope."

Alan studied her face in the moonlight, the shadows that made crevices on her cheeks and heightened her wide innocent eyes and perfectly sculptured lips. Long tendrils of her hair framed her heart-shaped face and sloped over the swell of her ruffled bodice. He felt the strong stirring of desire as he watched her, and yet something about her held him back. He had to smile at himself, for he would have had any other woman on her back in the deep hay before now.

"How did you learn to speak so much better than the others?"

"By working at it. When I came to Thornwood as a child, I noticed that all the important people spoke clearly and correctly, and I decided there and then I was going to be like them. It took a lot of work and I earned a lot of teasing, but I did it. Now nobody even notices."

Alan was intrigued. "You did that on your own?"

"Yes. I used to practice reading from the penny plays, and that helped a lot."

"You can read, too?" he said with surprise.

"Not really well, but enough to make out most of the words."

Alan laughed and lay back with his fingers laced

beneath his head. "Upon my honor, you are truly amazing, Maud Mellingham. But I'm surprised you ever found penny plays around here, with that harridan of a Squire's wife. I should have thought she wouldn't allow them on the place."

"Oh, she doesn't know anything about them! Squire Bexley loves the plays, and he brings a new one home nearly every week. He was the one who insisted your company should come here. It is one of the few times he has overruled her. He usually throws the plays out after he has read them, and one day I found them and kept them instead. Now I look for them every week."

"What about the better writers? Have you ever read Shakespeare?"

"Indeed yes! When I went to the Glebe School before my parents died, we used to recite passages aloud. I loved it, though I didn't always understand them."

She leaned back on her elbow, studying him. "Do your players perform Shakespeare's plays?"

"Why, we wouldn't be professionals if we didn't. Every company performs Shakespeare. But the quality of our performance is sadly lacking when it comes to most of the great dramas, so I prefer to keep to the lighter plays."

"Which you write yourself."

"As a matter of fact, yes. It's not unusual, you know. At the moment England is teeming with playwrights. Besides, I happen to think my efforts are extremely good."

"I thought so, too. At least, I liked the one we saw tonight. But how did you get to be a playwright? I've told you all about me. I'd like to hear something about you."

"There isn't much to tell that would interest you. I'm just a wandering player, who happened to visit Drury Lane one evening to see the great Garrick as

34

Macbeth, and realized I would never come close to being that good an actor. I decided then and there that I would prefer to direct and write plays rather than act in them."

"You've been to Drury Lane! How wonderful! Tell me more about London."

Alan laughed but willingly launched into a description of London's theaters, particularly the one his company was headed for at the end of this tour. Maud's enthusiasm and interest kept him talking much longer than he intended, and by the time a slow gray dawn began to creep over the fields, he realized with a start that his seduction had never taken place. Maud had eventually succumbed to sleep and had nestled in the crook of his arm with her head against his shoulder, her soft breathing warm against the thin fabric of his shirt. She appeared so young and virginal, that he could not believe he hadn't even wanted to take advantage of her. In his experience, most pretty young serving girls expected him to take advantage! Yet how different Maud was from most young serving girls, he thought, as he lightly smoothed a long strand of golden hair across her forehead.

When Jeremy crawled over the edge of the haystack to tell Alan that they had better be getting the wagon ready to leave, he looked at Maud sleepily picking the hay from her hair and shook his head. Alan preferred not to disillusion his friend. No one would believe he hadn't had the girl.

In two hours the barn was cleared of all the players' paraphernalia, and the wagon was piled high. Just before the caravan was ready to pull out of the yard, Maud walked out in the courtyard carrying her basket of the morning's egg collection, and watched as Alan gave last-minute directions.

It was all just as yesterday — Jeremy on the driver's seat with his hat pulled low, the women looking tawdry without their glittering costumes and heavy paint, sitting high atop the pile, the other men taking their places alongside, and Alan checking everything before mounting the wagon.

And yet how different it all was. Now she knew the little driver was a clever conjurer, the women were actually jealous and hard, and the grubby-looking barrels and crates carried the means to magically transform ordinary places into wonderful other worlds.

And Alan, that handsome man in his leather coat and high boots, his hair pulled back in a queue, so obviously in command, was the first man who had really kissed her, who had made her feel desire, who had taken the time to open up new worlds for her. She knew she would never be the same person again, now that she had known him.

She waited, leaning against the cold stones of the buttery, filled with a terrible sadness that he was going out of her life after so short a time, probably forever. And then he was there in front of her. He put his hand under her chin and tipped up her face.

"Goodbye, my sweet little Maud," he said, and lowered his head to touch her lips with his. Maud felt the moist warmth of them. Her body began to tingle with the animal magnetism of his nearness, his firm body pressed against hers. His mouth moved sensuously against her flesh, and her lips parted with the singing of her body. Then he lifted his head, his arms tightening around her, holding her trembling frame. There was a strange surprise in the look he gave her, almost a wariness. He squeezed her once more, then stepped back.

She could not speak. Her eyes filled with tears and she hoped the noisy chatter of the people around the caravan would keep anyone from seeing her distress.

"If you ever get to London, come and find me," he

added, but she knew how unlikely that was, and it only made her feel more forlorn.

He quickly raised her hand to his lips, as the players began to make catcalls and ribald remarks from their places by the wagon. Then he vaulted up onto the seat and waved his hat jauntily to the crowd as they rolled out of the yard.

Maud fled to the silent buttery, where she would not have to bear the knowing looks of her fellow servants or listen to their gossip. Everyone assumed that she and Alan had made love in that haystack, and they would never believe that nothing of the kind had happened. Alan Desmond had been a perfect gentleman. He had given her far more than a few blissful moments of passion, and she would always be grateful to him for that. Yet her heart had felt as though it would break in two as she watched him ride away, and she knew she would probably never see him again.

"You're uncommon quiet this mornin'," Jeremy mumbled, shifting the reins in his hands.

Alan stared at the road ahead, a narrow lane lined with hedges higher than the horses' heads. He didn't answer because he did not know himself why he wasn't more enthusiastic about the Stanbury Players' next appearance. It was to be in Thetford, a small town, but one with a real hall and that usually got his theatrical juices flowing.

"I suppose you didn't get much sleep last night, that must be it," Jeremy added, giving him a sideways glance that was more of a question than a comment.

"You're too inquisitive by far," Alan said, grinning. "I was only thinking of the best way to stage *Love For Love* in that small Thetford hall. The apron is quite shallow, as I recall."

Of course, the truth was that his mind was not

filled with the playhouse at all, but with the image of a perfect oval face, huge, liquid blue eyes, and abundant golden hair laced with fire. Those eyes—so innocent one minute, and so enticing and captivating the next. Maud Mellingham obviously had no inkling of the magic she worked on men. She was beauty and siren wrapped up in one, with the siren still only partially developed. But soon it would be crying for release. With the right man's encouragement . . .

God's teeth! What was he thinking? A common serving wench in a small manor house in a rustic little shire! He should be able to forget her with a snap of the fingers.

And yet he could not. It still amazed him that he had not even tried to seduce her. She was so full of curiosity and joy, that instead he had found joy himself in telling her about the world. No, it was more than that. She had a special quality of innocence and trust that he could not bear to destroy. Nothing like this had ever happened to him before. Women were to be enjoyed and, most of the time, they enjoyed being enjoyed.

But Maud was different. And, after all, no one knew better than he, how terrible it was to have your faith and trust destroyed in a few careless moments, and how bitterly it could affect the rest of your life.

The wagon rolled to one side and Jeremy jostled against him, breaking into his thoughts. "That was a pretty young thing you were with last night," he said lightly. "Might it be that it's she that's got your tongue tied?"

Alan laughed. "Since when have you known me to be tongue-tied over a woman? Though I will admit, she was rather special. And you have been reading my mind again."

"I thought as much. Was she . . . all you expected?"

There was an edge to Jeremy's voice. How unlike him it was to ask such a question! "Nothing happened," Alan answered. "We spent the night talking. And if you ever breathe a word of it, I'll drum you out of the company."

Jeremy chuckled. "I'm relieved to hear it. There was an innocence about that young girl, for all that she was the prettiest little thing I've seen this age."

"Yes, she was pretty," Alan said with an air of nonchalance. "And if we ever get back this way again, possibly I'll look her up. Of course, by then she probably won't be so innocent."

Chapter Three

It did not escape Squire Bexley's notice that Maud had disappeared last evening with the handsome playwright. All the better, he thought, for it suggested that little Maud was both willing and experienced. Once the handsome Desmond moved on with his shabby collection of actors, he would make his move.

The first step was to convince his dear Julia that the girl belonged in the house instead of the kitchens. From long experience he knew he must walk this road carefully, for if Julia suspected he had his eye on the girl, she would pack her off to the Running Man Inn in the village, where Maud would be subject to the attentions of half the riffraff of England. For several weeks after the presentation of the play, he kept his eye on Maud while biding his time. The girl grew more lovely every day. Her porcelain complexion — so unusual in this age when two-thirds of the village bore the ravages of smallpox on their faces — was enough to make his mouth water. And although she seemed to grow thinner after the acting troupe left, it did not affect the ripe fullness of her breasts, so delectable under the low ruching of her blouse. It only served to add a touch of wistfulness to her pale cheeks, while emphasizing her round, luscious lips and wide, blue eyes.

More and more Squire Bexley licked his lips thinking about Maud, and agonized over the best way to approach his wife. And then, the opportunity fell into his lap like a gift from heaven.

"I don't know what I am going to do about that Hetty," Julia said one evening as she sat at the supper table, picking listlessly at a plate of roast fowl. "She gets more slovenly in her work every day. And yesterday, I caught her leaving the closet just after I passed William, the footman, in the hall. I could tell by her face what they had been up to. I won't have such immorality in my house, and yet if I turn her out, I have no one to take her place. It's very aggravating."

Squire Bexley looked up from his full plate to stare at his wife. "Hetty? That dark-haired young minx with the mole on her chin?"

"Yes, that's the one. Surely you've noticed," she said archly.

"Barely. You know the servants are your concern, my dear. And I quite agree. We must observe a high standard in the home."

"My dear papa, Lord Bambridge, would expect nothing less."

Squire Bexley silently ground his teeth over the way his wife never spoke of her father without mentioning his title. He had long ago recognized that it was her way of reminding him how she had married beneath her rank. "Well, you needn't put up with such deplorable activity, simply because you have no one to take her place. It happens that only recently Cook spoke to me regarding one of the girls in her kitchens. She's done so well and has been so exemplary, that Cook wondered if she might not be better used inside the house as a chambermaid."

"Really? I shall speak to Cook first thing tomorrow."

"No need to do that, my love. I'll have a word with her myself, since I was the one she approached. Let's see now, I believe the girl's name was Maud. Yes, that's it. Maud Mellingham."

"That little ragamuffin we took in as an orphan? Well, now that you mention it, she has been rather dependable as a kitchen maid. I wonder why Cook didn't speak of it to me."

Squire concentrated on his plate, not willing to point out that Julia knew very well Cook detested her overbearing ways so much she would never venture more than a "Yes, ma'am" and "No, ma'am," to her. For once, however, that was going to be to his advantage.

Julia smiled to herself as she envisioned sending Hetty packing while, at the other end of the table, Squire Bexley all but rubbed his hands together in anticipation. It had gone much easier than he dared hope.

Maud found herself plucked from the cozy confines of the kitchen and promoted to the shadowy halls of the great house, with a speed that left her head reeling. She had expected the most difficult part of her new position would be to see Hetty leaving in tears, carrying her pitiful little bundle of personal belongings under her arm. As it turned out, Hetty was pleased for Maud and quickly arranged a wedding for herself with Jimmy Corcoran, the blacksmith in the village who had been pestering her to marry him for months.

"Just don't let that old witch bully you, Maud," Hetty said as she was leaving. "You're much too trusting. You got to stand up to 'em, these gentry. Especially an old harridan like Mistress Julia."

"Oh, Hetty," Maud cried, hugging her friend. "How am I going to get along without you? You're just about my only friend here."

"Cook'll watch after you, like she's always done.

Listen to 'er, Maud. She knows what's what. You just bob to the mistress and do like she tells ye. And don't never be alone with Squire, and you'll do well enough. And come see me in the village on y'er 'alf-day off."

Once Maud got over the loss of her friend, she found she liked being a house servant. She enjoyed the blue serge dress with the starched white apron and the cap and the filmy fichu she now had to wear. She loved working in high-ceilinged rooms among beautiful things. She polished the silver trays and teapots until she could see her reflection as clearly as in a pool of water, and she did it, not out of fear of Lady Julia's wrath, but out of the joy of seeing how beautiful they could be. She watched the older servants and studied how they spoke when they announced a guest or brought in a card from a caller or greeted someone at the door, and she quickly picked up the proper way to do it all. She watched the way the table was laid, and what dishes were used to serve the different concoctions that Cook sent up. She even watched the way the Squire and his wife used their utensils, and the way Lady Julia took tiny spoonfuls and left half her meal on her plate. This must be the way proper folk ate, she thought, ignoring the way the Squire dug into his food.

Her happiest moments were when visitors came for meals. She greeted them at the door, noting what they wore and how casually they handed their cloaks and hats to outstretched hands. She studied them at the table, especially the women. The men had none of these graces—with the exception of Lord Bambridge, who somehow never lost his dignity, even when the other men were sliding drunk under the table.

But the women—ah, it was an education in itself to watch them. She noted the fashions, the fabrics, the colors, the paint on their faces, the outlandish hats; and her greatest wish was to someday dress like them.

One afternoon when guests were arriving for a birthday supper, she found herself taking Lord Bambridge's heavy cloak at the door.

"Well, you've come up in the world, Maud. I'm pleased to see it," the old gentleman said kindly. He patted her gently on the shoulder. "I always thought you'd be better used in the house than in the kitchens."

Maud bobbed him a curtsy, blushing with pleasure that he remembered her. "Thank you, sir. I'm very happy to be working here."

"Don't let my daughter browbeat you, my girl," Bambridge said, winking at her. "She's got a fierce bark about her, but she won't bite."

"She's been very kind to me, sir," Maud answered, as she took the lawyer Ramsey's overcoat and draped the two garments over her arm.

"Ha! We know better than that, don't we Ramsey?" Bambridge said. "But you're a good girl to say so." He turned to go down the hall while Maud hurried to dispose of the coats and run to announce them, nearly colliding with the lawyer as she passed them in the hall. The thin little man looked down at her, his narrow face scowling in annoyance.

"Sorry, sir," Maud muttered and hurried on. Ramsey was a frequent visitor to Thornwood, and yet as far as Maud knew, he never seemed aware that she was there. She had long ago decided that was a characteristic of lawyers who, the Squire said, only existed to swindle people or cart them off to jail.

On the whole, even lingering thoughts of Alan Desmond could not dampen the enthusiasm she felt for her new position at Thornwood. When she crawled into bed at night, weary and sore-footed, he came vividly back, his warm lips, his strong arms, his tall, lean, hard body evoking a stirring need and a longing that made her ache all over. It filled her with sadness to know that she would probably never see him again, and more than once she had to remind herself that, after all, there *were* other men in the world. She would move among the lovely rooms of Squire's house, admiring the elegant furniture and beautiful pictures, and she would force herself not to mourn. If she had to spend the rest of her life at Thornwood, better to spend it as a house servant than as a kitchen maid.

If there was one troubling problem about her new position, it was that Squire Bexley was paying her a great deal more attention than he ever had before. It seemed to delight him to find her by herself in one of the rooms or in a darkened hall, and he would grab and tickle and pinch her in a way that made him laugh uproariously, and made her extremely uncomfortable. Maud was confused at first about how to handle the situation. She was grateful to Squire for moving her out of the kitchen and into the beautiful house, but even though she owed him for bettering her station in life, she did not owe him her body! Yet how to convince him of that? Cook had warned her about this, and Maud had naively believed it would never be a problem.

Of one thing she was certain — she was not going to be sent packing like Hetty. With no willing blacksmith to marry her, she would go straight to the workhouse, if she was thrown out of Thornwood. Better to deal with Squire Bexley than that. She would simply have to try to stay out of his reach, and pray that in time he would look to one of the other servants for his pleasure. It was her only hope.

For the first few weeks, her plan seemed to work. The Squire paid her little mind, largely because his wife, feeling poorly, stayed closer to home than usual. Maud went diligently about her work, minded her own business, and kept her own counsel. Her problems appeared to be solved.

Her problem with the Squire, at least. His wife was another matter altogether. Lady Julia had suffered a spell of the quinsy, which only served to make her none too pleasant disposition even more strident. Up until now Maud had quietly borne the mistress's contentious scolding. There was no pleasing Lady Julia, for if you did what she told you with great care, she would harp on something she had not told you but expected you to know anyway. Her disposition was reflected in the perpetual scowl on her thin face, and at times Maud did not wonder that Squire sought his pleasure with the servants, so cold must his marital bed be.

Though she did nothing to provoke her ladyship, it seemed her very presence was enough to set her mistress off. Of course, Maud told herself, Lady Julia was just as abusive and mean to all the other servants, but Maud had expected that she might earn a little measure of goodwill by quietly and diligently going about her work. All it seemed to do was make her mistress's inspections even more critical, and cause her to add to the list of Maud's duties.

Yet she refused to be discouraged. She worked hard and was quietly obedient, because she felt that eventually Lady Julia would recognize her worth.

"Ye're too optimistic for ye're own good," Cook warned her. "Ye always was. An ould sow like the mistress is never goin' to be grateful for a good, quiet girl, because then she would na' 'ave the chance to rant and yowl and carry on, and everybody knows, that's her biggest pleasure in life."

"All the same, I intend to prove to her that I can be a valuable servant, no matter how long it takes."

She didn't add that proving this to their mistress was necessary, if she wanted to keep her place secure. And with every day she became more convinced that her pleasant new position was one she wanted to hang on to at all costs.

Nevertheless, when Lady Julia announced that she was feeling so much improved that the following day she would be off to Thetford again, Maud breathed a sigh of relief and began looking forward to a quiet day puttering among the Squire's lovely rooms.

Early that morning she was sitting in the kitchen have a bowl of milk gruel with Cook, when the Squire entered. Without even acknowledging Maud's presence, he announced that he would be seeing his wife off to Thetford and might even be away overnight, and Cook must prepare a simple supper for her ladyship's return.

"Oh," he added, almost as an afterthought. "And while I'm gone, Maud, I'd like you to clean my room. It is in a dreadful state—ashes in the hearth, bedding in need of airing, dust everywhere."

"Of course, sir," Maud said as he swept out of the kitchen.

Cook gave her a thoughtful glance, but since both the Squire and Mistress would be gone, she couldn't think of any warning that might be necessary.

Sometime later, armed with broom, bucket, brushes, and cloths, Maud tripped up the stairs to the Squire's bedroom. It was the first time she had ever been inside, and she peeked around the door with awe, tempered by caution. A huge tester bed stood against one wall, the hangings close around it. Velvet drapes were pulled over the windows, shutting out the light. Clothes lay scattered everywhere—a coat half-lying over the arm of a chair, a cambric shirt on the floor, a wig carelessly thrown on a wooden stand, and two pairs of breeches tossed in the corner. Even from the doorway she could see the thick dust that covered nearly every surface. The room looked like its owner—unkempt, zestful, and hearty.

Closing the door, she set down her brushes and began picking up the clothes, holding them in clipped fingers at arm's length. She had a small pile atop the clothes press, when she heard a suspicious noise behind her. Turning, she gasped in surprise as the hangings on the bed came alive, two hands poking between them, shoving them apart just far enough for a head to poke through.

"Squire!" Maud cried, too astonished to move. With a burst of flaring white linen, Squire Bexley jumped to the floor.

Maud stood frozen as he bounded to the door and turned the key in the lock. He was a comical figure with his bony, hairy legs protruding from the length of nightshirt, and — had she been less horrified — she might have laughed. Then she realized what he had in mind and, with a piercing cry, she bounded across the room to grab the key from his hand. The Squire laughed with delight and hid it behind him, while Maud tried first one side, then the other. When he reached for her, she nimbly jumped away and ran back to the other side of the room.

"Really, sir, you were not supposed to be here."

"Yes. Isn't it a great joke? I sent Julia off with that lawyer, Ramsey, and stayed behind just to catch you when you came to clean my room."

Maud frowned angrily at him. "That was not gentlemanly of you, sir. In fact, it was very wrong."

"Oh, pooh, Maudie, my girl. There's nothing to enliven a gray day like a little romping among the feathers! You must learn to be more accommodating. Take it all in stride."

"Sir, I insist you give me the key and allow me to leave this room," Maud said with as much authority as she could summon.

With a nimbleness she hadn't dreamed he possessed, the Squire leaped up on his knees on the bed and jerked the hangings apart. Chuckling to himself, he pulled back the covers and threw the key far underneath.

"You'll have to come and get it, my girl."

Maud began to feel very uneasy. "Pray, Squire, give me the key. This is not to my liking."

"Am I holding you here? I most certainly am not. You are free to unlock the door and leave anytime you wish. All you have to do is climb up here, and retrieve the key."

She eyed him with suspicion. "You know very well—"

"Here, I'll help you," Squire Bexley cried, and with great enthusiasm snapped the curtains open on the other side. When he bounded down beside her, she darted around to the other side of the bed.

"You get it for me," Maud said, hardly daring to hope it might work.

"No, no. That will never do. But I promise you faithfully, that if you retrieve it yourself, you can open the door and leave at your leisure."

"Sir, I am a good girl. None of this is to my liking."

"Yes, yes. I know you are a good girl. But even good girls have to learn the ways of the world, and who better to instruct you in those ways than me, your benefactor?"

Tentatively, Maud reached out and lifted a corner of the bedclothes. The big brass key was lying far underneath, buried near the foot of the bed and nearer the Squire's side than hers. Keeping a wary eye on the Squire, she leaned toward it and found it was too far away to grasp. Lifting her skirts and keeping a watchful eye out, she set one knee on the feather mattress and stretched out across it. The Squire watched her every move, still chuckling to himself at his little game. Very carefully, she lifted the other knee.

"Ah ha!" he cried, and in an instant was up on the

bed, grabbing her around the waist. They fell back together on the covers, his heavy, flabby body pinning her down. As he jumped up to snap the curtains shut, Maud scrambled to the end of the bed, where her weight sent the feather mattress folding around her like a cocoon.

"Now, my luscious little plum," the Squire boomed, reaching out to grab at the laces of her bodice. Maud clenched them in her hands.

"Faith, Squire, this isn't right—"

"I'm not going to hurt you, my beauty. Just lay back and put yourself in my hands . . ."

The sides of her sacque fell apart as the laces were torn away. Maud clutched at her bodice, but the Squire bent his big, hairy face and clamped his wet lips on her skin, licking at the cleavage between her breasts and smacking to himself as though tasting one of Cook's concoctions.

Maud glimpsed the white nightshirt slipping up over his bony knees and thick thighs, and panic swept over her. With a tremendous lunge she shoved him back and rolled to the side of the bed. As he fell back against the pillows, the shirt went flying over his head and she glimpsed with astonishment the stiff, blood-red prong that thrust out from a thicket of hair between his legs.

He quickly regained his balance and grabbed for her—as she was half off the bed—trying to drag her back on the mattress. Panic rose to consume Maud, and she screamed, flailing at him with her hands.

"What is going on here!"

They hadn't heard the key in the door, or even the noise it made when it was flung open. Frozen, Maud and the Squire both stared openmouthed as Lady Julia's tall form filled the doorway. She was wearing her cloak and a riding hat with feathers too tall for the frame.

With a gasp the Squire dropped Maud, and she

rolled off the bed onto the floor in a heap. Clutching at her bodice, she scrambled as far from him as she could get and began fastening her clothes.

Julia's cold eyes never left her husband's astounded face. "Need I ask what is going on? It's obvious. You . . . you lecher!"

Recovering, Squire Bexley tried to reclaim the shards of his dignity. "What the devil are you doing here? You are supposed to be in Thetford by now."

Julia swept into the room like a warship in full sail. "That's what you were waiting for, wasn't it? I suspected as much when you fobbed poor Ramsey off to do your duty. Get up at once, you disgusting old reprobate, and put on your clothes. What would my father say to see you acting so disgracefully!"

Squire slipped off the far side of the bed and reached for a robe, mumbling to himself how that frozen old man was too proud for anything as human as an afternoon's romp in the hay. But Julia was too busy directing her fury on Maud to hear.

"And you, you hussy," she snapped. "I imagine you led him on to this, except that I'm familiar enough with his lecherous ways to know he doesn't need any encouragement."

"But Mistress, truly I didn't—"

"Don't speak! You are just as decadent as he is, and I don't want to hear any of your excuses. Go downstairs at once! I'll decide what to do with you later."

Glaring at the Squire, Maud slipped past Lady Julia, knowing it would be useless to try to protest her innocence now. Perhaps later, when her anger had subsided—if it ever did—Lady Julia might listen to the truth. In the meantime, Maud could have gladly thrown the first thing at hand at the Squire's red, disappointed face.

With her cheeks burning, she fled to the attic room she shared with one of the parlormaids. She was relieved to see it was empty. She scrubbed her face in the washbowl, as though to cleanse it of the embarrassment and horror she felt, but it did no good. She sat on the bed, twisting her hands in her lap and thinking.

If Lady Julia had been hard on Hetty, Maud could now expect ten times that wrath to fall on her own head. *If* she even deigned to let Maud stay. That was a chilling thought, but one that had to be faced. It seemed she had but two choices: she could endure her ladyship's mean, vindictive ways and try to reestablish her place here at Thornwood, or she could try to find another position before she was thrown out on her ear.

Of the two, the second seemed far the best. But where could she go? All her life had been spent on the Squire's land or in his house, and she knew very little about the rest of the countryside. Julia's haughtiness was based on the belief that most of the people who lived near Thornwood were not good enough to entertain. And those she would accept were inclined to stay away, because of her unpleasantness. The upshot was, very few of the local gentry crossed the portals of Thornwood.

Except . . .

Of course, Lord Bambridge! It's true that he was Julia's father, but he had never shown any of her proud ways. In fact, he had often gone out of his way to speak a kind word to Maud, even when she was a kitchen maid. Perhaps he would take her into his house.

It was a comforting thought. She wouldn't even mind being demoted back to the kitchens, if she could only get away from Squire Bexley and his horrible wife.

The more she thought about it, the more she was convinced it was her only hope. But she wouldn't go right away. She would wait awhile, look for the right moment, and hope that Mistress's anger would fade in time. No matter how badly the Lady Julia might treat her, it gave Maud courage just to know that there was something she could do when she couldn't bear it any longer.

In three more days the Stanbury Players would arrive in London. As Alan Desmond rode his solitary horse along an empty road outside the small village of Pinner, it gave him a sense of relief to know the great city was not far away. This tour had been long and taxing, and he would be glad to hang his hat in his rooms at the Lamb and Flag and stay in one place for a while.

Not that the time had been wasted. He had three new plays in his saddlebag, ready for the printer the moment he unpacked. And they were especially good plays, too. They were funny with a dash of poignancy, and filled with double entendres that skewered the House of Hanover, while subtly praising the Stuart Cause. It was going to give him great satisfaction to see them come to life on the stage of the Chelsea Theater.

A magpie fluttered abruptly out of the hedgerow lining the row, and his horse shied into a nervous little dance. Alan smoothed the sleek neck and calmed the beast, until it resumed its leisurely plodding. He pulled his hat closer down on his face against the bright sun, while his thoughts went wandering once again.

The only problem with his new plays was how to cast the lead. Frances was too long in the tooth, and Kitty was too obviously a wanton to bring the right touch of youth and innocence to Perdita. Besides, the two of them were so competitive, that were he to favor one over the other, he would risk being in the middle of a real cat fight. He would simply have to peruse the other playhouses, to see if there were any new actresses around who might be lured to his company.

Lord Stanbury's Company, he reminded himself. Though the good Earl was content to bask in the Italian sun and let Alan run things back in England, still, it was his money that kept the company going. Of course, even that was providential, since it allowed Alan to use his own money for the things that mattered the most to him.

His horse followed the road down a long hill that led to the main street of the village. As he had hoped, there were not many people about for a warm early afternoon, though far off to the right he could see men working in the fields. He ambled off the main road at the first narrow path leading to the left, and reined in beside a shabby wooden lynch gate. After fastening his horse, he passed through the gate and walked the short path to the old medieval church; its square tower loomed heavy in the lazy afternoon. When he had chosen this place to meet the Earl's cousin, his greatest fear was that the vicar might be lurking about, and he was relieved to see no one in sight. The old man was probably having a little nap somewhere in his vicarage.

His soft leather boots moved quietly over the stone floor of the porch. Pushing open the door, Alan slipped inside the dark, quiet church, looking around quickly to make sure he was alone. The interior was refreshingly cool in contrast to the warmth outside, and Alan removed his hat and wiped at his damp brow with his sleeve.

How peaceful it was here, an oasis of tranquility and quiet. He stared at the long nave and stone sanctuary, thinking that a prayer might be appropriate, if only he were a praying man. In this stillness one might believe that the world was actually an orderly and caring place—if one did not know better. Images rose unbidden to his mind. They were not pictures of the hedonistic, pleasure-loving denizens of a corrupt London down the road. They were old memories of his home in flames, of his fourteen-year-old brother, Neil, struggling in one soldier's grip while another thrust a bayonet through his heart, of his mother wasting away with grief until life had become a burden gladly relinquished.

Alan shuddered and got a grip on his mind. It was never any good thinking about these things. His family was long dead now, and the only thing worth remembering was his determination to someday exact his revenge. And that he was never going to forget!

He jumped as he heard a muffled footstep on the porch. Quickly he faded into the shadows and watched as a man slipped through the door. The newcomer wore a short cloak with a hood that shielded his face and the top half of his burgundy coat, but Alan recognized the white silk stockings and silver buckles on his shoes.

"Good morrow, m'lord," he said in a low voice, and stepped from the shadows. The man looked quickly around, his faded gray eyes flickering with fright.

"Egad, you gave me a scare! And don't be so free with the titles. You never know who might be listening."

Alan smiled. "We're quite alone for the moment. When did you arrive back in England?"

The two of them slipped around the octagonal baptismal font and into the low recess of one of the stone arches, where they could watch the entrance without being seen and where they could keep their voices barely above a whisper.

"Two nights ago. Frightful trip. Bad weather all the way."

"Did you see the Earl?"

"Yes. And the Prince, too. Though I have to confess, it gave me no encouragement to be around either of them. Cousin Stanbury's all right, of course, but the Prince, well, he's all but given up, and seeks solace with his whores and his wineglass."

"He mustn't. There are too many depending on him."

"I tried to tell him that. But . . . well, as you know, at times it does seem like a hopeless cause."

Alan glanced away, refusing to let himself believe that. It couldn't be hopeless. They simply had to be successful.

"We're not giving up," his companion said, as if he had read Alan's thoughts. "I've brought money from the Earl, and letters which you are to pass on to Madam de la Trembrille." He reached under his cloak, and handed Alan a packet wrapped tightly in a chamois cloth and tied with a cord. "Can you get them to her?"

"Yes. We're going to be in London in three days, so it should be an easy matter. But are there no other plans? Nothing formulated yet?"

"You know how difficult that is going to be, and how much time it will take. We cannot afford another failure . . ."

"I know. Still, at times I grow impatient to act, to do something that would show our hatred and defiance openly. I grow weary of all this secrecy and skulking about."

The man laid a hand on Alan's arm. "Patience. It will come. And we must be secret, or everything will be lost. Now, I must go. You will be contacted again as soon as I hear from the Earl."

"In London?"

"Possibly. Possibly not. Your traveling around the country makes you very useful to our cause. Oh, and here. I brought you this."

He handed Alan a square wooden tray. It was simply made and rather ugly, with a circular smear of paint across its flat surface.

"What's this?" Alan asked, turning it over in his hand.

His companion gave a low chuckle. "It looks innocuous, doesn't it? But if you hold your goblet of claret just right, that smear of paint will be reflected as the face of our Prince. It's called an anamorphic portrait. Any kind of cylinder will do. We thought it particularly appropriate when you have to toast 'the King' in secret."

"That's clever," Alan said, smiling as he tucked the tray inside his coat. "I'll make sure it is used."

They left the church separately, allowing a lapse of time between them. Alan climbed back on his horse and started out of the village, before remembering that there was a tavern nearby. He was thirsty, and there was plenty of time to stop before heading back. Perhaps a pint might ease the slight depression he felt, when he thought how slim were the chances of the Prince taking his rightful place in Scotland, much less in England.

If there were not many people around, he might even take the risk of laying his tray on the table and quietly making a toast to the anamorphic portrait of Prince Charles Stuart.

Chapter Four

It did not take Maud long to figure out that Lady Julia had decided her best revenge was not to send Maud packing, but to keep her nearby, where each new day presented countless opportunities to make the girl's life miserable. Determined to endure, Maud quietly bore the increased work, Mistress's close supervision, the eternal dissatisfaction with everything she did, having to do her work three times over before it was acceptable, even the occasional switch which Mistress used on Maud's hands when she thought she could get away with it.

Many times Maud thought she could not bear it any longer and would run away, but each time the memory of Hetty trudging away from Thornwood with her miserable little bundle of belongings under her arm revived her determination to stick it out. Surely after a suitable time, Lady Julia's temper would improve. Maud received no help from the Squire, who seemed to blame her for what happened and scarcely gave her a civil word. Finally, after several weeks had passed in which Lady Julia's needling grew worse rather than better, Maud decided that there was nothing for it but to seek out Lord Bambridge. If he could not help her, there would be nothing to do but resign herself to a miserable life.

On her next half-day off, she put on her only good dress, a dark blue fustian, tied a spotless white fichu across the low front of her bodice, set her straw hat on top of her linen cap, tied it with a ribbon across the top, pulled the sides down around her face, and fastened it in a bow under her chin. When she was satisfied with her appearance, she put on her wooden clogs and walked seven miles to the beautiful, sprawling manor house, Denton Hall.

It took her half an hour to get inside, talking her way past the footman, the butler, and the housekeeper. Finally she was left in a small dark winter parlor off the servant's wing, which appeared not to have seen a dustcloth for weeks. There were two shabby armchairs flanking a round tea table, obviously castoffs from the main wings of the manor house. Maud was too nervous to sit, so she spent the time walking around the room, resisting the urge to clean it as she would have at Thornwood. She waited so long that her stomach became a mass of churning nerves, and she decided she'd been put there and forgotten and might as well leave. Then she heard the clip of Lord Bambridge's heels on the tiled floor outside.

The door opened and he was there, filling the room with his bulk, a big, dignified man in a powdered tie wig, a sky blue coat worked with silver lace and white stockings embroidered with silken clocks. Maud shrank back toward the window, and mentally cursed herself for coming to Denton Hall.

"I was told you wanted to see me," Lord Bambridge said kindly. His smile widened as he recognized her. "Why, it's Maud, isn't it, from Thornwood?"

Maud peered at his face with the heavy jowls and little laugh lines around his eyes, and was encouraged. "Yes, sir. Maud Mellingham, your grace."

"Come now, Maud, I'm not a duke, you know. Just plain sir will suffice. What can I do for you?"

He flipped up the tails of his coat and settled in

one of the chairs. Maud took a deep breath and gripped her hands in front of her stomacher. "I . . . I shouldn't have come, your grace—sir. It was a mistake. I'll just go—"

"Now, now, I'll wager you didn't walk all this way over here for nothing. What is it? Trouble with my daughter?"

Maud caught her breath, wondering how he could have known. "Well . . ."

"Yes, I suspected as much. Go ahead. Tell me about it."

Suddenly uncomfortable, Maud fastened her gaze on her hands. "Well, sir. I . . . I don't seem to be able to please her ladyship very much."

"Ha! You mustn't let that bother you. No one has been able to please Julia, since she was in leading strings."

She breathed a sigh of relief at his sympathetic response and, to her shame, tears burned behind her eyes. One of them slipped out and slid down her cheek, and she bent her head lower to hide it.

"I can see this has affected you deeply," Lord Bambridge said more quietly. "I should not make witty comments about something you feel so sorely. Forgive me, my child."

His kindness all but undid her. Getting a grip on her emotions, Maud tried to explain. "Mistress expects perfection, sir. Not that I mind doing things well. And it's so much nicer being in the house than working in the kitchens. Truly, I enjoy making beautiful things look gleaming and spotless. But . . ."

Lord Bambridge eyed her closely. "But I suspect she is taking out her anger on you. Is it about that dreadful business with the Squire?"

Maud's eyes flew open. "You know about that? Oh, sir, I was innocent. I never had any idea Squire was in that room. He told me he was going off, and I should use the time to clean it."

Lord Bambridge waved a hand. "You don't need to explain, my child. I know Anthony Bexley far too well not to understand. And you strike me as a good girl, Maud. Not one who would encourage such shenanigans."

"Oh, sir. I am. Truly."

"But Julia is exacting her revenge by making your life miserable, is that it? It would be just like her. My daughter was never one to turn the other cheek."

"I do not wish to speak against Mistress, sir . . ."

"I understand, and that is to your credit. But what do you want me to do? I could speak to her about it, of course, but that would only make her bad temper worse, and I fear your life would become even harsher. I'm sure you can understand that."

"Pray, sir . . . I . . . I wondered if perhaps you might have a place for me here at the Hall." The words sounded horribly presumptive to her ears, and she went on quickly. "Not as a housemaid, I'm sure you have as many as you need. But I would gladly go back to the kitchens just to work here. There is always a need for another pair of hands in the kitchens, and I would be so grateful and so willing . . ."

Again he waved his hand, bringing her rush of words to a close. His thick brows knitted over his high forehead, and he rose and walked around the table, pausing by the window.

"I wish I could help you, Maud, but it is quite impossible that I bring you here. Julia would never allow it, of course, and though I might insist on it, it would be so obvious to everyone that it would embarrass her. I cannot do that."

Maud gripped her hands tighter, fighting back tears. She bent her head again to hide her disappointment, and fought down the wave of hopelessness his words sent through her.

"I understand, sir. It was good of you to see me at all."

She waited to be dismissed, but he continued to stare through the lace curtain, saying nothing for several minutes. Then he turned back to her.

"I could tell you to bear your suffering like a good Christian, but, faith, I won't allow Julia another chance to take out her bad disposition on an innocent person. Especially on a girl who seems as intelligent and willing a housemaid as you are. No, I think there is only one solution. I shall send you to my other daughter to serve her household."

Maud looked up in surprise. "You have another daughter?"

"Yes. Cynthia is a firm taskmaster, but there is no meanness in her, as I fear there is in Julia. I think you will be happy there, and I'm sure you will suit Cynthia. She leads a busy life, and is constantly discharging servants and hiring new ones. Yes, I think that will be a suitable answer. Everyone will think Julia sent you away, and few will know where."

Maud herself did not know where, but was afraid to ask. While she stood trying to absorb this good news, Lord Bambridge rubbed his hands together and chuckled with satisfaction. "I shall give you a letter of introduction to take with you, explaining why I am sending you to her. Can you be ready to leave in a week's time? There will be a stage from Norwich then, and we'll find a place for you on it."

"A stage? In a week? Will her ladyship allow it?"

"Oh, yes. I'll see to that. You just go home and begin packing your things. I'm sure you can't have much. And you'll need a little traveling money. I'll give it to you, and Bexley can pay me back with whatever is due from your wages. Yes, that will do nicely, I think."

He laid a hand on her shoulder and propelled her toward the door. With eyes like blue saucers, Maud looked up in to his smiling face. "But, sir, traveling where? Where does Miss Cynthia live?"

"Oh, didn't I tell you? She has a country home in the next county, but her primary residence is her London house, and she spends most of her time there. That's where I shall send you. To London!"

Maud's feet barely touched the ground during the seven miles back to Thornwood. London! It was more than she had ever dared hoped for, more than she dared to dream. She would be in that wonderful, exciting city with a secure place in Lady Cynthia's town house, and leisure time to look for Alan Desmond again. Surely he had mentioned that the troupe was going there. It might take her many weeks but eventually she would find him; she felt it in her bones.

If only Lady Julia would really let her go. It would be just like her to refuse her father's request out of sheer meanness. If she did, Maud thought melodramatically, life would not be worth living.

For the next few days, she went about her duties very quietly, trying not to call attention to herself and, when she was alone in her room, carefully sifting through her belongings to see what she would take with her. There was very little worth bothering with. Her one good dress, two patched dimity fichues, a small ring that had belonged to her mother, and other odds and ends.

She felt certain that Lord Bambridge had told his daughter of his plans, because Lady Julia went out of her way to make Maud's life even more miserable. When, on the day before the week was up, her ladyship finally called her into the parlor and informed her she would be leaving on the stage the next day, she looked as though the words were stuck in her throat.

"It's far more than you deserve, you wicked girl. I hope you know that! You should get down on your knees and thank God for my father's tender heart, for you can be sure I would never do you such a kindness."

"No, ma'am," Maud muttered, feeling quite certain that she wouldn't.

"But Papa, as usual, knows what is best, and it is better for this household to have you out of it. You would always be a temptation my weak, stupid husband could not forgo. The workhouse would be more appropriate, but Papa would never send anyone there. Sometimes I fear his compassion will be the death of him."

Maud stopped listening, and forced herself not to let her face show the happiness she felt. Madam Julia was far more likely to pack her off, if she thought Maud was frightened to death of a big city like London and it was a form of punishment for her to be sent there.

All at once she was aware that Julia had stopped speaking, and was looking at her with such venom in her eyes that Maud was certain the woman had read her thoughts.

"You think you are very clever, don't you? I know what girls like you are like. You use your beauty and youth—while it lasts—to get favors from silly men like my husband and father. Well, it won't work with me. I see right through you. You may think you have got the best of me now, but you are very mistaken, I assure you."

Maud's happiness began to wither under Julia Bexley's cold glare. The woman could not have looked more sour if she were sucking on a lemon. Yet, determined not to let Lady Julia think she was quaking under all that icy anger, Maud straightened her shoulders and lifted her chin.

"Does that mean I will not be allowed to leave?"

Julia waved a thin hand. "No. Papa says you must go, and go you will. Besides, I prefer to have you out of my house. Wickedness earns its own reward in the end. But you haven't heard the last of me. Remember that!"

Maud breathed a sigh of relief. She could stand any amount of abuse, as long as she knew she would be leaving soon.

So it was that early the next day, Maud found herself tearfully enveloped in Cook's massive embrace as she left Thornwood for the Running Man Inn in the village, where the London coach wagon would stop for passengers. It was hard to leave the woman who had been almost like a mother to her for so long, and she was struck for the first time with a pang of fear and nostalgia.

"God bless ye, Maudie, me girl," Cook said, wiping a tear from her own eye. "Ye be a good girl, and don't let them London swells shove ye around."

There was no way Maud could tell Cook all she had meant to her these ten years since her parents had died, so she simply flung her arms around the woman's neck and hugged her tightly. Grasping her bundle, she turned and ran from the yard. At the gate she stopped long enough to turn back and wave to Cook, who was still standing by the kitchen door. A flutter at one of the upstairs windows caught her eye, and she glanced up to see Lady Bexley standing at the casement, one hand holding back the lace curtain, and looking down at her. Her ladyship let the curtain drop and moved quickly away, but not before Maud saw that she was smiling a curiously smug smile. Too excited to give it much thought, Maud waved to Cook again and ran through the gate toward the village.

Hetty was at the Inn to give her another embrace, before Maud was handed up to the roof of the great coach where she found herself scrunched in between two other young girls—mirror images of herself, in straw hats tied with ribbons over their ruffled caps, white kerchiefs tucked inside their laced bodices, and bundles of their meagre belongings tightly held in their laps. Maud waved, as the coach pulled away in a cloud of dust and with a blast from the long horn. She watched behind her as the familiar thatched roofs and low houses, rolling green fields lined with hedges, and the high hayricks dotting the landscape slipped away. Tears burned behind her eyes as she thought about how she was leaving everything she knew behind, but she forced herself not to cry.

As the countryside began to grow strange and unfamiliar, her sense of adventure took over and transformed her sadness to elation. After all, she was young, pretty, and healthy, and she had a letter in her tattered reticule that promised her a place in the city. Somewhere down that long winding road over which the coach was flying lay London, the most exciting city in the world, the place where she, Maud Mellingham, was going to find the only man she had ever cared for and, with any luck, her place and fortune in life.

During the third stop to change horses, she discovered the brooch. It was tightly wrapped in a lace handkerchief, which was much finer than any she had ever owned. Once she felt the unfamiliar hardness of it, she slipped into a shadowed corner to unwrap it and see what it was. She gave a gasp of dismay when she looked down and saw the beautiful thing in her hand. The gold loops glinted, and the red stones gleamed fire even in the shadowy corner. Maud wrapped it up quickly and put it back in her purse. Then she found a place on the end of a bench and thought hard.

Where had it come from? It certainly did not belong to her. She could make no sense of its presence in her reticule, until a horrible possibility rose like a spectre in her mind. Perhaps Lady Julia herself had placed it there! Not out of kindness or generosity, but to accuse Maud of stealing and have her dragged back to Thornwood! It would be so like something she would do. The punishment for stealing was often as not hanging, and certainly her ladyship would enjoy seeing Maud on the gallows.

It was a horrible thought, but one that was all too possible, and it took much of the joy Maud had felt up to this moment out of the day. She shoved the hateful thing as far down in her reticule as it would go, and made up her mind to keep it hidden until she got to London. Once there, her very first act would be to post the thing back to Thornwood.

Maud remembered Alan saying that one of the newfangled "Flying Machine" coaches could make the trip to London in the astounding time of little more than a day! She, however, had no such luxurious accommodations, and the wagon coach on which she traveled promised to take twice that time. But this was no deprivation to Maude, who watched in utter fascination as the miles rolled by. Having never been beyond the limits of her parish, she found everything new, fascinating, and completely delightful. Each village and hamlet was a fresh experience. A town, with its cobbled streets branching off in every direction, lined with shops and crowded with houses, was truly amazing. As the countryside grew more lush beyond Newmarket, she could not have been more intrigued with the landscape if she had suddenly been transported to another planet. When, near the end of the day, rain began to fall and a heavy fog rolled in, she was grateful that the coach stopped for several hours at a thatched roofed inn to wait for better weather.

The next day, when the wagon resumed its journey to creep through Epping Forest, its occupants hunkered down on their seats, praying that the highwaymen who made their living by robbing travelers along this desolate area would conclude that they were not worth bothering about. Maud remembered Alan telling her that the ghost of Dick Turpin on his black charger haunted this road, and she anxiously watched the trees for any sign of a spectre.

She was almost disappointed when they left the forest without a ghostly visitation, but then, when she realized that they were on the outskirts of London, her excitement and wonder grew with every passing mile. They crawled through quiet hamlets to skirt Hackney Marsh, then crossed the fields of Bethnal Green, dotted with grazing cattle. Soon they were winding along narrow, cobbled streets lined with houses crowding close on both sides. As they neared Shoreditch, the houses grew taller and closer, their upper stories overhanging streets made even more crowded by a profusion of sedan chairs, carriages, drays, and wagons. The stench created by massed humanity mingled with poor sanitation assaulted her nose; the roar of ironshod wheels on cobbles roared in her ears. Yet still Maud watched round-eyed and enchanted, until the coach rolled into the yard of the Ram's Head Inn and she knew she had arrived at last in London.

Only then did she remember that unless she found Cynthia Wiltshire's house by evening, she would not have a place to stay. As she was handed down off the coach and into the crowded yard, the enormity of her situation suddenly swept over her like a cold wash. She was alone in a strange city, knowing no one and little of its peculiar ways. Somehow she had to make her way through the twisting, crowded streets to the Wiltshire home, and hope that Lord Bambridge's letter would get her inside. It was a frightening thought.

Yet she was here, and there was nothing to do but

go forward. Perhaps a friendly innkeeper might give her directions, though if the gentleman who ran the Ram's Head was anything like the ill-tempered Jonas Sourby who ran the Running Man back home, she was going to be in trouble. Still, it was a place to start, and she moved forward to join the clusters of people streaming into the Inn.

She was nearly to the door when she felt something bump against her, nearly knocking her against a door post. Though she quickly caught her balance, she realized immediately that the weight of her bundles was different. With a cry she saw the dangling string where her reticule had hung from her waist. Looking back, she caught a glimpse of a young boy darting through the crowd and into the street.

"Stop! Stop that thief!" Maud cried, running after the child. But it was hopeless. He was swallowed by the mass of people in the street before she reached the road. She looked in dismay both ways, knowing she would never be able to find him. The other pedestrians gave her cursory glances, too absorbed with their own concerns to bother with hers.

Maud looked around and saw that she had become the object of interest to a group of men lounging around the yard. Embarrassed, she hurried back inside to a bench along a wall, where she sat, trying not to attract attention and fighting her inner panic.

Her purse was gone and with it her letter of reference, the little money Lord Bambridge had given to tide her over, even Madam Julia's brooch. What in the world was she going to do now? Cynthia Wiltshire would probably slam the door in her face, without that letter from her father explaining who Maud was. And with no money at all, she couldn't even rent a room for the night, or buy a ticket on the next coach back home. Not that she wanted to go back — that was unthinkable. Yet the more she examined her situation, the more desperate it seemed to be.

No, I won't give in to this panic, she thought, gritting her teeth and lifting her chin. Sitting prettily on the bench, Maud arranged her skirts, straightened her hat, and made up her mind to use these few moments to strengthen her determination and plan what her next moves should be. Perhaps a few judicious questions to a few innocent-looking people might help her find an answer.

Glancing around the yard, she noticed that most of the people there were wandering about their own business and paying her little mind. The only exception was a stout woman standing near the tavern door, listlessly fanning herself as her tiny eyes darted around the yard, often flickering back to Maud. Maud looked quickly away in embarrassment, for she had never seen an apparition like this woman, and her lingering gaze made her uneasy. Yet, when a few moments later, the woman waddled across the yard to take a vacant seat on the bench next to Maud, she decided that perhaps here was someone she could ask for directions to Grosvenor Street.

"Just arrived in London, 'ave ye?" the woman said before Maud could speak, smiling at her in a way that Maud supposed was meant to be sympathetic. With the white paste that smeared her face and the painted red slash that passed for her mouth, the smile looked more like the grimace of a jester.

"Yes, ma'am," she replied politely, knowing full well the woman had seen her handed down from the coach.

"Someone comin' to meet ye, then?"

"Well . . ."

"My, but if someone do be comin', he do seem to be a bit late. I wonder that he don't know when the wagon were due to arrive."

"He might have been held up by the . . . the crowds in the street."

The woman arranged the long tabs of her cardinal

cloak over her arms and lapsed into silence, as Maud debated whether this lady might be a dependable person to ask questions of. Her appearance was not one to encourage confidence. Fat almost to the point of grossness, her massiveness was exaggerated by yards of faded satin and tattered ruffles. Even Maud recognized that they were more tired than fashionable. The red puffs of curls that peeped from under her hood were obviously false, while her white face was dotted with several little black satin patches that only served to make her face look more grotesque. Her huge hoops took up so much of the space on the bench, that Maud was forced to shift to the end where she clung precariously.

"Ye appear to be a country lass," the woman went on, opening a faded chicken-skin fan and flapping it about as she studied Maud. "From Somerset, is it? Or perhaps Devon?"

"Suffolk," Maud replied tentatively, trying not to gaze in wonder at the woman.

"Now there, I knew it! I says to Jack, I did, when I first saw ye step off the coach, there's a Suffolk lass or I'll lay down and die. I can always tell. Why, I'm a Suffolk lass meself, though I been in London these many years."

Maud's smile blossomed to its full loveliness at the thought of meeting someone from home in the strangeness of the city. Of course, the woman's accent did not resemble a Suffolk burr in the least, but that could be because she had lived so long in London.

"Forgive me, my girl," the woman went on, before Maud could ask what part of East Anglia she came from, "but I could not help but notice ye're a stranger here. And I saw that young cutpurse make off with your reticule. I do hope it didn't leave ye with no way to support yerself in this wicked city?"

Maud looked down at her hands, fighting back the

tears that sprang to her eyes. "It was so unexpected . . ."

"Allow me to introduce meself. I'm Eliza Finchley, and I am completely at y'er service." She extended a clawlike hand to Maud, who took it gingerly.

"Maud Mellingham," she said as her fingers were gripped by the clutching claw.

"Maud! Why there's another happy coincidence. Maud was my dear sainted mother's name, and has always had a special place in me heart." She leaned close into Maud's face, still gripping her hand. "And who did ye say was meetin' ye here? What was the name?"

"Well, I'm not sure," Maud said, certain the woman knew as well as she that no one would be coming to meet her.

"Yes, I can tell by yer innocent sweet face that ye're alone in this sea of iniquity called London town. But God has favored ye, my child, for he has sent ye straight into the arms of the one person who is willin' and able to help ye. Faith, but I make it my life's work to seek out sweet young girls like yerself, and offer them a place to stay until they've got theirselves established in this city."

Maud's heart gave a leap. What luck to stumble on the very person she needed most, until she could find Grosvenor Street and convince Cynthia Wiltshire she was worthy of employment. "You have a boardinghouse?"

"That I do. You see, many years ago I was sitting here just like yerself, wondering what was to become of me. I, too, had a 'cousin' who was to come and meet me," and she tapped Maud's arm with her fan, smiling at her little joke, "but the wicked man never showed up. Yes, my dear, Madam Eliza knows what it is to be cast penniless and alone on the mercy of this great city."

A tear broke free and rolled down Maud's pale

cheek. "I wasn't penniless until . . . And even now, once I begin work I shall be able to pay for my keep."

"Why, I wouldn't hear of it. Not until ye're truly hired and earnin' wages, and then you may repay me with some little trifle. But we won't worry about that now. You need a place to lay your head, a bit of food, and a warm glass now and then to tide you over until you can get established. And Madam Eliza's House for Young Ladies is just the place."

Before Maud could reply, the Madam waved her fan at a slim fellow across the yard who came scuttling over, running in a disjointed way. He looked almost as grotesque as the Madam with his thin face, jutting chin, bowed shoulders, and hands that never stopped moving. He bobbed up and down obsequiously, as the Madam heaved herself to her feet, still gripping Maud's arm.

"Jackie, we've a lass here who needs our help. Let's escort dear Maudie back to the premises."

"But . . . I really don't think . . ."

"Jack, you take Miss Maud's bundle. Come along, my girl. Ye'll never regret this, I'm sure."

Maud was not at all certain that going with this strange woman was the wisest thing for her to do, yet her options were extremely limited at the moment, and the woman was very forceful. Her native wish to be obliging won over her discretion, and she fell in beside the Madam as they walked toward the open gateway. They had not gone ten steps before a gentleman in a grand red velvet coat and plumed hat swept up before them, stepping into Eliza's path.

"Mrs. Finchley, good day to you," he said, sweeping off his hat and making an elaborate bow. "May I say how very fine you are looking this afternoon."

Madam glared at him. "Good afternoon," she muttered.

"And are you going to introduce me to your charming companion?" he went on, eying Maud. He grabbed for her hand, but Eliza yanked it away.

"Maud, this is Sir Witherstone. Sir Witherstone, Maud Mellingham."

"Maud. A charming name. I shall have to remember it."

"You've no need," the woman said pointedly. Maud, who could not understand Mrs. Finchley's sudden anger, bobbed him a curtsey.

"We must be on our way. I'm sure ye'll excuse us, Sir Ralph," Eliza snapped, pushing past him. He waved his hat in their direction and bowed again. "Good day then," he called, as they hurried through the gate and into the street.

"Who was that?" Maud asked as she was bustled off.

"No one you wish to know," came the curt reply. Though Maud wanted to ask why, there was no more time for questions as she fell in line between Eliza in front and Jack behind, carrying her bundle.

"Keep to the wall, my dear," Eliza cautioned, as they started down the street. Madam's considerable bulk was enough to heave any interlopers out of the way, clearing a path for her. All the same, Maud found it hard to watch where she was stepping, for there was so much to see all around her that she seldom looked down.

The street between the narrow walkways was a heaving sea of carriages, sedan chairs, and pedestrians, all jostling one another for space. Shops lined both sides, their windows filled with all kinds of luscious wares, their doors spilling out furniture and other assorted goods onto the walkways. Overhead a jungle of huge signs marked the various establishments like massive banners, creaking on their rusted hinges. Often the crude pictures were enough to tell what was made there, but she found it interesting to read some of them as well. They were caught in a crowd that stopped their progress long enough for her to glance up at the wig-maker's sign, where she read:

> *A.S. Holden & Son,*
> *makers of Fine Hair pieces and Perukes*

and underneath:

> *O Absolem, O Absolem,*
> *O Absolem, my Son;*
> *If Thou hast Worn a Periwig,*
> *Thou hast Not Been Undone.*

Maud chuckled to herself as Eliza, finally pushing through the crowd, dragged her across the street. But her smiles soon turned to dismay as the roads grew narrower and darker, and the houses cramming them on both sides more shabby. The streets became a jumble of squalid rookeries and alleys, jammed with people and vehicles. Street-criers shouted their wares, and now and then, Maud caught the fragrant aroma of a tray of pies or a basket of apples. It was a pleasant diversion from the stench emanating from a trench that ran down the middle of the street. Occasionally, with a loud cry of *Ware below!*, someone would open one of the windows jutting over the walkway and dump the contents of a slop bucket or chamber pot into the street. It did not take Maud long to realize the wisdom of "taking the wall."

The noise, the crowds, the miasma of odors, the contrasts—such as a gorgeously robed gentleman in brocade silk, poking the end of his ebony and gold walking stick at a dead cat rotting in a doorway—soon had Maud so confused, that by the time Eliza stopped in front of a rickety timber building with several grimy steps leading to a low porch, she was grateful just to think they had arrived.

"Well, my girl, here it is. Mrs. Finchley's Home

For Homeless Young Women. And glad I am to see it. Me feet is pinchin' something 'orrible."

Maud looked up at the soot-blackened walls and the tiny windows, and her heart sank. She watched with dismay as Eliza pulled a very large key from the front of her dress, heaved herself up the low steps, and fitted it into a brass doorplate that looked as though it had never seen a polishing rag. Throwing the door open, Eliza stood back and beckoned for Maud to enter.

The entrance hall was as dark as nightfall. Maud took one last glance at the fading sunlight in the street, and reluctantly walked up the steps and into the gloom of the house.

Chapter Five

As the door closed behind her, Maud saw a woman waddling down the hall. She was almost as fat as Eliza, but she had none of Mrs. Finchley's tattered elegance. Homely, with puffy features and stringy hair beneath her wilted mobcap, she wore the apron of a servant, but the air of one who knows she is something more.

"Gertrude, we have a new guest," Eliza said, stressing the word guest in a way that made Maud uneasy. "Take her to the kitchen and see that she has something to eat. Then she can come upstairs and meet some of our other girls."

Gertrude motioned Maud down the hall. For a moment Maud was reminded of Cook at Thornwood, but where Cook's brusqueness had an underlying layer of kindness, this woman was obviously hard and mean. When she laid a chunky hand on Maud's shoulder and propelled her toward the kitchen, Maud eased away from her.

She was led into a room smaller and dirtier than any kitchen she had ever seen before. The plate of meat and bread she was served tasted delicious in spite of its poor quality, since she hadn't eaten anything since that morning. Maud polished off every bit, downed a glass of watered ale, and then followed Gertrude upstairs, curious to see what she would find. After climbing two flights of stairs, she was led into a small parlor at the front of the house, overlooking the street. Her first glance took her breath away. Gaudily upholstered chairs, a gold brocade sofa, candelabras dangling crystal drops, and gilt everywhere, on walls, mantel, mirrors, tables; it was the most garish room she had ever seen. Mrs. Finchley was ensconced on the gold sofa, while around her stood several other women in various degrees of plumage.

"Come in, Maud, my dear, and meet some of our other guests." Her voice oozed sweetness. "We are about to have a little tea, aren't we, girls? Pour dear Maud a dish, will you, Patty, there's a dear."

Maud made her way uneasily to the nearest chair and perched on its edge. One of the women who appeared to be near her own age — yet whose paint and limp feathers suggested a weariness that was worlds away — handed her a small handleless cup which held the palest tea Maud had ever seen.

"This is Patty," Eliza said, "and over there's Adeline . . ." She gestured toward a very pretty girl half-asleep on a love seat near the window. "This here is Catherine, and that's Min over there with the scowl on 'er face."

"And well you know why, you old —" Min snapped.

"Now, now, mind yer manners. We don't wish little Maud to think we're not civilized, do we now?"

Mrs. Finchley's pleasant words were belied by such a chilling flintiness in her eyes, that Maud's heart sank. The girl to whom she had spoken so harshly was a thin creature in a soiled white wig that was at least a foot high. Under it, her face was a mask of fury directed at the fat old woman lounging on the sofa. Mrs. Finchley grandly ignored her.

Maud concentrated on her cup and cast furtive glances at the other women. Patty was dark-skinned with large, brooding eyes, while Adeline — the one who seemed about to doze off — was a brunette with heavy-lidded eyes and a pert, round mouth. Though all four women had different coloring and features, there was something very much alike about them, too. They each wore the same type of dress, satinette and taffeta that appeared elegant from a distance, but stained and worn close up. They each wore a lot of jewelry, and all but one, the angry Min, had heavily painted faces. And all four wore the same collection of black satin patches on their faces as Madam Finchley. One of them had several on her arms as well.

"Drink up, Maud, girl," the Madam went on, "and then Min will take you up and show you where you're to sleep. I believe I'll have a refill as well. Hand me the bottle, will you, Min, dear."

"Get it yourself, you lazy old witch!" Min muttered. Quickly Patty reached for the bottle and slopped the contents into Eliza's glass. Eliza glared at Min, but then gave her grimace of a smile and raised her glass toward Maud. Maud lifted the cup, took a tentative swallow, and began to choke.

The liquid seared her throat all the way down. Gasping, she tried to set the glass down, but only managed to drop it, spilling the contents on the carpet.

All five women went into hysterics as Maud fought to catch her breath. "That's not tea—" she gasped.

"Of course not," Patty answered, as her laughter revealed several missing teeth. "Hadn't you ever had gin a'fore? You must be a bumpkin, if you hadn't had gin a'fore."

Gin! No wonder, Maud thought. According to Cook, gin was the devil's own invention, and the streets of London ran with it. Here she hadn't been in the city a day yet, and already she was being undone by gin! "I don't think I want anymore," she said, still rasping.

"Nonsense," Eliza said, waving the decanter in her

direction. "You just ain't got the knack of it yet. Take my word, Maudie, there's no comfort in life like Holland gin. Drink up now, like a good girl."

Reluctantly Maud took a sip. It warmed her insides as before, but was not quite so damaging to her throat. By the third sip she was beginning to feel much better, and by the fourth, decidedly improved. When the room began to grow blurry and she heard herself laughing vacantly like the others, she decided she had better not take anymore, and she only pretended to swallow it. To her relief, Eliza soon lost track of who was drinking and who was not, when a visitor, Lord Ponceford, was introduced.

The gentleman who swept into the room looked more grand than anyone Maud had ever seen. She was familiar with the comfortable elegance of Lord Bambridge, but this man shone like the sun against his lordship's tiny moon. No quiet understatement here — the silver embroidery and brushed velvet of his coat were exquisite. His white wig sparkled like diamonds, and the lace at his throat and wrists was as white as alabaster and as delicately spun as spiderwebs. A jewel on his jabot flashed like a comet, when it caught the light.

And yet, though Maud was impressed with Lord Ponceford's elegance, there was something about him that turned her flesh to ice. His heavy jowls sagged between the curls of his wig, and his protruding, thick lips seemed perpetually moist. His eyes were small, and the lids hung over them like a tortoise, while his hand, as he took Maud's, was soft and spongy. She had to repress a shudder as he lifted her fingers to those wet lips.

Eliza at once began to impress Lord Ponceford with Maud's virtues, embarrassing her even more. "Is she not a ripe, young beauty?" she asked, forcing Maud to stand and pirouette. Maud could not help but notice that while Mrs. Finchley made her the object of attention, the other women stood about glaring angrily at her. "Wait until you see her spruced up a bit," Eliza went on. Maud wanted to protest that she would soon be leaving, but she wasn't allowed a word as Eliza and his Lordship went on appraising her as though she wasn't even there.

"Pray, take tea with me," Lord Ponceford said in a sultry voice, leering into her face.

"Now, don't be hasty," Eliza said quickly. "At the soiree tomorrow evening, you shall be allowed to monopolize her. But you must wait until then. After all, she's only just . . . joined us."

Lord Ponceford devoured Maud with his eyes. "I only hope I shall be able to contain myself until then."

A few moments later, Eliza sent Maud upstairs with Min to find her bed.

"The old bitch!" Min hissed once the door was closed behind them. "She wants me out of the way so her darling Adeline can have his lordship all to herself. Damn her eyes!"

Astounded at such language, as well as the anger that inspired it, Maud timidly followed Min up two flights of stairs. "Well, come on then," the girl snapped at the way Maud lagged behind. "I don't have all day. I have my own gentleman friends to entertain."

The top floor of the house was one large room under the eaves, with several cots lining each side. Maud saw her bundle on one of them and thankfully eased herself down beside it. Although Min was anything but friendly, Maud had some burning questions she wanted answered before the girl could turn on her heel and leave.

"Have you just come here, too?" she asked as Min started toward the stairs. She was relieved when Min stopped and turned back.

81

"Me? Blister me, no. I've been here nearly two years."

"Two years! But I thought . . . Mrs. Finchley said . . ."

Min crossed her thin arms over her chest and laughed at Maud. "She told you that you would only stay until you got your own place, didn't she? That's what she tell 'em all, the lyin' bitch. But that's only to get poor simpletons like yourself into her clutches. You're never goin' to leave this house. You might as well know that now."

A cold chill gripped Maud's chest. "What do you mean?"

"She told you that you could sleep here just to lure you inside! But now that you're here, you'll never get out. Nobody ever does."

"I don't understand . . ."

Min softened a little at the distraught look on Maud's innocent face. "Don't you know what you've walked into? Don't you have any idea what kind of house this is?"

Maud turned her luminous gaze on the girl, afraid to answer for fear that her worst imaginings would be confirmed.

"You don't know anything, do you?" Min said more gently. "You country girls—you're all alike. You come to London thinking you're going to find the world waiting for you with open arms, and instead you walk right into the clutches of a money-grubbing old whore like Eliza Finchley. If I didn't hate her so much—"

Min caught her breath at the sudden thought that this lovely, innocent wench might be a means of getting her revenge on Madam Eliza, who obviously expected Maud to be a pliable girl. But what if she wasn't so ignorant or soft? Perhaps the Madam's expectations might not be met in quite the way she expected.

Walking back to the bed, Min laid an arm across Maud's shoulder in a gesture of sympathy that brought tears to the girl's eyes. "Now, don't cry. It's true you got yourself into a flash house, and not such a good one neither, but if you face up to that old woman, you might be able to keep her from getting the better of you."

"How?" Maud asked in a choked voice.

"Well, to begin with, watch out for the gin. The more you drink it, the more you want it, and pretty soon, that's all you want. That's how she gets you on her string, and keeps you there. So, that's the first thing — don't let her get you on the gin."

Maud nodded, recognizing good advice.

"Second, like as not she'll take every penny you earn. Oh, she'll tell you that you get to keep a third, but don't believe her. Cheat and lie, if you have to, but put some by for yourself. That's your only hope of getting out of here someday."

"Earn — ?"

"On your back, nobby. What else do you think we do here? Now, third. Are you a virgin?"

Maud nodded again, still trying to come to terms with the fact that the horror she had suspected since she walked into the parlor below was now confirmed.

"You country wenches! You all *say* you're virgins, even when you're not."

"No, it's true. I really am."

Min thought a moment. "I think I believe you. It explains why Eliza was buttering you up to Lord Ponceford just now. He'll pay a pretty penny to deflower a virgin — that's his specialty."

Maud stared at her in horror. "You mean . . ."

"I do indeed. And he'll only be the first. After that you'll have to serve all the gentlemen callers, just like the rest of us."

She was beyond tears now. Rage, slow and smouldering, seeped through her distress. "I didn't like

83

him. In fact, I thought he was the most repulsive man I've ever met."

"What's that got to do with anything? Nobody likes him. He *is* repulsive. But he's also very rich, and if you played your cards right, you might be able to get out of here sooner rather than later."

"Never!"

"Oh, you will all right. In fact, you'll let him do anything he wants, and some of these gentlemen have strange tastes. Believe me, I know."

Maud's blood turned to ice. She jumped up, pacing the small space between the cots. "Is there no way I can get out of this house? No escape?"

"None that ever worked. Between old Gertrude and Jack Smirk, you'll never leave the premises without them seeing you or going with you. As for the gentlemen, there's only a few days of the month when you're allowed to put them off. Your best trick would be to accept your fate and make sure you get the ones that pay the most. Now, I'd better go back downstairs before that slut Adeline robs me of my best customers. She may look like she's half-asleep, but don't believe it. She's a cat, always ready to pounce."

Maud stopped her pacing long enough to grip Min's hand. "Thank you for being so honest with me."

For the first time the girl's hard face softened a little, and Maud realized they were nearly the same age.

"Too bad we can't be friends," Min snapped, "but you can't have friends in here. We all have to look out for ourselves."

When Min was nearly out the door, Maud called her back. "Min, what are those patches everybody wears? And why do they wear so many of them?"

"Don't you know about the pox?"

"The smallpox?"

"No, ninny. The French pox! Merciful heavens, you *are* ignorant! Everybody gets the pox in these houses. It will give you sores—though not at first—so you cover the sores with patches."

"But I've seen them on gentlemen, too."

Min shrugged. "They like to say it's us whores that gives them the pox, but like as not, it's the other way around. Anyway, you can't avoid it. You'll get it too, mark my words."

The blood drained from Maud's face and she raised her hand to her smooth cheek. "Is there no way to avoid it?"

"None that I know. There's a few things you can do to cure it, though. A dose of quicksilver every morning helps, and a salve made from bruised nettles and brandy applied to the sores helps them heal quicker."

"It sounds terrible!"

"You'll get used to it. Everybody does."

For a long time after Min left, Maud sat on the edge of her bed and thought back over their conversation. One thing was certain—she had to escape from this awful house. But how, when she was constantly watched? And where could she go? Without that letter, Cynthia Wiltshire was never going to take her in. Especially if she learned Maud had been taken in by Eliza Finchley.

She fought down the urge to grab her bundle and run for the stairs, and decided that it would be best to wait until early morning, when everyone was asleep. In the meantime, she must not allow Lord Ponceford to lay a hand on her, if she wanted to avoid getting the pox. The only way to do that was to convince Eliza that she had her monthly flux, even if she didn't. Just in case the old harridan wanted proof, she would slip down to the kitchen and steal one of the poultry gizzards she had noticed there earlier. Applied to a few old rags, it would serve her purpose.

A short time later, having carried out the first step in her plan, Maud returned to her room and fell into an exhausted sleep. After the first drugged restful hours passed, she was awakened by noise from the downstairs rooms; after that, she only slept fitfully. Music, laughter, thumping, and loud voices roused her intermittently, until she could see the first gray lights of dawn seeping through the room. Still, she was thankful no one had come to fetch her downstairs during the night. Mrs. Finchley had at least allowed her this night to herself, whatever her reasons.

As the light increased in the room, she began to see the other women creep to their beds. The noise below had quieted by now, but with the other women in the room it was going to be difficult to slip out. She sat on the edge of her bed and fought down the urge to flee from this awful house, no matter who might see her.

She had no money, no prospects, no place to go. She was adrift in a dangerous city where she had no one to turn to for help. Suddenly, fleeing to the streets did not seem a viable alternative.

Perhaps she could stick it out here for one or two days, long enough to get her bearings and try to beg, borrow, or steal enough money to get by, until she could throw herself on Cynthia Wiltshire's mercy. If she pretended to be as ignorant and naive as they believed her to be, perhaps she could manage to stay out of Eliza's traps and find a way to escape.

She went downstairs to the kitchen, determined to butter up the horrible Gertrude, if it would help her find a way out of the house. She quickly realized this was not possible. Gertrude had nothing but contempt for the ladies of the house, and she was not about to be softened by a stupid country wench like Maud. Breakfast was hardly finished before she was summoned by Mrs. Finchley.

Maud spent the morning with Eliza and Min, having her hair arranged in elaborate puffs and curls, and choosing a tired satin dress with lace flounces and hoops so wide she had to turn sideways to get through a door. It had a shocking decolletage that exposed her swelling breasts almost to the nipples. She was given a paste diamond necklace to set it off, a silken patch on one flawless cheek, and two rather limp feathers to raise her hair even higher.

"There, now. Old Queen Caroline herself never looked no better. In fact, that German sow never looked as good. God rest 'er soul," Eliza said, chuckling at her little joke. "I want you to be on yer best be'aivour today, for ye'll be entertaining Lord Ponceford this evening."

Maud took a deep breath, and confessed to Eliza that this was the wrong time of the month to be entertaining a gentleman. Though she did not believe her at first, and claimed to be shocked that Maud ever dreamed she expected such a thing of her, she finally shrugged and said:

"No matter. Two days' delay will only whet his appetite that much more. Play y'er cards right, Maud, my girl, and ye'll have his lordship wanting you so badly that he'll give you anything you ask. He's very rich. Ye're a fortunate girl, and I hope you know it."

Maud smiled, hoping she looked sufficiently bedazzled by her good fortune.

But later that morning, when she was forced to spend time alone with Lord Ponceford in the salon, her resolution began to waver. He appeared before her garbed in an embroidered coat stiff with gold lace and with a brilliant sapphire at his throat. Yet his devouring eyes and wet lips seemed more repulsive than the day before. His chunky hands were all over her, stroking the nipples below the ruching of her gown, sliding up under her skirt, pinching, grabbing, clutching, grasping. Maud began to think he must have eight arms instead of two. Though he wore no telltale black patch, she was terrified that his hands or his foul breath would give her the pox. Yet the more she evaded him, the more insistent he became. Finally, when it became apparent that there was no other way to put him off, she fell into a swoon that sent him running in great agitation for a burnt feather or some vinaigrette. No sooner had the door closed behind him, than Maud was peeking through it, waiting for him to disappear down the hall so she could dash off in the opposite direction. She had hoped to run upstairs to the attic room, but she heard voices coming down the stairs and instead made a dash to the floor below, darting through the first double doors she could find. She closed them tightly behind her and leaned against them, hardly daring to breathe.

She was in some kind of drawing room, very large, elegant, and, thankfully, empty. Four rows of gilt chairs were arranged facing the other end of the room, where several velvet curtains were hung around a low dais. A ladder stood on one side of the dais and a table on the other, covered with a long black cloth embroidered with gold symbols.

She stiffened as she heard her name being called outside, followed by footsteps on the stairs.

"God's blood!" she exclaimed aloud. "I'll never get away!"

Frantically she looked around the room. The drapes were too narrow to conceal her hooped skirt, and the covered table was too small. "There must be someplace to hide," she cried, darting toward the dais. She was stopped halfway down by a sudden trilling sound of bird song.

"Chirp, chirp . . . good morrow . . . chirp chirp."

Then she saw the bird cage. A great hoop of interlaced wire sitting near the covered table. With a shock of recognition, she stared at the little bird inside, hopping around and trilling merrily.

"Chir-rr-up, hide here . . . hide here . . . chirp . . ."

"Everarde! Is that you?" she gasped.

"Up here . . . chir-rr-up. Hide here."

Without another word Maud rushed to the dais and darted behind the curtains. Just as the doors to the room were thrown open and Eliza sailed in, a strong arm suddenly clasped Maud around the waist and pulled her farther into the gloom. She looked up, stunned, into Alan Desmond's smiling, mischievous eyes. His hand went over her mouth to muffle her shocked cry. Together, they froze. Eliza's wooden heels clattered on the floor as she approached the dais.

"Maud!" Eliza called in a voice full of indignation. "Where are you, you naughty girl. Come here at once!"

Maud sucked in her breath and shrank back against Alan. From the other side of the dais, she saw a familiar figure emerge from behind the velvet hangings opposite her, as Jeremy stepped out and made Eliza an elaborate bow.

"Good morrow, Mrs. Finchley."

"Oh, it's you, Jeremy. Have you seen a girl running through here? Very fair, red-gold hair, wearing a green dress."

"Why, no, ma'am. There's been no one here to keep me company but my faithful Everarde." He gestured toward the bird cage, and the bird broke into frenzied chirping.

"Now none of yer conjuring tricks on me, you rascally rogue. This girl's new and headstrong, and she must be taught a lesson."

"Why, Madam Eliza, would I tell you a lie? Perish the thought! Everarde, perhaps, but never me."

"Not I, chirp, chirp," the bird echoed. "Jeremy, perhaps, but never me, chirp, chirp."

"Humph. Ye're both rogues, as is that handsome

ne'er-do-well, Master Desmond. Very well, but if you do see her, keep away from her, you hear me? And tell Master Desmond the same. I'll deal with Mistress Maud meself."

Turning on her heels, she clumped to the door and slammed it behind her.

Maud let out a sigh as Alan's arms released her. She stared up at him, her eyes round as saucers, still not believing he was there. Yet surely that was his handsome face, looking down at her with a surprised but mischievous smile on his lips and a glimmer of delight in his eyes.

"Well, Mistress Maud," he said, grinning at her. "We meet again. And under most unusual circumstances, I must say."

Relief flooded over her. "Alan!" she cried, throwing her arms around his neck. "You can't know how glad I am to see you!" She pressed her face into the hollow of his neck, rejoicing in the feel of his strong body. His arms went around her waist, and she was filled with both comfort and delight. Just being close to him again made her feel that now everything was going to be right again.

Alan tightened his grip around Maud. He had recognized her the moment she stepped into the ballroom, and he was still dumbfounded, both at seeing her again, and in such a place as this! He'd never forgotten the time they spent together in Suffolk, and had taken it for granted that she would still be there one day when he happened back that way. What luck to come across her again in teeming London! He pulled her closer, reveling in the feel of her small waist, the pressure of her breasts against his chest, her cheek against his skin above his linen neckcloth. Getting a grip on himself, he put his hands on her shoulders and stepped back, just as Jeremy came running over, his eyes full of questions.

"I can't believe it, Miss Maud," Jeremy cried.

"You, here in a flash house like this 'un? How'd you ever come to be here?"

"Yes, Miss Maud," Alan added. "I was wondering that myself. How did you come to be in London, much less in the clutches of an old witch like Eliza Finchley?"

Maud felt her knees begin to give way and sat down on the dais, her skirts billowing out on either side. To her consternation, she began to cry.

"Oh, my dear," Jeremy said, hovering over her. "I didn't mean to upset you. Don't weep. We won't ask anymore questions."

"It's all right," she said between sobs. "It's just that I've felt so alone, and then to see friends again . . . I'm so relieved and happy. But I didn't mean to cry."

Alan went down on one knee before her and handed her his large linen handkerchief. "So, Mistress Maud. Madam Finchley is very angry with you? Why? Were you running from her?"

"No, not exactly. I was running from Lord Ponceford, though I would not be sorry never to see either of them again. They're both horrible."

"Let me guess," Alan said, taking a seat beside her on the dais and resting his elbows on his knees. "You had only just arrived in London, and Eliza swooped down and offered you a place to stay."

"Yes, just until I found something else."

"Only you have no other place to go."

"That's because a vile little cutpurse stole my reticule almost before my foot touched the ground of the coaching inn. Otherwise, I never would have come here."

"How very convenient. Did you tell Eliza this?"

"She was there. She saw it."

Alan and Jeremy exchanged knowing glances. "And she stepped in like a fairy godmother. It's her way of snaring penniless girls and keeping them here.

Poor Maud. I'm afraid you've got yourself in something of a fix."

The tears fell soundlessly on her pale cheeks. "I didn't realize it was a . . . a flash house, truly I didn't. Lord Bambridge gave me a letter to his daughter, and I was supposed to work in her household. But that was stolen along with my money."

Alan reached for his damp handkerchief and gently dabbed her cheek with it. "Well, don't cry. You're not helpless or alone any longer. Fate has sent you to Jeremy and me, and we'll see that you are saved, both for your sake and to spite that horrible old harridan."

Maud's eyes glistened as she smiled her gratitude at him. She was struck once more by what a pleasant face he had—generous, wide mouth, merry eyes, and a strong chin with a cleft in the center. He looked very fine, too, with his hair pulled back and tied in a queue, his long black coat, and his buckled shoes with the red heels.

Jeremy laid a sympathetic hand on her shoulder. "We've seen this happen to other girls, Miss Maud. Most of them get sucked into this terrible life and never escape. I dare say we won't let that happen to you."

Maud's heart swelled with gratitude, and she reached up to squeeze his hand. "But . . . Jeremy, Alan, why are you here? I never thought to find you in a place like this." She had a sudden, horrible thought. "You're not . . . customers, are you?"

Alan laughed. "Customers? Egad, no. We're not warm enough in the purse for her tastes. We were hired to perform at the soiree tomorrow evening, and we were just setting up for it."

"Everarde loves to put on a show, mistress," Jeremy said, trilling a few notes of bird song.

"The acting company!" Maude cried, clapping her hands. "Are they coming here?"

"Not this time. It's just Jeremy and me. He does his conjuring tricks, and I assist him behind the curtain." Alan cocked his head to one side and studied Maud. He had forgotten just how beautiful she was, with her porcelain skin, large blue eyes the color of periwinkles, petal-soft lips, and creamy breasts swelling above the ruching of her dress. Even the tawdry satin set off her loveliness in a way the country fustian never had. No wonder Eliza wanted to keep her under lock and key.

"Look here, Maude," he said, "What will you do if we get you away from Madam Finchley? Do you want to go back to Thornwood?"

"Faith, no. I want to find Lady Wiltshire, and convince her that her father really did send me to work for her. Though I doubt she'll believe me without his letter. Most of all, I want to leave this house, where everyone gets the pox and I have to be fondled by gross old men like Lord Ponceford."

"Well, I certainly cannot blame you for that. Come, Jeremy. We must put our heads together and figure out a way to help Mistress Maud escape."

"Faith, we must," Jeremy said, and threw in a few trills for good measure. Getting to his feet, Alan clasped his hands behind his back and took a few strides back and forth before Maud.

"It won't be easy. Eliza watches her girls like a vulture. And yet, we should have a better chance of rescuing you than anyone else. She does not take either of us very seriously and, as far as she knows, we've never even met you, Maud." He stopped rubbing his chin. "Truth to tell, I wouldn't mind giving the old biddy a little of her own medicine for once. In payment for all the lives she's ruined."

Maud was filled with hope for the first time since she entered Eliza's house. "Oh, Alan, thank you," she cried, jumping to her feet and impulsively kissing him on the cheek.

"What about me?" Jeremy asked shyly. "Don't I get some thanks, too?"

"Yes, indeed," Maud answered, giving him a peck on his round cheek. "I'm so grateful to you both."

"We'll have to plan carefully, for Eliza is nobody's fool. You must pretend to go along with her little plan, I think, Maud. At least until tomorrow night. Do you think you can fend off his lordship for that long?"

"Yes. I'll find some way to handle him."

"Good. Go back now and tell her you're sorry. Then tomorrow come down here again. By then, we'll have worked out a way to whisk you out of this house."

Maud glanced at the door, her face turning a shade paler. To encourage her, Alan took her hand and pressed the fingers to his lips. Looking down at her, his eyes full of promise, he smiled and said, "Courage. It won't be for long."

Maud gave him a dazzling smile in return. "I'll be all right, as long as I know there is hope. You've both made me so happy."

"It gives me great happiness to see you again."

She started toward the door as the little bird hopped about in its cage. "I'm happy too, chir-rr-up," Everarde sang.

Chapter Six

For the rest of the day and most of the following morning, Maud endured Mrs. Finchley's scoldings and bided her time until she could escape to the ballroom again. Though Eliza was very angry with Maud, she felt the girl was still too new and untried to vent her displeasure on her too much. She also had great plans for her, and was not anxious to ruin them by setting the girl against her right at the start. Once Lord Ponceford had had his fun with her, Maud would still be young and pretty enough to become a drawing card. Eliza could almost hear the coins clinking when she thought about it.

For her part, Maud played the part of the repentant young girl who had allowed fear to get the best of her. Keeping her fingers tightly crossed behind her back, she promised to be good and not irritate Lord Ponceford ever again. Mrs. Finchley decided that Maud and his lordship would share a private supper in her own quarters following the entertainment, so Maud was spared having to fend him off during the afternoon.

She slipped away after the noon meal, when the first callers were beginning to fill the parlor, and quietly opened the drawing room doors, then closing them tightly behind her. Jeremy was fussing about on the dais, but Alan was nowhere in sight, and for a moment her disappointment welled. Then he appeared from behind the curtain, walking toward her to clasp her hands.

"I was afraid you wouldn't come," he said, kissing her cheek lightly.

"I was terrified I wouldn't be able to get away. I kept wondering if it was a dream that I saw you and Jeremy yesterday."

"Not a dream," he answered, raising her hands to his lips, "but real flesh and blood. How is everything going? That old witch didn't hurt you, did she?"

"No. I convinced her that panic had overcome me for a little while, and promised to behave myself. But what will I do now? She has arranged a private dinner for me tonight with Lord Ponceford, and you and I both know where that is supposed to lead. My knees tremble at the thought."

Alan laid an arm around her shoulder and led her to the dais. Jeremy, among trills from the bird cage, gave her a warm smile. He had filled the table with all kinds of contraptions that were new to Maud, but she was too engrossed in her own problems to be very curious about them.

"A supper party," Alan mused. "That could be to our advantage. Yes, Madam Eliza could not have planned it for us any better if she tried."

"But I'll be alone with that man for hours! I'm afraid."

"Don't be, my girl. We won't leave you alone very long. But food and drink raise all kinds of possibilities. Do you think you could slip something into his wine?"

"I could try."

"Oh, Mister Desmond," Jeremy said from behind the table. "Not that old sleeping-draught-in-the-wine trick! Surely, you can do better."

Alan waved his hand. "It may be hoary, but it still works beautifully. Now listen, Maud. Tonight at the soiree, I'll slip you a small vial. Somehow you must introduce the contents into his lordship's wineglass at supper. Once he's out cold, we'll have you whisked out of here before you know what's happening."

It sounded a little too easy. Maud bit her lower lip nervously. "But what about Mrs. Finchley? You know she'll be watching me like a vulture all evening."

"Don't worry about Eliza. I'll take care of her. In fact, it shall give me great pleasure to do so. Now, you'd better get back before you're missed. We'll see you tonight."

Maud clung to Alan's hand for a moment. He seemed so strong and capable, like a lifeline in a turbulent sea. "Tonight, then."

Alan kissed her cheek again, and gave her a little pat on the back of her skirt to send her toward the door. "Tonight!"

It took hours for Maud to dress for the evening's party. Madam Eliza had made up her mind that no more time should be wasted, and she set about trying to make Maud look as gloriously overdressed as possible. This frock was newer than the green satin, and so heavily embroidered that it could almost stand alone. Her white throat, her ears, her arms, wrists, and fingers were heavy with jewels, all of them paste except one brilliant ring which Eliza made certain Maud knew had been borrowed from Eliza's personal hoard. Her hair was lifted, piled, and supplemented with puffs and curls, until it stood nearly two feet high. Then ornaments, artificial flowers, and feathers were woven into it to make it even taller. She wore stockings with embroidered clocks, and shoes with bright yellow heels. All in all, she had never looked so fancy or been so uncomfortable in her life. Still, she might have enjoyed it except for the nagging thought of the supper with Lord Ponceford which was to end the evening.

So laden with finery that she could hardly move,

she went through the motions of enduring his lordship's attentions in the parlor, until the whole crowd headed downstairs to the large ballroom for the entertainment. There were not enough chairs for everyone, and Maud managed to take the last one in the third row, leaving Ponceford to stand behind her. She expected to see everyone's attention focused on the performance, but all around her the ladies and their gentleman friends were so busy talking and laughing and fondling each other, that not much attention was paid to what was happening on the dais.

It was too bad, for Jeremy was really quite good. He had Maud openmouthed with wonder at the amazing things he could do with his magic lantern, conjuring tricks and, of course, Everarde's antics. However, the rest of the audience only focused on the stage during the times Alan appeared to read several poems and passages. Several of the poems were quite bawdy, and had the women and men guffawing while Maud squirmed in her chair. He looked so absolutely handsome in his old-fashioned periwig, satin breeches, long flowing cloak casually thrown back over one shoulder, with a sword by his side and a feathered Cavalier hat held in his long fingers, that even Maud might have swooned if she had not been so full of trepidation.

Then the performance was over, and the audience crowded around Alan and Jeremy. Min and Patty were quite open about inviting Alan to enjoy their company, and even Adeline flashed her sultry gaze at him and pointedly rubbed her ample bosom against his arm. Maud would have fled the room, except she knew she had to retrieve that vial from him somehow.

To her horror she saw Eliza swoop down and bear Alan off. Though revolted by the way the old woman simpered at the handsome actor, Maud's disgust quickly turned to panic when she saw Mrs. Finchley leading him toward the door. Lord Ponceford had already grabbed her arm and was running his clammy fingers along her bare shoulder. "I can hardly wait," he said breathily, leaning against her to plant a moist kiss on the nape of her neck. Maud shuddered and watched Alan Desmond's retreating form with increasing alarm. Surely, he was not going to desert her! Was this his idea of helping her, to leave her in the hands of this lecherous, horrible man? And how was she ever going to get the vial from him, if he disappeared upstairs with Eliza Finchley?

Anger and fear set her heart thumping, even as she tried to evade Lord Ponceford's grasping hands. Quickly she swung behind on one of the spindly chairs, keeping it between herself and Ponceford.

"Don't be coy, child . . ." his lordship said, giggling. Maud gripped the back of the chair, determined to make a run for it. Then she saw the crowd parting and Alan pushing his way back to her, Eliza firmly on his arm.

"Mister Desmond expressed a wish to meet you, my child," Eliza said in a clipped voice. "She is beautiful, is she not, Alan? You of all men would appreciate that."

"Very beautiful," Alan breathed, taking Maud's hand and raising it to his lips. When he lowered it, she had the tiny vial clasped firmly in her hand. "You grace this house, Mistress . . . what was the name?"

"Maud. Maud Mellingham."

"Come along, Maud," Lord Ponceford exclaimed, yanking her arm away. "I believe we have supper waiting."

"I should be honored to take you into supper, Miss Maud," Alan offered.

"Never mind," his lordship snapped. "She's coming with me. Miss Maud's taste doesn't run to actors," he sneered, looking down his long nose.

"And you are taking supper with me, you naughty boy," Eliza added. "You promised you would, and heaven knows how long I've been trying to entice you to do so."

"I have a capital idea," Alan exclaimed. "Why don't we all take supper together? Think what fun that would be."

Eliza's jaw dropped. "No, no. It's not possible. Lord Ponceford and Maud have an . . . an arrangement tonight. Their supper is very private."

"But they can still have their arrangement following supper. I wouldn't dream of interfering with that."

"It's out of the question, dear boy," Ponceford said in a steely voice.

Alan turned to Eliza. "Oh, I think it would be lovely, the four of us. And then we can all go on to our separate . . . arrangements." There was just enough of a hint of promise in the way he said it, to make the old woman's heart leap with anticipation.

"Well, I suppose it might be arranged," Eliza grudgingly agreed.

"I insist . . ." Alan said, focusing his gaze firmly on Eliza's fat face.

"Now, your lordship, we'll just have a quick bite with you and Maud, then be on our way," Eliza promised a fuming Ponceford. "I promise you it won't interfere with your night's pleasure."

To Maud's disgust, Alan laid a possessive arm around Eliza's plump shoulder, and smiled like a simpleton as he pushed her toward the hall.

"It had better not," Ponceford snapped, following Maud.

Supper had been laid in a curtained alcove of the most gawdy bedroom Maud had ever seen. The walls were covered with flocked paper interspersed with framed paintings depicting lovers in assorted lewd positions. A tall tester bed hung with pink satin curtains dominated the room. The furniture was white and gold, but there was little of it. Tall ornate mirrors filled the spaces between the paintings, reflecting the candles on sconces and the chandelier. Maude assumed it was Eliza's own room, until she heard the Madam effusively confide that her own bedroom lay beyond the closed door on one wall.

It quickly became obvious that supper was to be little more than a prelude to other things. A platter of cold meats, a tray of cheeses, and a bowl of fruit filled the spaces between china and silver. There were several glasses, and no less than four bottles of wine on the sideboard near the table.

"I've sent the servants away," Eliza said, lifting her hoops to settle on one of the spindly chairs. The only servant Maud had seen since coming to Mrs. Finchley's house was the gross Gertrude, so she knew this was said to impress the gentlemen. Yet she was so grateful that Eliza and Alan were in the room, that she wisely kept quiet. Alan fell on the food as though it was a feast for a king, filling Eliza's glass with every sip she took and entertaining them all with stories of the stage. Eliza's laugh grew more raucous, and her perch on the chair more precarious with every glass. Yet to Maud's rising consternation, Lord Ponceford refused to take more than a sip from his wineglass. He preferred to concentrate on pawing her, rubbing her arms, giving her neck slobbery kisses, even slipping his hand up beneath her skirt—not an easy feat considering the wide hoops she was wearing. Alan did his best to divert him, growing more garrulous as Eliza grew more intoxicated and Ponceford more amorous.

Finally, in a desperate move, she managed to knock over Ponceford's glass, spilling the dark liquid on her skirt. "Oh, good heavens, how clumsy of me," she cried, jumping away from him.

"Don't bother with it," Ponceford said, taking advantage of the situation to rub her skirt with his napkin. "You won't be wearing it much longer anyway—that is, if this boorish actor will realize he is unwelcome and take Mrs. Finchley off."

"Boorish! Sir, I resent that . . ."

Maud threw Alan a warning glance. "At least allow me to replenish your glass," she said, evading Ponceford's hands. Taking his glass, she turned her back to him, filled it, and added the liquid from the vial in with the wine. She swirled it a few times—hoping it would mix—and took it back to the table.

"I demand an apology," Alan said, playing his role to the hilt.

"What you will get is a thump on the head, if you do not leave this room at once. Can't you tell when you're not wanted?"

"Yes," Eliza said in a slurred voice. "Let us be off, dear Mister Desmond. Off . . . next door . . ."

"An insult cannot be tolerated, sir. I demand satisfaction!"

"Oh, be off with you. This is not the stage of Drury Lane. Besides, I never fight anyone who is not a gentleman, and preferably an Earl."

Alan knew Maud had drugged Ponceford's wine, but he was as aware as she that his lordship was not taking much of it. Yet he had diverted Ponceford about as long as he could. A little longer, and the man would probably try to toss him through the connecting door himself. Not that he could actually do it, but the trouble it would cause would make it damnably hard to spirit Maud away quietly. He decided he had to risk letting the girl take it from this point.

"Come along, Mrs. Finchley," he said, dragging Eliza up. The chair toppled backward as she leaned against him. "Let us withdraw."

"Yes, oh, yes. Right through . . . there . . ." she said, lifting a limp hand to point. Maud looked frantically at Alan, begging him with her eyes not to leave her alone with Ponceford.

In despair, she watched him half-drag Eliza through the door and close it.

"Egad, my sweet. At last we are alone," Ponceford cried, closing his arms around her. "I thought I could bear it no longer!"

She ducked away from him, sitting back down at the table. "But we haven't finished supper, my lord. Look, you've barely touched your wine."

"Bah! Who wants food or wine, when there is a sweet morsel like you to taste instead?" He came up behind her, leaning over to reach beneath her bodice and grasp her breasts, lifting them upward and clutching at her soft flesh.

"Please, your lordship," Maud cried, slapping his hands away and darting out of the chair, closing her hands over her breasts. "Really, you go too fast."

"Ah, but I've waited so long," he cried, running after her. She ducked behind the table and he jumped in front of it, darting after her whichever way she turned.

"Oh, it's a game. I like that, really I do! Makes it all the more exciting."

In desperation Maud reached for his glass and held it toward him. "Come now, just a few sips and the game will be over."

"And you promise to behave?"

"Absolutely. I'll be good and do whatever you want."

Carefully he reached for the glass and raised it to his lips. Maud inched around the table, hoping to get by him, but he immediately set the wine down again and grabbed her arm. "You are all the wine I want tonight, my pet," he said, pulling her to him. All subtlety flew out the window, as Maud found herself clutched in his enormous grasp. She fought in vain. Between his impatience to have her and his excitement caused by her attempts to flee, she was powerless. Screaming and fighting, she was dragged over to the bed, her dress ripped down the front, and she was thrown on the covers in a heap.

"Damned hoops," Ponceford cried. "Inventions of the devil! Take them off at once."

Tangled in the wide hoops and the long skirt of her dress, Maud struggled to the other side of the bed.

She felt his hands climbing her legs, thrusting between them and moving upward to deftly untie the tapes of her hoops. Frantically she pushed the wire contraption downward and slithered out of it, yanking up her skirts and throwing the hoops over Ponceford's head. He laughed at her antics and tore them away, while she went bounding off the other side of the bed, running for the door. Without her hoops her skirt was twice as long, and halfway across the room she became tangled in the hem. He dove after her and they both landed on the floor. Ponceford was breathing hard, but more excited than ever.

"I must have you," he cried. "Now . . . now! Can't wait . . ."

Clasped together they rolled over and over back toward the bed. "For God's sake, be still!" he yelled, pulling at his own clothes and trying to hold on to her at the same time.

"Let me go!" Maud screamed, slapping at him with her fists. With a sudden lunge she managed to break free and rolled over to the bed, trying to scramble to her feet. She was breathing hard now herself. She knew she would not last much longer. Then her hand grasped something and she pulled, dragging a long-handled warming pan out from under the bed.

Dragging herself to her knees and gasping for air, she saw him scuttling along the floor after her.

"Don't come any closer!"

"But, my little pet, I can't wait any longer."

Maud struggled to her feet, swinging the warming pan like a flail. "I warn you . . ."

"Enough of this playacting. It's time for the serious—"

Maud swung the pan without looking, acting from pure instinct. She heard the loud clunk of the brass as it encountered his lordship's head and stopped, looking on horror-struck as he fell back on the floor. In the sudden silence she lowered the handle and stared, her heart pounding. "Oh, my God. What have I done?"

"You've given him a sound bashing, I should say," Alan spoke from the doorway. "Congratulations, my dear. No one ever deserved it more."

Maud turned in fury. "You viper! How could you leave me alone with him? I thought you were going to help!"

He hurried to her side. "You've managed very well without me. Besides, I had to tend to dear Eliza. My, look at you. I heard the thumping in here, but I had no idea it was as savage as all that."

Maud got a glimpse of herself in one of the long mirrors. Her hair was tangled and drooping around her face. Her dress was torn at the top and hanging like a stage curtain around her legs. She looked almost comical, if she had been in any state to laugh.

"Where is Mrs. Finchley?"

"Passed out on the bed, as soon as I laid her down. What about him? Did he drink the wine?"

"He wouldn't touch it. I didn't know what else to do."

He took the pan from her trembling fingers. "An admirable weapon. I couldn't have thought of a better one myself. But he'll awaken soon. We'd better think of something else."

Maud's legs refused to move, even when Ponceford gave a low moan. She watched as Alan fetched the wineglass with the drugged wine and knelt beside the comatose man, lifting his shoulders and cradling his head.

"Oh . . . what happened . . ." Ponceford moaned.

Alan winked at Maud and answered in a high voice that mimicked hers. "You fell and hit your head. You'll be fine in a moment. Just drink this."

Still half-unconscious, Ponceford sipped the wine. Though he tried to push it away, Alan managed to get most of it down his throat, then laid him gently back on the floor. "Throw me that pillow," he said to

Maud. Gently settling Ponceford's head on the pillow, he rose and took Maud's arm.

"In a few minutes, he'll be out for hours. Come on, let's get away from here."

She clung to his strong arm, only able to move by leaning on him. They were almost to the door when she remembered Eliza's ring.

"Wait," she said, pulling it off her finger. "I must return this. I don't want her calling me a thief."

"You've earned it this night."

"No. She'd use it to bring charges against me. I'll only be a moment."

Feeling stronger, she fled next door to Eliza's room, and saw a large chest on one of the tables. Ignoring the heavy breathing coming from the bed, she slipped open one of the drawers and laid the ring inside. She was about to close it, when she spied a familiar piece of jewelry. With a cry she lifted it from the drawer.

"What is it?" Alan whispered from the doorway. "We must hurry."

"My brooch! That is, Lady Julia's brooch. But that means—"

Throwing a furious glance at the somnolent figure on the bed, she began pulling out the drawers, one by one. Near the bottom she found what she was looking for. "It's Lord Bambridge's letter. Why, that wicked old hag! All this time it was *she* who robbed me! Where is my money, I wonder."

But Alan gripped her arm. "It won't be here. You'll never get that back. Come on, we need to escape from this house, before either of them wakes up and realizes what has happened."

Reluctantly, Maud agreed. It was more than she ever hoped just to get the brooch and letter back. She paused only long enough to yank a sash from one of the curtains to tie up her drooping skirt, and followed Alan into the hall. They slipped downstairs to the ballroom without seeing anyone, and were quickly across the dais and behind the curtains.

"I was beginning to think you weren't coming," Jeremy commented dryly. "A little longer, and I might have gone to see for myself what this house is like."

"You wouldn't care for it, believe me," Alan replied.

Jeremy had been busy while they were upstairs. The paraphernalia of the magic show was boxed, folded, and crated, ready to be taken away. Alan lifted the lid on one of the tall baskets and yanked out several velvet curtains.

"Here, this will just fit."

"I'm going out in that?" Maud said in a small voice.

"What better way? Climb in."

She was in no mood to argue. Yanking up her skirts, she tried to climb inside, but it was a tight fit.

"You'll have to leave the dress. It's torn anyway. Take it off."

A little embarrassed, Maud slipped off the dress and stood in her shift and petticoat. It was an easy fit without all the yards of fabric. Alan laid one of the velvet curtains on top, scrunched it around her, then replaced the lid. "Don't worry, my pet. We'll carry it carefully," he said, tapping the lid down.

It was stuffy in the basket, but Maud kept very still as she listened to the two men carrying the other boxes and baskets to the door. They took her last, knocking the basket around pretty violently, in spite of Alan's words. But she stayed still and quiet. When they finally set the basket down, she could tell the door was open by the chill night air that seeped through the weaving. Then she heard Jack Smirk's voice.

"So you're off, are you? Well, it's about time. How much did the Madam pay you for that bit of trickery?"

"I'll thank you to hold your tongue," Jeremy answered. "I consider myself an artist. A conjuring artist."

"Artist my grandmother's teats. It's all tricks. I know your lot. Actors! None of you is worth hanging from Tyburn Hill."

She heard Alan say in a level voice, "Would you like to inspect our things? Just to make certain we're not carrying off the silver?"

"Naw. You may steal from the madam when she pays you to perform, but you're not thieves. Go ahead and load this stuff up and get out."

Maud breathed a sigh of relief as the door creaked open wider. Outside she heard a low whinny from a horse, and knew Alan had a cart waiting. With any luck they would put her inside it first.

"Hold on there!"

Gertrude's voice! Maud froze as she heard the thumping of the servant's heavy feet coming down the hall.

"Just a minute. Did you check these crates over, Jack Smirk? No, I didn't think so. Couldn't put the gin bottle down long enough, could ye? I'll just have a little look, if you please, sir. Actors ain't no better than thieves."

Maud held her breath. She could make out the sounds as Alan lifted the lids and Gertrude went thrusting through the contents. "You don't have to turn them all topsy-turvy," Jeremy said irritably. "I packed them very carefully."

"All a bunch of nonsense, anyway," Gertrude snapped, as Maud felt Alan lift the lid of her basket. The curtain over her head moved slightly as a sudden trilling began.

"Chirp . . . chirp . . . lovely lady . . . lovely lady . . ."

"What's that then?" Gertrude said, turning from the basket. "How did you do that? Lovely lady, indeed."

"Everarde's my name, chirp, chirp. What's

yours . . ."

"It's a trick, isn't it? You think you're so clever, you conjurers. Ought to be hung, drawn, and quartered for all the trouble you cause."

When Gertrude turned back to the basket, Alan had replaced the lid on Maud's and was holding up the lid of another. She plunged her arm into it, muttering to herself. "Charlatans! Tricksters!"

Maude remained very still. Then she felt her basket jerked up as Alan and Jeremy carried it through the door and dumped it onto a cart waiting outside. She heard them make several more trips before the wagon shifted under their weight as they climbed aboard. Though she couldn't see, she knew Gertrude had followed them out to the street, when her voice came clearly:

"You . . . conjurer! Can you talk with the dead, then? I'd give something to hear me old mother again . . ."

"That's a trick we've never managed," Alan called, as Jeremy slapped the reins and the wagon rolled away over the cobbles. For another five minutes Maud fought to keep her balance, while the wagon rumbled from side to side. Then the lid was lifted, the velvet curtain thrown off, and Alan was reaching down to help her out.

"Are we out of there?" she cried, as the cool night air bathed her face with joy.

"We're gone. You're free of Mrs. Finchley."

"God be praised!" she cried, laughing as she threw her arms around Alan's neck and pulled him backward off the seat.

Chapter Seven

Holding the tankard with both hands, Maud sipped at the warm wine. Every now and then she would look around the cozy, comfortable room, just to make sure she was really there. Across from her Alan Desmond sat resting one hip on a table, his hands crossed on his thigh, watching her and thinking how lovely she looked in the candlelight. Though the strain of the night had left dark circles around her eyes, they only emphasized the golden lashes on her white skin, and the largeness of her eyes in her small, oval face. She had slipped one of his banians loosely over her shift, shaken all the feathers, pins, and false curls from her hair, then brushed it, and tied it at the nape of her neck with one of his laces. It fell in a golden cascade down her back, glinting red flames of fire in the glow from the candles.

Maud looked up at him, caught him studying her, and blushed prettily. "I still can't believe it."

"That you got away?"

"Yes. And that I'm really here with you. Do you think she'll come after me?"

"I shouldn't think so. Country wenches with no place to go arrive in London every day. She'll have another one trapped in her clutches before the sun sets. And by then, Madam Eliza won't even remember you."

"I hope you're right, but Min said she could be vindictive."

He suppressed an urge to reach out and touch the flame of her hair. "Don't think about her anymore. You've a whole new world ahead of you."

Maud set the tankard down on the table beside her chair. In the silence she could catch the dim sounds from the tavern below, not raucous, but homey and comfortable. It was Jeremy who had told her Alan was taking her to his rooms, and at first it made her apprehensive. But now she was so relieved to be away from Mrs. Finchley's flash house, and so weary with all that had happened—so eased by the warm wine— that she didn't really care anymore. Besides, she trusted Alan Desmond. She knew he would not hurt her.

"What will you do now?" he asked.

"I'm not sure. That new world you spoke of rather frightens me. I think I would like very much to sleep, and when I wake, find something decent to wear and then go round to Lady Wiltshire's house and give her Lord Bambridge's letter. With any luck I'll be established in her household by tomorrow evening."

Alan abruptly rose to stride to the hearth and reach for a pipe. His back was to her, and she could not tell what he was thinking. She waited while he lit the pipe with a spill from the hearth, then sat down in the only other chair in the tiny sitting room, opposite her.

"You don't have to be a servant, you know."

Maud laughed. "Faith, I don't know anything else. And I'm fortunate to have a place that might take me. I know that now, even though I didn't when I first arrived here."

"Oh, I agree that it is helpful to have some hope of employment before coming to a city like London.

But have you ever thought of doing something else?"

Her eyes grew round. "Like what? I know nothing else."

"Well . . ." He took a long draught on his pipe. "What about playacting? Have you ever thought of going on the stage?"

She looked at him incredulously. "Playacting! I don't know anything about the stage. Why, I'd look ridiculous."

Alan removed his pipe and stared at her. She was surprised to see that he was really serious. "Let me tell you a little about an actor's life. There are some people who are born with the talent to entrance others, to lift them out of their own meager little lives for a time, and carry them to heights never dreamed of before. Those are the real actors, like Garrick and Quin. Then there are many others who enjoy playing parts, learn their lines diligently, and perform adequately. Lots of those. And then there are some who are not born with talent at all, but with such beauty that audiences will flock to see them just to admire their loveliness. I think you could be one of those."

"But even an actress with a pretty face has to speak a few lines. Why, I wouldn't know where to begin!"

"You can always learn lines, and how to walk properly, where to stand, when to sit, and when to rise. That takes no talent at all." He rose and moved to her chair, bending over her, his hands resting on the arms. "I think I could make you a shining star of the stage, Maud, if you would let me. Think of it. Adulation, applause, playing a different part each day, maybe even a little money accumulated along the way. More than you could ever dream of earning as a housemaid."

Maud turned away from his earnest eyes. "It's preposterous."

"All right," Alan said, throwing up his hands and walking away. "If you want to be a servant, be one.

I'll take you round to the Wiltshires tomorrow, and leave you there."

"Now I've made you angry."

"Not angry, just disappointed."

Tentatively she rose to stand beside him. "Is that why you took me from that house, to put me in your company?"

He looked down at her and smiled his charming smile. "No. I helped you because you needed help, and it's really too bad of me to try to bribe you this way. You must do what you feel is right for you."

Maud reached up and kissed him on the cheek. "I'll always be grateful to you for taking me out of there. Let me think about it. I'm too tired right now to make any decisions. Perhaps it will all look different in the morning."

He ran a finger down her smooth cheek, thinking how tempting she was. His brightly colored robe was far too large for her, and had slipped down over one shoulder, baring the creamy perfection of her skin. Shadows from the candlelight emphasized the perfect planes of her cheeks, and heightened the violet blue of her large eyes. She had pulled the long train of her golden hair over one shoulder, and it swept provocatively down the swelling mound of her breast. Alan caught his breath and, with great self-control, forced himself to turn away.

"I'll sleep in Jeremy's room, and leave you to your dreams. In the morning, then."

Her eyes flashed with relief just for a second. "In the morning."

When she woke, daylight was streaming through the windows, and she could tell from long experience on a farm that the morning was half-gone. She was splashing water from a washbowl on her face, when she spied a dress draped over the chair. It was of some poor fustian cloth, dark blue with an embroidered stomacher and matching underskirt that showed signs of wear. Probably one of the dresses used in Alan's plays, she thought as she squirmed into it. Yet it fit tolerably well, and she was grateful to have it. She was starving, and certainly could not go downstairs in her shift.

Entering the tavern room a few moments later, she looked around in awe. The paneled wood, black with age, low ceilings, and uneven floors attested to the building's long history. There were small windows with leaded glass that glowed a mellow amber in the sunlight, and handsome copies of Mister Hogarth's prints along the walls. Maud stepped inside tentatively, grateful the room was nearly empty, and wondering if she might be allowed to put her breakfast on Alan Desmond's bill. Then she saw Jeremy.

He was sitting at a corner table with a large tankard in front of him. When he saw her, he rose and beckoned her over.

"I was beginning to think you were goin' to sleep the day away."

"What luck to see you here. I'm starving, and I didn't know how I was going to pay for my breakfast."

"Not luck," he said, sitting opposite her. "Alan told me to wait here till you came down. He had business in London, so he couldn't stay. But he knew you'd be hungry, a healthy country wench like yourself."

"He thought of everything. This dress . . ."

"Just one of the costumes. Here, girl," he said, waving over one of the serving girls. "Bring the young lady the same as I had. Except for the ale. She'll have . . . what will you have, Maud? Tea? Coffee?"

"I'm used to ale," Maud said to the girl, "but I'd prefer coffee, if you please."

"We don't serve it much here, miss, but I'll find you some."

When she left, Maud leaned across the table and whispered to Jeremy, "What am I having?"

"Porridge and bread and a piece of ham. A good English breakfast."

"It sounds delicious. But I shall have to keep account of the cost to repay Mister Desmond. It can come out of my first wages."

"So, you're still set on staying a serving wench, are ye? I rather hoped the Master had talked you out of that."

"He told you about the preposterous idea?"

" 'Twas I who suggested it, though he would have thought of it himself sooner or later. You're uncommonly pretty, you know."

Maud felt her cheeks warming. "Thank you. But *me*, on the stage! I just can't picture it."

Jeremy chuckled and leaned back in his chair. "That's because you never met any of the ladies of the theater. If you had, you would know they're nothing special. Just people, like you and me."

Maud cocked her head to look at him. His round face and ready smile always made her want to smile back at him. His arched brows gave him a perpetually startled expression, yet underneath them his gray eyes sparkled with a curiosity and liveliness she had never seen equaled. "I don't think you're a bit ordinary, Jeremy. In fact, you're really quite special. I never knew anyone who could do the things you do."

"Just a few tricks of the trade, as we say in the theater. But thank you for the compliment."

The serving girl returned with Maud's meal, and for the next ten minutes she concentrated on nothing else. When it was completely finished, she sat back in her chair and resisted the urge to loosen the laces on her borrowed stomacher.

"I never saw anyone enjoy food so much," Jeremy commented. "Come up for air, have you now?"

"Yes. One of the lesser horrors of Mrs. Finchley's house was the terrible food. This is like heaven itself." She sat quietly for a moment, reveling in the joy of having been delivered from that ghastly house and into such pleasant circumstances. "Jeremy . . ."

He looked up and waited for her to go on.

"Do you think I really could be an actress?"

"Indeed, I do. You're able to read, you speak very well already—though how you manage to learn that at Thornwood, I'll never know—you have a pretty voice and a beautiful face. You walk well, you even managed your hands in a natural way."

"Merciful heavens, you make me sound like a paragon."

"No, I'm just pointing out all the natural abilities you already possess. You can always learn the rest."

"But, Jeremy, I was always told actresses are . . . are not exactly respectable."

"Like Mrs. Finchley's whores? You very nearly became one of them, you know. And most of the serving wenches I've known cared little about respectability."

"That's true. But it always mattered to me. I guess I learned it from my parents."

"Why didn't your parents keep you from coming to London then?"

"They're dead. They both died from the plague when I was seven."

"Oh. I'm sorry." Suddenly he bent his head for a moment, then lapsed into Everarde's chirping. "Chirp . . . ye have a loose tongue, Jeremy Oaks . . . chirp . . ."

Maud laughed. "No matter. This is all just foolish talk. I was born a serving girl, and that's what I shall remain. Anything else is just idle wandering thoughts. Now, did Mister Desmond leave any other instructions for me?"

Jeremy reached into his pocket and laid a half crown on the table. "He said that if you decide you want to go to that lady's house to be hired, you should take this and hire a ride. You can return the dress to the Chelsea Theater once you're settled, and if you insist on it, you can pay him back the half crown someday from your wages. Breakfast was his, however, and you're not to worry about it."

Maud's face fell. "He . . . he isn't coming back here?"

"Not until later. He said if you didn't want to work with him, then you might as well go on about getting settled in your new position. But . . . I'll go round with you, if you'd like me to. It's the devil for a stranger to find his way around London's rabbit warrens."

She only hesitated a moment. "No, I'll get there all right. Please tell Mister Desmond how grateful I am for all that you both did for me. And I shall certainly return the dress and the money. I promise him that." She rose, filled with a sense of disappointment after the euphoria of the previous hour. He rose as well and she reached for his hand. "Goodbye, Jeremy. And thank you, with all my heart."

Even Jeremy's bright little eyes seemed to grow dimmer. "I hope we shall meet again, Miss Maud."

"I hope so, too, but it's not very likely. Well, I'd better go collect my things."

Once back in the upstairs rooms, Maud fought not to give way to tears. She would not allow herself that luxury. It was very small of Alan Desmond to practically turn her out because she would not do what he wanted, but if he was like that, then so be it. He had done her a wonderful service, but she had to follow her own path. Yet she kept his handkerchief from the night before, wrapping it around the brooch and placing it along with the letter in the inside pocket of her skirt. Then, with a last look around, she left the warm, cozy room and ventured outside into the noisy, dirty, crowded streets of London.

It took her the better part of two hours to locate the house, and then it was only by asking directions of several persons. London was a confusing, congested tangle of streets, and when she started out she did not even know in what part of town Grosvenor Street was to be found. By trial and error she finally made her way to the new section of Mayfair, where expensive homes were being built among the quiet fields as the city boundaries pushed farther out.

It was a beautiful street lined with row upon row of spanking new brick houses. Like its neighbors, number 315 had a marble facade with low steps leading to a wide door, whose polished brass handle and door pull gleamed brightly even from where she stood across the street. Over it a lovely fanlight spread its glass panels in an inviting welcome. In the windows above, lace curtains moved lazily in the slight breeze and glass windowpanes reflected back the green of the trees along the walk in front of the house.

A beautiful house, a comfortable house, a house in which it would be a joy to work. Maud fingered the crisp edges of Lord Bambridge's letter in her pocket, and fought down the panic that set her chest pounding. It was foolish to be frightened now. Her fear must be the lingering effect of all that had happened since she had arrived in the city. With the letter and the neat dress Alan had loaned her, she should have no trouble at all convincing Lady Wiltshire that she really had been sent to her by her father.

Just as she took a deep breath and started across the street, the door opened and a footman stepped out. Maud recognized the green and white livery of Lord Bambridge's servants, and the rather smug, obsequious air of the servants at Denton Hall. He stepped briskly aside and pushed the door open for another man who stepped out, speaking quietly to the footman. Maud froze where she was standing. He was a short gentleman, rather shabby and stringy-looking, and the stance was familiar. Then he took his hat from the footman, turned, and started down the steps, while Maud quickly shrank back behind one of the narrow trees across the street.

Lawyer Ramsey! There was no mistaking that severe face. But what on earth was he doing here in London, and at Lady Wiltshire's house?

The horrible answer came sweeping over her. She caught her breath and turned her back against the tree, facing away from the house. Of course. He had come to reclaim Lady Julia's brooch, and cart Maud off to Newgate Prison for stealing! Naturally the first place he would come looking for her in London would be Cynthia Wiltshire's home.

Maud held her breath, afraid to look to see if Ramsey was storming across the street, ready to drag her out from behind the tree. After a few moments, she sneaked a glance and saw that he was far down the street, striding away toward George Street. She waited until he turned the corner, then quickly ran in the opposite direction as fast as she could go, darting down streets and alleyways without caring where she was going, as long as it was away from Lawyer Ramsey. When her breath was tearing at her chest, she was finally forced to stop, lean against the wall of a house, and try to figure out what she was going to do next.

It was no good allowing fear to take control like this. Better to think the thing through, and then decide the best course of action. She could go back to Lady Wiltshire's, tell her the truth, and throw herself on the lady's mercy. If she was like her father . . .

But suppose she was more like her sister! Maud had no doubt at all about how Mistress Julia would handle the problem, nor what kind of revenge she would seek. And even if she assured them the brooch had been taken without her knowledge, would they believe her, since she had it in her possession?

No, she could not go back to the Wiltshire house ever again. Fortunately, she had an alternative, and right now it looked very appealing.

Her return journey to the Lamb and Flag Inn took half the time it had taken her to leave it. Jeremy was nowhere to be seen, and Maud feared both he and Alan might have already left for the theater. When she asked the innkeeper whether Alan Desmond was expected back that night, he casually informed her that Mister Desmond was upstairs in his rooms, no doubt getting himself worked up for the histrionics at the theater that evening.

Maud barely noticed the sarcasm or the man's knowing leer, as she turned away to bound up the stairs and down the long hall to knock on Alan's door.

"Who is it?" a muffled voice sounded behind the door.

Maud didn't answer. Instead she tried the lock, found it open, and stepped hesitantly inside. "It's me, Maud Mellingham," she said, leaning back against the door for support. "I've come back."

Alan had been sitting in one of the armchairs, reading from a small, leather-bound book. When he saw her, he started up, then caught himself and sat back, watching her suspiciously. "What's wrong? The lady didn't choose to hire you?"

"I never saw her. I . . . I decided I'd rather be an actress."

"Oh? Rather an abrupt change of heart, wasn't it?"

"Yes." She took a step inside the room. "No. That is, oh dear, I might as well tell you the truth. I had no more than reached the street in front of her house, when I saw Mister Ramsey, the lawyer from

Thornwood, coming out of the front door. Don't you see what that means! He's after me to arrest me for stealing the mistress's brooch. I can't go to Lady Wiltshire's now. I can never go there!"

"What brooch? The one you found at Eliza Finchley's?"

"Yes. I'm certain Lady Julia slipped it into my purse before I left Thornwood, so she could accuse me of stealing! It would be just like her. She even told me I'd not seen the last of her."

She sat down on the edge of the chair opposite him, twisting her hands in her lap. Alan, who had prepared to be stern and uncaring, found himself moved by her hopelessness. If she started to cry, he would be completely undone.

"Well, perhaps it's a good thing. I would have preferred you to join us with a little more enthusiasm, but even without it, I still believe I can make you a popular attraction and an asset to the company. You'll have to work very hard, you know."

Maud brightened at once. "I don't mind that. And I promise you I'll try very hard. Only, you *are* going to leave London very soon, aren't you? I can go with you, can't I?"

Alan sat forward and tipped up her chin, inspecting her face as though he was seeing it for the first time. "We leave for Cambridgeshire the day after tomorrow. Until then, you'd better stay here so no one will see you. Yes, you're a beautiful girl. A minimum of paint, I think. The simpler the better, so as to allow the natural beauty to show through. Let's see, your first role should be Portia . . . no, much too difficult. Perhaps one of my own plays, *The Knight Errant*. Yes, Lydia would be perfect for you. I'll give you the role to study, while you're cooped up here."

Maud patiently allowed him to turn her face first to one side, then to the other, feeling a little like a side of meat on display, but so relieved just to be here out of sight, that she didn't really mind. Perhaps eventually she might even enjoy learning to be an actress. If the tingling sensation she felt from the touch of his fingers on her flesh was any indication, she was going to enjoy it very much.

Alan found his enthusiasm growing as he studied her profile. "Lovely, really lovely," he murmured and fought off a desire to kiss her warm, luscious lips. "Stand up. Walk back and forth. Mmm. That'll need some work. You still walk like a milkmaid. And how's the voice? Stand over there, and say something as you would on the stage."

Maud grew suddenly self-conscious. "What should I say?"

Alan bounced across to the other side of the room. "Try: 'the quality of mercy is not strained. It droppeth as the gentle rain from heaven upon the place beneath.'"

Maud murmured, "The quality of mercy—"

"No, no, with much more breath. 'The quality of mercy . . .'" he said, raising his voice to a level that Maud thought would rouse the neighbors. "And use your hand like thus . . ."

She took a deep breath, extended her hand as he had done, and said the line as though she were calling in the cows.

"That was terrible. I can see we have a lot of work ahead, but in the end, you'll be a triumph. I feel it in my bones."

Maud smiled at him shyly. "Do you really think so?"

He came up to her and slipped his arms around her waist, pulling her close. "When I'm through, you're going to be the toast of the provinces, Maud, my girl. Trust me. You have a great future. We both do."

His lips met hers, sending a jolt of sensation through her. His grip tightened, and she melted against his hard body, afraid and yet wanting to be even closer to him. When the warmth surging through her grew to clamoring proportions, she pulled away.

Alan let her go. He was more than a little overwhelmed himself at his reaction to having her so near. Though he was accustomed to young actresses melting in his arms, somehow he was not willing to rush Maud. It was that quality he had noticed in her at Thornwood: the innocent and the siren, mingled in one perfect woman. He adored her charming innocence, and his blood warmed at the thought of the siren awakened. But he sensed that she was not ready yet, and it seemed important to him to wait until she was.

Besides, the more he studied her, the more he really believed all those encouraging words he was telling her. She *could* have a future with his company! Her youth and beauty would be a big drawing card, if rightly developed. And she might prove very useful in other ways as well.

"Yes," he said, gripping her arms and smiling with encouragement. "Lydia will be just right for your first role. And after that, perhaps Belinda. We'll wait until you are ready, and then put broadsides all over the towns we go through, announcing a bright new addition to the company. Maud—what is your last name again?"

"Mellingham."

"Maud Mellingham. No, that won't do. Much too provincial and not provocative enough. I know . . ."

He bounded to the chair where the book he had discarded was lying on the seat. "When you came in, I was just reading a history of Edward II. Horrible story but that's neither here nor there. Yes, here it is. A wardrobe item, dated 1298, of a payment of two shillings to Maud Makejoy for dancing before the prince—that's the young Edward—in King's Hall at

Ipswich. What a dance that must have been, to earn such a timeless place in the household accounts. Must have put Solome to shame. But that's it. 'Maud Makejoy'! That should attract an audience, from curiosity if nothing else."

"It doesn't sound quite . . . well, quite decent," Maud protested.

"Decent!" He threw the book down, clasped her in his arms again and swung her around before giving her one more quick kiss on the lips. "Forget decent, Maud. You're an actress now. Decency has no place in the theater!"

Chapter Eight

Decency has no place in the theater!

The words echoed in her mind, while she watched Alan bound over to a bookshelf and sort through a haphazard stack of narrow paperbound books. She took a step closer and, through the open door to the next room, caught a glimpse of the corner of a heavy, old-fashioned tester bed. Its massive posts were hung with a faded burgundy velvet cloth, which had been pulled back to reveal the round end of the bed, covered with a rather handsome cotton bedcover.

Maud caught her generous underlip in her teeth, thinking hard. All her life, first her mother and later, kind and dear Cook, had drummed into her that she must remain true to herself. "Never let some worthless man steal your self-respect from you," her Mam had told her. And Cook, once she realized Maud was not just another shallow, flighty wench after everything she could get from life, took over the admonitions where her mother had left off.

And so, even though she was surrounded by bawdy people, and lived in a bawdy age, she had clung tenaciously to her self-respect. In fact, she realized, up until now she had never known a man she considered worth losing it for. Until she met Alan Desmond.

From what she had learned about life in the theater, liaisons came and went like chaff blowing on the wind. Would Alan expect her to become his mistress, in return for making her an actress? Was that what she wanted?

She silently shook her head. No, she would prefer to lose her virginity in the marriage bed, but that was a lot to expect of this worldly, independent man. Yet, he had almost single-handedly saved her from Eliza's flash house, and now was promising her a career in the theater. He would certainly expect something in return. Watching the way his hair fell over his forehead as he bent toward the book, the way his shirt strained over his broad shoulders as he reached for another, her blood went singing. She glanced again at the bed in the far room, and felt her legs tremble.

"Here it is. *The Knight Errant*. Take it and study it. Especially Lydia." He straightened and handed her the little book. Maud collected her wandering thoughts and took it as though it were straight off the stove.

"Is it . . . a large part?"

"No. Mostly Lydia must stand around and look beautiful—that's why I chose it for you. She has to have that blend of innocence and allure that draws men to her like flies to honey, but she holds them at arm's length at the same time. It should be perfect for you."

He tipped up her chin to study her profile again. "Perfect. Beautiful and virginal at the same time. You'll have the men writhing in their chairs."

Maud lowered her lashes and smiled provocatively. "I was told one could not remain innocent for long in the theater."

Alan caught his breath at the flirtatiousness in her eyes. "Nor will you. But by then I shall teach you how to act innocent, even if you aren't."

His arms slid around her and, for the first time,

Maud did not stiffen and try to pull away. He could sense the difference in the way her body slowly, shyly melded to his. Her hands slipped hesitantly upward to his shoulders. Her fingers lightly touched his hair, then, with more assurance, stroked the long strands as though she were feeling some rich fabric for the first time. Alan reached up to loosen the bounded roll of her hair, and it fell like flame to her shoulders, framing her face in a golden nimbus.

He caught his breath, still expecting her to turn away. She looked directly into his eyes, and in their blue depths he saw the siren stir and warm to life for the first time. Gently he pressed her closer. She moved against him, murmuring little sighs of surrender. He could feel the hard points of her breasts against his chest. His hands explored her back, the long sinuous curve beneath her bodice, then deftly, hesitantly, slid along her waist and up to cup her breast. She tensed, but only for an instant, then her body mellowed in his hands, reveling in the feel of them.

Her lips were so close, so tempting, that he could not resist tasting them. He traced the outline of their curves, then closed over them, drawing from their sweetness. Her mouth parted slightly, and his tongue darted against the opening, wanting to go deeper, to explore every part of her mystery, but still holding back, waiting for her invitation.

Maud felt her body consumed with a growing warmth, that set her trembling down to her toes. Reason and caution were quickly slipping away, succumbing to a delightful joy she had never before experienced. What wonderful sensations he could evoke with his wandering hands, his insistent lips. What happiness to be in the hard, strong arms of this man, to be a woman responding with all her body to a man's wonderful masculinity.

Alan released her lips to lightly drop soft kisses on

her chin, along the curve of her neck, and into the hollow of her throat. Her body arched with a shudder, as his fingers slipped beneath the low bodice of her blouse to stroke her breast and lift it, encased in its soft muslin, warm and glowing to his lips.

A stab of sheer delight coursed through Maud's body, as the last of her resistance was swept away. Alan felt her tremble and sink against him, as he teased the taut nipple with his tongue, supporting her increasingly weak body with one arm. With a shock of surprise and pleasure, he realized that she was going to be his, that her need for him was growing as strongly as his for her. He murmured against the pink delicacy of her breast, "I know a better place for this." Lifting her, limp and trembling, in his arms, he moved toward the door of the bedroom. Maud clasped her arms around his neck, and nestled her head in the hollow of his shoulders. Her lips lightly coursed the long line of his neck beneath the open collar of his shirt, thrilling at the scent and taste of his maleness. Her growing desire to be needed, to be loved by this man, shouted down any other qualms, and the last of her resistance melted away.

A soft rapping brought Alan to a dead halt in the bedroom doorway. Maud barely noticed it, until he set her down on her feet and stared back at the closed door of his rooms, listening. It came again, three quiet raps, followed by two, and then two again.

"Whoever it is, tell them to go away," Maud whispered, her arms tight around his waist.

Alan looked miserably at the closed door. "I have to answer it," he said finally. "Wait here."

Stunned, Maud watched him walk across the room to open the door barely an inch. He stood talking to someone she could not see, so quietly that she could not make out the words. Then he closed it and returned to her.

"I have to go out for a while. Hell and damnation! It could not have come at a worse time."

She stared at him, unbelieving. "You're going out? Now!"

"I must. I'm sorry, my dear. I'll be back after tonight's performance, and I'll make it up to you then. Believe me, I wish I could stay, but there are some things more important than love."

"What things?" Her words were strangled. She felt debased for having thrown herself at him, only to be discarded when someone came knocking at the door.

"Nothing you would understand." Hurriedly he slipped his coat over his shirt and waistcoat, and fastened the jabot at his throat. Reaching for his hat, he stopped long enough to clasp her against him and kiss first her lips, and then the still erect nipple of her creamy breast. "Keep this warm for me," he murmured, and moved away to slip through the door.

As the door closed behind him, Maud gave way to her anger and hurt. This was appalling! After all these years, when she finally had made the decision to give herself to a man, he walked out, leaving her for something or someone else before barely getting started! No wonder Cook had warned her to beware of men. They were only after their own selfish pleasure!

Well, it wouldn't happen again. If Alan Desmond thought he was going to find her waiting around for him when he finally got around to seeking her, he had another thought coming. Rummaging around in her reticule, she found the loathsome brooch that had been the cause of all her troubles, and slipped it in her pocket. After making sure that there was no one around, she walked downstairs and talked the landlord into accepting the brooch in return for a small sleeping room in the attic for the next two nights. Then, without even leaving Alan a note to say where she was, she caught up her few belongings and moved up two flights of rickety stairs to a dormer room, which she would share with two of the serving girls later in the evening.

Plumping up the pillow, she settled against the wall and opened *The Knight Errant*. Without the distraction of Alan Desmond, she ought to have her part memorized by the time the troupe left London.

Although Alan's mind was able to swiftly focus on the summons he had received, it took his body a lot longer to simmer down from the incipient boil his blood had been racing toward when Maud was in his arms. He had been waiting several days for a packet of letters which he was to pass on, and he knew that when the moment came, he must not allow other distractions to interfere. An intricate network of faceless, nameless couriers was all that kept many of the people who felt as he did out of the Tower. Many of them were known Catholics, and so already under suspicion. But Alan Desmond, with his murky past and his reputation as a wandering playwright and actor, was a useful man for assignments like this one, a go-between whom no one bothered to suspect. To treat these duties with anything less than the seriousness they deserved was to put other, more prominent people in great danger.

And so, without a backward glance, he left Maud to wait for him while he carried out the duty he considered his destiny. Besides, they would still have the rest of the night. The important thing was that she was willing to stay with him, and his blood warmed again at the thought of sharing his bed with her. He was certain that once he had got past her shyness and reluctance, she was going to be a willing and skillful pupil. He could hardly wait!

He had to follow the man who had knocked on his

door through two dark alleys, before they found one empty enough to speak to each other in safety. The message he received then sent him to the stable to saddle his horse for a trip out the Chelsea road to a small, grubby tavern set well back from the highway. He waited there nearly an hour at a plank table under a dim lantern burning one candle, before a stranger joined him. When the stranger left to go on his way, he casually picked up Alan's saddlebag, leaving his own for Alan to throw over his shoulder as he left.

By the time Alan returned to the Lamb and Flag, the watch was crying ten o'clock, and the streets echoed with the occasional clatter of a carriage or the loud cries from a group of boisterous young men making the rounds of the public houses. Still carrying the precious saddlebag, he took the stairs two at a time and fitted his key in the lock with a hand that almost trembled from anticipation.

The sitting room was dark, but that might be because Maud had already gone to bed. So much the better, he thought, as he removed the packet of letters and locked them in a wooden chest on the bookcase. He would wake her gently, with wandering hands and light kisses . . .

He lit a candle and carried it to the bedroom, quietly pushing open the door. Setting it on the table beside the bed, he bent to look for the mound of her body beneath the covers.

Nothing. No one! He couldn't believe it. He ran his hand across the coverlet to be sure, his brow furrowing with surprise. Where in the world was she?

Going back to the sitting room, he checked the chairs just to be certain she was not curled up in one, then stood looking around and wondering. Had she gone off again to that woman who was supposed to hire her? That did not seem likely, considering how frightened and disturbed she had been earlier over seeing the lawyer from Suffolk. Would she have sought out Jeremy? Not likely. Besides, Jeremy would never take her in when he knew she had come to Alan first. Would she have gone out on the streets? Not Maud. She was ignorant of life on the London streets, but wise enough to realize the dangers.

Irritation, disappointment, and a burgeoning anger began to displace the delightful anticipation he had felt on returning to his rooms. It was unfair and unkind of her to leave him like this, so suddenly and with no explanation. How like a woman! And after he had taken her in and befriended her, not to mention offering her a whole new career! It would serve her right if he shrugged her off as good riddance and went to bed.

But he could not do that without knowing she was safe. He made his way downstairs, where he found the tavern's night watch and learned that Maud had rented a room in the attic. Full of righteous indignation, he stalked up the three flights of stairs and knocked on the door. When no one answered, he found it unlatched and walked inside.

There were three beds, all of them occupied. Near the window Maud was sitting up on one elbow, the covers pulled up around her chin. She watched him stalk toward her, the dim glow of the single candle throwing macabre shadows on his face. Her mouth opened in surprise.

"What are you doing here?" she said in a loud whisper.

"I might ask you the same thing. Why did you leave?" His voice was thick with irritation, though he had come in with every intention of simply seeing that she was all right.

"Why do you suppose?" she answered, squirming away from him.

"For God's sake, woman, I wasn't going to hurt you! I thought we had an understanding."

"Well, we don't. Go away."

Alan set the candle on the window ledge and sat down on the bed. To his consternation, Maud pulled the covers higher around her chin and scrambled up against the wall, leaving a wide space between them. He could see from the daggers in her eyes that she was still very angry with him.

"I don't understand why you should react so strongly. I had to leave. I had important business to attend to."

Maud, still chagrined at the way he had walked away from her when she had practically thrown herself at him, pushed back against the wall. "And I have my self-respect. I intend to sleep here as a proper girl should."

"God's blood, you weren't thinking 'proper' before that knock on the door came."

"That's because you tried to seduce me. It brought me to my senses."

Alan started to laugh, but a movement on the next bed reminded him they were not alone. He glanced over to see one of the chambermaids peeking at him with wide eyes from behind the coverlet, while beyond her another maid stirred restlessly. "This is not the place . . ." he said lamely.

"No, it isn't. Go away."

Alan fought down the urge to grip her shoulders and shake some sense into her head, after which he would kiss those pouting lips until she begged him to carry her to his bed. A quiet giggle from the adjacent cot dispelled that notion, and he settled for a hard glare. "I'll see you in the morning," he snapped, and grabbed up the candle to leave.

He was nearly to the door when he heard Maud speak.

"Does that mean you still want me for your company?"

"Yes, though I don't know why I should bother

with you, except that it will be good for business." He deliberately stressed the word. "Be there early and be prepared to work."

He slammed the door behind him and stalked down the stairs, still grumbling about the ingratitude of women.

Maud slept very little after Alan left. If he only knew, she thought, how much a part of her had wanted to stay and wait in his bed for him, or even how she longed now to leave the dark, cold attic and flee to his rooms. Yet, that she would not do. Alan Desmond might as well learn right away that she was not one to give herself lightly. As attractive as he was, and as much as she longed to have him teach her the delights of love, it must happen at the right time, and when she knew him better. In a way she really *had* been saved by that knock on the door. When Alan left her, he gave her the chance to step back and see more than just the flaming needs of the moment.

There were dark shadows under her large eyes when she trudged back up the stairs that morning, after a light breakfast in the dining room of the inn. Alan had said to be there early, and to Maud, who had worked on a farm for most of her life, early meant rising with dawn and the chickens. When she roused him out of a deep slumber, it only added more fuel to his annoyance. He set her to memorize several pages from Farquhar's *The Beaux's Stratagem* as punishment, while he went downstairs for a leisurely breakfast.

The company was to leave London for the provinces in two days, and Alan made good use of them to get even with Maud. She worked all of both days and into the night, never leaving his rooms except to fall exhausted into her attic bed for a few hours' rest.

He launched her into an intensive course on how to walk, how to speak clearly, how to enunciate, how to throw her voice, and how to tantalize an audience with movements and eye contacts.

She was made to memorize songs and long passages, then worked mercilessly on the best way of presenting them. She was brought near to tears over and over by his ceaseless criticism, and no matter how hard she tried, nothing pleased him. If she had not finally become furious with him, she might have walked out sobbing by noon of the first day. Yet, instinctively, she knew he was giving her sound advice, and besides, she had no other place to go. She was not going to let him know that, however.

"Try it again. You're waddling like a cow."

"What do you expect, when I spent my life tending cows?"

"No one's going to make allowances for that, when you walk across a stage. The audience looks for grace and wit and charm. Without it, you'll be pelted with vegetables before you get halfway across. And for God's sake, lower your voice. You're not tending pigs."

"I *did* lower it. You told me I couldn't be heard."

"Lower it in the correct way. Breathe. Raise your shoulders. A good actor can make a whisper heard in the last tier of boxes."

And his criticisms continued:

"I've never seen such a poor excuse for a dance."

"You call that grace? My horse has smoother movements."

"Stop flailing your arms! You look like a puppet doing the Saint Vitus dance."

"That passage was absolutely garbled. How do you expect to recite anything, if you cannot remember the words!"

Several times she reached the breaking point, and screamed her frustration at him. "I can't stand this!

Raise your head, lower your head, lean forward, lean back, throw your voice, swallow your voice. I don't think you know what you want. Certainly I don't."

Alan felt a slight tinge of guilt over the way he was driving her. He knew there was an element of revenge in it, yet there was also the need to teach her a great deal in a little time. The truth was that he was amazed at how quickly she was picking up the beginnings of stagecraft, and with every hour, he was more convinced that his original estimation of her had been correct. She was going to be very good at this — but he wasn't about to let her know that.

"All right, take a few minutes to have supper. But then be right back. We've still got Lydia to work on."

Those were the longest two days of Maud's life, and when the Stanbury Players finally climbed aboard their wagon before dawn to leave the City, she was too tired and angry to even be exhilarated. To add to her misery, it was drizzling rain from skies that looked like gray soup, and a chill in the air reminded her that autumn was around the corner.

Alan accompanied her silently to the theater, where the rest of the company waited. He had relented enough to bring her a massive, warm woolen cloak with a large hood that shadowed her face, but when they reached the coach, he handed her up without even introducing the rest of the players.

Because of the rain, no one sat on top of the heavily laden wagon. Instead they dug burrows for themselves among the clutter inside, and sat dozing against the bales or staring morosely at the walls and each other.

Maud made a brief effort to introduce herself, but gave up when she met with a solid wall of indifference. She recognized the two women she had seen at Thornwood and briefly hoped there might be a flicker of warmth there, but unfortunately the reverse was true. Their indifference was closer to outright hostility; no doubt, she reasoned, because they resented another young female being added to the troupe.

So she kept her peace and studied another of the plays Alan had given her. She knew he was angry with her, but she didn't care. She was just thankful that his anger had not prevented him from taking her with him.

By the time they were nearing Hertford on the Stamford Road, she had begun to sort out the members of the company. The women were Kitty Thomas and Frances Gibbon (known by the stage name of Mrs. Macauley). Though Kitty was not much older than herself in years, the hardness of her face even in repose made her seem older. Frances Gibbon was probably nearing thirty, and had the professional demeanor of an actress of long standing. Maud remembered Alan telling her that Mrs. Macauley was the tragedian of the company, and Maud could see why. Her whole manner was artful—even the way she used her hands when she was arranging her shawl suggested she was still on a stage.

There was an older woman, Eva Graham, a lady of considerable girth who spent the morning snoring gently against the shoulder of a plump little man who turned out to be her husband. Graham, as he was called, sat staring at the floor and smiling now and then to himself. Ever so often he would remove a flask from his coat pocket and take a long swig, smiling even more broadly.

There was another drinker in the group—Coram Dodd, a once handsome man whose edges had been blurred by his love for the bottle. He sat in a stupor most of the way, weaving back and forth with the motion of the wagon, occasionally lapsing into long, half-muttered passages from one of the plays. One of them Maud recognized as a long speech from *The Knight Errant*, and she had to catch herself from giving him the answering lines. The company was rounded out with one other man, Rowland Hervey, a thin, wiry fellow of indeterminate age, who gave Maud a pleasant smile, then pulled his hat down over his eyes and slept the entire morning.

Maud looked around at this group of self-absorbed and sleeping men and women, their drab cloaks pulled around them, their eyes, when they were open, focused inward, their mouths turned downward, and she marveled at the memory of these same players cavorting in the barn at Thornwood with such glamour and energy. Is this what an acting company is like, she wondered? All light and glory on stage, and drab emptiness off?

Of course, Jeremy and Alan were not like that, she remembered. It was unfortunate that the two people she knew best in this group chose to ride outside in the drizzling rain, leaving her to make what she could of the rest of the company.

By the time the wagon pulled into a shabby inn in Hertford, the rain was coming down in sheets, and Alan made a decision to stay there for the night and resume their journey the next day. The old inn had seen better days, but it was dry and comfortable, and even their horses deserved to be out of this weather.

The players dragged themselves into the darkly paneled serving room, while Alan made the arrangements. The men would sleep in the barn, and the women all together in one of the upper rooms that had several beds. On announcing this he gave Maud a vengeful glance, which she did not fail to notice. Nor did Frances Gibbon. She pulled her gauzy shawl around her throat and decided not to complain. If Alan Desmond was sleeping in the barn instead of in her bed, at least he would not be sharing one with this little upstart, who was too pretty for her own good.

The food at the old inn was surprisingly good, and

the company seemed to revive with the meal.

"Ye'd better have some more of this kidney pie dearie," Eva Graham said, shoving a large round pan toward Maud. "Ye look like ye could use some more flesh on those narrow bones. Actresses have to keep up their strength ye know."

"And are you an actress then, Miss . . . uh, what was the name?"

Maud smiled at Rowland Hervey, who had leaned across the table toward her. "Not yet, but I hope to be."

"Oh, God!" Frances Gibbon cried, raising a limp hand to her forehead. "Not another apprentice! Does Alan never tire of foisting these rank amateurs on us? Must we endure their miseries and mistakes, only to lose them once they've learned the minimum of their craft."

Kitty Thomas smirked at Maud. "They always run off when they realize Mister Desmond does not intend to set them up. It's an affront, really, to us professionals."

Maud recognized the spiteful tone of Kitty's remarks, but her words smarted nonetheless. "I've heard about you *professionals*," she said with asperity. Kitty's pitted cheeks went white, and Maud realized she had probably made a mistake by getting off on the wrong foot with these ladies. Yet they might as well learn right at the beginning that she would stand up to them.

"Ha!" Coram Dodd laughed, waving a tumbler. "That put you in your place, Kitty luv. Very good, my dear Maud. I can see you are going to be a welcome addition to the Stanbury Players."

"Oh, go back to your gin," Kitty snapped, glaring at Dodd.

"Pay them no mind, dearie," Eva said warmly. "You've a rare pretty face and a smart figure. You should do well as the 'ingenee' or whatever Mister

Desmond calls it. We've all got our little roles, you know. I'm the tiring woman, and take a few of the lesser parts as needed. Corum here is our leading man, except when Mister Desmond has an urge to walk the boards."

"Which he does now and then," her husband added.

"Frances—Mrs. Macauley—takes the tragedies, and Kitty, here, does most of the comedies. Hervey is the second lead, and my own dear Mister Graham takes the older gentleman's parts."

Hervey leaned over the table again and waved his spoon at Maud. "And when we have too many roles, we double up or seek out local talent. Can you sing, Miss Maud? Or dance?"

"I can sing a little—country airs mostly. And dance reels and jigs."

"Much good that will do you," Kitty said. "He means, can you sing and dance for an audience?"

"I don't know. I've never tried."

"Egad!" Frances moaned. "Just as I thought. Why on earth did Alan drag you along?"

"That ought to be obvious, my dear Mrs. Macauley," Coram answered. "All she has to do is stand on the stage and look beautiful, and she'll have the gentlemen jumping up and down on their seats."

"Very perceptive of you, my dear Coram," said a voice from the doorway.

Maud looked up to see Alan Desmond entering the dining room. He had evidently come in from outside, for his hair lay damp against his head and the cuffs of his coat were wet. He slipped off the coat and threw one leg over the bench at the table. "I suppose you've all met Maud by now," he said casually, drawing up a plate.

No thanks to you, she wanted to say. Instead, Rowland Hervey broke in.

"The good Eva Graham has made us all known

to each other. Your Maud is delectable, Mister Desmond. Good thinking on your part."

Maud caught a glimpse of Jeremy, who had followed Alan into the room. He gave her a warm smile as he shoved Hervey over so he could sit next to her.

"Well, no doubt you've learned by now," Alan added between mouthfuls of the pie, "that Maud has little knowledge of the stage. So I propose to begin her apprenticeship right away. Since we're forced to remain in this grubby little place until the weather permits us to move on, we'll use the time to best advantage. Rehearsals begin following this meal."

There were outraged groans from everyone around the table. "Jeremy," Coram said in an aggrieved voice, "can't you talk this monstrous tyrant into allowing us one day's respite? I planned to rest this afternoon."

Jeremy, who knew what "rest" meant, gave Maud an encouraging smile. "You have to start sometime, my girl. It might as well be today."

The rehearsal was not half-bad, Maud thought, even though her part was even less demanding than she expected. Lydia was almost an ornament, little more than a statue without personality, whose sole purpose in the play was to personalize beauty. As the play was written, she would have had several long passages to speak. By the time Alan got through cutting, she was reduced to little more than standing around. Still, since it was Maud's first time on the stage, perhaps it was better to start with something small.

At least, that's what she tried to tell herself. When one passage—so important to the action of the comedy that it could not be cut—was given to Frances, she almost walked away. Only the satisfied smirk on Alan's face prevented her from speaking her mind

141

and leaving. A reassuring grin from Jeremy reminded her that she would be alone in a strange town if she left the company. Besides, she would not give Alan the satisfaction of knowing he had wounded her.

The company started out again the following morning, under a gray sky that was still threatening, though less than the day before. Inside the wagon the company, in marked contrast to their first morning, played cards, told bawdy jokes, argued, and studied their scripts. Little attention was paid to Maud, but she did not mind. Still smarting from Alan's indifference and the petty little revenge he had taken by cutting her part, she sat quietly all the way, lost in her own thoughts.

Once Hervey tried to draw her out. "You're very quiet today," he remarked, sliding closer to where she was wedged in between two large bales.

"She thinks she's too good for the likes of us," Kitty said with a humorless laugh.

Maud started to protest that that wasn't it at all, but she did not have the will to argue. Let Kitty think what she chose.

By noon, when they finally reached Peterborough, the clouds had cleared and the day promised to be fine. Unlike most provincial towns, this one had what passed for a real theater—a kind of town hall, with a raised dais at one end and a few small cubicles behind to serve as tiring and greenrooms. Maud was thankful that her first dramatic appearance before the public would not be in a barn, though that was sure to come on this tour.

Alan procured rooms for them at a rather grubby inn near the hall, and they spent the rest of the afternoon setting up the machinery for the play. As the fateful hour approached for her debut, Maud found her stomach turning flip-flops, and her heart pounding every time she thought about it. By that evening, she decided that the whole thing had been a horrible mistake, and if she could only come across Lawyer Ramsey at that moment, she would throw herself on his mercy rather than endure the coming horror.

Eva was encouraging as she helped Maud into her elaborate dress and fussed over her hair.

"You'll be the envy of every woman in the house," she said, adding another artificial flower to the pile of her hair. "And the gentlemen, why, they'll have their breath fair taken away! Mark my words."

Maud stared into the wavy, undulating surface of a tinned mirror, wishing she could see her reflection more clearly. The paint with which Eva had decorated her face, while extremely gawdy, still enhanced her features in a most attractive way. For a few moments she almost believed Eva's encouraging words, but the thought of stepping out in front of all those people quickly wiped away any exhilaration she felt. Besides, Eva's effusive comments only seemed to make Kitty and Frances more tight-lipped.

She had hoped for an encouraging word from Alan, but since he was speaking the prologue and taking two of the minor parts in the play, he was much too busy to spend time with her. As the moment approached for her entrance, she stood in the wings, fighting down flutters and wondering if any actresses had ever fainted from heart failure while facing an audience for the first time.

And such an audience! Before the first act, she watched with amazement as the benches began to fill. There was the expected assortment of country types noisily taking over the rear rows, pulling out baskets of food and passing bottles among themselves. But closer to the stage and arriving later, came what surely had to be the provincial equivalent of the London fops and their ladies. Many of them were the local gentry attired in their best finery. Some of the gentlemen, with their painted faces and outlandish dress, followed players around the countryside, or were practicing to become the more refined version in London someday. They laughed, called to each other, flirted shamelessly with the ladies, and made a generally good-natured din which barely subsided once the play began. The idea of stepping out in front of that mob was even more frightening than she had expected.

When the time finally came, she hesitated, frozen to the floor so long that Eva had to shove her out the proscenium door on the side of the stage. Once the lights fell full on her, she took a deep breath, raised her chin, and walked down to the front of the apron, where Alan had told her to stand.

A strange quiet descended on the hall. Maud stood quaking in her shoes, afraid to look up into the audience, which was horribly closer to her than she had expected it to be. For an instant she wondered if there was something wrong with her dress, then she took a deep breath, forced her head up and her eyes open, and smiled directly at the front rows.

A great roar went up, punctuated with applause that grew in volume. Some of the men climbed up on the benches and began to cheer. She caught a few of the phrases being thrown at her:

"What a beauty!"

"Why've you kept her behind the scenery!"

"A veritable Venus."

"Sing us a song, lovey."

"What's the name . . . Maud. Maud Makejoy! Aptly named!"

"Hooray for Earl Stanbury!"

Maud listened to all these encouraging comments, and her self-esteem went soaring. Being an actress was not half-bad, she thought, growing more delighted with her new career by the moment. Her smile grew wider as, behind her, the faces of the other women who had been dominating the play settled into raging scowls. Alan, who was standing toward the back of the stage and who had the next line, let the applause go on while the rest of the company looked to him to stop it. He took some satisfaction in knowing that his judgment had been right. If Maud could just carry off her few lines as well as she was handling all this acclaim, her future in the company was going to be very successful indeed.

He let the applause go on long enough to enrage Kitty and Frances even further, then continued with the play. For Maud, who had begun soaking up the attention like a sponge, the rest of the play was a terrible letdown. The whole time she was onstage she had to contend with Kitty placing herself directly in front of her, even though that was not where she was supposed to be. And because Kitty's hoops stood out nearly four feet on each side and her wig was almost three feet high, she was very effective in blocking Maud in her slim grecian skirt from the view of the audience. Then Frances, who fed Maud three of her lines, began adding others that weren't supposed to be there, confusing Maud so much that she fluffed one of her lines badly. The last and longest of her speeches was interrupted in mid-sentence by Mrs. Macaulay, who was by now dominating the play. Maud looked to Alan, hoping he might do something to control these ladies, but he only gave her an enigmatic smile. By the time she finally left the stage, she was near tears, and did not even notice the farewell comments from the audience.

She was somewhat mollified when, after the play, a group of gentlemen and three of their ladies came to the greenroom to seek her out and pay her all kinds of effusive compliments. She knew this was not going to endear her to Mrs. Macaulay or Kitty Thomas, but by now she did not care. If they wanted war, then war it would be. Certainly they had not received an ovation anywhere near as enthusiastic as the one given her. They were just jealous.

She put off her new admirers, wiped away the paint, donned her everyday dress, and went to find Alan Desmond with fire in her eyes and murder in her heart.

Chapter Nine

There were ten grogshops in the vicinity of the Peterborough Hall, and Maud looked inside all of them without finding Alan. She did find Jeremy in the fifth one, well into his cups and happily entertaining a goggle-eyed group of farmers. He had no idea where Mister Desmond had gone.

After searching the smoky common room of the last tavern, Maud walked into the night, resigned to having to sit on her anger until morning. It was then that she spotted him.

It had begun to drizzle again, and the wet cobbles glistened in the shadowy moonlight. He was standing at the end of the lane with two other men, their cloaks tight around them and their hats pulled down over their eyes. Maud didn't recognize him in the dark until she caught the timbre of his voice, carrying clearly even though he was speaking very quietly.

She threw her hood over her hair, caught the edges of her cloak in her fingers, and swooped down on him.

"I want to talk to you!"

Alan looked up in surprise. The faces of the other two men were in dark shadows, but she sensed the question in their glances and ignored it.

"You can see that I'm involved at the moment. We'll talk later."

"This is important. And there might not be a later."

"Nevertheless it will have to wait," Alan said, making no attempt to introduce her to his companions. He shifted the saddlebags draped over his arm and turned away from her. "I'm going on a short trip. We'll talk first thing when I get back."

His casual dismissal infuriated her even more. "Trip? What kind of a trip would you be taking at this hour? Surely you can spare me a few moments before you leave. What I have to say won't take long."

The moon slipped out from behind a wispy gray cloud, illuminating the mouth and chin of one of the men watching. Maud caught the smirk on his lips, and her irritation climbed upward a few notches.

"I said I'm busy," Alan snapped, sensing she was not going to be gotten rid of easily.

"And I said I have something to say to you *now!*"

With an exasperated sigh he turned to the two men. "We'll talk later," he murmured in a low voice as the men slipped off into the shadows. He gave Maud a withering look and started off in the opposite direction, taking long strides. She followed closely on his heels.

"Where are you going? Talk to me!"

"I'm going to get my horse. Really, Maud, where are your manners? I'm sure this can wait until tomorrow."

Maud skipped to keep up with his long legs. "Manners! You snake! You deliberately stood there tonight, and let those two witches make a laughingstock of me in front of half the town! And just when things seemed to be going so well."

"I didn't notice anyone laughing. In fact, I think

you could consider the evening something of a triumph."

He hurried his strides, causing her to run to keep up.

"What triumph? I flubbed my lines. And it was my longest speech, too!"

"Everybody flubs their lines. God's blood, Maud! One would think you were 'the Darling of the Theater' who had been acting on the stage since your cradle. Forget it. You'll do better next time."

"There won't be a next time!"

He stopped at the door of the stable and lifted the latch. Maud stood and watched, trying to catch her breath while he disappeared inside. She ran after him, glad to be in the dark warmth of the stable after the chilling rain. She stood waiting and fuming, while Alan pulled the stub of a candle from underneath his cloak and fussed with a flint until he got it lit. The horses, disturbed in their slumber, stirred restlessly and craned their heads to see who had entered.

"Did you hear what I said?" she asked.

"You mean about there not being a next time?" Alan said dryly. "I heard."

He threw the saddlebags over one of the stall doors and walked to the end of the row, where the saddles were lined up on long wooden pegs.

"Well, don't you care?"

Alan turned to see her standing in the dim light of the tiny candle, hands on her hips, her full lips pursed, her eyes blazing, and her hood pushed back to allow damp tendrils of red-gold hair to frame her face. She was absolutely enticing, and so beautiful that for an instant he regretted having to leave.

"Why won't you answer me? Why didn't you stop those women tonight? Is this what acting on the stage is going to be like all the time?"

Alan gave a sigh and walked back to her, lightly laying his hands on her shoulders. "Listen, Maud, Frances and Kitty were only reacting in a natural way, to the extraordinary attention you got just by walking out in front of an audience. They got back at you the only way they could. But don't let that blind you to that wonderful response. Those people sitting out there saw a potential in you that I suspected was there. It was just what I hoped for.

"As for Kitty and Frances, you'll have to deal with them yourself. I never get involved in cat fights between my leading ladies."

His words were as soothing as the nearness of his body was intoxicating. His hands resting lightly on her shoulders were like hot brands against her flesh. She wanted to melt into his arms, feel his warm breath on her cheek, his lips against her own. Then he dropped his hands and walked back to pick up one of the saddles.

Maud's resentment flared into life again. "I'll wager you've been involved with them in other ways — and many times, too," she said venomously, following him.

"And what is that supposed to mean?"

"How many times have you bedded them? That's what actresses do with their leading men, isn't it?"

"That is hardly any concern of yours."

"I'll wager that's the reason you didn't stop them from humiliating me. Isn't it!" Blindly she struck at him with her fist, knocking his arm hard enough to dislodge the saddle which nearly slipped from his hands. "You couldn't stand up to one of your whores, could you!"

"Young woman, you are badly in need of a good caning," Alan said, throwing the saddle over the top of the stall.

"And I suppose you think you're man enough to

give it to me." She shoved him again, but he grabbed her arm, imprisoning it in his grip, holding her tightly for a moment before shoving her away.

She staggered backward, lost her balance on the uneven floor, and fell headlong into a large bin filled with hay. Alan walked up to stand over her, saw that she wasn't hurt, then laughed. "I'm more man than you've ever had, my girl."

"You beast! You're . . . you're no gentleman!" Maud cried, as she struggled to dig herself out of the yielding hay.

He laughed again and climbed into the bin, dropping on one knee beside her. Catching her hands, he forced her down on her back and imprisoned her hands above her head. His face was very close.

"It's not caning you need, it's kissing. Aye, that and more, much more. You've held yourself back too long." His voice was husky with his swelling need for her.

"Let me go!" Maud cried, writhing in his grip. Instead, he lowered his body over hers, pressing her deeper into the fragrant hay. His lips poised above hers, then slowly, languidly, covered her cries.

Maud fought to resist him, until the soft murmuring of his kiss gradually overcame her, turning her resentment to waves of warm desire. Her body slackened, and her hands, released now, slid over his shoulders and caught his silky hair between her fingers. His lips held her prisoner, as her body flamed and her arms sought him, drawing him down against her.

His tongue flicked against her lips to search the sweet depths within, lightly touching, exploring. She almost opened her lips to him, but the memory of Frances's vindictive face and Kitty's mean smile brought her anger sweeping back, and doused the warmth Alan's touch had flamed. She pursed her lips tightly, and turned her head back and forth trying to escape his insistent tongue.

"Mmmm," Alan murmured, chuckling to himself and nuzzling the hollow of her neck. "Not still reluctant, surely . . ." He moved to her mouth and lightly licked her taut lips, savoring them. Maud shuddered as his warm tongue traced the outline of her mouth, flicked against her lips, and softly probed between them, until she lost all thought but to welcome him within. She opened to his vibrant, probing tongue, that sought to seek and taste her hidden depths.

When at last he released her mouth, she gave a shudder and lay quiescent and willing, while his hands took up the exploration of her body his tongue had begun.

"We always seem to end up in the hay," Alan murmured against her silken throat. Maud could not answer, for his nimble fingers had found the taut nipple of her breast beneath the edges of her gown, and were lightly circling and stroking it with feathery motions that sent her reeling. He stretched out full length against her, and pulled her on her side to face him. While his hands teased her breast, his lips drew a course along her throat and down her chest. She arched against him, lifting her chin to allow him full access.

"Your . . . trip . . ." she managed to say.

He nuzzled the erect point of her breast with his lips. "What trip?" It was forgotten in the joy he experienced as all the barriers fell away, and he knew with an exhilarating thrill that she was his for the taking.

Deftly he untied the laces of her bodice, letting it fall open until he could lift her full, wonderfully soft breasts free. He bent over them, savoring them with his lips, teasing them with his tongue, until she thought she could not bear it any longer. He took a long strand of hay and drew it in concentric circles around the aching nipples, until she was ready to plead with him to take them and suckle.

Getting beneath all the petticoats and skirts was harder, but Maud was so consumed with the music he was evoking from her body that she was barely aware when his hand slipped through. She slipped off her shoes and raised her leg to his searching fingers. Caressing it, he ran his hand along the calf, caught the edge of the garter that held her black stockings in place, slipped above it to the warm fullness of her thigh. Maud gave a shudder as she felt him move higher to the hollow between hip and limb, then into the moist depth of her womanhood. Deftly he stroked, massaging and drawing into life the flame of need that swelled within her. She cried out, drawing him against her to muffle her moans, but the insistent fingers refused to cease.

He shifted his weight above her, and she realized his hands had been replaced by a hot, stiff rod that plunged into her with driving thrusts of passion. She felt the barrier give way with a pain that was almost pleasure, and he drove deeply into her, riding the crest of glorious sensation. He, too, was beyond thought now, as carried on the waves of desire as she. They moved as one, thrusting and receiving, until, when she could bear it no longer, they went crashing into a void of delight like none she had ever known. She clasped him to her, merging her flesh into his, wanting to be forever part of him.

As their breathing subsided, that clasp eased and, with some sadness, he pulled away to rest beside her, his arms still holding her.

"Oh, my goodness . . ." Maud breathed.

"Now you know what you've been missing," he said, kissing her forehead chastely.

Maud smiled into his eyes, still cloudy with satiated desire. "I think I made a mistake waiting so long."

"No," he said, stroking her hair away from her face. "You waited for me, and that is as it should be."

She lay against him, breathing in the musk of his scent with the fragrant hay. His collar had come open, and the light hairs on his chest tickled against her skin. She felt more complete, more whole, and more satisfied, than ever before in her life. She was a woman in the arms of a man, a man she cared for deeply. For the first time in her life, she felt completely and utterly feminine. She was part of the mystery of the universe, where male and female joined to become one whole being. It was the most common experience in the world and, at the same time, the most awesomely beautiful.

Gently he drew her hand down to clasp his maleness, limp and exhausted now. Gingerly at first, then with increasing wonder and awe, she stroked and explored it, sensing the tiny murmurs of life returning as she touched him. "That is a most wondrous thing," she said, giggling.

"I'm glad you like it."

"I like it very much."

He laughed and pulled her close, kissing her again. "You are enchanting, Maud. A wonderful blend of innocence and seduction. You're going to be a very popular attraction."

She pulled back. "Is that why you're making love to me? Just to get me to bring in customers for you?"

"That might be a dividend, but, believe me, it's

not the primary reason." He dropped his head to nuzzle her breast. "Do you believe that?"

She gave a cry as he caught one nipple between his teeth and lightly pulled on it. "I believe you, truly I do!"

"Good." He laughed again, clasping her in his arms and rolling over, until he was on his back and she lay full length on top of him. "I have so much to teach you, and not only about the stage. Do you still think you want to leave the company?"

Taking his face between her hands, she brushed his lips with her own. "Perhaps I shall reconsider it."

"It would be unfortunate if you did leave, for then you would not get to read the new part I've written for you."

Maud pulled back, scrambling to her knees. "You've written something for *me?*"

"Just for you. It's a new play, and I had you in mind for one of the leading characters. It won't be too demanding, and it will show you to advantage."

"Oh, that's wonderful," she cried, clapping her hands. "Then I really can do more than I did with Lydia?"

"Of course. You didn't think I'd keep you standing around in a Grecian dress looking beautiful forever, did you?"

"I wasn't sure, especially after tonight. That seems so far away now. But won't Kitty and Frances be jealous — a part just for me?"

"Now, before you start crowing, remember, I've written parts for them in the past. Every company manager does."

Maud caught her breath, then fell beside him, reaching for his hand and placing it on her bare thigh. "And did you teach them this, too?"

His other hand slipped around her neck, drawing her lips closer. "Neither one of them ever needed lessons from me, believe me." His hand slid up to clasp her hips against him, as the need for her grew again from a low murmur to a swelling torrent.

"Oh, Alan," Maud sighed, arching her back to lift her breast to his ministrations. "I do care for you so."

He nuzzled her breast. "And I care for you. 'And I yield my body as your prisoner.' That's Congreve, by the way. *Love For Love.* You must learn it someday — you'd make a wonderful Angelica."

"I don't feel very angelic right now," Maud cried, as the growing swell of desire threatened to overcome her again.

He drew his finger down her stomach, to cup her between her legs with his hand. "That is too bad, for you've certainly shown me something of heaven!"

When she woke, the first threads of light were beginning to weave their way between the loose boards of the stable wall. Maud, remembering where she was, sat up quickly and saw that she was alone. The hollow indenture where Alan had lain was still visible, but he was nowhere to be seen. Pulling the strands of straw from her hair, she saw that one of the horse stalls was empty. So he had gone on his short trip after all. How long since he left her there alone, she wondered.

This time she could not be angry, for she still had too much of the comforting residue of their lovemaking within her. She smiled to herself as she straightened her bodice and tied her laces, hoping her satisfaction and happiness would not be too evident. Not that she cared about Kitty and Frances — in fact, she hoped they would realize she had been with Alan and burn with jealousy. Yet, somehow, she did not want Jeremy to know. She had a feeling he would not be pleased, though whether that was from envy or because he knew too much of Alan's ways, she could not be sure.

She slipped from the stable just ahead of the young men coming to tend to the horses, and made her way back to the tavern where the troupe had their rooms. Most of the players were still sleeping off the effects of the parties that had followed the play, so she was able to slip upstairs and into her tiny room without being seen. She fell on the cot, still smiling to herself, and was soon asleep again.

Alan had not meant to be so late leaving Peterborough. The house that was his destination was not far from town, but it was slow going in the dark. At least the rain had let up, and although it left the road a slew of mud, still the scudding clouds allowed the moonlight to bronze his path more than it would have an hour ago.

And what an hour! Alan smiled to himself, remembering the feel of Maud's soft body in the hay. A warm glow of satisfaction spread through his body at the memory of all that warmth and exhilaration. She was everything he thought she might be. Her responses were given with her whole body, and with a joy of surprise and delight unbounded. Even better, there was a hint of pure abandonment in her, which he suspected would increase with time. His loins warmed at the thought.

But was it wise to get so involved, a tiny voice at the back of his mind warned. Maud was not like Kitty or Frances, or like any number of women he had known over the years. There was a strong streak of integrity within her. She would give herself completely, and only to one man. Was it really wise of him to let her think that he could be that man?

He still had not answered that question, when he turned down a path leading off the road to the dark shape of a house looming ahead. Since he was so much later than he intended, he was apprehensive when it seemed that the house was shrouded in darkness. Then he caught a glimpse of a faint light behind one of the downstairs windows. Satisfied that Menzies was still waiting, he tethered his horse to a post near the low porch and knocked softly on the door.

He had expected a sleepy servant to answer, and was surprised when it was opened by a woman in a long pink robe. She closed it quickly behind her and leaned against it, looking up at him. Her dark, unbound hair fell in long strands around her face and across her breasts, which were barely concealed by the loose opening of the robe. He caught a glimpse of white flesh in the dim candlelight, pink lips parted provocatively, and dark, hungry eyes fastened on his face.

"I thought you would never come," she whispered.

"Margaret, what are you doing still up?" Alan said lightly. "You should be in bed, not answering the door at this hour. Where are your servants?"

"I sent them away. I've been waiting for you. And I don't want to be in bed, unless you're there with me." With a smooth movement she threw her arms around his neck and pressed her mouth to his. Her tongue darted against his lips, seeking entry.

Alan reached up to remove her arms with a firmness that surprised even him. Ordinarily he would have responded with enthusiasm to Margaret Bowman's advances. He had done so in the past. Tonight, for some reason, he was not interested.

"What would your father think, if he saw you?"

"He went to bed hours ago," she murmured, coursing his face and neck with her hungry mouth.

Alan gripped her shoulders and stepped away from her.

"Look, I've come a long way to see Menzies, and it's late. Let me handle that before thinking of pleasure."

She cocked her head, studying him. "Then you'll come to me afterward?"

"If there is time," he said, being deliberately vague.

She frowned, but there was little she could do. Stepping closer to him, she ran her finger down his chest to his breeches, stroking him. "Make the time. I promise you it will be worth it."

Alan pushed her hand away, smiling at her. "You're insatiable."

"It's one of my best qualities," she said, lightly kissing him. "Menzies is in the library."

He gave her a quick squeeze as a sop to her vanity, and hurried away toward a door at the far end of the entry hall. Knocking softly, he entered a room where a fire crackled in the grate, throwing dark shadows on heavy chairs and shelves of books. A man looked around from one of the chairs and got to his feet, placing a small book on the table where a lamp burned.

"It's about time," Joseph Menzies said, extending his hand to Alan. "I'd about given you up."

"I was . . . delayed," Alan answered, and sank into the chair on the other side of the small table.

"Not by the luscious Margaret, I trust." Menzies picked up a crystal decanter and poured wine into two goblets on a tray beside the lamp.

"No, but not because I wasn't offered the opportunity. A damned handsome woman, that. I can't think why I didn't want to take her up on her offer." Except for the memory of huge violet eyes and a cloud of red-gold hair. And a freshness as far from

Margaret's worldliness, as a daisy is from a rose past its bloom.

"Better to avoid that one," Menzies commented, as he handed Alan one of the goblets. "Her father ought to marry her off soon, or she'll have no reputation left to speak of. She has almost none now."

"Her father once suggested that I be the lamb led to slaughter, but I begged off. I told him I wasn't the marrying kind, and never intended to be."

Menzies settled back in the deep comfort of the chair. "He would never have asked, except that he knows you are not the penniless playwright you pretend to be."

Alan ran his finger down the stem of the glass. "Yes. There aren't many people in England who know that. I'm afraid if I married the luscious Margaret, people might begin to wonder."

"Perhaps not. Another year, and they'll assume Sir Lawrence would take any husband he could get for his wayward daughter."

Alan downed the glass and reached for the decanter. "Well, that's not what we are here to discuss. Did you have a good trip?"

"As well as could be expected. My Scottish burr seems to arouse suspicion wherever I go in this country. How did you learn to disguise yours? I can still detect a trace of it, but I doubt that most people could, who do not know where you began life."

"Through hard work and determination. How are things at home? Any better?"

"Worse, if that's possible. Bad weather has severely hampered the crops. The fishing continues well, but the English collector is always there with his hand out to grab the profits. Between taxes and excises, most of the crofters and fishing folk are near to starvation."

Alan sipped at his wine, staring thoughtfully into the fire.

"You ought to come home, you know," Menzies added quietly. "It would at least give your people hope to know that their laird was there, sharing their suffering."

"I can never go back."

"But it's been over ten years. Surely you would be safe now."

For the first time Alan turned to face his friend, smiling sadly. "There may not be a price on my head any longer, but how long do you think I could live quietly without feeling the shadow of my father's death. And even if I could, burying myself in the desolate highlands is not what I want from life."

"Your father died honorably, fighting for his Prince."

Alan gave a bitter laugh. "Tell that to the Hanovers. No, a part of my life ended on Culodden Moor. I can never go back. Nor do I want to."

Menzies sat forward in his chair, his hands clasping the stem of his wineglass. "My boy," he said earnestly, "I know why you won't return. You are centering your life on one thing—revenge. That is not Christian, nor is it wise. It can only lead to disaster."

Alan rose abruptly and went to stand near the fire, resting his arm on the marble mantel. "And who has a better reason for revenge? I saw my young brother's arms pinned behind him, while a bayonet was thrust through his heart. I saw my mother—as gentle a creature as ever walked—waste away and die from grief. I watched my home go up in flames, my people driven from their farms, my stock stolen and scattered. I don't ever want to go back!"

Menzies's voice remained calm and dispassionate. "Many others suffered in the same way. Yet they stay."

Alan turned from the old visions in the flames and laughed. "They did not decide to hound the man responsible for their suffering. Well, *I* know him. I have followed his movements these many years, and I will have my revenge when the time is ripe for it. So help me, God!"

The transformation on Alan's face—from his usual smiling, carefree manner to this hard, cold determination—always surprised Menzies, even after he had seen it so many times. He shook his head. It was always the same. Why did he even bother to try to persuade the young laird to return?

Alan shivered. "Well, let us speak no more of returning. How goes my cousin? Is he managing well?"

"Oh yes. He does a fair job of keeping your interests sound. I brought you the latest proceeds," he added, setting a heavy leather pouch on the table. "I wish it were more."

Picking up the pouch, Alan bounced it in his hand. "It feels quite substantial for my needs, thank you. I trust my cousin kept out enough for himself. Someday, perhaps, he will be the laird."

"Not while you live. Dear boy, can I not persuade you at least to visit?"

"I have no wish to see Scotland again, and certainly not while there are things to be done here in England. Give my cousin a free hand in all things, and tell him I thank him and support him in all decisions."

Menzies shook his head again. "Things to be done in England—dangerous things! Crazy, foolish, dreams that can only lead to more bloodshed."

Alan moved to clap the thin, older man on his

shoulder. "Come now, don't be morose. Nothing you can say will turn me from my purpose, so let us speak of lighter things. I see you so seldom, and I long to know what is happening with my friends in Scotland."

He resumed his seat as Menzies began speaking of the people around his old home. Though Alan was interested, he found his mind wandering at times, back to that delightful romp in the stable at Peterborough. Strange how it left a lingering smile on his lips, and a singing in his heart. That had never happened before!

Silently he got a grip on his thoughts. Maud was a tantalizing girl, but he must not let visions of her interfere with the mission he had set himself. Perhaps he should be careful about when and how often he made love to her, so that might not grow more important than other concerns. And he had a suspicion that such a thing could happen with a girl like Maud.

As Menzies's voice droned on, Alan's thoughts wandered to Margaret, waiting for him upstairs in her white and gold bedroom. Should he spend the rest of the night there, or take the tiring, lonely trip back to the inn at Peterborough?

No, he decided quickly, he would do neither. He would bed down with his horse in the stable until dawn, and then return to town, leaving word for Margaret that he was called back. Though such a thing had never happened in his life, he could not face the thought of another woman so soon after being with Maud.

The company stayed in Peterborough for four days. Maud repeated the part of Lydia once more, and during the other performances she watched from the sidelines or filled in as a court lady or part of a crowd. In the meantime, she concentrated on learning more parts, including the new play Alan had written for her. It was a delightful comedy with no long speeches for her, but many lines that bounced off other characters. She was so consumed with stage fever by now, that she could hardly wait to perform in it.

She had gained a modest amount of notoriety from playing Lydia, enough so that after each performance groups of men, young and old, came backstage seeking her. She found it easy to put them off, even when they blatantly offered her gifts. It was enough for now that Maud Makejoy was a name that was beginning to be known.

It was far more difficult to handle her new relationship with Alan. When they were with the other actors, he treated her just as he did everyone else, and gave her no more attention than he did the others. He had not come to her rooms at the inn, and she was beginning to wonder if their night in the stable had been a dream, when, one evening, he passed her in the darkened hall on their way to supper. There was no one else about and he seemed ready to move on, when all at once, he stopped beside her and pressed her against the wall, covering her face with his kisses. Maud had longed for him so, and had felt such confusion over his indifference, that her heart swelled near to bursting with joy at being in his arms again. A flaming desire engulfed them both, so strong that nothing could extinguish it. Alan crushed her against the wall, his eager hands roaming her body.

"Come to my rooms," he breathed, and led her back to his door. Closing it behind them, he turned and pressed her against it, pushing aside the shoulders of her dress to bury his lips against her throbbing breast. Almost without realizing it, they had discarded their clothes; he lifted her in his arms and carried her to his bed. The joy of searching, exploring, tasting her eager, naked body, was even more intoxicating than the first time, especially for Maud who had never known what pleasures could be shared on a feather mattress.

They never made it to supper.

Yet the following day, it was back to the same diffidence and distance. Not by so much as a secret smile did Alan betray the wild joy they had shared a few hours earlier. The succeeding days took on a pattern of cool objectivity in the daytime, and secret, passionate, wild coupling in the night. She did not know what to make of it.

Though Maud was not aware of it, Alan was as confused as she. He had steeled himself against getting involved, yet now he suddenly found that he was helpless to prevent it. Just the sight of Maud in her simple gowns taken from the company wardrobe was enough to stir his blood. Everytime they made love, she responded with more eagerness and warmth, sometimes growing as wild for him as he was for her. She was as intoxicating as rare, fine wine, and in spite of all his intentions to remain objective, he felt himself growing more addicted to her every day.

They left Peterborough for Leicester on a fine, sunny morning. Maud rode on the top of the wagon along with the rest of the troupe, just as she had seen them arrive in Thornwood only a few months before, and she could hardly believe she was really there. She had never been so happy.

The following weeks tested that happiness, for Alan drove her relentlessly to learn the basic standards of her craft. If it had not been for the searing nights of love she shared with him, she thought she might despise him by now. Most frustrating was the way he seemed determined to keep her as a stage ornament, until he was satisfied she could really play a part, and, of course, she felt she was ready far sooner than he did. No matter how she pleaded or cajoled, he would not allow her to take on a role until he was sure she could handle it.

"I don't understand him!" Maud complained to Jeremy one afternoon, after a grueling rehearsal when everyone had left but the two of them. "He's mean and cruel! I'll never be up to his standards."

Jeremy sat down on an upended drum and began weaving a long strand of rope into a coil. "He's only being careful. If you went out there and made a disaster of your part, it might hurt your reputation and that of the company. Not to mention the fact that your confidence would be in shreds. He doesn't want to risk that."

"You always defend him," Maud said, pacing up and down the cluttered floor. The performance that night was to be given in a barn not unlike the one at Thornwood, and it brought back unpleasant memories which had not been helped by the difficult rehearsal. "But then he's never as hard on you, nor on anyone else for that matter, as he is on me. It's not fair."

"Chirp, chirp . . ." Jeremy broke into one of Everarde's songs. "Not fair . . . not fair . . ."

"Stop that! I'm serious. Why is he so hard on me?"

"My dear child, look at the rest of us. We're all old hands at this, having walked the boards since we were out of leading strings. We've completed our apprenticeship. You're just learning, and Alan wants you to learn properly. In the end, you'll thank him for it."

"Pooh!" Maud scoffed. Yet she knew Jeremy was

right. It amused her the way Jeremy talked like an old man, when he probably had no more years on him than Alan. She pulled up another of the drums and perched on it. "You really admire him, don't you?"

"Yes. We've been together for some time, and I have a great respect for him. He's very good at what he does."

"Jeremy, has it ever struck you that there's something peculiar about Alan? Something, well, mysterious?"

"Mysterious?" Jeremy concentrated on pulling the rope through his nimble fingers. "I don't know what you mean."

"The way he always goes off. The way he meets these mysterious people on the street, never in the open. He gets messages sometimes; I've been there when they came. And then right away, he's out, and nothing or no one can stop him."

Jeremy gave her a crooked smile. "I think you managed to keep him around at least once."

Maud felt a flush on her cheek. "How did you know about that? I suppose there are no secrets in a company like this. But that was the only time. For the most part, there is nothing he won't leave to go on one of these mysterious errands."

Jeremy shrugged. "Whatever it is, I'm sure Alan knows what he's doing. I wouldn't worry about it. More important . . ."

He paused. Maud glanced at him, bent over his work, a lock of blond hair falling over his forehead. "What?"

"It's not my concern, of course," he said in a rush of words, "but I'd be cautious, my dear, about getting involved with Alan Desmond. He's not, well, he's got more on his mind than falling in love."

"You say that because he has so many lady

friends. I'm aware of that."

"No, that isn't what I meant. I really can't say anymore, except that you should be cautious about giving him too much of your heart. I would hate to see you get hurt."

Maud caught her underlip in her teeth. Was Jeremy saying this because he might want her heart himself? She had caught him looking at her a few times with longing in his eyes, yet he had never by so much as a breath attempted to express what he obviously felt. Or did he know some dreadful secret about Alan that he was unwilling to share?

"He cares for me. I know he does," she said rather plaintively.

"How could he not? Besides, he knows how popular you are going to be. You're already as well known as Mrs. Macauley in the places we visit. By the time we reach London, you'll outdistance us all. Just be patient with him, and do as he tells you. In the end you'll be glad you did."

Maud reached out and squeezed one of his hands lying on the rope. "You're right. I'll try to be more patient. But I'm awfully glad you're here to encourage me, when I'm ready to give up."

"Chirp, chirp . . ." Everarde sang. "You flatter me, lady . . . chirrrp."

Through the rest of the fall, the company traveled the towns and shires of central England. Maud's reputation grew with each performance, until it began to precede their arrival. By the time Alan allowed her to actually appear in a real role, she was so schooled in her craft, that even her extreme nervousness and Kitty's efforts to upstage her could not ruin her performance. After that, her confidence and ability grew stronger with each appearance.

Alan began adding songs to the productions for her to sing, and he started writing another play which would be more of a challenge for her. She was confident in a number of roles now, even two minor Shakespearean ones. She even felt secure enough to stand up to Alan, when she disagreed with his direction.

Though they were not together at night as often as she wished, when he did come to her or draw her away with him, their lovemaking deepened and matured in a way that left her limp with wonder. She knew she was falling deeply, hopelessly in love with this man, and she was powerless to stop it. That he did not necessarily feel the same way about her, was something she tried not to think about.

Then they were ready to return to London for the winter season. She was no longer simple Maud Mellingham, but Maud Makejoy, confident, enthusiastic, more happy than she had ever been. She just knew she was going to have the city at her feet, like no one ever had before.

Chapter Ten

The Chelsea Theater sat midway down Catherine Street, one of the narrow lanes that spun off like spokes from the wheel of Covent Garden. From the front it appeared old and shabby, but Maud soon realized that the backstage area was far superior to the provincial theaters where she had cut her theatrical teeth. There was a real greenroom with pewter wall sconces and gilt chairs, a large tiring-room, and elaborate machinery, painted flats, and reliefs that left her eyes wide with awe.

Her first performance was to be in Alan's new comedy. Unfortunately, there was more of being seen than of speaking in her role, but Jeremy, who played her elderly foreign suitor in a padded costume that increased his girth by half, was on stage with her most of the way, and that gave her confidence. Still, she was so nervous the first night, that he came near to dragging her through the proscenium door and out onto the stage. The hall was filled, but the audience—more jaded and accustomed to theatrical opening nights—was lukewarm in its enthusiasm. It even seemed to Maud that at times they were almost hostile.

The first week's group of plays were given without much improvement in audience response, and Maud began recalling with some bitterness how she had expected to have London at her feet by now.

"Not so easy, is it, dearie?" said a smirking Frances. "London audiences, who are used to the likes of Mrs. Pritchard and Susannah Cibber, look for more than a pretty face."

Though Maud would not give Mrs. Macaulay the satisfaction of a reply, it was gall to her soul that she should fail in her efforts to surpass these older ladies of the company.

Then, after a second lukewarm week, Alan wrote a special epilogue for her to deliver between the play and the musical number that followed it. The verses were witty and clever, and she delivered them with such enthusiasm and charm that for the first time, she felt a surge of warmth from the house. By the second night, the men were stamping and clapping their approval, and by the third, she was on her way to becoming the success she had hoped to be. Maud Makejoy was soon a name that resounded through the theater district. Crowds of admirers lavished praise and gifts on her following the performances, and she suddenly had more invitations than she could ever hope to fill.

Alan surprised her after the third week by renting a small house near Leicester Square expressly for her. It was tiny and exquisite, with a graceful fanlight over the wide front door and a hall that led to a drawing and dining room on the first floor. Both were covered with flocked Chinese paper and furnished with gleaming cherry wood pieces.

"It's beautiful," Maud breathed, wandering between the rooms to admire the silver epergne and candlesticks, the crystal drops on the chandelier, the sculptured plaster moldings, the flowered chintz upholstery, and turkey carpets. "I've never seen anything so lovely!"

He laid an arm around her shoulders and

squeezed. "You deserve it. Our little company has never been so prosperous, nor had the promise of becoming more."

She lifted her radiant face to his lips. "Oh, Alan, I never expected to have a whole house to myself—especially one so beautiful!"

"Well, it's not exactly for you alone, for I intend to spend a good deal of time here, too. There is a small room downstairs, which I shall appropriate as my workroom."

Her heart gave a leap. She had never hoped for such a lovely house, much less to share it with Alan. She ran a finger down his cheek, tracing the line of his lips and the tiny cleft in his chin.

"Write me another epilogue as good as the last one, and you will be able to rent another house. I guarantee it."

Although Alan was in effect living with her in the lovely house on Leicester Street, Maud soon realized that he was going to be gone far more often than he was going to be in. She soon became accustomed to his slipping into her bed in the early hours of the morning, waking her from an exhausted sleep with his hungry embrace, drawing her response with deft fingers until she needed him every bit as desperately as he needed her. And after sleeping satiated in his arms, she grew used to waking when the light was streaming through the curtained windows to find his place empty beside her.

During afternoon rehearsals and evening performances, Alan treated her with the same firm but polite courtesy he showed to Frances and Kitty, and this soon had her feeling frustrated and confused. She endured his strange behavior and turned away suitors who became more ardent with each passing day, until she could stand it no more. Finally, late one morning, she stormed into his little workroom, pulled the quill from his fingers, and angrily demanded his attention.

"I don't understand what is bothering you," Alan said, after recovering from his first surprise. "You have this house, you are on your way to becoming one of the better-known names in London, and I'm with you at least two nights a week. What more can you want?"

"I never see you," Maud said lamely.

"You see me all the time."

"In a professional way. But what am I to you? Some kind of secret mistress? No one would know it unless they saw you sneak into my bedroom in the middle of the night. I'm certainly not your wife. Am I simply your—what do they call it—your protegée?"

"You are all those things, except my wife, and I have no intention of marrying anyone, ever. Everybody knows we live here together. Naturally they all assume that we are lovers."

"But we don't live together. You're *never* here."

Alan's face hardened. "I have other interests besides the theater, Maud. They demand a certain amount of my time, and I intend to see to them."

Maud flounced to the window. "Other women, I suppose!"

Alan sat back in his chair and folded his arms across his chest, smiling, much to her irritation. "How can you imagine I have any energy left for other women, when you know how much of it you receive?"

He studied her expressive face, which even when scowling was lovely against the light. "I think perhaps we both need a change of routine. What if we took a night off, and saw something of London? I'll take you to Vauxhall Gardens. You've never been, have you?"

Maud looked quickly around, almost afraid he was jesting. A great weight lifted from her heart. "No, but I've heard so much about them. They are said to be wonderful!"

Alan rose to place his hands on her shoulders. "They're that and more. Everyone should see them at least once. We'll go tomorrow evening."

"Oh, Alan. That would be lovely!" She threw her arms around his neck and kissed his lips. "I can't wait!"

Gently he steered her toward the door. "Tomorrow night. I promise. But now you must let me finish my work."

She left him and bounced up the stairs, feeling much relieved. It was clear to her now that her unhappiness stemmed mostly from the way he never appeared openly with her, acknowledging to the world that they shared a special relationship. Of course, she never expected or hoped for marriage. Nor was she bothered by the fact that everyone around them assumed that they were lovers. Since they *were* lovers, she wanted the world to know it was true. She wanted to be seen with him in public, to be known as his, and to have him known as hers. Without really sensing all this, Alan had hit on just the right solution.

Vauxhall Gardens was everything and more than Maud expected. From the moment she walked under the door in the walled entrance on Alan's arm, until they left six hours later on a barge down the Thames, she was completely enchanted. She had long-ago heard of the Gardens, since they had existed before she was born. In fact, they went back to old King Charles's reign. But during each new decade since those early days, they had been enlarged and expanded to reflect the latest in modern taste. Now one could wander through triumphal arches or along sheltered paths where Grecian grottos sat hidden among the foliage, or listen to an orchestra (that even included an organ) in a Gothic rotunda. Along the Rural Downs, musicians were lodged in a pit in the ground, so that their music seemed to magically emerge from a clump of "musical bushes." Along the graveled walks, strolling visitors could pause among statues representing mythological gods and goddesses, or take a seat in one of the amphitheaters to hear the best singers in London. There were pavilions for supper parties scattered among the greenery, waiting for those who could afford to hire them. Once it was dark, firework spectacles lit up the night sky. And along the walks, one could meet the very highest of London society — nobility, members of Parliament, clerics — or the very lowest — including hordes of the better class of London prostitutes and their pimps. To Maud it was an enchanted garden, and just being there with Alan made it all the more wonderful.

They had just passed on from admiring one of the painted frescoes that adorned a small temple, when Alan stopped suddenly, staring ahead. "Bless me, there's someone I would like you to meet."

Taking her arm he drew her through the crowd, towards a couple standing a little farther down, near one of the porticoes. The woman was striking — of middle years, but with the vestiges of what must once have been a stunning beauty. She wore an embroidered scarlet dress over a flowered underskirt, and had feathers in her piled hair. Her fine eyes peeked out from behind a sequined black mask, which she lowered in delight once she spied Alan coming toward her.

Her hand lay lightly on the arm of her companion, a tall, heavy-set military man with a pronounced paunch, wearing a brigadier wig and a scarlet coat with cuffs nearly a foot wide. Exquisite lace at his throat was largely covered by a wide silver gorget that gleamed in the light of the lanterns.

"Alan Desmond," the woman cried, giving him a brilliant smile. "Why, you saucy fellow, I didn't know you had returned to London. How good it is to see you again!"

Alan lifted her fingers lightly to his lips. "The Players returned almost four weeks ago. Louise, you seem younger every time I see you."

"Liar! As romantic as ever. And only now are you getting around to seeing me," she said, laughing with pleasure and scoldingly tapping his arm.

Alan drew Maud forward. "May I present Maud Makejoy, the newest sensation of our company. Maud, this is Madam Louise de la Trembrille."

The women nodded suspiciously at each other. "And may I present Major General Ambrose Wilkes," Louise said, motioning to her companion. "Alan Desmond, General Manager-Actor-Playwright of Earl Stanbury's Players Company."

The General's tiny eyes bounced quickly off Alan to fasten on Maud. He reached for her hand to enclose it in his beefy paw. "Enchanted, Miss Makejoy. I've seen you perform. You are even more beautiful in private than you appeared on stage."

Maud preened under his compliment and threw a glance at Alan, which said she hoped he had heard it. However, her delight turned to dismay a moment later, when Alan fell in beside Louise to walk ahead of Maud and the General, who quickly drew her arm through his own.

"We were just going for a little supper," Louise said, throwing her remark over her shoulder. "You'll both join us, of course."

"Well . . . I don't know," Maud said hesitantly.

"But naturally," Louise went on quickly. "I wouldn't hear of anything else. How often do I have an opportunity to visit with my old friend," she added, squeezing Alan's arm.

Wilkes leaned toward Maud, speaking in a quiet voice. "You don't know how I've longed to meet you, Miss Makejoy. May I call you Maud?" With her eyes fastened on the two people ahead of her, Maud nodded absently. "I could have come backstage, of course," Wilkes went on, "but I hate competing with all those fops and roués. I was hoping for just such a chance meeting as this. How fortunate that it happened tonight."

"What? Oh, yes. Fortunate indeed."

He deliberately fell a few steps behind the others. "Louise is an old friend, of course, but the truth is, as I languish here in London between commands, I have often felt the sad need of a new . . . uh . . . interest. An enchanting creature such as yourself—"

"Command? You have an army then?"

He gave a deep chuckle. "My dear, all generals have an army, or they would not be generals. Unless they are retired, of course, and I fancy I'm not ready to be put out to pasture quite yet. At the moment my army is idling its time near Bristol awaiting orders."

"But who do you fight?"

His tiny eyes widened with amazement. "Why, Maud, my child, don't you ever hear anything of the real world, while you are engaged in your theatrical pursuits? The French, of course. Always causing trouble, those Frogs. And now they are threatening to relieve us of our American colonies and, more importantly, our West Indies sugar islands. Those rogues must be taught a lesson."

"And you are just the man to do it," Maud said, trying not to giggle. The idea of this fat, pompous man leading a heroic charge to rid England of a French threat was almost laughable.

Wilkes drew himself up like a preening cock. "I fancy that I am. And so does the King."

Maud's smile was lost in dismay as she saw Alan leaning close to Louise, their heads together in quiet conversation as they walked. She tried to concentrate on General Wilkes, whose innate egotism was tempered by just enough bluster to make him almost comical. He was a solid, heavy man with wide jowls, thick lips, and heavy brows that hung over small eyes so close together as to seem almost unnatural. He obviously felt that his rank and prestige should make up for all other deficiencies and, it was clear, he expected her to be impressed. Well, why not go along, she reasoned. Perhaps a little flirtation might remind Alan that he was not the only one who could look elsewhere.

By the time the two couples moved up the low steps to a pavilion draped in red velvet and surrounded with a canopy of thick trees and shrubs, she was regaling the General with stories of her first attempts at acting. Her bubbling rendition and his rumbling laughter were in sharp contrast to the quiet murmurs of the other couple. The pavilion was furnished with a linen-covered table and several chairs, and once they all sat down to supper, Louise seemed to brighten. A bevy of waiters appeared from nowhere to set cheeses, fruits, breads, and cold meats on the table, and to pour wine from three standing coffers. With the food and wine the laughter picked up, and soon all four were enjoying themselves. The conviviality increased a little later when another group of Louise's friends strolled by, and she invited them to join the company.

Everyone seemed to know everyone else, except for Maud, who sat quietly observing the new arrivals. They included a brother and sister, Emeline and Frederick Lewiston: she, small and pretty, and he, short and paunchy and filled with a sense of his importance over recently being elected a Member of Parliament. The tall gentleman in the lavishly embroidered coat turned out to be a peer, an earl, no less. He was paying assiduous attention to Miss Lewiston, which seemed to please her to no end. There was also a young man, Justin, Lord Hansome, whose outlandish dress rivaled the most outré of the fops who attended the Chelsea Theater. But Maud soon found the most interesting person among the new arrivals to be a Frenchman, the Chevalier Hippolyte de Prevaloir. Of middle height and stocky build, Monsieur de Prevaloir had a long, darkly handsome face, and flashing black eyes that seemed to undress her on the spot. His English was impeccable, and his manners, aside from his daring eyes, were most pleasing and correct.

"Forgive me, Monsieur Prevaloir," Maud said quietly to him, while the others were enjoying an animated discussion on the near hatred the king had felt for his deceased eldest son, Prince Frederick. "I don't pretend to understand politics, but General Wilkes told me earlier that your country was at war with mine."

"And you are wondering why I am here, in enemy territory, so to speak," the Frenchman said, smiling at her. "Unfortunately, it is true that a war exists between our two homelands. But I, Mademoiselle, am a man who values the profit over politics. You English have an appreciation for such, and so allow me to continue with my business and trust me not to engage in animosities."

"And what business is that?"

"I import fine French wines, Mademoiselle Makejoy. Since the enjoyment of fine wine is one thing your King and his son did agree on, I am allowed to continue doing business. Quietly, of course, since officially there is no trade allowed between our countries."

Maud sighed. "I cannot understand why His Majesty had such a hatred for his own son. To me it seems unnatural."

"Mon Dieu, in one so lovely and untouched as yourself, it would be unnatural," he said, reaching out to stroke one of the long curls that fell over Maud's shoulder. "But princes are not subject to the same standards as mere mortals, as I'm sure you know. And the King is inordinately fond of his grandson. I am sure he prefers that young George is his heir, rather than Frederick."

"As we all do," the Earl broke in, having caught the tail end of de Prevaloir's remark. "George II will always be a German at heart, while his grandson promises to be the first truly English monarch since old Queen Anne."

The discussion was quickly taken up at full voice by the rest of the party. In the middle of it—and to Maud's surprise and delight—Alan changed places at the table and came to sit beside her, unseating General Wilkes and putting Monsieur de Prevaloir at a distance. The crowd was so congenial and intent on enjoying themselves, that she soon found herself one with them, laughing, drinking, and eating with gusto.

They stayed until nearly two in the morning, then took a slow barge back down the river to the city. She lay back in Alan's arms, resting on huge cushions as the boat drifted among the other barges, dark shapes on the silver river.

"General Wilkes asked me to ride out with him in the park tomorrow," Maud said after a long, blissful kiss.

"Will you?" Alan shifted his weight a little away from her. His voice was casual—too casual, Maud thought.

"No. I told him I had to be at rehearsal. However, he kept asking until he finally discovered when I next have an afternoon free, and insisted that I save it for him."

"I think you should go."

It was not what she had expected to hear. "Why? He's pleasant enough, but I don't see any point in encouraging him."

"My dear, half of an actress's success lies in the people she knows. The General can open doors for you. Significant doors."

Maud sat up on her elbow, peering down at him. "Do you want me to take him as a lover?" she asked in a low voice, bending closer to tease him with her soft breath on his cheek.

Alan's arms went around her in a sudden vise, pulling her down on his chest. "If you do, I shall have to kill you both!"

There was a low fire burning in her bedroom to take the chill off the evening. Alan lit a single candle near the window, closed the drapes, then walked back to where Maud stood near the bed, and slowly undressed her, taking the time to stroke and kiss and fondle each newly uncovered part of her, until she was in such a wild need of him she could barely breathe. Then he lifted her in his arms and carried her to the high, pillowed bed.

She stretched the length of her body, filled with a wild joy that he wanted and needed so strongly. She had been half-afraid that after the happiness of their evening together, he might leave her to go off on another of his secret trips. But from the moment they left the barge, Alan had hurried her to their door and up the stairs to the bedroom, his urgency driving them both. His long, leisurely undressing and eager exploration of her body had been controlled to build a consuming excitement in her, as well as fueling the need for her he felt so strongly. His hands seemed to want to touch every part of her, the long line of her waist and the swell of her hips, the smooth creaminess of her thighs, the moistness between them that he gently probed., She lay white and lithesome on the coverlet, her redgold hair spilling around her shoulders. As he struggled with his own clothing, Maud scrambled to her knees to watch. The shadows fell on the crevices of his body, the lean, hard body that she loved so much. She loved to watch him, the broad shoulders and strong arms, the long torso, so solid and firm, his flat stomach and lean hips, his muscular thighs, and his throbbing, erect maleness thrusting toward her in eager anticipation.

Alan threw aside his clothes and gripped her shoulders, pushing her back across the bed. She forced him over and, with her hands on either side of his shoulders, rose above him to allow her breast to tease his lips while he murmured his pleasure. Gently she allowed her hips to caress him, until he was as wild with the need of her as she with him. Still he waited, enjoying the exquisite ecstasy of prolonged excitement, the building of their mutual need.

With his hands on her shoulders, he turned her to lie beside him, cradling her in his arms. His fingers probed, seeking the soft warmth between her silken thighs, thrusting within as she opened to him. Her body grew into a flame under his insistent fingers. Then he shifted his weight and drove into her, his rhythm carrying them both along, clutched tightly together, driving them both to heights of pure feeling, until the world shattered in ecstatic shards, drenching them both with its fragmented lights.

Satiated, Maud nestled her head in the hollow of his shoulder. "Would you really mind if I took General Wilkes for a lover?"

"How can you ask such a question after the last hour?"

"Well then, what about de Prevaloir? He seemed interested, and he's a Frenchman, after all. I'm told they're experts at making love."

"He would be worse than Wilkes! Besides, I hadn't noticed any deficiencies in my performance. What more could a Frenchman give you?"

Maud nuzzled his throat. "I have no complaints."

He settled back with his arm around her, enjoying the feel of her soft body stretched alongside his own. "No, my wanton. I think you should encourage the General, lead him on, take his gifts, be seen in public with him, tease him all you like. But save this bewitching, enticing lovely body for me. No one but me!"

Maud's soft laughter was drowned by the press of his lips.

The following morning they were awakened near noon by an insistent knock on the bedroom door. When Maud finally roused enough to slip out of bed and step to the door, she found her housemaid standing in the hall.

"Pardon, m'lady, but there's two gentlemen downstairs who wish to see Mister Desmond. Very demanding they are, too."

"Oh. Well, I suppose it is rather late. Show them into the parlor and offer them something to drink. Oh, and Betty, bring up some chocolate, please. I'm famished."

By the time the maid returned with the steaming chocolate, Alan had already dressed and gone downstairs. Maud gave the visitors little thought, until she went to take her seat at a small round table near the window and glanced out to see two soldiers standing at her front gate. She did not know enough about colors and uniforms to recognize which regiment they were from, yet she knew enough to realize that when one had soldiers with long rifles standing at one's gate, it was not exactly a welcome sight.

"Did those soldiers accompany the visitors downstairs, Betty," she asked, trying to sound casual.

"Yes, ma'am. They came together, but I heard one of the gentlemen tell them to wait outside. Gave me a start to see them, too, I must say."

"Never mind picking up those things now," Maud said, making a sudden decision. "Help me dress."

She slipped down to the first floor, only to find the parlor and dining room empty. One glance through the windows told her the soldiers still waited outside, so she took the stairs to the floor below and started down the hall to Alan's little study on the pretense of offering the men some refreshment. As she neared the door, she saw that it was slightly ajar. The voices from inside the room were low, but very clear, and Maud, though she hadn't planned to eavesdrop, was completely unable to turn and walk away. Instead, she stood quietly listening.

Though she could not recognize the voice of the gentleman who was speaking, his displeasure and anger were all too apparent.

"You'd be wise to heed what we say, Desmond. Men have gone to the Tower for worse."

"Come, gentlemen," Alan said, his voice thick with a mocking good humor. "A few buffoonery characters. Who could possibly take offense?"

"Easily recognized characters. I suppose Lord Stanbury has no idea what you're up to."

"You know Lord Stanbury has not been in England for over a year now."

"Yes, and I know how foolishly lenient he is about allowing his people to make decisions and give vent to their follies. It won't be so pleasant, however, when he's called to account for it."

Alan's voice took on an icy edge. "My work is my own. I have his lordship's full consent to write what I please."

The second man spoke in a high-pitched, whining tone. "Have you his consent to be thrown into the Tower?"

"Really, this is all a tempest in a teapot. You are reading meanings, where they don't exist."

One of the men stepped closer to the door, and Maud moved away. But not before she heard what he was saying: "The Crown doesn't like it, Desmond. And when the Crown doesn't like something, it has very effective ways of ridding itself of it. You'd do best to remember that."

She was around the stairs as the door opened. There was no way she could face these men after what she had overheard, so she dashed back upstairs to her bedroom, closing the door behind her. While she did not understand what they were talking about yet mention of the Tower and the Crown was enough to throw an anxious cloud over what had promised to be a lovely day. Politics was not something Maud had ever been interested in, even when they occasionally intruded on the confined world of Thornwood. Yet even she remembered how in '47 the last of the Scottish rebels had been beheaded in a public execution on Tower Hill. And hangings at Tyburn were still a popular spectator sport. Just the thought of such things becoming a part of her life or Alan's life was enough to send her into tremors.

Later, when she asked Alan what the visitors had wanted, he gave her a brief, evasive answer and hurriedly left the house. It was obvious he was not going to explain the problem or share his concern with her.

"Very well then, don't tell me," she said to herself, as she watched him dodge among the sedan chairs and drays that filled the street. "I'll ask Jeremy."

The servant in lavender satin livery who answered the door, looked down his nose at Alan as though he smelled some offensive odor in the street. "Madam is not yet receiving," he said in sepulchral tones.

He must be new, Alan thought. "Madam will receive me," he snapped, and pushed by him to enter the marble hall. "Tell her Alan Desmond is here, and it is important. I'll wait in the morning room," he added, to show the footman that he knew his way around. The small parlor was drenched with sunlight. Alan poured himself a glass from a decanter and settled in one of the two wing chairs. A newly printed broadside lay on the table, but he was too absorbed in this own thoughts to glance through it. Ten minutes later the door opened, and Louise de la Trembrille swept in. Her face was pale without its usual paint. Her hair was caught up in a long silk kerchief, and she wore a brocade robe over her nightdress.

"So early in the morning, Alan! You roused me out of my beauty sleep."

"It's already afternoon, Louise. Time you were roused."

Louise settled on one of the chairs as a maid followed behind her, carrying a wooden tray with two cups of chocolate. The maid set the tray on the table, before scurrying quickly out and closing the door. "You know I never rise before two o'clock. Now, what is so important that you felt you had to drag me from my bed?"

"I had two visitors this morning, from the Admiralty's office."

Louise gave him a long, silent stare. "Have a cup of chocolate," she finally said, as she reached for one herself.

"Thank you, no. I already poured some of your excellent Madeira. It's more to my taste right now."

"What did these two men want?"

"To warn me that my charming little plays were getting very close to the cutting edge, and I had better back off. They were really quite pathetic.

They have no real basis for any suspicion, except for my obvious sentiments which are clearly shown in what I write, and in England, that does not make enough of a case for treason. Not yet, at least."

Louise studied him over the rim of her cup. "Do you really believe that is all they have?"

"It must be, or they would have done more than simply give me a warning. However, it does suggest they might be watching me, and perhaps my usefulness as a courier is not as great as it once was."

"Yes, that is true. It might be as well to have someone else take over for a time."

Abruptly Alan rose and walked to the window, pulling aside the lace curtain to stare out at the busy street. "To tell the truth, I am beginning to wonder if all our efforts are really worthwhile anyway. With every year that passes, the Hanovers become more entrenched, and it appears less likely the Stuarts will ever return. When this King goes, his grandson will take the throne, and already he is more an Englishman than either of the other two Georges. I don't see much opportunity for change, especially now with Pitt as prime minister. This war he has launched us into will make public sentiment more conservative than ever. No one wants to force radical political change when the country is threatened."

"Bah! What threat? This war is nothing but an effort to wrest rich colonies from France." She set her cup on the tray and sighed. "However, in the end it may force me to leave England, where sentiments toward the French grow more hostile every day. It is too bad. Everything was working so well. At least it had the advantage of forcing General Wilkes to return to England."

Alan dropped the curtain and moved to the empty hearth, resting his arm on the mantel. "Yes, that is true."

"I suspect that is where your real interests lie now, no? This warning comes at a good time. It allows you to set aside our purpose and concentrate on your own."

Alan smiled. "I won't deny that. What a buffoon he has grown into! I watched him last evening, and could barely believe this was the same man who brought all that ruin on my family. Age has turned him into a fat, silly, posturing rake."

"Nonetheless, he is still a dangerous man. If he had any idea who you really are . . ."

"Oh, I intend him to know that, but not until the right time."

Louise studied Alan as he stood casually leaning at the hearth. With his tall, graceful body and easy stance, heightened by the simple green coat and long patterned waistcoat he wore, he might be a man of mode discussing something as frivolous as the latest fashions. Until one looked closer at that lean, handsome face with its brooding mouth and dark, green, intense eyes. A wave of dark hair fell over his forehead, while the rest of the long strands were pulled back and tied in a ribboned queue. His linen stock fell gracefully over the bands of his coat, which fit his muscular frame to perfection. His long fingers and elegant hands moved with an actor's grace, yet there was strength there as well. Strength, too, in the muscular thighs and calves, so evident under his nankeen breeches and simple, plain hose. If she were a younger woman . . .

"Is that why you were throwing that pretty little actress of yours at him? Is she part of your plan for revenge?"

Alan looked quickly away. "She may prove useful."

Louise laughed and fussed with the sleeve of her robe. "She may prove *too* useful. She is quite beautiful, but not unintelligent, I think. And not a little headstrong. She may have her own ideas on the subject."

Alan moved back to sit in the chair opposite Louise, crossing one hosed leg over the other. "Maud will do as I ask. She feels a sense of gratitude toward me, for making her the success she is."

"You should take her out more often. She is still a little shy in public, and I think that with a little more guidance and experience, she could have the town at her feet. The General could be good for her."

"That is not what I intend," Alan snapped. "She's not going to have an affair with him. She's just meant to lead him on, until I can step in."

"Oh, Monsieur Desmond," Louise said, laughing. "You are so clever about some things, and so blind about others. You have no idea how much you care for this Maud, no?"

"Of course, I care for her," Alan replied, not looking at Louise.

"A great deal more than you realize, I think."

"That is not what I came here to discuss."

The truth was that he could not bring himself to talk about his feelings for Maud with Louise, for he did not understand them himself. He would rather die than involve her in the danger he willingly accepted, and yet he was determined to use her as bait to hook General Wilkes. But only in a general way, he told himself. Just enough so that he could stay on Wilkes's trail and eventually hunt him down. The idea that Maud might actually end up in the General's bed was completely unacceptable. In fact, it was appalling. That must not happen!

Yet how was he to avoid arousing her suspicions or antagonisms? Mentally he shook himself. He must not allow a woman, any woman, to interfere with the goals he had set himself.

"Unfortunately, Maud saw those men arrive this morning. She is beginning to ask questions about why I disappear so suddenly, and am away so often."

"And you told her it was none of her concern."

"As a matter of fact, yes."

Louise picked up his glass and moved to refill it, pouring a second one as well. "That is what I would expect of you. You should think of something else, something that will satisfy her questions."

"Such as . . . ?"

"That is for you to decide, my clever playwright. I am certain you can think of something. Here, let us make the toast, and then you can go back and create some kind of story for your little Maud."

"I don't think so," Alan said, taking the glass. "I would like to stay here for the next few days. I am just finishing a new play, and I think it might be better to avoid the Admiralty's men."

"And your actress? What will she think?"

He shrugged. "I'll give her some sort of explanation. She's accustomed to my disappearances."

"My house is yours, for as long as you want it," Louise said. "Perhaps it is just as well that you do stay. You can help me plan the best way to distribute this latest packet of letters."

She reached down and removed a lace doily from the tray, revealing a smear of bright paint across its dark, wooden surface. As she lifted her glass, the distorted perspective rearranged itself into a shimmering picture of a young man in a white wig, with a lace jabot at his throat, and a blue ribboned sash across his chest.

"To the King across the water, and his bonny Prince Charles," she toasted.

Alan lifted his glass out next to hers. "The King and the Prince."

Chapter Eleven

Alan did not appear at the theater at all that day, nor at the performance that night. In fact, it was two full days before Maud saw him again, and that was when he appeared briefly at a rehearsal to announce that the company would be leaving London in two weeks on another tour. As he left the theater, he handed her a newly printed pamphlet.

"A new play. Your character dominates, so you'd better begin learning it right away."

Before she could answer, he was down the steps and out the door. With a mixture of emotions, she leafed through the play. *Perdita, The Watchman's Daughter.* Another challenge to the King's authority? she wondered. She might have been hurt at Alan's indifference, had she not been so angry with him, both for the shabby way he treated her, and at the way he flirted with danger. And just when things had seemed to be going so well!

Jeremy had been little help to her in explaining what Alan was about. "You'd better ask *him*," he said, when Maud drew him aside and told him about the angry visitors.

"But they seemed to be important men. And they had soldiers with them! What on earth would they want with Alan?"

"Were the soldiers wearing the uniform of the King's Guards?"

"I don't know. One uniform looks like another to me."

"Pity you couldn't tell," Jeremy said, thoughtfully rubbing his chin with his finger. "Well, I can tell you this much. You know these comical foreign figures Alan peoples his plays with—like the one I'm playing tonight. More often than not, they are Germans and ridicule the fat, pompous, ribald, thickheaded German squire. Now who does *that* remind you of?"

Maud's eyes grew round. "Hanover! Of course. They're a caricature of King George."

"Exactly. And while there is no law against poking fun at kings and their ministers—Walpole was slanderously ridiculed on the stage twenty years ago—still, in these unquiet times, it does not pay to make your satire too obvious. Alan slices quite close to the edge at times."

"But why does he not take more care? Why antagonize people who have the power to throw you in prison? He could write funny, entertaining characters without going so far."

"Well, for one reason, audiences love to see the powerful being pricked. The more obvious the power, the more they enjoy it. And this is England, after all. Even George II is not going to throw Alan into the Tower for poking fun at the Crown. No, it would take something more serious than that," he added softly.

Maud picked up the straw country bonnet she was to wear in the play, and impatiently tied the strings under her chin. "It sounds like a tempest in a teapot to me—just as Alan said. Yet, you should talk to him, Jeremy. Make him see reason. This new play he has just given me is worse than any he has done before. The foreign squire is not only ridiculous, he's also villainous. *Perdita* might land him in more trouble than ever."

Jeremy gave her a crooked smile. "Alan has written a wonderful description of the King. He's a stupid man, but he's also a complicated man. There is no more dangerous combination."

Alan eventually returned to rehearsals, but not to Maud's little house. Finally, angry, hurt, and pretending an indifference she did not really feel, she accepted General Wilkes's invitation to ride with him in St. James Park. It was a beautiful, sunny afternoon, and she wore a new cloak and muff of deep forest green velvet, lined with soft reddish brown fox fur. The brisk air gave a touch of color to her cheeks, and she felt very pretty and flirtatious in spite of her heavy heart.

General Wilkes was entranced. He claimed her hand during the entire ride, releasing it only to slide his fingers along her knee. Casually, she brushed him away, but it only seemed to encourage him more.

"We'll have dinner together," he breathed into her ear. "We'll go back to my town house . . ."

"Oh, I'd prefer not," Maud said easily. "I have an invitation to a party, which I simply must honor."

"At Madam Louise's home, right? Yes, I have one, too. We'll go together then. I know you don't have to be at the theater tonight, and I insist you spend some time with me. I've earned the right by being so patient."

Maud laughed and ran her gloved finger down his cheek. "Very well. We'll go together." But don't get any ideas about what happens later, she added silently to herself. It was obvious General Wilkes thought the evening would end with her in his bed since that was how things usually progressed with actresses and their admirers. But he was in for a surprise, if he thought to lead her along that path. She might be furious with Alan, but she was not yet ready to fall into someone else's arms when the thought of him was still so strong. And certainly not those of this arrogant, fat, unattractive general.

Actually Maud had not planned to go to Louise's party that evening. It was just another of the many invitations she received, which she usually ignored. But as a way out of spending the night alone with General Wilkes, it had some advantages, so she dressed in her best ball gown, decked herself with her finest jewelry, and rode in the General's carriage to the glittering entrance of Louise's town house.

She was surprised to see that it was one of the finest houses in London. The columned entranceway led to a wide hall that shimmered with candlelight from more than fifty silver candelabras. The large ball room was hung with tapestries and paintings and lined with gilt chairs. An orchestra played on a small balcony overlooking the glittering assembly and wide French doors opened onto private gardens that were illuminated with colored lanterns.

By now Maud was able to recognize the members of the ton who had gathered there. The room was thick with nobility. Those she did not know, General Wilkes did, and he took great delight in pointing them out to her. Never before had she seen so much gorgeous finery and gleaming jewels assembled in one place, and she soaked up the sights with enthusiasm.

Until she felt a slight tapping on her shoulder and turned to look up into Alan's face.

While she searched for her voice, Alan spoke politely to General Wilkes.

"You will allow me to partner Miss Makejoy for this next dance?"

Without waiting for a reply, he grabbed her hand and led her out onto the floor where partners were assembling for a stately old-fashioned pavane. Maud pursed her lips while the music began, and did not speak until the patterns brought them close together.

"I didn't expect to see you here," she said with quiet bitterness.

"Obviously. Why else would you have come with that gross militant."

The steps took them apart, and it was several minutes before she was again close enough to him to hiss:

"Perhaps you think I should have stayed by myself at home, wondering where you were. As I have been doing most of this past week!"

Alan had the grace to look a little guilty. "No," he said when she came around again. "Just to have chosen a more suitable escort."

"My choice of an escort is my business."

"Not while I pay the rent!"

Furious, it was all she could do to smile thinly at the other men who took over the patterns of the dance. At last the closing strains signaled the end, and she was returned to Alan while they both gave the required dignified bows. To her surprise, he gripped her hand and yanked her through the wide double doors and into the subdued darkness of the garden. Once outside, he pulled her down the walk.

"General Wilkes will be looking for me," Maud spluttered as she was dragged farther along the path. "You are supposed to return me to him."

"You've become very conscious of social etiquette for a former farm girl," Alan snapped, stopping finally at a small marble bower deep into the garden.

Maud yanked her hand away and rubbed at her wrist.

"Enough to know boorish behaviour when I see it."

He leaned against one of the pillars and folded his arms across his chest, giving her a humorless smile. "Oh, and if I am a boor, then you are a wanton. Look at you in that dress! It's enough to drive men wild."

His backhanded compliment almost made her forget how angry she was with him. "That was why I wore it," she said tauntingly. "To drive General Wilkes wild."

His eyes flashed fury. "And I suppose you intended to take him home and into your . . . my bed as well."

"Isn't that what all these people do? You told me yourself these balls are nothing more than a flesh market."

Reaching out he gripped her arm, his fingers digging painfully into her flesh. "I did not intend for you to put yourself on the block!"

"Why not?" Maud said, her eyes blazing. "You're not interested in me any longer. Why not sell myself for the best offer? A girl has to make her way in the world."

The foolish words had barely left her lips before he pulled her to him, crushing her against his body. His arms went around her, pinning her to his chest in an iron grip. His face was so close to hers, she could see the tiny flecks of anger in his eyes that quickly merged into desire so strong, it took away her breath.

"Never say that again, Maud. Never!" His lips sought hers, hard and insistent. For a moment she fought against him, but it was futile. His lean, hard body, his lips on hers, his swelling need for her, quickly spun the familiar magic, and she reached up to clutch his hair in her fingers and pull him even closer into her. It was so much what she wanted, what she had longed for these past days, that she could no more turn from him in anger than she could deny her own flesh. His tongue darted against her lips, then plunged to explore every part of her mouth. Maud gasped and sank against him, her body melting within his arms. A flame burst within her, setting her blood racing. She arched against him, and his hands, not gentle but hard and demanding, searched the bodice of her dress to cup her breasts, kneading and stroking.

Alan swung her around so that her back was against the column. Pressing against her, his hips ground into hers, and she felt his swelling hardness through the fabric of her skirt. Maud groaned with the need of him, while his mouth bruised her parted lips, claiming her as his own.

She fought to turn her face away. "No . . . not here . . ." she gasped.

He released her at last to bury his face in her hair. "Maud, my dear. I didn't realize how much I've missed you until now, when I hold you in my arms again. I only wish I could take you right here."

She tried to pull away. "Where have you been?" she said, trying to make anger cover her own burning desire for him. "Here, with Louise?"

"Some of the time. Working on my latest play. Trying to decide what to do."

"That is no reason to leave me alone, wondering where you were, what you were doing. And without a word of explanation! For all I knew, you might have been arrested."

His head shot up. "Arrested! Why should you think that?"

"I saw the soldiers outside that morning, remember."

Alan shrugged. "Oh, that. I told you it was nothing important. Besides, you *have* seen me. I gave you the new play. And I told you about leaving London."

"Me and the rest of the company. Oh, Alan, I thought I meant something special to you. That we . . . that we two . . ."

Alan pulled her back inside the circle of his arms. "I know. I have neglected you, but it could not be helped. There were things I had to see to. Important matters. I meant to come home soon."

"And in the meantime, I am supposed to sit at my tatting and wonder where you are. How much of that time were you with Louise?"

"I've told you before, Louise is just an old friend. I should have sent you word, but I've been so busy. And then when I saw you come in tonight with that fat old man and looking so ravishing—well, it reminded me of what I've been neglecting."

Maud broke away from him and turned her back, fighting with herself. He really had treated her shabbily, and she was half-determined to snap her fingers in his face and go back to General Wilkes, just to teach him a lesson. And yet . . .

What was the use? She belonged to him totally and completely. She was his, and she wanted no one else. Least of all General Wilkes.

"I thought you wanted me to encourage the General," she said lamely.

Alan moved to her, circling her waist with his arms and pulling her against him. His breath was warm and enticing on the back of her neck, like feathery down against her skin. "Encourage, not invite. Those invitations are for me alone."

She turned in his arms, lifting her lips to his.

"And would Mister Desmond like a little supper at my . . . our house?"

"Now there is an invitation I cannot refuse. Come on. There is a back gate in this garden that lets out onto the street. We'll slip out and leave General Wilkes to wonder how you disappeared."

As it turned out, once they stepped inside the darkened hall of the house on Leicester Square, neither one thought about supper. Alan felt such a burning need for Maud, heightened by the time he had spent away from her, that he could barely contain himself from taking her in the darkened coach on the way back to the house. Partly to prolong the exquisite agony and partly out of propriety, he had contented himself with pressing her against the seat, kissing her as deeply as possible, and allowing his roaming hands to explore her breasts beneath the satin fabric of her bodice.

When they stepped inside the silent house, his need for her was almost unbearable. The door had barely closed before he shoved her against the wall, his mouth open against hers, his tongue seeking to explore the deepest mysteries of her body. At length he forced himself to pull back, took her hand, and led her—almost at a run—up the stairs to their room.

Once behind that door, he was consumed with the joy of freedom and privacy. With a moan he folded her in his arms again, pressing her back against the closed door. His mouth sought hers, drinking, drawing as one who seeks life from another, as her own ardor rose to match his. He pushed down the bodice of her dress to expose her breasts, and buried his head in their creamy softness, lifting the globe of one to his lips to suckle and nip.

Maud arched against him, and he knew the wild

joy of her need for him. Hurriedly, agonizingly, he unfastened the tiny buttons of her dress, while she, in her own need for haste, tried to help him. The satin folds billowed around her feet, followed by the petticoats and hoops. Before they touched the ground, Alan's hands were on her thighs and moving to cup the mystery of her womanhood, while his own body throbbed and expanded with his need for her.

He never remembered how he had got out of his own clothes. He only knew that by the time she stood there, pristine and glowing in the moonlight, he had rid himself of any barriers, and the blood was drumming in his head. He pressed against her, his member thrust between her legs, ready to take her there.

Maud gave a flirtatious laugh and teasingly pushed him away, long enough to run to the bed and grasp the post.

"Why, you little minx," Alan said throatily, and chased after her. He nearly had his hands on her waist, when she slipped out and darted to the other side, clasping the bedpost and giggling mischievously. "Not so quickly, my lover," she said, laughing. But he was not finding her game so pleasant. Moving first one way, then the other, he managed to catch her arm, pull her around, and toss her on the bed, where he fell above her. Entwining his fingers in her long hair, he murmured against her cheek, "You can't escape me," before thrusting inside her, driving deeply. With a moan of sheer pleasure, Maud arched her hips against him, and he forced himself farther into her, trying to meld with her body, as his ecstasy built and fired to a heat so all-consuming, all else was forgotten. Her fingers dug into the flesh of his back, as the flame consumed them and carried them over the edge of paradise to merge with the stars in sheer delight.

Alan collapsed against her. His brow was beaded with perspiration, and his breathing was labored. He rested his head against the hollow of her neck and clasped her to him, rejoicing in the feel of her and the consummation of the love he felt for her.

Love? Was that what this was? This compulsion for one woman, this need to have her in his arms, to meld his body with hers?

The quiet of the room was broken only by their shallow breathing, and the muffled sounds of a carriage passing on the street outside. Alan rolled onto his back, pulling her close and circling her with his arm. Her breath was warm on his neck, and her long hair fell in strands across his chest. He thought he had put her out of his mind those days he spent at Louise's, until he saw her tonight. Then, the sight of her looking so beautiful, the jealousy at seeing her on another man's arm, the need for her that rose up like a volcanic roar within him, had overwhelmed any other concern.

And yet, was not that the very danger of falling in love? Was he ready to let his need for one woman push aside the important work he had to do, and the goals he had set for himself so many years ago? Was he ready to abandon the work of avenging his family, for one girl with a cloud of flaming hair and eyes like the color of a clear, cold sky over the highlands?

With a slight shiver he pushed such thoughts from his mind. They were absurd, anyway. Of course, he was not going to abandon his goals or his work. He would find a way to complete them both and have Maud as well. That should not be so difficult.

Maud nestled closer and tightened her arm over his chest. "Cold?"

"A little," Alan said, stroking the hair away from her brow. "However, I was just thinking of some clever ways to warm us both up again."

Perdita debuted the following week, and was an immediate success. It made no sense to Maud that the company should leave London just when things were going so well, but Alan was determined. Perhaps he was right, since this new play poked even more glaring fun at the foibles and denseness of the King and was even more scathing toward William Pitt, his ministry and his war.

Still, it was difficult to think of leaving the city, with its wonderful entertainments, enthusiastic audiences, hordes of backstage admirers, sophisticated residents, and a growing circle of influential friends. She would not miss the other side, of course: the ever present threat of cutpurse and mugger, the army of prostitutes and pimps, so reminiscent of Eliza Finchley's flash house, the teeming slums of St. Giles and Saffron Hill—which she seldom entered—the dirt and squalor, ramshackle ancient houses alongside the handsome public buildings such as Wren's St. Paul's Church, elegant town houses, and superb public parks.

The city was such a vibrant, wonderful mixture of the great and the gawdy, the rich and the poor, that she knew she would miss it sorely until the next time their tour brought them back to it.

To Maud's surprise, General Wilkes appeared at her door two days before they were to leave. She had heard nothing from him since the ball, and assumed that he was thoroughly miffed with her. Yet, though he sat rather stiffly in her parlor and would accept no refreshment, he was polite enough. He even invited her to ride out with him again the following afternoon.

Maud considered it. "Well, tonight is our last performance, and I do have the day free. I *could* ride with you, but I shall have to come directly back here afterward. There's so much to do, you know."

"I quite understand," Wilkes said, pulling a handkerchief from the wide cuff of his coat and opening it with a flourish. "Feeling a bit under the weather myself. It's the damned cold. Hate winter."

Did he know about Alan? How could he not, after the way he was deserted at Louise's ball?

Yet the next afternoon, during their long ride through the park, the General was very careful never to mention Alan. He talked nonstop of awaiting word on his next command, of how he hoped to be sent to India where Clive was making such astounding inroads for England, of almost every subject he could summon up except her company of players and its playwright manager, Alan Desmond.

Maud was polite and friendly without, she hoped, being too encouraging. What Wilkes seemed to want most, was a sympathetic listener and to be seen with a beautiful woman, and those two things she was happy to oblige. He kept his hands to himself and did not insist that she return with him, and for that she was grateful.

In fact, she was thinking the afternoon a complete success, when the open curricle rolled out of the drive to the street and she looked up to see a group of people standing on the walkway waiting for the traffic to subside. One of the sedan chairs at the intersection had dropped a pole, and the men retrieving it got involved in an argument that stopped all movement for a few moments. As she sat in the carriage waiting, her hands clasped together inside her muff and the long fur of her hood lifting in the cold wind around her face, Maud idly glanced across at the group of people on the walk, and froze.

Not ten feet away stood a thin, little man intently watching the chair bearers' argument. Maud sat forward on the seat and gasped as she recognized Samuel Ramsey, the lawyer from Thornwood. Quickly she slid downward on the cushion, pulling her hood closer around her face and turning in the opposite direction. General Wilkes went on chatting without noticing anything, except that she seemed to lean closer to him. For several endless moments they waited, while Maud, unable to look, felt the lawyer's eyes boring into her. But when the street opened and they moved on, she glanced back long enough to see him hurrying across, intent on some errand of his own.

Though she felt sure he had not recognized her, she returned home with a profound sense of anxiety. Was he still looking for Maud Mellingham in order to put her in jail for theft? The loss of the brooch seemed so long ago, that she wondered if he would even bother. And yet, knowing Lady Julia, it seemed all too possible that he was still pursuing her. Lady Julia would never forget or forgive! The sooner Maud got out of London, the better.

That evening Jeremy dropped by to pick up some of her boxes in order to begin packing the tour wagon.

"It must be difficult for you to leave this lovely little house," he said, looking around the exquisite entrance hall. "You'll not have anything nearly so nice on tour."

Maud took his arm and drew him into the parlor.

"I know. It is hard, and yet, perhaps it's time to go. London is an exciting place, but at times it is also overwhelming. I cannot always deal with it. I am still a novice at this, you know."

Jeremy chucked her under the chin. "It's wise of you to remember that. I've seen adulation such as you've received go to the heads of more foolish girls. A little fame, and they think they are the only actresses who ever walked the boards."

"That can't happen to me, with both you and Alan to remind me of how little I know. Won't you have a warm drink before going back out into the cold?"

Jeremy sat on the arm of a chair and eyed her as she perched on the edge of a brocade love seat. "No, thank you. I've too much to do before it gets dark."

Maud stretched her legs out before her, and studied the tips of her satin slippers. She failed to notice Jeremy struggling to pull his eyes away from her trim ankles, encased in white stockings embroidered with little black flowers. "You know how fond I am of you, Jeremy," she began.

Jeremy fussed with an imaginary particle on his sleeve. "Oh?"

"Yes. You're like . . . well, like the brother I never had. Tell me what to do about Alan."

Jeremy's face fell. "My dear Maud, surely there is little I could tell you about Alan that you don't already know."

"But you've been friends for so long. Does he want to leave London because he is in danger?"

"I suppose you'd prefer to stay here in the city?"

Her blue eyes grew round. "No. On the contrary, I want to leave as much as he. Perhaps more. It's just that since those gentlemen came here to speak to him, I've worried that he might do or say something foolish that would bring the authorities down on his head."

Jeremy's eyes lingered on her profile against the diffused, gray light streaming from the curtained window. "It does seem as though their warning has only served to make him more stubborn. But that's his way. I've never known Alan to take the easy way on anything."

"But doesn't he see that what happens to him affects us all? Especially me!"

On an impulse he moved to the love seat and sat close to her, taking her hands in his own. "Maud, you have a lot of naivete and a charming innocence. I'd hate to see you get hurt."

"I know I am naive, but I'm learning!"

"Indeed you are. It's wonderful how you've put both Frances and Kitty in their place, and kept them there! But Alan . . . well, he's not like other men. For one thing, he has always loved women.ABreath he's not really a lighthearted roué. There's much more to him than that."

"Oh, I know. All these mysterious comings and goings. At first I was sure he was seeing other women, but now I'm certain it's not that."

Jeremy released her hands and sat back. "Do you know what it is?"

"No. I only wish I did, because I'm terribly afraid it is something that will involve him in some horrible trouble."

"You really do care for him, don't you?" he said softly.

Maud flounced off the sofa to stand at the window, staring through the lace curtain. "I don't know why I should," she said with bitterness. "He disappears and never says where he is going. He almost never wants to be seen in public with me. And he has practically thrust me into General Wilkes's arms, yet orders me not to encourage him. He's overbearing, arrogant, and inconsiderate!"

She was so concentrated on Alan's shortcomings, that at first she did not notice that Jeremy had moved to stand close beside her.

"It's just his way," Jeremy said quietly. He reached up to tentatively, lightly, lay his hands on her shoulder. "I don't suppose you would prefer a more ordinary fellow — one who would rather cut out his heart than see you hurt—"

Maud looked up in surprise.

"No," he said quickly, and moved away from her to cross the room. "Of course not. Ridiculous idea. Should never have mentioned it. Never will again."

"Jeremy," Maud managed to mutter. "My dear friend . . ."

With a flourish Jeremy picked up a corded box standing near the door, and tucked it under his arm. "If you want to know what is in Alan's mind, my dear, you'll have to ask him. I've never been able to decipher it in all the years I've known him. Just don't let him think . . . don't let him take you for granted."

"No, no, I won't."

"Now, I must be about this business of loading the wagon, or we will never get to Windsor in time for tomorrow evening's performance."

He fled the room leaving Maud to stare after him, feeling more perplexed and confused than before.

Early the following morning, in a cold, drizzling dawn, the Stanbury wagon rolled down the Great West road to Hounslow Heath. The players huddled inside against the bitter cold, scrunching between the chests and bales, or clinging together in a vain attempt to keep warm.

Maud burrowed into her warm fur-lined cloak in a corner, her hands twisted together inside her muff. Her spirits were as bleak as the dreary day promised to be. It had been hard to say goodbye to her little house, especially when Alan had not appeared at all during the night. Her only consolation was the conviction that she would return there some day. This tour might not last too long, and by the time they returned, spring—with all its promise and hope—would surely be on the way. Perhaps by then Alan would have reconciled himself to the government, and he could live with her in their lovely house without any fears or threats. She felt certain in her heart that this would be so.

Her optimism had been sorely tested when she got to the wagon that morning, and found that Alan was not there. He had sent word for them to go ahead, and that he would meet them at Windsor that evening. In spite of her brave words to Jeremy that she was not really worried about other women, she could not help but wonder if it was the warmth of some lady's arms that held him in London.

Then Jeremy had treated her so strangely. He barely spoke to her, and refused to look directly into her eyes. The invisible barrier that suddenly existed between them gave her a terrible sense of loss.

Maud closed her eyes and laid her head back against the jolting wall of the wagon. Jeremy would get over his embarrassment. She would see that he did. She would pretend that nothing had been said between them, and they still had the comfortable, lighthearted friendship they had always enjoyed. He would come round.

And Alan? Well, that would take more thought. But she would find some way to draw him back to her. By the time they returned to London, she was determined to have lured him from any other concerns that claimed his attention. She would convince him that his happiness lay with her.

Yes, by the time they returned to London, everything would be better. She was sure of it.

The rain, a light drizzle when Alan left London, had grown into a drenching downpour by the time he reached Windsor, and he was wet through by the time he glimpsed the round tower of the castle through the sleeting rain. He went straight to the stable, where he knew the Stanbury wagon was stored for the night, and spent half an hour drying and feeding his exhausted mount. The stable was warm and comfortable. Dreading the walk in the rain to the inn, he sank instead onto a bin filled with sweet smelling hay to rest for a while, before once again going out into the weather.

Alan pulled his cloak around him and lay back with one arm beneath his head, listening to the pattern of the rain on the roof. His thoughts wandered aimlessly, but kept returning to one pair of huge violet eyes framed in a white oval face. Lustrous pink lips and a cloud of red-gold hair intruded, when he would try to force his mind to more practical things. He smiled to himself as he realized that Maud probably seemed so near, because the hay reminded him of their first time together. And what a time that had been!

As he had suspected, with each experience the siren in her grew more evident. There was a wild abandonment in her passionate response, a willingness to learn, and an eagerness to match his own needs that left him completely fulfilled and with a strange sense of awe. He had never felt that way about a woman before.

Why, then, wasn't he running through the rain to hold her in his arms? It had been several days since he last saw her, and even longer since they had shared the warm bed in the neat little house on Leicester Street.

Why indeed! Face it, Alan Desmond, he told himself. You care too much, and that is a most disquieting thing. Putting too much of his heart into caring for a woman was to draw it away from other, more entrenched concerns. It also meant having to think about the future, something he had not done for a long time. Revenge for the hurt he had experienced years ago was all the future he had needed. He did not want to change that now, when revenge was almost in his grasp.

He was startled by the barn door creaking open. Sitting up, he watched as a small man wrapped in a cloak with a hat dripping rain slipped inside. Alan had his hand on the handle of his small sword, when the man pulled off his hat, and he recognized Jeremy.

"What brings you here," Alan said, rising from the bin.

Jeremy jerked quickly around. "Ecod! You gave me a fright." Throwing off his cloak, he walked over to sink down in the hay, while Alan drew up a small tub and sat on it, watching his friend. Jeremy carried a squat green bottle, and from his appearance he had been drinking from it for some time.

"Want a dram?" Jeremy asked, holding out the bottle.

"Thanks. It might help against the damp." Alan took a long swig from the bottle and coughed. "Ugh!" he exclaimed, handing back the bottle. "Where did you get this? I never knew you to care for brandy before."

"I'm developing a taste for it. It's the strongest thing I could get."

Alan picked a few strands of hay from his sleeve, wondering that his friend—who had never cared much for drink of any kind—should have taken such a sudden liking for something so potent. "You'd better be careful," he said lightly. "Brandy's been the ruin of better men than you or me."

Jeremy smiled at him, his faded gray eyes crinkling in amusement. "Don't worry about me, old friend. I always land on my feet. But why are you here, instead of up at the inn?"

"I rode in a short while ago and took care of my horse. It was raining so hard, I thought to wait a while in the hope it might slacken." Alan folded his arms across his chest. "You've had a bit of that already. You'd better go easy on the rest."

"I'm not drunk," Jeremy said defensively, jamming the stopper back in.

"You know, I only remember seeing you drunk once before, Jeremy. Do you recall that time?"

Jeremy laughed. "Could I ever forget it? It was the first time we met. At the Durham Fair. That rascally magician challenged me to a contest."

"Yes, and you beat him so soundly at conjuring, he determined to drink you under the table. He was much more proficient at holding his liquor than he was at performing magic. And you, by the way, were the most astounding magician I had ever seen. You still are."

Jeremy felt his cheeks warm at the compliment. "You are too kind, sir," he said, giving Alan a flourish of the bottle. "I wasn't so drunk as to notice what you were like. I never saw such a rawboned young man. You had a Scotts burr so thick, y'could cut it with a knife. And you were so angry at the world, thrashing around trying to find a way to get even with everyone who crossed your path!"

"I remember," Alan said, his eyes darkening. "Those were bad days. I was like a boiling stream, looking for a river in which to channel all my turbulence. You gave me that when you introduced me to the Earl."

"I only showed you a path. Your own talents and ambitions have enabled you to use it."

Alan studied his friend. Only a little older than himself, at times Jeremy seemed like an old man. When he was performing, either as a character in a play or as an entertainer between acts, he was as riveting and charming as any man. It was only off the stage that he seemed, at times, unfocused and a little lost. But never before had he sought solace in a bottle.

"We had some good times in those early days, didn't we," he said. "The traveling around the country, the thrill of writing a play and seeing it come to life . . ."

"The grungy inns, the frolics, the women . . ."

"I don't recall so many women."

"That's because you took them for granted. Once you lost a little of that burning anger and took to the stage, they were drawn to you like flies to honey. I just enjoyed the ones you did not have time for."

"Nonsense. Well, perhaps there is a little truth in that, but we were younger then. Things change," he added, thinking of Maud.

"Yes, they do, don't they," Jeremy muttered, also thinking of Maud.

Alan's horse in the stall nearby shook his head and snorted restlessly. Alan walked over and ran his hand down the velvet nose, before pulling a broken piece of carrot from his pocket and offering it to the animal. "You know, Jeremy, you could do better than the Stanbury Players. With your abilities, you could have your own benefits. Rich patrons pay well for such entertainments."

"Yes, and charlatans are paid well to predict the future. That would be the next step."

"Not necessarily. I only mean that your talents far surpass the meager gifts of most of our players. They might even make you rich, if you used them in the right way."

"And what about you? Has writing plays made you wealthy?"

"You know I don't do it for the money."

Jeremy took another swig from the green bottle, wiping his sleeve across his mouth. "Nor do I. I've always enjoyed being part of the Stanbury Players." Until now, anyway, he added silently. "Besides, I long ago decided someone had to be around to prevent you from being destroyed by your political persuasions. There did not seem to be anyone but me."

Alan pulled at his horse's ears. "Am I supposed to thank you for that?"

"No need. It's been my pleasure." He began pulling the stopper out of the bottle.

Abruptly Alan reached over and took the brandy out of Jeremy's hand. "Come along, old friend. I think we both need a good supper, even if it means going back out in the rain. It's much too wet and gloomy to be so nostalgic."

Jeremy's protest turned to a weak smile, as he looked up into Alan's sympathetic eyes. "You're the director," he said, and staggered to his feet.

Chapter Twelve

Though Maud had left the city with no idea where the Players were going, somehow she never imagined they would end up in Bristol. She had heard of Bristol, and what she was told made it sound like the last place the Stanbury Players would want to visit. It was a port city with all the evils that came with that designation. York, Oxford, Lincoln—almost anyplace else would have been preferable.

Yet they headed for Bristol in an almost unvarying western route: Reading, Newberry, Bath, Wells, then up to Bristol, and all of it was at Alan's insistence. When they arrived in the town, they did not even have a proper booking, though Alan felt sure it would be easily arranged. She had been there two days, when a visitor walked into the hall where they were rehearsing, and she began to understand why they had come.

"Why, General Wilkes," she cried, walking to the edge of the stage to peer down at him. "I did not expect to see you here."

"My pleasure, Miss Makejoy. I am delighted that our paths should cross again in this unlikely place." He beamed up at her. "You'll take supper with me tonight, of course?"

Before Maud could reply, Alan walked up to stand beside her. "Good afternoon, General," he said coolly. "You're rather out of your usual routine, aren't you?"

"Your servant, Mister Desmond. No, as a matter of fact, I am here awaiting passage to my new command. The Foreign Office finally made up its collective mind where to send me. You must have noticed the abundance of soldiers in the town."

"I did, but I rather thought that was typical of a city such as Bristol, that sends ships out all over the world."

"No. Those idle fellows are waiting along with me for our ships to be outfitted." He beamed at Maud. "Though I confess, the annoying wait has now taken on a completely different complexion."

Alan gave Maud a searching glance. "Oh, yes. You two know each other, don't you."

"I was just inviting Miss Makejoy to supper tonight. Of course, you can join us, too, if you like," he added without enthusiasm.

Alan rubbed a finger along his square chin. "I'm afraid I have already made arrangements. But Maud is free. Why don't you go along, Maud, and enjoy yourself."

She glared at him. "As a matter of fact—"

"Nonsense," he said, taking her elbow and propelling her closer to the edge of the stage. "It will do you good to relax. You've been working too hard. A tour is exhausting, General, as I'm sure you can imagine."

"Oh yes, I can. I can. About eight then, Miss Makejoy? I shall send a chair for you."

Angrily Maud yanked her arm from Alan's long fingers. "Eight. Yes. That would be fine. Send it to the theater. I'll be here."

"Wonderful! Wonderful. I shall see you tonight then." He gave her a flourishing bow, and waddled back up the aisle humming to himself.

"I don't want to have supper with him," Maud said through clenched teeth. "Why did you push me into it?"

217

"I've told you before, that you should encourage people like Wilkes. He can open a lot of doors for you."

"In this town? Besides, he's about to leave for India."

He chucked her under the chin before she could knock his hand away. "Then he won't have time to bother you for long, will he?"

Maud glared daggers at him as he went back to directing the play. At least her anger was strong enough to drive away some of the hurt his behavior caused her. And that behavior had been stranger than ever on this terrible tour. How many times had he slipped between the covers of her bed to arouse and fondle her until she was ready to give him her life, only to treat her the following day like she was no more to him than Kitty or even Eva! It was so frustrating and confusing, that she was about ready to begin locking him out of her room. Perhaps it would not be so bad to have supper with General Wilkes. Though she did not want him as a lover, still he treated her with respect and courtesy and, that would at least be a welcome change.

She was relieved that evening when the chair Wilkes had sent delivered her to one of the fashionable inns not far from the waterfront. A young potboy led her directly to General Wilkes, ensconced in a small private room on the first floor. Maud moved straight to a long window that looked out onto the quay. Even at this hour the dock was a busy place, stacked with goods recently unloaded or ready to be shipped out, thick with people — workers, pursers with their lists, merchants, ships' captains and sailors. A long string of lanterns threw a golden light on the shimmering cobbles, and touched the tall masts of the ships moored alongside the dock.

"Somehow the quay looks prettier in the lamplight than it does in daytime," Maud said absently, as

Wilkes took her cloak from around her shoulders.

"Pretty has little to do with it," he said, stepping up beside her to glance through the windowpanes. "There is more wealth represented on that quay than anywhere else in England. Much of the world's trade comes through this port. Fortunes are made and unmade down there every day. But come, I have everything set out. I hope you like baked oysters and capon. It's the best the house has to offer."

He pulled out a spindly gilt chair for her at the small round table.

"It smells delicious," she said, arranging her wide skirt. "I'm sure I shall love it."

Though she did not really like Wilkes much, it was quickly obvious he was going out of his way to make her feel pampered and welcomed. She was relieved that he kept his hands to himself. Of course, she knew now that if the General liked anything more than a pretty woman, it was food, and he soon concentrated on that so much that he barely had time to talk about himself.

"Are those ships out there being outfitted for you?" Maud asked more to make conversation than from any real curiosity.

Wilkes tore off an end of crusty bread and stuffed it into his mouth. "No. Ours are farther down. They are almost ready, except for my flagship. I'm having it completely refitted. Why, no gentleman in his right mind would have sailed under the primitive condition it was in. It should be ready in the next four weeks, they tell me."

"Things in India must not be too pressing, if you can allow so much time."

"Oh, I'm not headed for India. Dear me, no. The Foreign Office would never be so obliging as to send one of its own where he wanted to go. No, I'm headed for the Colonies."

"The Colonies?"

"America. Philadelphia, to be exact, though we shan't be there long. It's those damned Frenchies, causing no end of trouble in the godforsaken wilderness. Stirring up the aborigines and such. Yes, they're counting on me to put them down, and put them down I shall."

"But isn't America very . . . well, primitive? Indians, wilderness, pathetic little towns . . ."

"Oh, all of that. Yes, we shall indeed be leaving civilization behind, except for that part of it we can carry with us. But duty, you know. The King speaks and the King must be obeyed . . . though in this case, the voice is more Mister Pitt's than the King's. Aren't you going to finish that capon, my dear? No? Then I'll oblige you, if you don't mind . . ."

He leaned over and speared the half of the fowl that Maud had left on her plate, and tore into it with gusto. She watched him, hoping that all the food and the quantities of wine he had consumed would do away with any longings for any other entertainment he might have in mind.

As it turned out, her hopes were realized. By the time they had eaten the last of the little ices and drained the tiny cups of coffee, General Wilkes was so stuffed, he could barely keep his eyes open. It was an obvious effort for him to continue making conversation, and with only a little encouragement she led him to the small settee that took up one corner, and lightly rubbed his forehead until he was soon snoring. Then she blew out all but one of the candles, picked up her cloak, and slipped downstairs. Through the window she could see the men still waiting with the chair. Hurrying outside, she ordered the startled bearers, who obviously had not expected her so quickly, to take her to her rooms. As she was about to step inside, she heard someone call her name.

"Why, I do believe it is Mademoiselle Makejoy,"

said a smooth voice in a cultured French accent. "How delightful . . ."

"Monsieur de Prevaloir," Maud cried, recognizing the Frenchman at once. "You're here in Bristol, too?"

He reached for her hand to lift it to his lips. The long hairs of his moustache tickled her skin. *"Mon dieu,* I spend half of my time here! Imported wines, you recall? But you, mamselle . . . what bring you to this town?"

Maud gently recaptured her hand. "What else? The Stanbury Players are touring, and have scheduled a round of performances."

"Then I shall have to attend the theater," he said, sweeping off his hat, fashionably cocked with three buttoned loops. "I had no idea . . ."

"Yes, please do come," Maud said quickly, while pulling her cloak around her shoulders. "Forgive me," she said with a glance at the still darkened window above, "but I really am in a frightful hurry. I hope I shall see you again."

"Yes, Mademoiselle," he said, gripping her hand again to help her up. "I'm sure you shall."

Maud took her seat, then leaned back out the narrow window. "Good night then, Monsieur."

"Good night, mademoiselle."

As the bearers went lumbering off down the street, Maud, still intent on keeping an eye on the darkened window of the inn, did not see the Frenchman glance up at the window and smile to himself. Nor did she hear his muttered comment, as he entered the building: "Oh, yes, Mademoiselle Makejoy. You shall certainly see me again."

The next morning was so fine, that Maud decided to walk to the hall where the plays were presented. As she neared the building, she saw Alan crossing the pavement toward the door. He was deep in conversation with another man, and the two of them had to jump to dodge a heavily laden cart that careened suddenly around the corner. The driver shook his fist and threw them a few pungent comments, which they both ignored.

As she drew near, they stopped and waited for her. Alan towered over the other man, who was short and spindly, but had a round, pink face with kindly eyes of pale green. He was dressed entirely in black, and for a moment Maud thought he might be a clergyman. Alan's first words changed that.

"This is our newest member of the company, Mister Bennett. May I present Maud Makejoy, singer, dancer, and actress *extraordinaire*."

Maud extended her hand and gave a short curtsy.

"The heavenly Perdita! Your servant, ma'am," he said in a strange accent, barely lifting her fingers to his lips. "Josiah Bennett of New York. So pleased to make your acquaintance."

"A colonist!" Maud exclaimed. "I've never met anyone from the Colonies."

"You won't find us so different, I fear. My, Desmond, but she's lovely. I can see that she is a great addition to your company."

Alan laid a possessive arm around Maud's shoulders. "She is indeed."

"She would be a sensation in New York. Take the town by storm. You'd never regret it, I assure you."

"Josiah is trying to talk me into taking the Players to the Colonies. New York, to be exact. I told him it was out of the question."

Maud had a sudden image of a very large, very strange, and very fearful ocean lying between England and America. "I'm relieved. New York is too far from home to my liking. But I would love to hear about the town and about the Colonies. I hope you will indulge me in that, Mister Bennett."

"In anything you ask, Madam. I shall be in Bristol

for at least another week, hoping to change Alan's mind before I sail for home. Perhaps I can improve your opinions of America, while I am at it."

Maud smiled to herself. If he thought changing *her* mind was going to lead to changing Alan's mind, he was sorely mistaken. "I don't think you shall, but I will enjoy having you try," she said, giving him one of her most captivating smiles. "Are you coming to the rehearsal?"

"We will be there eventually, but for the moment, we are going to find a coffee house and spend time catching up," Alan said before Bennett could reply. "Josiah and I have known each other for years. He has been trying to talk me into crossing the Atlantic, since he first started making these tours to England."

"I have always felt the Stanbury Players are a cut above most touring companies, though I don't think Alan believes me. I manage a small theater in New York, where you would be very well received, I promise you."

"Do you write plays as well?" Maud asked, for it was becoming more and more evident that Bennett was a creature of the theater.

"A few trifling things. Nothing as good as Desmond's here. We colonists have a great affection for Shakespeare and Pope and Fielding, as you would see if you visited our shores. We also appreciate beauty, as you would soon find out as well. I do hope you will consider coming."

Alan drew his friend away. "Enough of that, Josiah. Flattering my leading lady will not get you your way. Come, let's go have that coffee. I want to hear all about what's happening over there in the wilderness."

"Wilderness! You mock me, Desmond. Why, New York in its own way is as lively and sophisticated a city as . . . well, as Bristol."

"You shall have to convince me of that. Be a good

girl, Maud, and tell the others I'll be along presently."

She watched them as they headed down the pavement and wished she could go along. Unfortunately, coffeehouses were not very receptive to women. With a sigh, Maud picked up her skirts to enter the hall. She might not want to travel to a place as far away as New York, but she certainly was anxious to hear all about it. She hoped she would have a chance to before Mister Bennett sailed for home.

Somehow the days passed without presenting an opportunity for Maud to visit with Josiah Bennett. When she heard he had left Bristol to travel to Wells, she began to think she would never have a chance to talk to him. She said as much to Alan one evening while they were having supper alone, but he only scoffed at her disappointment.

"Believe me, you don't want to listen to Josiah. He will tell you only one side of the story. He tries to paint a glowing picture of a colonial city, but the reality is far different."

"How would you know that?"

"I talk to everyone. Josiah, after all, wants us to think highly of his little town, because he'd like to get us there. Anyone without an ulterior motive will tell you that it's a rustic, dirty, little port with extremely puritanical ways. Josiah won't mention, for example, that his little theater is routinely closed by the town fathers, who fear its evil influence. He can only arrange a limited number of plays, before the churches come down on him and force the actors out of town."

"Then why would he want to bring us there?"

"Because before that happens, he makes quite a tidy little bundle of coins. It keeps him going until the next time."

Maud sat back in her chair. "I don't believe it."

"Well, it's true. It's the reason I never wanted to go there." He looked over the table at her, at the way the candlelight bronzed the gold in her hair and set

The Publishers of Zebra Books Make This Special Offer to Zebra Romance Readers...

AFTER YOU HAVE READ THIS BOOK WE'D LIKE TO SEND YOU 4 MORE FOR *FREE* AN $18.00 VALUE

NO OBLIGATION!

ONLY ZEBRA HISTORICAL ROMANCES "BURN WITH THE FIRE OF HISTORY" (SEE INSIDE FOR MONEY SAVING DETAILS.)

MORE PASSION AND ADVENTURE AWAIT... YOUR TRIP TO A BIG ADVENTUROUS WORLD BEGINS WHEN YOU ACCEPT YOUR FIRST 4 NOVELS ABSOLUTELY *FREE* (AN $18.00 VALUE)

Accept your Free gift and start to experience more of the passion and adventure you like in a historical romance novel. Each Zebra novel is filled with proud men, spirited women and tempestuous love that you'll remember long after you turn the last page.

Zebra Historical Romances are the finest novels of their kind. They are written by authors who really know how to weave tales of romance and adventure in the historical settings you love. You'll feel like you've actually gone back in time with the thrilling stories that each Zebra novel offers.

GET YOUR FREE GIFT WITH THE START OF YOUR HOME SUBSCRIPTION

Our readers tell us that these books sell out very fast in book stores and often they miss the newest titles. So Zebra has made arrangements for you to receive the four newest novels published each month.

You'll be guaranteed that you'll never miss a title, and home delivery is so convenient. And to show you just how easy it is to get Zebra Historical Romances, we'll send you your first 4 books absolutely FREE! Our gift to you just for trying our home subscription service.

BIG SAVINGS AND FREE HOME DELIVERY

Each month, you'll receive the four newest titles as soon as they are published. You'll probably receive them even before the bookstores do. What's more, you may preview these exciting novels free for 10 days. If you like them as much as we think you will, just pay the low preferred subscriber's price of just $3.75 each. *You'll save $3.00 each month off the publisher's price.* AND, your savings are even greater because there are never any shipping, handling or other hidden charges—FREE Home Delivery. Of course you can return any shipment within 10 days for full credit, no questions asked. There is no minimum number of books you must buy.

shadows on her pale cheeks, and something stirred within him. On an impulse he reached out and took her hand in his. "You're looking particularly enchanting tonight. I love seeing you in that shade of green. It's very becoming."

Maud smiled. "It's called sea green."

"Oh, no! How appropriate. Are you going to badger me, too?"

"No," she replied more seriously. "I have no wish to leave England, especially for a place so far away. But I do wonder why we are still in Bristol. I thought we were only supposed to be here a few days. It's already been far longer than that."

Alan's face became suddenly guarded. "Oh, I'm just enjoying the town. We'll move on soon. In the meantime, I thought the company might like sitting still for a time."

Maud reached for the wine decanter, filling his glass and then her own. They were in a small private dining room of the inn where they were staying, not unlike the one she had shared with General Wilkes, except that this place was not as grand nor as comfortable as that more fashionable hostelry. Yet it was cozy and it was shared with Alan, so she did not mind.

"How's the General?" Alan said, as if he had read her thoughts. "Has he asked you to supper again?"

"You know very well that he has, and I've had to make so many excuses that I'm embarrassed. I wonder he doesn't get discouraged."

"He doesn't seem in a great hurry to move his army, does he? Probably doesn't want to give up the comforts of England for the hardships of India. Can't say as I blame him."

Maud opened her mouth to correct Alan's mistake, but then thought better of it. What did it matter where Wilkes was going? She would just be relieved when he left, and she would no longer have to think of ways to avoid him.

"I suppose you still wish me to encourage him without really encouraging him? It's a delicate task."

"Well, it can't hurt. Lead him on as much as you want, as long as you don't let him drag you into his bed. I enjoy seeing him suffer."

"You might have a little more consideration for me. Sometimes I think I'll give in to him, just to get even with you. It's not a pleasant thought."

Alan gripped her arm and pulled her toward him. His face was very close to hers, his eyes boring into her own. "That would not be wise. I would not like to think of you in the arms of a boor like Wilkes."

"Perhaps that is my decision," she said angrily.

His face softened. "I would not like to think of you in anyone's arms but mine," he whispered, and leaned closer to kiss her lips. His mouth began to work its magic and she softened, melding into his lips, reveling in the hard feel of them against her own. When he released her, she sat back, angry at herself, yet helpless against the love she felt for him. Why must every endearment he gave her be wrung from his attempts to throw her at another man?

Alan ran his finger down her cheek, fully aware of the effect he had on her. "You've come very far, Maud, my girl. You are more successful than I dared to imagine. You can wrap these pompous, rich men around your little finger, and have them crying for more. Use your talents to get even."

His words confused her. "Get even for what? For being wealthy and powerful? What do I care about that?" I only want you, she almost added, but thought better of it. He already knew too well how she melted in his arms. There was no need to make it more evident. Annoyed at herself, she rose from the table and walked to the window to pull back the curtain and stare down at the quiet street. "What about Monsieur de Prevaloir? He's made no secret of the fact that he would like to get me in his bed."

Alan sat back and stretched out his long legs. "He's a Frenchman. I think it would be wiser to stay away from him."

"There's something else that bothers me. Have you noticed the way Jeremy has been acting lately? How he has changed?"

"Yes, I have. It bothers me as well. I tried to talk to him about it, but he wouldn't discuss it. It's so strange. I've never known Jeremy to drink so much, in all the time we've been friends."

"He was so drunk yesterday at rehearsal, he could barely stand! I really hate to see it."

"Yes, but he sobers up enough to perform as well as ever, so I cannot fault him for that. Yet such behavior is not typical of him. I wish I could understand it."

Should she explain, she wondered? Better not, considering how jealous Alan was of the way other men courted her. It might create an unpleasant barrier between the two friends. Besides, she had no way of knowing for certain that Jeremy's strange behavior was a result of that conversation in London. It had been such a short, simple exchange, that surely it could not be the cause of so much pain.

Alan reached out his arms to her. "We've talked enough about your admirers. Come, fill my glass and sit on my lap, and let's think only about ourselves."

She studied his smiling, self-assured face. It would serve him right if she poured the wine on his head and stalked out, leaving him alone for once! But she knew she would not. The thought of lying in his arms for the rest of the night was too enticing. Crossing the room she dropped to his lap and slipped her arms around his neck. He pulled her against him, and she leaned back, dangling her feet across the arm of the chair.

"Fill your own glass," she muttered.

"Minx!" Alan replied and bent over her, running his hand up her bodice to cup her breast. Working the laces free, he lifted one creamy globe from its confining stays and began to lick the pointed nipple with his tongue. Maud stifled a cry, as a wonderful magic began to seep its warm way through her body.

Alan reached across her for his wineglass. There were still a few drops in the bottom and he dribbled them on her breast, then bent to taste and suck the drops. "Oh . . ." Maud sighed and went limp in his arms.

He caught the taut flesh lightly between his teeth. He slipped his free hand underneath her dress, and began a slow exploration that worked on her like an exquisite torture. Writhing, Maud cried out for him to stop, but it was his pleasure to keep driving her, working her like a precious instrument, forming her like a sculpture under the hands of a master, until her whole body was as taut as a bowstring. Not until she cried out for him, begged for him, did he pick her up in his arms and hurry to the settee under the window, where he went thrusting within her, driving himself to that same height where they climaxed together in one glorious meld.

He sank back, his heart pounding and his breath coming in long drags.

"The next time . . ." he gasped, "I ask you to fill my glass . . . will you do it?"

Maud had to wait a moment for her own labored breathing to ease.

"Anything you want, my love," she said with a quiet laugh.

The following week General Wilkes decided to hold a party for the entire company, at the home of the

Lord Mayor of Bristol. This time, Maud knew, she could not put Wilkes off, and, as it turned out, she did not mind. The party was a glittering affair. Most of the local gentry had been invited, along with several ships' captains, wealthy merchants, and a few ladies of questionable reputation. The more refined of Bristol society had made polite excuses, but that seemed to bother none of the guests. Maud found herself enjoying the dancing, gaming, and good-natured flirting far more than she had expected to.

If Alan had been there, it would have been perfect, but she had not seen him since early that morning, when he left the theater to look for Jeremy. As the midnight hour approached, she was having such a good time that she forced him from her mind and gave herself over to pure pleasure.

After a long siege at the faro table, where she won enough to put her ahead of the game, she even allowed Monsieur de Prevaloir, who had been standing at her elbow for two hours, to lead her outside for a walk in the garden. It was cool and refreshing after the closeness of the gaming room, and Maud did not object when he drew her arm through his as they ambled along the darkened paths that wound among the boxwood hedges.

"You play very well," Prevaloir commented, looking down at her. The moonlight made crevices on his lean face, silhouetted against the massive, old-fashioned wig he wore. "It must be the actress in you. You betray nothing on that sweet face."

Maud laughed and pulled away a little from his long body. "It did not take me long to learn I would never win a sou, if I did not keep my cards to myself. It is great fun, but I would not want to become overly fond of playing. I have heard too many stories of fortunes won and lost on the turn of a card."

"That's very wise of you. The more I see of you, Mademoiselle Makejoy, the more impressed I become, not only of your beauty and charm, but of your good sense as well. It is a rare combination."

"You are too kind," Maud murmured, growing a little uncomfortable with his flattery. "Perhaps we should go back inside. The wind seems to be picking up."

"In a moment." His fingers grew strong on her arm. Stopping alongside a small marble colonade, he turned suddenly, pinning her against the stone. Maud tried to squirm away, but his body pressed her firmly back. He leaned close to her face, his breath warm on her cheek. "You must know how I feel about you. Since the first moment we met at Vauxhall, I have wanted you more than any woman in England."

Maud pushed against him, but could not dislodge herself. "Please Monsieur. You are ruining what was a pleasant walk—"

His arms tightened around her. "I cannot hold back any longer. Your nearness is like a strong wine. I've tried to pursue you with polite words and all the other silly trappings of society, but I weary of that." His lips laid a wet pattern on her cheek, moving everywhere at once. "Let us be done with this nonsense. I'm determined to have you at all hazards!"

She twisted her head in a vain effort to avoid his ubiquitous lips. Then he found her mouth, forcing her head against the column, thrusting his tongue deep inside her mouth.

Utterly revolted, Maud shoved with all her strength, pushing him back just far enough to allow her to slip from underneath his body. Furious, she rubbed the back of her hand over her mouth. "How dare you, sir!"

Monsieur de Prevaloir laughed, his eyes shining in the moonlight as he grabbed at her arm and pulled her against him again. "I like a girl who puts up a fight. It makes the final conquest so much more satisfying!"

But she was not pinned against a column now. She swung her arm and slapped him across the face with all her strength. When he fell back, startled, she shoved him and sent him careening into one of the hedges. Then she turned and ran for the house. Her last glimpse was of the Frenchman trying to extricate himself from the boxwood, his wig askew and his dignity in shreds.

Serves him right, she muttered to herself, as she paused on the terrace just long enough to straighten her gown and her hair. Hoping she did not look too disheveled, she entered the bright ballroom and wove her way among the dancers toward the door. She had not gone ten feet, before General Wilkes bore down on her.

"Maud, where have you been? I've looked everywhere for you. My dear," he added, taking her arm, "you look quite pale. Is the evening wearing thin? Come, I'll take you home."

"That won't be necessary," Maud said, but he draped an arm around her shoulders and steered her toward the hall.

"Nonsense. This party was really for you, you know, and I insist I be allowed the favor of seeing you home. I've earned it. I've been very patient."

Maud saw that she was going to have to do some fancy footwork tonight, if she wanted to get rid of Wilkes without offending him forever.

"You see, my dear," he said, speaking softly into her ear, "I've just heard tonight that we are ready to sail. The Foreign Office sent word that we are expected to be in America by next month. Our ships are ready and we must get underway, if we are going to meet that date. So, this is my farewell to you, and one I shall want to remember while I am tramping the wilderness of America."

They were in the hall. Wilkes kissed her hand and

told her to wait, while he went to arrange for their carriage. Maud stood frozen while a footman draped her cloak about her shoulders, wondering how she was going to extricate herself from this dilemma. Perhaps it no longer mattered if the General was offended. He was about to sail away, and once he was gone, Alan could no longer have an interest in her relationship with him.

"Maud!"

Alan's voice! She looked up to see him slipping around the footmen and through the entrance. "Thank God, I've found you. Come with me. I need your help."

"Where have you been? I waited for you all evening. Now General Wilkes is bringing round the carriage to take me home."

"I saw him out front. Come on, we'll find a way through the back." He grabbed her hand and half-pulled her toward the rear of the hall, where a door led onto the private rooms of the house. Maud struggled after him. "But what will he think—"

"It doesn't matter what he thinks. We have more important matters to deal with."

The door closed behind them, revealing a flight of steps which led to the kitchen and serving areas. Alan hurried her ahead of him.

"What do you mean? What kind of matters?"

They emerged out on the flagstone floor of the kitchen, where Alan glanced around long enough to note the door at the far end which led outside. Grabbing her hand, he rushed toward it.

"It's Jeremy. he's disappeared."

Chapter Thirteen

He must have left his coat in one of the taverns. Because the night was so mild, Jeremy did not notice its loss until well into the evening, and by then he was almost too drunk to care. Waterfront grogshops were always too hot anyway; hot, steamy, filled with the heady odors of stale beer and ale, and riotous with the noise of drunken revelers—just the kind of atmosphere he craved.

He had been at it since early afternoon, making the rounds of one dingy public house after another. Unfortunately, he was still sober enough to realize it. Oblivion had not yet taken him out of himself, and so he must keep stumbling along the waterfront, until it managed to overtake him. He could still remember too much. He could still recall speaking something of what was in his heart for almost the first time in his life, and that memory was still too painful to be borne. How careful he had been since he was old enough to know better, to never allow anyone to know what lay behind that gay, entertaining facade. Everyone, Maud included, thought he was the best of fellows, the most talented of magicians. No one ever bothered to see the pain behind it all, and until that unguarded moment in Maud's house, he had never invited anyone to.

And all he got for letting down his guard was a look of such surprised horror, he would never be able to erase it from his mind. If he had half the courage he ought to have, he would throw himself in the canal and drown. That was all he deserved—miserable, unlovable coward that he was!

He shoved open the door and walked into a wall of light. This appeared to be the worst of the lot, not too surprising since it was near the end of the waterwalk. A few yellow faces turned his way, but for the most part the drinkers were too far in their cups and engrossed in their false hilarity to notice another shuffling, half-drunk arrival. Jeremy weaved his way unsteadily between a row of tables, and almost fell against the bar.

"Got a pint?" he mumbled.

The beefy man behind the bar turned tiny, hard eyes on him. "Got the coin?"

Jeremy slapped a few pence on the counter and slid it toward him. It disappeared in the barkeep's big paw before it was halfway there.

"Between you and I and the pot, you look like you've had enough already," the man said, pushing a squat green bottle toward Jeremy. He gripped it by the short neck.

"Not quite, my good man," he muttered, and slipped the bottle under his arm. Looking around the room, he saw two men leaving a table in one of the dark corners, far away from the swinging lanterns that illuminated the front of the room. He picked up a glass and made for it, anxious to claim the space before anyone else could. He had just slipped into the chair, when a man sitting in a nearby booth grabbed at his sleeve.

"Gor', it's the birdman from the playactin'. I seen 'im t'other day. Give us a few birdcalls."

Jeremy yanked his arm away. "You got the wrong fellow," he muttered, and bent over the bottle.

A woman who was sitting inside the booth leaned

over her companion to stare goggle-eyed at him. "I recognize 'im. Joey's right. Where's y'er little fellow in the cage, what talks and sings. 'Ave ye brought 'im along?"

"I knew it was 'im. Come on, be a good bloke and give us a few calls—"

"Let me be!" Jeremy snapped. "You got the wrong man!"

"Well, I never!" the woman said with a sniff. "Thinks 'e's better than the rest of us poor mortals, I suppose."

"Ah, come along, now. There's a good fellow. We could use a little conjurin' in 'ere. Entertaining, an' all . . ."

"Let 'im be, Joey," the woman said, as Jeremy glared at them both. " 'E wants to drink alone, so let 'im. I'm sure I don't care."

To Jeremy's relief they turned back to their own concerns, and allowed him to pour his drink in peace. He downed the first glass in its entirety, choked and gasped at the burning trail it left down his throat, and filled the glass again. Not much longer now and oblivion would come. In this dark corner perhaps no one would bother him, and he could lie on the table and sleep it off until tomorrow.

Tomorrow. The same memories, the same ache, and the same solution to be sought. And the day after that, and the day after that . . .

He downed the second glass. There ought to be a better way to deal with this, but he was damned if he knew it.

His eyes were beginning to blur and the room to swim. There was a shattering noise near the front of the room, but he could not focus clearly to see what had happened. The room was filling with people, men in bright red coats, with long rifles . . .

He was just sober enough to feel the cold chill that

shot through him, as he realized who they were. There was a lot of movement now and a lot of shouting as the men went through the room, yanking up anyone who could move and dragging them toward the front, where the lantern threw its grim light on their frightened faces. Jeremy looked frantically around for another door, and saw a dim hallway with a flight of steps leading down to the ground floor. It was in almost total darkness, but if he could get that far, surely it would lead to a way outside. Hunching down, he slid along the front of the darkened booths, making for the stairs before he could be seen.

"Well, well, look what we 'ave 'ere!"

A burly hand grabbed Jeremy's collar, dragging him backward, then lifting him clear off the floor, where he squirmed in the air. He could make out a huge, red-coated figure holding him and a grinning, fleshy face. He swung his arms helplessly, trying to strike that hateful face, but the man only held him at a greater distance.

The woman who had been sitting in the booth began to scream, as another soldier dragged Joey away from her. She grabbed at his free arm and the two of them pulled Joey between them, with her screaming all the while.

"Let go of me!" Jeremy struggled to yell through his strangled throat.

"He's such a runt, don't know as the Captain'd want 'im," another of the men said, laughing.

The soldier holding Jeremy lifted him higher off the floor. " 'E's breathing, ain't 'e? That's all that matters. We got a quota to make."

He dropped Jeremy suddenly into a heap, then yanked him up by his arm and propelled him toward the tavern door. Jeremy swung furiously at him.

"No damn press gang is going to drag me off—"

The soldier laughed. "What's wrong? Don't want to

do y'er duty for y'er God and King? Too bad." He shoved Jeremy against the wall, but he came off it flailing his arms and managed to strike the huge man full in the stomach.

"Damn the fiesty little bastard," the soldier gasped, and threw Jeremy against the wall, slamming his head against one of the oak beams. The room began to swim as all the strength went out of Jeremy's legs and arms. He felt himself yanked up again and shoved forward. The last thing he remembered as blessed oblivion swallowed him, was the light gleaming like moonbeams on the cobbles outside the tavern door.

To Maud's surprise Alan had a carriage waiting. He had not dared to bring it up to the door, so had left it at the end of the street. He bundled Maud into it, shouted directions to the driver, and climbed in beside her.

Maud recognized the address. "Why are we going to the waterfront? Is that where Jeremy was lost?"

"He's not lost. It's worse than that. He's been pressed into the army. He was drinking in one of those grungy alehouses, when a press gang came in and rounded up every man who could walk. They're sailing with the tide, and they needed to fill out their ranks."

"Then he's not murdered or dead. When you said he had disappeared, I feared the worst."

Alan's face was grim. "He's not dead yet, but he will be. I know Jeremy. He's clever, but he's not made of the kind of stuff that would enable him to survive a voyage to India, much less life in the army. He'll be dead within a month, I guarantee it."

Maud was both surprised and moved at Alan's obvious concern. She knew the two men were friends, but she never suspected Jeremy's welfare meant that much to Alan. She opened her mouth to tell him that the army was not headed for India, but he broke in before she could speak.

"Now here's what I want you to do. You're going to put on the performance of your life! We're going down to that ship, and you're going to tell that Army Captain that you are Jeremy's wife, that the two of you have ten children, and that they will all starve if he isn't allowed to return home. Do you think you can do it?"

"I think so. But will he listen to me? Does the army allow some men to escape impressment, if they have obligations at home?"

"The Navy, never, but the Army . . . I just don't know. But it's worth a try. We've got to do something. I won't allow this to happen. I won't! Come now. Let's practice. Pretend I am the officer, and you are trying to save your husband."

They worked on her story while the coach careened down the darkened streets to the waterfront. By the time it pulled up opposite the huge lumbering shape of the moored schooner, she had almost worked herself up to real tears.

She saw that she would need them if she was going to convince the cold-eyed, officious officer in charge. Thankfully, he was on the deck along with several of his men and a swarm of pig-tailed sailors. They were waiting impatiently on the tide. It was obvious that another half-hour and they would have been on their way.

Maud threw herself at the officer in charge. Weeping, pleading, dropping to her knees, and then clinging to his arm, she begged him to release her poor husband. The officer shook her off.

"Who allowed this woman on deck?" he snapped to his subordinate.

"She pushed by me," the man answered. "I tried to stop her."

"And who are you?" the Captain said, eying Alan.

"This poor woman's brother. You must believe her, Sir Captain. This suffering family needs their father."

The officer beckoned and a huge sergeant stepped forward. "Where is this man? This . . . Jeremy Oaks?"

The sergeant leaned forward and spoke softly: "Below, sir. He was well, a little injured comin' aboard. It's his head."

Maud felt Alan grip her arm, and she began to wail loudly.

"Stop that racket! Has this man taken the oath?"

"Oh, yes indeed, Captain. First thing."

"Then there is nothing I can do about it. Your husband is in the Army, madam, and you must accept it. Your 'brother' here looks to be in fine shape. Let him take care of your poor, suffering family. Now both of you leave this ship. We are about to get underway."

He turned his back on them. Maud threw Alan a desperate glance and began to sob once more, as two of the soldiers stepped forward to shove them both toward the gangway.

"You can't do this," Alan cried. "India will kill Jeremy. He'll never survive."

"Put y'er mind at rest then," one of the soldiers quipped, "for we're not bound for India. We're bound for America."

At the gangway Alan grabbed the ship's railing and held on. "What did you say? You're not going to India? But I thought—"

Maud clung to his arm. "I tried to tell you. General Wilkes's orders were changed. He's going to fight the French in Philadelphia."

"Philadelphia? Stop manhandling me," Alan said,

shoving the soldier back. "Just hold on a moment. America?"

"That's right. And if you don't want to go along, you'd better get down that gangway now."

"Wait just a moment." He ducked from behind the soldier and darted over to the Captain. "Do you need another recruit?"

The Captain looked up in surprise as Maud gave a horrified scream.

"If you mean yourself, why yes. We can always use a strong, healthy man."

Tearing her arm away from the soldier's grasp, Maud ran to Alan. "What are you doing? Are you out of your mind?"

"I'm taking the king's shilling. It's the only way I can think of to see that Jeremy doesn't get killed."

"But what about me? Alan, you can't just go off like this and leave me!"

The Captain stared down his nose at her. "Your 'sister' seems to have a very strong affection for you."

"May I have a moment, sir, to say goodbye?"

"You'd better hurry. I have no room for a woman on this ship."

Alan took Maud's elbow and propelled her toward the railing. He leaned close to her startled face and whispered: "Go find Josiah Bennett. Tell him I've changed my mind, and we'll take his offer. But we want to go to Philadelphia, not New York."

"But suppose—"

"There is no time to discuss it! Bring the company to Philadelphia. Once this ship gets there, Jeremy and I both will find a way to be separated from the Army, honorably or not. I'll meet you there."

"Alan . . . I don't know . . ."

He caught her in his arms and kissed her. It was a long, hard kiss that held no promise and much of farewell.

"I'll see you in America."

Before she could speak, he turned and was gone down the hatchway. Maud would have followed him, but for the soldier who pulled her down the gangway. He shoved her onto the cobbles and ran back up to the ship. Immediately the long, ladderlike plank rose in the air, as the sailors began to draw it onto the deck.

Maud watched helplessly as the activity on board ship increased. Sailors swarmed up the rigging, ropes were unfastened and thrown up to waiting arms, the timbers creaked and groaned, as the sails fell and fluttered into life. In horror she saw the great ship move slowly, sluggishly out into the canal and down toward the open sea.

She still couldn't believe that Alan and Jeremy were on that ship slowly slipping away toward America, leaving her alone. How was she going to manage? What if the rest of the company didn't want to go to America? Suppose Mister Bennett decided he no longer wanted the Stanbury Players?

A welcome anger began to seep through her confusion. How like Alan to traipse off on some crusade of his own, leaving her to pick up the pieces. It would serve him right, if she turned around and went back to London and made her own way there.

And never see him again? The thought was unbearable. She stamped her foot and shook her fist at the huge shadow of the ship, then went off to find Josiah Bennett.

Although Alan had imagined himself standing at the ship's rail watching the last sight of England fade from view, he learned very quickly that was not going to happen. He had no more than signed his name to the roll of paper before the Captain, than a beefy hand gripped his shoulder and thrust him toward the hatchway. He looked around at a huge man with a beet-red face, a slash of a mouth, and tiny eyes peering coldly at him from beneath heavy, black brows.

Alan slapped the hand away. "You don't have to push."

"Oh, and it's a gentleman, is it? An' I'm supposed to ask all nice and everythin'." The sergeant leaned into his face, his thin mouth grimacing. "Well, I've a lesson for ye. Yer first one. Y'er no gentlemen now. Y'er a private in the King's Own, and that's the lowest form of life next to cockroach. An' I'm yer Sergeant, and that's the highest form of life 'cepting the Captain here, who ain't going to care if I grind you under my boot heel, same as I would a cockroach. Now get below with the rest of the vermin!"

Gripping Alan's shoulder, the sergeant shoved him toward the hatchway ladder. Alan stumbled, caught his grip, and was about to pound into the man, before getting hold of himself. It would serve nothing to cause a scene before he even knew where Jeremy was, or if he was all right. Bullies like this sergeant loved to provoke a man into striking back, since it would give them even more reason to bully. He straightened his waistcoat and gave the sergeant a thin smile. "Yes, sir. Right away, sir," he said, and disappeared down the ladder before the disappointed man could come at him again. The cold reality of his impulsive action was slowly sinking in, and he began recalling all the horrible stories he had ever heard about life in the Army. By the time he reached the second deck where most of the men were quartered, he had got a grip on himself. It was done now, and he would have to make the best of it. How long did it take to reach America? Six weeks? He could endure that, and once this voyage was over, he'd find a way to get out of this situation.

He found Jeremy in a small group of men still

dressed in civilian clothes, huddled at the back of the deck. It was close and dark and thick with the offensive smell of slop buckets set at intervals. The men were so jammed together that Alan had to shove them aside to sink down beside his friend. He pulled out a handkerchief and held it to his nose, as the strong odor of stale ale added to the rest of the miasma.

Jeremy looked over at him and stared, his mouth gaping. "God's toes and fingernails—!"

"Is that all you can say?"

Jeremy looked around. "What are you doing here? You weren't pressed, too?"

"No. I took the shilling."

"You what!"

Alan peered closer at Jeremy's battered face. "Beat you up a little, did they? Was anything broken?"

"No. If I hadn't been so drunk, I might have got away. It made me just a little too slow."

"Not exactly sober yet, are you," Alan commented, noting Jeremy's slurred speech. "I've a feeling that by tomorrow we'll both be *too* sober."

"Why'd you do it? I thought you had better sense."

"Somebody has to keep an eye on you. Besides, I had a sudden itch to see the Colonies. What's going on here? Do we spend the voyage crushed together like this on the floor of a lower deck?"

A man leaned around Jeremy, holding a hand to his head. "One of the regulars told me they'd rig slings for us to sleep in tomorrow. Issue uniforms, too. And muskets."

"This is Joey," Jeremy muttered. "At least, I think it is."

"That's right. Joey Stapleton," the man said, bobbing his head at Alan. "I was in that taproom with me wife, when this bunch came in and dragged us off. Bastards!"

Several of the other men spoke up, comparing the experiences that had led to their being thrown together on the darkened, close deck. Alan listened, thinking that already there was a budding camaraderie among them, men who shared a common outrage and fate. Most soon lapsed into silence, as they thought about the people they were leaving behind. A few fell into alcoholic stupors. Even Jeremy nodded, leaning against the plank wall, lulled by the gentle motions of the ship.

Alan settled beside him and was soon lost in his own thoughts. Unlike most of the others, he was clearheaded, and knew very well how he had come to be here. Yet it had happened so suddenly, that he still could not fully realize the implications. He had no illusions. That brief brush with the bullying sergeant was enough to tell him that he was in for a hard time. He could handle discomfort, and he knew enough about people to feel confident that the sergeant would not get the better of him. Unlike the others, he had chosen this willingly, and not had it thrust on him.

The hardest thing about the voyage, he suspected, was going to be his separation from Maud. Six weeks or more, without seeing her or holding her in his arms! Six weeks to wonder if she had done what he asked, and was crossing the ocean behind him. To question whether or not he would ever see her again. He had grown so accustomed to having her beside him when he wanted, that the pang of being apart was something he felt as a sudden searing pain in his chest.

Yet it could not be helped. Jeremy had survived the press gang, but there were going to be hard days ahead, and he knew they would both get through them together better than apart. Besides, Jeremy had once stepped in and saved Alan, when he was angry and lost. Returning the favor was the least he could do.

He leaned back against the plank and closed his eyes. A thin smile fluttered on his lips. There was really nothing else he could have done. Once he knew Wilkes was going to America, he would have found some way to follow him, whether it was in the army or not. His life was never going to be complete until the day he looked the fat, ugly General in the eye and told him why he was going to kill him. Until Alan reminded him of that brave, handsome young boy he had so callously destroyed, and the beautiful woman he had driven to an early grave. Nothing and no one was going to prevent that from happening.

Yet with all his heart, he hoped that Maud was even now looking for Josiah Bennett and making the arrangements to follow him.

On further reflection, Maud decided it might be best to wait until morning to confront Josiah Bennett. After a few hours' restless sleep, she dressed carefully to look her best, and walked to the inn where he was staying. She found him in the sunny dining room having breakfast.

"It's out of the question," he mumbled, between mouthfuls of kidneys and eggs. "My theater is in New York, not Philadelphia. Although, to be truthful, I do know the city, and I *could* arrange for you to appear there. But it's not a town that's known to be particularly hospitable to traveling players. It's full of Quakers, and they are notoriously opposed to anyone having a good time. Our Anglican churchmen in New York are prudish enough, but they're satyrs compared to the psalm singers of Philadelphia."

Though he spoke with conviction, Maud detected a hesitancy underneath his words. She leaned across the table and batted her eyelashes at him. "But there is a war going on in Philadelphia, isn't there? And soldiers need entertainment. I've heard they are very fond of plays and the theater."

"Egad, woman, we're not fighting the French in the streets of Philadelphia. The war is in the provinces, out in the forests. Still, there is something in what you say. The Army will have to spend some time in the city, waiting to depart for the frontier, and plays are a popular amusement with idle soldiers and their officers."

Maud gave silent thanks for Bennett's ability to see two sides to every statement. "And I fancy I might be something of a drawing card," she said, giving him her most beguiling smile.

He chucked her under her chin. "You would be even more popular than you are here in Bristol, for you would have no competition. But what about Desmond? Why isn't he here making these arrangements?"

Maud dabbed at her chin with her handkerchief. "He's already sailed," she mumbled.

Josiah gave her a searching look. "If he's already sailed, then he must have been on one of those transports. Don't tell me he took the king's shilling!"

"Well, yes, but only temporarily. You see, Jeremy was pressed, and Alan went along to watch over him. Once they're in the Colonies, they'll join the Players again."

"So that's what this is all about," Bennett said, flinging his napkin on the table. To Maud's relief he gave a low chuckle. "He wants his company to join him for an American tour. Poor deluded fool. If he thinks he is going to be able to walk away from the Army so easily, he's in for a surprise."

He studied Maud's face. The poor girl was so besotted with Desmond, she was willing to follow the fellow across an ocean to a world she obviously knew nothing about. Yet she was so pretty and had such a presence on stage, that he suspected she would do very well, even among the straightlaced Philadelphians. Especially if she had the right material. "Very well," he said with a sigh. "I'll stake your Players to a Colonial tour, but only if you pay your own passage. Do you have any money?"

Maud's spirits soared. "I have some of my own. And I know the company has a little. We'll get it together somehow."

"Good. Be at the quay two days from today. We'll sail on the *Marie Louise,* a packet ship. She's not too comfortable, but you can't expect that. I'll make the arrangements, and you bring me the money tomorrow morning. Agreed?"

"Agreed." She left soon after, her feet barely touching the ground. Now all she had to do was persuade the company to go along! When she faced them later that morning on the dais of the hall they were using for their performances, that proved to be easier than she expected. Both Frances and Kitty were enthusiastic about the idea, seeing new worlds to conquer in the Colonies.

Eva and her husband had a few reservations, but were not opposed. "As long as we can get back," Eva said, crossing her arms over her ample chest. "We would not want to be marooned in such a primitive environment, would we, Graham, love?"

"No, no. Quite. Did Mister Bennett tell you how we return, Maud?"

"We will get a percentage of the profits. If we let them accumulate, we ought to have enough for a return passage. That is what other companies have done."

Coram Dodd grumbled in his usual slurred voice.

"Well, it's not for me. Boats make me deathly ill. I'll stay in jolly old England, if you don't mind."

"Oh, but you must come," Maud cried.

"We can manage without him," Kitty said, in a voice edged with contempt. "There must be a drunk or two in the Colonies who could take his place. We don't need him."

Coram glared at her. "Dearest Kitty. I'm tempted to go along just to see you fed to the Indians. I hear they have a taste for ham."

"Then they would certainly prefer you to me!"

"Stop it," Maud cried. "This is no time for bickering. If we're going to meet Alan in Philadelphia, we're going to have to move very quickly."

Frances sniffed. "I do think it was very ungenerous of him to strike off on his own without first asking us. How could he be so sure we would go along? And then, leaving you to make the arrangements . . . He could at least have asked me."

"It was all very sudden," Maud mumbled. "Coram, if you're really determined not to go, I imagine we can arrange to find someone to take your place over there. What about you, Rowland?"

Rowland Hervey unwound his cadaverous form from a chair near the edge of the stage. "Oh, I'm always game for an adventure. I think it's a cracking idea. I know a couple of other fellows who might be induced to go along, if Coram here is serious about staying. Do you want me to ask them?"

"Yes. It can't hurt. And we will have plenty of time to rehearse on the ship. Very well, then, it's decided."

Later, when she went to look inside the company strongbox, she realized that there would not be enough money to cover their fare, even with her own little savings. Maud mentally went over every possible way to raise the remaining funds, but could only come up with one solution. It was a hateful one, and did not hold much possibility of succeeding. Still, determined to make the effort, she threw on her cloak against a rising wind from the east, and hurried to the quay. Thankfully, General Wilkes's flagship had not yet sailed, though it was only waiting on the tide to take advantage of the favorable wind.

She would not have been surprised if he had refused to see her at all. As it was, when she was ushered into the cramped cabin where he sat behind a desk, she stood for a long few minutes while he concentrated on some papers he was writing. She knew this was his way of taking revenge, so she patiently waited until he finally looked up.

"Miss Makejoy. I am surprised you have the audacity to come here. I am very annoyed with you, Madam. Extremely annoyed."

Maud looked down at her hands, trying to appear remorseful, even if she did not feel that way. "You have every right to be annoyed, General," she said demurely. "It was unforgivable of me to run off as I did. But truly, an emergency arose that required my presence. I would never have left but for that."

"The 'emergency' involved Alan Desmond, I take it. I saw him enter the house as I was fetching the carriage. Afterward I looked for you in vain."

"General, I truly regret offending you. The truth was, it was Mister Jeremy Oaks who was in trouble. He had been taken by a press gang, and we were trying to rescue him. There was not even time to explain."

"A press gang? The Navy, I suppose. They're always dragging fellows away to man their ships." He eyed her suspiciously, but felt the old charm of her lovely face eroding his righteous anger. "And were you successful?"

"No. In fact, Mister Desmond ended up going with him."

A thrill of hope went through Wilkes's ample chest. "You mean, he's gone?"

"Completely gone, General. And now, our Players Company have an opportunity to travel to Philadelphia to perform in the Colonies. All we need is part of the passage fare. I thought you might . . . well, that you might like the idea of having me come along to America, since you are going there . . ."

Her voice trailed off, but her hopes rose as she saw the sudden excitement that lit up his eyes.

"You want to come to America?" he said, rising from his desk.

"If I can find the rest of the fare."

"Well, well," Wilkes said, beaming. He walked around the desk to capture her hands in his. "Do I dare expect that if I help you, my patience will be rewarded at the end of this journey? You know I have waited a long time . . ."

Maud looked down at the toes of her slippers. "Well . . . I cannot promise anything, but . . ."

It was all the duplicity she could manage, but it seemed to satisfy him. He grabbed her in his arms and pulled her to him, planting a long, very wet kiss on her lips. Trying not to let her revulsion show, she managed to extricate herself before his passion grew to disturbing proportions.

"I am on my way now to arrange for passage on the *Marie Louise*. That is, if you could see your way to lending us the balance."

"Of course, my dear little Maud. I know the ship. It will probably be trailing along with our convoy for safety's sake. So, we shall be journeying together, how delightful! How much do you need?"

She gave him the figure and watched as he opened a strongbox with a key from around his neck and counted out the amount. "I think we might even consider this part of the expense of the army," he said, chuckling. "Entertainment for the troops in Philadelphia, you know. Here it is, my dear, and I look forward to the repayment."

"Thank you, General Wilkes." Reluctantly she reached up and gave him a quick peck on the cheek, then darted out of the way of his groping hands. "We'll talk about it in Philadelphia."

Once outside she took a long, deep breath of the clear air, pocketed the coins in her reticule, and wrapped her cloak closer against the cold wind. The things she endured for Alan Desmond! she thought, as she hurried off to find Josiah Bennett.

She was feeling more confident now that everything seemed to be falling into place. There was all the packing still to be done—the company's and her own, and there was very little time to do it in. Yet Maud was not worried. Better to be kept busy until they sailed, so she would not have time to think about what she was doing.

As she entered the hall of the inn to return to her room, a man rose from a chair to block her way.

"Madam," he said in an icy voice, giving her the shallowest of bows.

Maud stepped back. She knew she had seen him before, but she had to rifle through her memory to think where, until she glimpsed two soldiers standing in the doorway off to the side, wearing the colors of the Guards that she had seen on Leicester Square. She felt the blood drain from her face, as she recognized one of the men who had come to speak to Alan at their house in London.

"Sir?" she mumbled.

"Your servant, ma'am. Jeffrey Everley, Secretary to Lord of the Admiralty, Villiars. I am looking for Alan Desmond."

"He's not here."

"I am aware of that. Would you please tell me where he can be found?"

"Why, I don't know. He could be . . . anywhere."

He was tall enough that when he leaned forward, he towered over her. He had a lean face with small eyes close together, bridging a long, sharp nose. His heavy eyebrows came together in a scowl that seemed to form one straight line across his forehead. Maud took a deep breath and stared belligerently back at him.

"You live here together, do you not?"

"Alan stays here some of the time. But he is often out on concerns of his own, and he never tells me where it takes him."

"That does not surprise me. However, Madam, this is a very serious business. You will be making a severe mistake if you know where he is and do not tell me."

Maud's courage faltered for a moment. "I cannot help you. What kind of serious business?"

Everley waved a thick fold of paper in her face. It had a massive magenta seal with dangling ribbons that waved ominously. "This is a warrant for Desmond's arrest."

Her palms went damp. "On what charge?" she asked, still facing Everley's frown.

"On the charge of treason."

Maud felt her knees waver. "Treason! For making fun of the King in a few paltry plays? Surely we live in a more free society than that!"

"This is not about characters in a play. We have proof now of something we have suspected for a long time—that Alan Desmond is part of a treasonous Jacobite conspiracy. This warrant will take him to the Tower, where he rightfully belongs."

She turned away to allow herself a moment to regain control. No matter what she did, she must not let this man realize how deeply his charges had affected her. "I can't help you," she said angrily, trying to push by him. "If you want to search my rooms, please do. You won't find Alan there." But they would find his clothes and plays, thank heaven. Enough to convince them that he was still in Bristol.

Her foot was on the first stair when Everley's cold voice stopped her. "You might find it to your advantage to help us, Madam. You are not without suspicion yourself."

Maud gripped the newel post and turned to face him. "What are you talking about? I don't even know what Jacobite means! How can I be involved?"

"Perhaps not in that conspiracy, but there are other ways of circumventing the law. Are you aware that there was a Suffolk lawyer making the rounds of the playhouses in London, asking about you? Or rather, asking about a Maud Mellingham. That is your true name, is it not?"

Her knees began to tremble, and she gripped the round wooden post more firmly. With her mind racing, she thought how to answer. Surely if this man knew why Lawyer Ramsey was searching for her, he would have another warrant for her arrest. She decided to bluff. "You know it is. What does that have to do with anything? Many actresses take a stage name."

"True. And some do so to hide their past. If you have anything in your past to hide, Madam, I suggest that it will be to your advantage to help us find Alan Desmond."

So he did not know about the brooch! She released the newel post and fussed with her sleeve to mask the relief on her face. "I have nothing whatsoever to hide. I told you I don't know where Alan is, but you are free to search my rooms to make certain he is not there. I can do nothing more for you."

Everley motioned to the two soldiers to follow him, as he started up the stairs. "Oh, I intend to search your rooms, both to look for Desmond and to find further evidence of his guilt. And I suspect," he added, stopping beside her to look down at her again with his fierce gaze, "enamored as you are of the fellow, you would not tell me where to find him if you *did* know."

Maud did not contradict him. She merely smiled and motioned him up the stairs, silently thanking God that Alan had already sailed with the Army. Of course, Everley would eventually learn the truth, but at least Alan would be out of his long reach for the time being. Only one more day, and she herself would be out of Lawyer Ramsey's long reach as well.

Thank heaven for the Colonies!

Chapter Fourteen

The enormity of what she had done did not truly dawn on Maud until nearly twelve hours later, after the *Marie Louise* sailed out of Bristol. The ship had taken the tide just after dark on a nearly moonless night, while the darkness hung around it like a solid, heavy object. Maud went down at once to the tiny, cramped cabin she would share with the three other women, and stayed there, either trying to sleep on the narrow wooden shelf that served as a bed, or sitting at the table fastened to the floor, watching the thin, bronze light from a lantern swing desolately across the wooden planks. With every creak of the ship's timbers, she expected to see Jeffrey Everley come crashing through the door behind his King's Guards, ready to drag her off the ship and carry her to prison. Packing her belongings and all the paraphernalia of the company, then storing it in the hold, had kept her fear at bay, until the ship finally slipped its cables and moved sluggishly out into the channel. At that point it swept over her again. She was convinced that with freedom so close, something was bound to happen to ruin her escape.

But nothing did, and in the small hours of the morning, after Kitty and Eva and Frances had thrown themselves on their cots, she finally fell asleep out of sheer weariness. When she woke, the dawn was inching through the narrow window to bathe the cabin in a soft gray light. Instantly awake, Maud threw back the covers, groaned as she realized her body was sore all over from the uncomfortable bed, slipped on a dress, and climbed up the hatch ladderway to the deck.

She stood entranced. A soft breeze nuzzled her cheeks and fluttered lazily in the sails over her head. The ship dipped and rose languidly in the fair wind, and she nearly missed her footing as she made her way to the rail to stare out at the water. The sea was everywhere she looked, rosy with the colors of dawn, undulating toward the horizon everywhere she turned.

It washed over her, the realization that she was out on this immense ocean on a tiny, bobbing sliver of wood. She looked to the east, where the shades of gold and gray welcomed the rising sun, and realized for the first time that she was leaving everything she had ever known behind. England, home . . . slipping away like sands in an hourglass. A terrible sadness brought tears stinging behind her eyes, as she turned to the dark western horizon where emptiness and an unknown country awaited. This was a new kind of fear, a different sadness, and for a moment she wavered. Then she got hold of herself.

If she could sail away, then she could sail back someday! England would still be there when she returned. The future was unknown, but at the very least it would not hold the threat of arrest, either for herself or Alan. Not for a long time, and perhaps never. They were free for the time being.

And the sea was beautiful! Beautiful!

"Good morning, Miss Makejoy."

Maud turned at the voice behind her, and saw Josiah Bennett standing near the hatchway. He was dressed in sombre black with a gray tie wig that draped beneath a wide-brimmed tricorn. She smiled at him, and he stepped up to the rail beside her and spoke. "I haven't seen you since we sailed, and I was afraid you were below with the *mal de mer.*"

Maud looked at him blankly.

"Seasickness. It happens often, if you're not accustomed to the movement of the waves."

"Yes. I was a little ill," she answered. Better to have him think that than know the real reason she stayed below. "But I feel much better now." She looked out at the deepening blue of the ocean. "Isn't it beautiful!"

Bennett's eyes never left her radiant face. "Yes, it is. This is your first voyage then?"

Maud brushed away a long strand of hair which the wind had lifted across her forehead. "It is my first voyage. In fact, I was feeling a little homesick, until the beauty of the morning drove out every other thought. It gives me a strange feeling to think that with every dip of the bow we're moving farther from England."

"You must love England very much. Where do you come from?"

"Suffolk. Thornwood Manor near Thetford. Actually, my parents died some years ago, and I don't have an excessive love for the place or the people. But it *was* home, while everything that lies ahead is strange and foreign."

He leaned on the rail, crossing his arms and watching the lift of the waves. "Oh, you won't find the Colonies so foreign. They are English, after all, and have most of the same vices and virtues as the parent country. With the addition of a few of their own, of course. And there will always be ships going back and forth, in case you are overcome with a longing for home."

"How long will the voyage take?"

"The better part of six weeks, depending on the weather. I've made the crossing four times now, and only once did we run into storms so dangerous we were blown off course. The Captain feels this should be a rather peaceful trip."

"I hope he's right. Is General Wilkes's convoy very far ahead of us?"

"Only about a day. The main body of the fleet waited for the flagship off the Scilly Isles, and that held them up. It's rather comforting to know they are so close, isn't it?"

Maud looked to the gray horizon where, over the rim of ocean and sky, Alan and Jeremy were dealing with their strange new life aboard ship. "Yes, it is comforting."

Though Maud could not know it, beyond that horizon Alan and Jeremy both sat near the railing of their ship, and watched the first rays of the same dawn throw a golden veil of gauze over the eastern sea. They had been up for two hours already, dragged from their miserable hammocks by Stacey, the sergeant major whose function in life it was to form wretched pressmen into something approximating a fit for the King's 8th Regiment.

Jeremy knew better than to linger over the rosy fingers of dawn, and quickly went back to cleaning his long Brown Bess flintlock. This was the second time, and he knew there would be at least two more inspections before it passed muster with Sergeant Major Stacey. His back still ached from the blows that accompanied each failure, and they would ache even more before it was acceptable. He supposed he ought to be getting used to it, but perhaps it was still too soon. Army life had come too abruptly and too recently for him to be adjusted to it.

He looked up in dismay as he saw Alan lay the barrel of his rifle across his knees, and rest his arm on the rail. "Where's Stacey?" he asked quietly.

"Just gone below." Alan answered, staring out at the gray sea.

"I wouldn't relax too quickly. It would be just like that devil to try to make us think he's below, when he's just waiting to see if we drop our guard."

"Yes," Alan drawled. "Someday, when this is over, I intend to kill that bastard. After I've dispatched my other quarry, of course."

"Egad, you're not still dwelling on that, are you? After all that's happened—"

"Because of all that's happened."

"Bless me, Alan Desmond, if I don't think you're the orneriest, stubbornest, damndest fool that ever walked! I've seen you do some fool things before, but comin' after me was just about the craziest! You should 'ave left me to stick it out by myself."

"How long do you think you would have survived a bully like Stacey without me around? Aren't I the one he really hates? Don't I take most of the blows he would save for you, if I wasn't here?"

"It would serve me right for gettin' so damned lost in my cups. Don't know what I was thinking of now, anyway."

"Nor I. It wasn't like you at all. But we've been through too much together to let you go off half-cocked now. Besides, if it wasn't for Stacey and a couple of his sycophants, this wouldn't be so bad. I was ready for a change."

Two red-coated soldiers climbed up from the hatch. Jeremy made certain Stacey wasn't one of them, then went on languidly buffing the barrel of his gun. "You don't pull the wool over my eyes, Alan Desmond. You may protest that you only came along to help me, but I know the real reason. Once you knew the General was going to the Colonies, nothing on earth would have kept you in England."

Alan gave him a thin-lipped smile. "I'll admit there is some truth to that. I wasn't really looking forward to following him to India, but America didn't sound half-bad."

Jeremy sighed. "When will you give up this foolish vendetta? It's been over ten years now."

Alan's face hardened in the dim light. "That you of all people could ask me that!"

A booming voice issuing from the hatchway prevented his reply. "Get yer arses up that ladder, you lily-livered, hog-swillin' sons of sedition! I'll make King's soldiers of ye yet!"

A group of men came stumbling out onto the deck. Pressed, as Jeremy had been, most of them still wore the country smocks and twill breeches they had worn to the taverns where the soldiers found them. Their yellow pallor was considerably more jaundiced than Jeremy's, and they appeared more cowed and confused at finding themselves in this hostile environment. Jeremy and Alan both, on reflection, thought they had adjusted much more quickly and much more adequately. Perhaps that was why Stacey was so much harder on them. Not that he was easy on the others. Still, the ten stripes Alan had already taken at some whim of sergeant-major Stacey's, was more than anyone else had endured, including Jeremy. Of course, it paled beside the fifty lashes one of the sailors had already received, but it was still bad enough.

"One of these days that Sergeant is going to have apoplexy," Alan said dryly, noting Stacey's red face and bulging eyes.

"Not likely," Jeremy muttered. "He enjoys his work too much."

Alan turned on his perch atop a tar barrel, so that his back was to the activity on deck and he was looking squarely into the rising sun. "I wonder if Maud is back there," he mumbled more to himself than Jeremy.

"What do you mean?"

"I told her to bring the company to Philadelphia. If she did as I asked, she should be sailing with Wilkes, two, maybe three days behind us. It was a lot to ask of her, but she's a capable girl."

Jeremy bent over his gun. "Yes, she is that."

"I tell you, Jeremy, the farther from England I get, the more the thought of seeing her in America keeps me going. It's strange. I never expected to feel that strongly about any woman."

"Perhaps it is the natural result of homesickness. I feel it myself at times."

"Yes, perhaps that is it."

"Or perhaps, well, perhaps you're in love with her."

"Oh, I do love her. But I love a lot of women. You know that. I've just never felt this need for anyone special before. I find it difficult to get used to."

"DESMOND!" Stacey's voice roared. "To the front. You and that snivilin' conjurer, both. And them guns better be clean!"

"We're being paged," Alan said through clenched teeth.

Jeremy propped the butt of his gun on the deck and swung to his feet. "I figure at least two more cleanings."

"I don't know. Judging from his temper, I'd say this might turn out to be at least a three-or-four-more-cleanings day!"

By the second morning, Maud found herself so busy she had little time to think about what lay over the horizon. Josiah Bennett took charge of the company in Alan's absence, and began working them long hours to prepare the plays which he felt might be best received in America.

"Shakespeare! There's a great hunger for Shakespearean dramas in the Colonies. I'm not sure if it is because they remind everyone of England, or because it gives them the feeling they're sophisticated in spite of living in a half-wild country, but it's there, nonetheless. Even the unlettered rustics love Shakespeare."

"But Mister Bennett," Maud protested, "the Stanbury Company is not known for its Shakespearean dramas. We're better at the lighter comedies, Congreve, Steele . . ."

"And Desmond. Oh, I know that. But bumbling foreigners making fools of themselves over fluffyheaded beauties are just not the kind of entertainment Colonists crave. Besides, there is a strong puritan streak in America, even in New York. If they think they're being exposed to culture, they won't be so quick to close the theater."

"Well," Frances drawled, as she fussed with a long gauzy shawl that the wind threatened to carry off, "I think Miss Makejoy should speak for herself. Anyone can tell you I am renowned for my Portia, and my Juliet."

"You're a little long in the tooth for Juliet, love," Hervey said dryly.

"Yes," Kitty added with a giggle. "More like Lady Macbeth!"

"Enough of that now," Bennett admonished them. "There will be plenty of roles for each of you. We'll begin with *The Fair Penitent,* then move on to *The Reluctant Husband.* We'll round out the bill with *The Merchant of Venice, All For Love, The Careless Husband,* and *The London Merchant.* We have two new cast members to work in. It's going to mean a lot of rehearsing."

Actually, Maud was grateful that Bennett kept them so busy. It meant that she had little time to wonder if she was doing the right thing by leaving England, or to worry about what was happening to Alan and Jeremy. Even the other members of the company quickly adjusted. Kitty latched on to one of the new young men who had joined the Players, while Frances made eyes at the handsome First Mate, who returned her interest with vigor. The only difficulty in crossing came halfway out, when they ran into several days of severe weather that tossed the boat about on the angry seas like a leaf in a wind. Maud then learned firsthand what *mal de mer* really meant. She never left her miserable cot, could not keep down a bite of food, and soon found herself wishing the ship would sink and end her misery.

Then the weather cleared, the ship returned to its gentle rocking, the sun came blissfully out, and rehearsals began on deck once again.

Bennett pushed them even harder to make up for the lost time. Only four days out of North America, they were becalmed, and bobbed listlessly for a night and a day before the wind picked up, easing Bennett's concern.

"I don't know," he went around muttering. "You're still not ready. There's so much still to do, and I wanted to start right in with performances, once we get a hall in which to play."

"Most of us have been playing together for some months now," Eva tried to console him. "We can't be too ragged. How hostile can American audiences be, anyway?"

"They've been known to throw things at players, when they don't like what they see."

"That happens in England, too, you know," her husband said. "I recall a barn in Shrewsburg, where you couldn't walk across the stage for the vegetables underfoot."

"Yes," Frances added, "and remember that time in York. The man with the leather whip? He was going to lash us all, if we didn't please him."

"He was just a tiny bit drunk."

Kitty laughed, remembering. "He would have done it, too, if Alan hadn't grabbed him by the collar and heaved him out of the hall."

"I wish Alan was here now," Eva said plaintively.

"He's supposed to join you in Philadelphia," Bennett said quickly. "I hope he does, because he will add a much needed presence, as will Jeremy Oaks. In fact, if I was sure Jeremy would be there with his bag of magic tricks, I would not be so concerned."

"But he will be there," Frances said. "Maud, you said—"

Maud gave Bennett a quick glance. "Alan said he would be." She knew that Bennett had little hope of the two men escaping the army, but she refused to believe they wouldn't. Alan believed they would, or he would not have told her to follow him with the company.

"Well, I'd like you to be prepared all the same, then so much the better if they do show up. Now, let's take that scene from the first act of *The Fair Penitent* once more."

Maud had grown so accustomed to the long expanse of rolling water on every side, that the morning land was sighted, it was almost as though the coast itself was a strange, foreign object. It was only a dark smudge on the gray horizon, yet when the land-ho call came from the crow's nest and she rushed to the rail with the rest of the deckside passengers, she felt a vibrant, surging thrill at the thought that she was actually about to set her feet on the soil of a new country, another land. The idea that for the first time in her life she would be stepping on earth that was not English, was both exciting and a little frightening.

"Is that Philadelphia?" she asked Josiah Bennett, who had stepped up beside her to gaze at the long, dark line with a satisfied smile on his face. This was home for him, Maud thought a little wistfully, remembering how far away from England they now were.

"Oh, no. That's the Jersey Province. We still have to cross a lot of water, and then follow the coast for a while before entering a bay and a river that will bring us to the Waterstreet docks. It will be some time yet before we'll be close enough to really see the coastline. But we've a fair wind. If it holds, we ought to dock by tomorrow morning."

It seemed a long time to wait. The dark smudge of land teased and cajoled her for hours, before they drew close enough for her to begin to make out the shapes of low hills and green forests. That afternoon she still stood at the railing, watching pasturelands emerge from the verdant slopes, making out the white shapes of farmhouses, with long slashing rows of fences lying haphazardly around houses and outbuildings as if they had been carelessly thrown there. Ragged strands of white beaches sloped up to forests thick with trees that were so huge, she studied them in awe. She had expected to see mountains, but there were none. Just low, undulating hills, higher than the Suffolk fens, and dryer, no endless channel of canals here. The thick forests looked as though savage Indians should come running out of them, whooping and hollering their warcries and brandishing their hatchets, as she had been told they liked to do. But none appeared. The coast seemed as benign and peaceful as any in England. Except for the high trees, thick forests, and verdant shades of green, she might have been watching the shires and farmlands of England slip by.

It was only by late afternoon, when Maud had been staring at the horizon for some time, that it dawned on her how vastly empty the land was that lay out there. The occasional small farm or dotted grouping of low houses were tiny oases in a sea of uncleared countryside. Nowhere in England were there forests such as these to be found, stretching for mile upon mile. Bennett had told her that the wilderness of America lay far to the west, many hundreds of miles beyond the seaboard, but to her it seemed as though the whole continent was wilderness. Compared to England, perhaps it was.

At dark the *Marie Louise* moored in the channel, to await the tide that would carry them up into Chesapeake Bay. Maud was too excited to sleep, and she rose before dawn once she heard the flutter of wind taking the sails. While the first rays of sunlight cast the sea in bronze, she stood near the bow, her hands gripping the round rail, and peered toward the coast, eager to make out the first signs of Philadelphia.

They moved sluggishly with the tide, following the bay toward an inlet that became a river. There were many more farms here than she had seen the day before. For the most part they were low, squat buildings, formed of gray stone that gleamed in the morning sun as if freshly whitewashed. They stood in grim defiance of the thick forests surrounding them, their fields still bearing the marks of blackened stumps where the land had been cleared. White paling fences lay in neat squares around them, defining meadows, outbuildings, or pens. Brown and white cows grazed on grass as green as in England, and, as she could tell even from the deck, more thick and lush.

She was amazed at the birds. They were everywhere, a convoy accompanying the ship as it moved up the channel, screeching their welcome, diving and rising on the fair wind. And the fish in the water around the ship were thick and large. Schools of them slapped up a foam twenty feet away or swarmed so close to the sides of the ship, she could almost count them from the deck—except that there were too many to count. By the time the first roofs of the town came into view, Maud already sensed that this was a virgin land, untouched by the years of wear and use that, by contrast, made England seem old and tired.

Philadelphia was another revelation. She smelled

the town before she could make it out, but that was true of any port city. It was an earthy smell, a combination of fish, cedar ships from the islands, and all the accumulated emanations from wharfs piled with sugar, rum, spices, tar, tobacco, and coffee. Signs of these trade goods floated on the surface of the river, long before she could make out the jagged forest of masts anchored close to the town. Out in the water more ships lay at anchor, waiting for longboats to carry goods and passengers back and forth from the wharfs. The *Marie Louise* became one of them, and Maud had to curb her impatience to get ashore when Bennett told her to wait there with the others, while he arranged a place for them to stay.

He did not return until early afternoon, and only then did she climb down a precarious ladder to sit in the longboat and be ferried through the winding waterways between the ships to the shore. Bennett gave her a hand out of the boat and up the short steps to the stone landing, and Maud stood and looked around her, trying to take everything in at once with shining eyes.

The wharf was a long cobblestoned street that stretched the length of the town. The water side was piled high with barrels, crates, boxes, and bales of all sizes and shapes. Opposite it stretched a length of buildings, many of them wooden but a few of bright red brick that appeared to be newly built. None were high, and none had that dark mahogany patina so common at home. Once they were all ashore, Bennett started the group down the street at a brisk pace, while Maud twisted and turned to look longingly at the windows of the shops and taverns, eager to see inside.

Her attention was quickly turned to the crowds through which they pushed their way. This foreign city was as unique in its people as in its buildings. She stared unashamedly at Negroes, women in bright turbans and wide skirts, and men in homespun smocks and round flat hats. She had seen a few Africans in Bristol, but never so many as here. Interspersed among them were paunchy men in severe black coats, housewives in crisp white caps under modest straw bonnets, fine gentlemen in powdered wigs and satin coats, country people in tabby dresses and linsey-woolsey shirts. Most of them were identifiable by their sounds, a combination of languages she had never heard before, even in cosmopolitan London. The singsong hybrid speech of the Africans, with its Caribbean lilt. Scottish burr mingled with heavy German and Scandinavian accents. Even their English was different. By the time they left the wharf and turned up one of the streets leading into the town, she had identified London, East Anglian, Cornish, and northern Yorkshire patterns of speech.

And there were the soldiers, their scarlet, green and deep blue jackets denoting their various regiments. They were everywhere, and Maud soon realized it was futile to search for Alan's familiar face among them. Besides, there was too much else of interest to concentrate solely on the military.

As they left the waterfront, the town took on a more gracious air. There were trees lining wide thoroughfares with a depression down the middle to catch wastes, and posts set in the stones near the houses to protect walkers from the street traffic. She had seen streets like this in London, but only in the better quarters. Most of the houses here were red brick or stone, all of them looking newly constructed. She marveled at the lack of green mold, so familiar on the buildings that had stood for centuries at home. It was refreshing to be in a place where everything appeared new.

She soon realized that, new as it was, this town had retained some of the more grim characteristics of its parent country. At one side of a wide green common they passed, she recognized a pillory, familiar from her small village at home. Close beside it stood the grim silhouette of the gibbet, apparently as much a part of life in the Colonies as it was in the smallest shire in England. When Josiah Bennett pointed out one large pile of gray stone as the local debtors' prison, she began to wonder if she was not expecting too much of this new country.

Oh well, so it was not paradise. It was still new and enchanting, and she intended to enjoy it.

On a quiet side street, they ended their walk before a two-story wooden house with brightly painted red shutters. It looked comfortable and inviting, and Maud was pleased when Mister Bennett told them he had arranged for rooms there for the women, while the bachelors would stay two houses down. A matronly woman in a huge mobcap and an apron as large as a bed sheet, welcomed them inside and took them upstairs. The house was more functional than luxurious, but it seemed comfortable enough. Eva and Graham were given one room, Frances and Kitty another, and Maud, to her delight, was ushered into a tiny room under the eaves, just large enough for a plank bed and a heavy chest of drawers. A tin mirror over the dresser reflected light from a dormer window, pleasantly framed in ruffled homespun curtains. After three weeks in a cramped ship's cabin, the thought of having this clean, sunny room all to herself was like a gift from heaven.

Bennett had been anxious to take the men to their quarters, so she only had time to pull him aside momentarily before he took off again.

"How can I find Alan?" she whispered, holding him back by his coat sleeve.

"He'll probably come to the theater, once I have one arranged for us."

"But where is he? Suppose he doesn't learn that we've arrived?"

"My dear Miss Makejoy," Bennett said, shaking off her hand, "don't worry about finding Alan. Let him find you."

She thought over his words in her upstairs room as she stretched out on the bed that seemed to roll and toss, even though it was anchored to the floor. She wished she could be so certain that Alan would know they were here. Anything was possible—he could never learn of their arrival, or not know that they were on the *Marie Louise*. He could even have already left Philadelphia for the great unknown spaces beyond the coast. She might never be able to find him, given this huge, unpopulated continent.

A terrible unease threatened to wash away all the joy she had felt in discovering Philadelphia. It churned up an anxiety that might have overwhelmed her completely, except that the bed was so soft, the sun was so drowsily warm, and she was so weary, that she dropped off to sleep before she could think about it properly.

Chapter Fifteen

She was awakened by a loud knocking on the door.

"Missy . . . Missy!" Maud recognized the voice of the African maid who had brought up her box earlier. "Someone to see you, Missy." The voice was muffled by the thick door.

Dragging herself awake, she stumbled to the door and opened it a crack. "Who is it?"

"Don't know, Missy. A gentleman. I put he in the pa'lor."

"Thank you. I'll be right down."

Maud peered in the little tin mirror and was appalled at her reflection. Her hair was tousled, her dress wrinkled. She dared not hope too much that the gentleman waiting for her would be Alan. She smoothed her dress and ran a comb quickly through her hair, pinched her cheeks to make them rosy, and splashed on a few drops of lavender water. Then, hoping she could remember where the parlor was, she went down the stairs.

At the top of the second landing, she paused. A man stood in the shadows looking up at her. He was tall, he wore a white grenadier wig, and the scarlet of his coat gleamed like a ruby in the dim light.

Maud gave a squeal and flew down the stairs and into his arms.

"Hold on there!" Alan cried, laughing as the force of

her body nearly knocked him over. He caught her up and whirled her around in the hall, stopping only long enough to plant a long, hungry kiss on her lips. Maud twined her arms around his neck and pulled his face toward hers, breaking her lips away to giggle and laugh and try to talk all at once.

"Oh, I'm so happy . . . I hoped you'd come . . . that you would hear we had arrived. Oh, Alan, I've missed you so much!"

He laced his fingers into her hair and drew her lips to his again, drinking of them. "God! And I've missed you. I went to the wharf every day I could get away, to ask if a ship from Bristol had arrived."

"Look," she said, reaching up to straighten his wig. "I've knocked your hair all askew. And it's so . . . so military, too! You make a very handsome soldier, sir."

"And you look good enough to put me in a passion."

His lips searched her face as he nuzzled her ear, then traveled to the hollows of her cheeks and neck.

"That'll be enough of that, thank you, sir," said a fierce voice behind them. They both looked up to see Mrs. Bracegirdle, Maud's landlady, standing in the parlor door, hands on her ample hips and a look of extreme displeasure on her round face. "This is a decent house, I'll have you know, and I won't put up with no improper goings-on, not from no actresses nor from no soldiers neither."

Maud took a step back, but held tight to Alan's hand. "I'm sorry, Mrs. Bracegirdle. It's just that we haven't seen each other in a long time."

"Y'er not married, I take it. This ain't no husband and wife reunion, I can tell."

Before Maud could answer, Alan swept the lady a deep bow. "Your pardon, ma'am. We certainly shall bring no disgrace on your house. Forgive the enthusiasm of two hearts deeply in love, who have for nearly a month not had the comfort of feasting on each other's countenances."

To Maud his flowery speech seemed so obviously false, she looked for the landlady to take offense. Instead she only smiled. "Oh, I've been there afore ye, believe it or not, and I know all about feasting and abstinence. But I won't have it here in the open for anyone to see. Nor," she added quickly, "will I have it in my upstairs rooms! Go feast on one another's countenance at the Indian Queen down the street."

Alan pulled Maud's arm through his own. "Exactly what I had in mind. Where's your bonnet, love?"

"Right there by the door."

When they reached the street, however, Alan did not start down the walkway toward the tavern one block away. Instead, he bundled her up into a small chaise waiting behind a large, roan horse with a black mane and tail. He climbed up beside her, picked up the reins, and slapped them on the horse's broad back. They moved out to join the other traffic—assorted wagons and shays and carts, interspersed with men on horseback.

"Where are we going?" Maud said, her happiness spilling over within her.

"To the country. Or, at least, away from the town. I want you all to myself for a little while, and there may not be time for it later."

She slipped her arm through his and leaned close against him, while he maneuvered the chaise down the wide street that led out of Philadelphia and into the neighboring, less populated areas. Occasionally they passed fine homes, set back in trees and adorned with formal gardens. Farther out they passed several substantial farms, sleek and fat and obviously well-to-do. Maud marveled at them, even as she reveled in Alan's nearness.

They stopped finally on the banks of a river. There was a grassy knoll there, surrounded by a forest of trees and thickets and shadowed by the overhanging willows. Alan spread a cloth for her to sit on, then brought out a bottle of Madeira and two pewter glasses.

"A toast to the successful completion of our mission."

"It hasn't been successful yet," Maud said, lifting her glass.

With the bottle still in his hand, he slipped an arm around her shoulders and pulled her head against his own. "Part of it has. You're here and I'm here. And Jeremy is still in one piece."

"But you're both still in the army. And Mister Bennett says he is not at all certain he can find a theater for us in Philadelphia."

"Oh, he'll find one. He's a very capable gentleman." With his arm still around her, he filled the two glasses. "I'd forgotten how beautiful you are," he murmured, kissing her lightly. His lips were gentle and warm, and she could taste the sweet Madeira on them. "You're going to be a great success in the Colonies."

An electric thrill coursed through her, as he lifted her hair and nuzzled the back of her neck. Her body warmed with the need of him, the joy of being on this grassy bank with him.

"I don't care about success," she breathed, as her body grew into one long sigh. "I just want to be with you."

It might have been better not to let him know that, she thought, but she was beyond caring. Alan set the bottle on the grass and turned to her, laying her gently down on her back. The deep shadows spilled around them like the gentle spread of a coverlet.

Bending over her, he pulled at the laces of her bodice. Maud was glad she had worn her simplest dress, as it fell away easily, revealing her ruffled white shift beneath. Alan bent his head and nuzzled her breasts through the cloth, sending currents of pleasure through her body. She knew he was holding himself back, for his need for her was like a live thing, calling in its craving to her own. Deliberately he took his time, tasting the softness of her skin, making little circles with his tongue that gave soft waves of ecstasy to her body. She sighed and turned to lift her breast to his lips, but he would not take it. With a maddening slowness, he ran his finger around the edge of her bodice and then down her chest to her waist. With his tongue he edged the cloth down and away, until her breast was exposed. Then, closing it gently in his hand, he lifted it, poured several drops of the amber wine on the erect nipple and, only then, licked them with his tongue.

Her body was growing into one long flame. She moaned as he fondled her breast, teasing the nipple with little sucking motions, flicking it with the tip of his tongue, until she wanted to cry out in desperation. Her hands reached for him, only then to discover that he had somehow gotten out of the confining breeches. Her fingers closed on the hard firmness of him, and she drew him to herself.

She did not know he had gotten underneath her skirts, until she felt them fall away. His insistent fingers probed and sought her, closing around her flesh, cupping her hips, searching out the mysterious depths of her to fondle and massage, driving out all thought of anything but the need of him. She tried to draw him into her, but he refused to come. Another minute, and she would be begging for him!

Then, with a suddenness born of his own need, he could hold back no longer. He turned her on her back and fell over her. She felt him enter, the driving thrusts of him. His breath was hot on her neck, as he muttered against her throat. She pressed him closer as the driving grew in intensity, carrying them both in its riotous spell. A cry that she recognized came from both their lips. Alan fell against her, and she could hear the wild throbbing of his heart. Her fingers dug into his shoulders as she clasped him, trying vainly to hold him there, a part of herself, entwined with her body forever.

But, of course, it did not last. His heart grew more quiet and her breathing subdued. Though they lay unmoving, two parts of a whole being, the moment of ecstasy was gone; and Maud knew, with a sadness, that soon he would pull away, and there would be no more unity, no more wholeness. How sad that something as joyful as the union of two people, should always be tinged with this separateness.

Still, there was happiness and contentment, too. Her joy at having him with her again, of holding him, of being given this much of him, would sustain her for a long time.

At length, Alan rolled onto his side and pulled her close. "I knew I missed you, but until this moment, I did not realize how much. We're very good together, aren't we?"

She kissed his temple. "Very good. But it isn't going to be easy. We cannot always take rides into the countryside. Perhaps we could rent a little house, like we did in London."

Alan smoothed a long strand of hair from her face. "I don't think so. Not this time. You see, one of the reasons I was so anxious to find you, was to tell you that the army is going to be leaving soon."

A chill went through her, washing away all her joy. "Leaving? Where? Not back to England?"

"No, no. We're expected to be sent to a place called Fort William. In one of the provinces called Maryland. I'm not sure where it is, except that it's south of here."

Maud pulled away and sat up, gripping the bodice of her dress in her hand. "But you can't! You can't go off and leave me here alone. Not after telling me to follow you across an ocean!"

Leaning on his back, Alan laced his hands under his head and smiled at her. "You'll hardly be alone, when you're with a whole company of actors."

"But you said . . . I thought you and Jeremy were

going to be with the company. We're counting on it. *I'm* counting on it!"

"My love, nothing would suit me better, but it isn't going to be so easy to leave the army. Men who desert are likely to be shot first and asked questions later."

"You should have thought about that when you joined!"

"Well, I didn't really know about the penalties for desertion then. I've learned since. Now don't get your wig all in a tangle. You know I'll join you when I can."

Angrily Maud laced up the ties on her bodice. "Oh, Alan, I should have known something like this would happen. Just when I think everything is going so well between us, you always go running off somewhere, leaving me to fend for myself. I hoped this time it would be different."

Reaching for her, Alan pulled her down against him, pinning her within his strong arms. "I'm not going to desert you. I'll come back as often as I can."

"How far away is this Fort William?"

"I don't know. A few miles." He smoothed her hair away from her angry brow, and kissed her lightly. "You don't think I'll be able to stay away too long, do you? Not with memories of what we just shared."

Maud found her resentment melting, and fought against it by trying to pull away. He held her fast against him, his fingers entwined in her hair.

"What about Jeremy? We need him in the Players. Mister Bennett expects him to play Lord Foppington."

"Mmmm," Alan murmured, taking her face between his hands and exploring her lips again. "Josiah will just have to find another Lord Foppington. Or take *The Reluctant Husband* off the bill. Oh, my, but your lips are soft and sweet."

The siren warmth went spilling through her body. She was helpless in his arms, and it both delighted and infuriated her. Bending her head, she coursed her lips across his cheek to nuzzle the hollow of his ear. With her tongue she explored the crevices and mounds of it, very much aware of the mesmerizing effect it had on him. "Mister Bennett is not even sure he can find us a theater," she whispered. "He says the Quakers and the Presbyterians will prevent us from performing."

Alan gave a long sigh as her head moved down to explore his chest. "He's wrong. A company played here just a few years ago. The Mayor himself found them a theater. God's eyeballs, where did you learn that!"

Maud smiled at his exclamation. Continuing her downward drift, she found that wonderful part of him that not so long before had driven into her and claimed her for his own. Now that it was drained and relaxed, she licked the length of it and felt him shiver. She was a little appalled at herself. This was something she had not done before, but had heard about from Kitty and Frances. It was rather satisfying to see him grow pliant and expectant under her ministrations, and she took joy in it. She lifted the tip and fit it lightly between her lips, drawing on it as she felt it throb into life again. Alan gave himself over to the flame that gradually consumed him, as she fondled and tasted and sucked. Maud knew the effect she was working on him, and she increased the intensity until she knew he was totally and completely given over to her hands.

"Time to go," she said, abruptly sitting up. Alan sank back.

"What! You can't—"

She got to her knees and pulled her skirts around her. "If we get started now, we ought to be back in time for supper."

To his horror she rose to her feet, picked up the glasses and wine bottle, and started for the chaise.

"You wouldn't!"

"Why, what's the matter? I can always do it again, the next time you pay me a visit from Fort William!"

He crawled after her, clasping her around the ankles. "Oh, so that's your game. Well, I won't have it, Miss."

She laughed and struck playfully at him, trying to knock him away. "Can it be you don't like being the one who's left? How sad." Slipping out of his grasp, she threw down the bottle and started running for the carriage. "Good day, Sir Ardent," she said, giggling.

"You won't get away so easily, Mistress Wanton," he said, jumping up to run behind her. He caught her before she reached the chaise and clasped her tightly around her waist. "A good performer should finish what she starts," he breathed, pushing her down amid the leaves and grass. Maud's laughter mingled with his groans as he threw up her skirts and drove his need into her waiting body. With every thrust the flame consumed her, until she, too, cried out her need of him, for completion. Gripping his shoulders she held him to her, while together they went soaring on wings of ecstasy to the explosive climax that joined them into one flaming being.

Alan fell against her, completely drained. "You minx," he muttered when he could talk again. "You deliberately led me on."

Maud twined her arms around his back, pressing him close. "Oh, Alan, don't go. Stay here in Philadelphia with me. I don't want to lose you again."

"You aren't going to lose me."

"But it's such a big country! Suppose we get separated, and are never able to find each other?"

"That won't happen. You know that I care for you, Maud. But I have other concerns as well, important concerns. Things to do."

It was no use. "Oh, very well," she said, pushing him away and straightening her clothes. "It's been a lovely afternoon, but we really should be getting back if we want any supper. Mister Bennett promised to come round this evening, and let us know where our first play will be put on."

He sat up beside her and laid an arm around her shoulders. "We'll come here again before I leave," he said, kissing her.

"That would be nice," she said dryly.

Not until they were nearing the city again did he ask about General Wilkes, and then it was almost apologetically. "I haven't seen him since Bristol," Maud told him. "I owe him some money, but he won't expect it until after we've earned something from the plays."

"So you're indebted to him. That's good. It means he won't be likely to let you get too far away."

"Have you any idea what he expects in return for this debt? He made it rather obvious to me."

"Well, don't pay him in that coin. Pay him from the proceeds of the performances as soon as you can, and keep him dangling."

The disappointment of knowing Alan was going away soon made her throw caution to the wind. "I declare, Alan," she said in exasperation. "I never have understood why you want me to be involved with that man. He only wants one thing from me, and I'm not willing to give it. Wouldn't it be better to just stay away from him?"

"No. It's important that you continue to lead him on."

"But why? What is it you have against him?"

Alan's face hardened. "I can't tell you that now. Be patient. Someday you'll understand."

"I wonder," she muttered, as the first rows of houses came into sight. She leaned her head on his shoulder. It was so good to be near him, to feel his body against hers, to have him close. At the same time, it was so painfully obvious that he would never be really hers. He would always take what he wanted of her love and be off, until the next convenient time brought them together again. She ought to snap her fingers and tell him to be on his way. But she knew she never would. At least, not yet.

* * *

Josiah Bennett had arranged for the entire group to meet for supper at the Indian Queen Tavern, where they would have a private room to discuss plans for the repertoire. The room was painted in rich, deep green with sconces set in the walls and sand covering the scoured plank floor. The food was plain but good. And the occasion was especially pleasant, because Alan stayed to join them. Halfway through, Jeremy also came in.

She gave a cry when she looked up and saw him standing in the door. The scarlet coat and tricorne did not sit as well on Jeremy's slight frame as it did on Alan's muscular one, and his clever, rascally face below the flat brim of his hat was completely at odds with the bearing of a soldier. But Maud hardly noticed it. She flew across the room to clasp her arms around his neck, and plant what she hoped was a sisterly kiss on his cheek.

"You look as though you've lost weight," she said, drawing him to the table where the others crowded around to welcome him. He beamed in the warmth of their obvious affection, even Maud's. Especially Maud's.

"That's because they work me so hard. You've no idea what it's like. Enjoy your life as an actor, my friends, for to be anything else is damned hard work, and that's all there is to it."

"I declare, Jeremy," Kitty drawled. "That uniform makes you look like you're right out of *The Humors of the Army*."

Jeremy made her a face. "Major Outside himself. I have a sergeant major who wishes I were 'outside.' "

"Then come and join us, Jeremy," Graham cried. "We need you. No one can do birdcalls like you, not to mention all those comedic roles."

"I wish I could," Jeremy said, pulling up a chair to

the table and helping himself to a portion of the large pigeon pie that was placed there. "But Alan has probably explained to you what a dim view the military takes of soldiers who walk away. I think I prefer to keep my head attached to my shoulders."

"But you were pressed, weren't you? They have no right to keep you in the Army."

"Come round tomorrow and explain that to Sergeant Stacey. Meanwhile, may I have a little of whatever it is you're drinking there?"

"Porter. There's not much of it, but you may have what you want."

Maud recognized from Jeremy's improved complexion and bearing that his drinking had eased off since Bristol. She was relieved when he only half-filled a pewter tankard and took a light sip.

"So," he said, digging into the pie. "Do you have a theater yet?"

"We do," Bennett exclaimed with pride. "And I'm much relieved, too. It seems that four years ago a traveling company was allowed to use Mayor Plumsted's warehouse as a playhouse, there being no other in Philadelphia. Of course, there was great objection to it by the religious sort who consider a theater the sink of sin, but the Mayor prevailed. Now he has again agreed to open his warehouse for the length of our tour, however long that might be."

"Not long from what I hear," Alan said, lounging back in his chair. "There are some bolder spirits in town who like to have entertainment, but they eventually cave in to the Quakers and Presbyterians, who can be fierce in their opposition. My advice is to put your best efforts right at the beginning."

"We'll stay as long as we can," Bennett said, "then be off for the far more friendly streets of New York. I've decided our first play will be *The Fair Penitent,* and I've written a prologue for Maud. You'll be setting the tone for all of us, my girl."

Maud took the long foolscap he handed her, stood near one of the sconces, and read in her sweetest voice:

"Too oft, we own, the stage with dangerous art
In wanton scenes, has play'd a Syren's part,
Yet if the Muse, unfaithful to her trust
Has sometimes strayed from what was pure and just
Has she not oft, with awful virtue's rage
Struck home at vice, and nobly trod the stage?
The Muse's friends, we hope, will join the cause,
And crown our best endeavors with applause."

'It's a little apologetic, isn't it?" Alan said dryly.

"Perhaps," Bennett agreed. "But better that than to be driven off with hisses and boos and assorted missiles from the pit."

"I like it," Maud said, folding the paper. "And I intend to speak it with all the sincerity I can muster."

Alan took the paper to look it over. "Don't worry about sincerity, my dear. Just look your prettiest and show them an ankle. That will have a better effect than all the prologues ever written."

Chapter Sixteen

Alan was right, as usual. *The Fair Penitent* opened a week later to enthusiastic acclaim from the more liberal folk of the city, who preferred entertainment to piety. Unfortunately, its success also brought a louder and more concentrated howl from those citizens who sincerely felt that by encouraging the theater, society was sending itself to the dogs. Everyone, from the manager to the actors and crew, knew the run in Philadelphia was going to be short, and their reaction was to cram as many tragedies and comedies into the brief run as possible. Maud soon found herself so busy with performing and rehearsing, she had little time to think about Alan being gone.

A letter came one week after the opening. She was surprised to learn that he had not gone to Maryland, but to New York, where with the rest of the army he waited for orders to move into the interior. Meanwhile, he wrote, once it was all together, the accumulated might of British military was impressive, even to Alan's jaded eyes.

"You would be amazed to see it," he wrote. "A sea of white tents, flags snapping in the wind, row after row of canons, magnificent horses, battalions of infantry as far as the eyes can see—it staggers the imagination! How a collection of ragged savages and a few Frenchies hope to stand against such an army is more than I can credit.

"New York is an interesting town. It appears to be more cosmopolitan than Philadelphia, and not so much under the thumb of black-coated Quakers. In other words, more 'wicked.' In many ways it reminds me of London, except that it is surrounded by water on three sides and woods on the fourth."

A second page with an additional scrawl had been quickly added. "We're going to a place called Albany, north of New York. Now that we've been ordered to move, both Jeremy and I are beginning to grow impatient to have at the Frenchies. Being in the army rather puts you in the mood to fight. Think of me running through the forest after some hatchet-waving redskin savage."

She was disappointed that there were no words of love or even of missing her, yet that was typical of Alan. What concerned her more was the lighthearted way he looked forward to fighting a battle. It would be just like him and Jeremy to get themselves killed in the first skirmish.

The second week of performances brought more opposition than the first. After Kitty and Frances were pelted with eggs while walking on the street one afternoon, Josiah Bennett decided it wasn't worth remaining in Philadelphia. The company finished the week, and then packed up and climbed aboard the stage for New York.

It was a three-day journey even with traveling eighteen hours each day. Maud was so anxious to get there before Alan left, that she paid little attention to the countryside. By the time they took the ferry that brought them into the harbor, she was as anxious to quit traveling as she was to see Alan. This harbor was even larger than Philadelphia's, and more crowded with ships of every size and fashion. She could sense the difference in the town even before she stepped ashore. Long rows of buildings were interspersed with houses of yellow brick and roofs that moved upward in steps to the cornice, Dutch style; tall church steeples towering over the squat chimneys, huge square buildings sitting in the middle of grassy plots, and busy streets whose clamor could be clearly heard from the harbor. It seemed both more worn and more hospitable than the town they had left.

She had barely settled in her rooms at one of the taverns, before she learned that Alan and Jeremy had already sailed upriver for Albany with the King's Eighth. Soldiers of those regiments which had not yet left the city were still everywhere to be seen on New York streets, and were a bitter reminder that she had missed Alan by only two days.

There was nothing to do, however, but go on with her work. At least this time they had a real theater. The Nassau Street Playhouse was not as grand as the London Chelsea, but an improvement over Plumsted's warehouse. There were tiers of boxes surrounding the apron that extended halfway into the pit, a large area backstage for scenery and primitive machinery, tiring-rooms for the actors to dress in, and even a greenroom. It was all shabby and badly in need of repair, but it gave the entire company a sense of being back in familiar circumstances.

Maud threw herself into giving her best performances, even though at the back of her mind there was always a gnawing sense of concern over where Alan was, and if he were safe. She had not worried about him when circumstances had forced him into military service, but once he began to like the idea of being in the middle of a fight, her fears mushroomed. He might be killed, and she would never have told him how much she loved him! She might not even know he was dead, considering the vastness of the wilderness he was going into. If only she could see him one more time, talk to him, kiss him once more.

Of course, she might go after him. There must be a way to get to this Albany. If the army had taken it, so could she.

But alone? And friendless? The virgin forests on the edge of the town stretched away in such dark mystery, that she hesitated even as she was drawn toward them. Her common sense told her the wisest thing to do would be to stay here, and wait until the army came back from whatever battles they were going to fight.

If they came back!

And then providence stepped in to solve her problem.

It was after a performance of *The Careless Husband*, near the end of the second week of their run. Maud had given Lady Betty Modish all the coquetry and charm which characterized her best roles, and had made the evening a huge success. She was in the tiring-room in her shift removing her paint, when the door was thrown open and a familiar figure sailed into the room.

"General Wilkes!" Maud said with astonishment.

"My pet, my sweet, you were magnificent," the General said, capturing her hand and planting a wet kiss on each of her fingers. "Never was there a more delightful Lady Betty! You completely won my heart, that part of it you did not already hold."

Maud yanked her hand away and reached for her robe. "Please, General, this is a dressing room. It's not seemly for you to be here."

Kitty laughed and fluttered her lashes at the General. "Oh, I'm sure he's seen ladies in a state of undress before, haven't you, General?"

"Many times," Wilkes answered, keeping his eyes fastened on Maud. "I could not wait in the greenroom with all those yokels. I had to see you again. You've captivated me, my dear. Completely."

"All the same," Maud said lamely, pulling the ties of her robe around her waist, "you must go and allow us to dress."

He grabbed for her hand again. "Only if you'll promise to take supper with me."

She shoved him toward the door. "Yes. I promise. Only please go."

"Wonderful. I'll wait for you outside. Don't be long, my pet."

Maud closed the door and, ignoring the knowing leers from the other women, quickly threw on her clothes. She had not seen Wilkes since landing in Philadelphia, and had assumed he had left with the rest of the army. For the first time since she had met him, she was actually anxious to talk to him. At least he might be able to speak to some of her concerns about Alan.

Yet she was hesitant to open the conversation, as he drew her arm through his and led her down the street to the closest tavern. It was only after they were seated at a table in a small room where the firelight from the hearth and candlelight on the table set flickering patterns on the paneled walls, that she found the words to begin.

"I am surprised to see you in New York. When you didn't come backstage in Philadelphia, I assumed our paths might never cross again."

"I was barely ashore before I was sent here. Even now I ought to be upriver, but when I read in the broadsheet that your company was coming to town, I deliberately managed to drum up some lingering business with the quartermaster in order to stay and see you. And it was worth it. You look positively ravishing, my dear. The Colonies have obviously been good to you."

"Not too good," Maud said, laughing. "In Philadelphia they all but escorted us to the edge of town, and sent us on our way."

"Ah, but New York will be kinder. The people here enjoy good entertainment. Truly, my dear, I have seen productions on the stage of Drury Lane in London that could not compare in quality with your Lady Betty tonight! It is a shame I have to take you away from the stage, when you grace it so beautifully."

Maud looked quickly up. "Take me away?"

Wilkes colored slightly. "Ahem, I did not mean to speak of it quite so soon, but having broached the subject, I might as well explain myself. I want you to come with me."

"With you where?" Maud said in a small voice.

He reached for her hand and squeezed it painfully. "On the march with me. And after that, to wherever in this godforsaken country we are sent. Say you'll come."

"But, General Wilkes. You're going off to fight a war, are you not? Are you saying you want to carry me into battle with you?"

"Not into battle, of course," he said, sitting back in his chair. "Just on the march. There will be other women. Many of the wives of the soldiers follow the army as a matter of course. And not a few camp followers. But naturally I wouldn't expose you to them. You'd be with the other, ahem, 'ladies' of the officers."

Maud looked at him in astonishment. "You mean the officers take their wives to war with them!"

"Well, not so many wives. But yes, it has been done. Braddock carried his mistress all the way to Fort Duquesne, I'm told. And I'm sure there will be a few along on this campaign as well."

"General Wilkes . . ." she said, looking everywhere

but at him while her mind raced. This might be the answer to her prayers!

"I've embarrassed you. Forgive me, my dear, I know how uncommonly sensitive you are about these things. But I don't want to lose you now that I've found you again. Say you'll go. All my happiness depends upon it." He reached for her hand. "After all, we made a bargain, did we not? In Bristol . . ."

Maud rose from the table to stand by the hearth, pretending to stare into the fire. "The money you loaned me will be repaid tomorrow. As for going with you, where would we be heading? I know so little of this country."

"I barely know much more. However, I can tell you that we will be going first to a little Dutch town called Albany on Hudson's river, then north toward New France. Our objective is to capture a trifling outpost called Fort Carillon from the French, and once that's done, we will probably slip right back here to New York. It'll be over in no time, and you'll be back in the comforts of town before you know it. You can even rejoin the company, if you wish."

Maud ran her fingers along the wooden mantelpiece. She was tempted to throw her arms around the General's neck and give him an enthusiastic yes, but she knew that would not be wise. Better to let him think she was hesitant. And, in fact, she was, if he thought that by going with him she was agreeing to become his mistress.

"I don't know . . ." she said coyly. "It's so—so dangerous out there! There is a huge French army, isn't there? And Indians. I've heard terrible things about them."

Wilkes waved his hand. The light flickered against a large ruby on one finger, giving it the deep glint of blood. "There are only a few Frenchies, and their officers are known to be highly incompetent. As for the

Indians, why, they are merely a parcel of ranting savages! Neither force will be able to stand against the might of the British Army that is assembling in Albany. Believe me, my dear, your safety shall be my first concern."

"Oh, I'm not afraid," Maud said, resuming her seat across form him. "Of course, I'll be leaving Mister Bennett in rather a bind."

"Nonsense. Other actresses can be bought for a tuppence. Though, I admit, none to compare with you. Do say you'll come. I command it!"

Maud flickered her lashes coyly. "Very well. I agree. I'll tell Josiah tomorrow."

"Capital! But no, it might be better not to tell him at all. I have to sail upriver tomorrow night, so we'll slip you away. I'll send one of my aides around after the play, to take you quietly to my ship. We can't be too obvious about this."

Maud grasped at her chance to evade his grasp. "No, I won't go under such circumstances. I insist that I at least be allowed to finish the week. Then I will meet you in Albany."

Wilkes's plump underlip turned downward. "Oh, very well. I'll arrange passage for you on one of the staff vessels leaving next Sunday. It's the *Lady Margaret*. And I'll assign Ensign Randall to watch over you. But promise me you won't be any later than next week!"

Maud picked up her glass and sipped the claret. "I promise," she said, looking up at him over the rim. "Now that I've agreed to go, I'm becoming rather curious to see this Albany."

Curious was not the word for it, she thought as the week wore on. All her thoughts turned northward up the long silver river, where Alan would once again be in her arms. Her indifferent performances prompted Bennett to ask if she was well, and, in response, she told him what she was going to do. She expected an angry tirade from him, but Josiah Bennett had worked too long with actors to be surprised by anything they did.

"I hope you know what you are getting into. That northern country has been little touched by civilization. It's nothing but forests and savages and a few Frenchmen trying to claim it for France. Are you sure you want to do this?"

"I want to be with Alan. I want to know that he's safe, that he's not lying dead in a thicket somewhere with his scalp missing. It would be bad enough knowing he was killed. But to *not* know . . . to always wonder what became of him . . . I couldn't bear it. Please try to understand."

Bennett patted her shoulder. "Oh, I understand. But does General Wilkes? Does he know you're only pretending to go along as his mistress, in order to find Alan Desmond?"

"Well, not exactly. I'm not sure how I'll get around that yet, but I'll find a way."

"I'm sure you will," Josiah replied with a laugh. "Just think of all the coquettes you've played, who managed to slip out of the grasp of lecherous old men without damaging their pride. You've had plenty of practice."

The summons came early Sunday morning, when the first rays of dawn were gilding the cobbles on Water Street with gold. Maud followed Ensign Randall on foot along the street to Peck slip, where a longboat waited to carry her out to the *Lady Margaret*, sitting out on the dark river like a sleek racing sloop poised for flight. She was helped aboard by sailors who treated her with more respect than she had expected, given Randall's rather hostile civility. He was obeying orders, but he made certain she realized that he did not consider her a lady of quality. It bothered Maud a little at first, but as the ship got underway she forgot about him.

By the time they sailed past the last outposts and farms of the city, she became so enthralled with the river, all else became irrelevant. With the growing dawn she could make out the tall, steep walls of rock on one side of the bank, and the rolling forests on the other. Farther north the river widened, only to narrow again between low-rising mountains tinged with gold and blue and dotted with tiny houses and farms. For the most part, the land was uncultivated, great soaring hills thick with virgin forests. The beauty of the river was overwhelming. Maud, who had never before seen real mountains, was captivated by it. Often, on the low banks before the rising ground, there were small towns whose waterfronts were a sea of masts and spars. The river itself was alive with small, one-masted sloops, whose colorful sails sometimes gave it the semblance of flowers scattered on the surface. Beneath the blue water were huge sturgeon, some of them sever feet long, swimming close to the ship. Dolphins somersaulted, setting up a crystal spray that flickered in the early light, and whole schools of smaller fish dappled the river's silver surface.

As the day wore on, one of the sailors brought her a chair and she stayed on deck, amazed at the richness and the beauty of this country. It might be savage and uncivilized away from the seacoast, but it was abundant with possibilities. No wonder the Crown had sent such a massive army to keep it in the fold.

They reached Albany three days later, after having lost their wind for several hours during one night. Ensign Randall made arrangements for Maud to go ashore, with all the enthusiasm of a man who is about to discharge an unpleasant duty. But Maud was so excited to be in the same town as Alan, that she ignored his poor manners.

She could tell at a glance that this little town was a far cry from New York. The sea of white tents on its outskirts spoke volumes of how completely the army had taken over the place. Once ashore, she saw red coats everywhere. They were interspersed with a great many blue coats as well, the color of the Colonial regiments. She was about to make her way among them, when she was stopped by a smartly dressed young man in a tall grenadier hat who handed Randall a message.

"I'm to take you to the Belle Sauvage," the Ensign said after scanning its contents. "The General has arranged rooms for you there."

"Oh. Very well. Do you know where it is?"

"Haven't the slightest. But this fellow will lead us there."

His reluctance was obvious. "Look," Maud said. "You've done your duty in getting me to Albany, Ensign Randall. Why don't you go on to headquarters, and let this young man show me where the tavern is. I'm sure I won't need both of you for protection with all these soldiers around."

Randall brightened up at her words. "Are you certain? I'll gladly see you to the door, if you wish."

"I'm certain." She did not add that she would be as glad to be rid of his disapproving presence as he was to leave her. He gave her a perfunctory bow and, after asking directions to headquarters from the grenadier, took off down the street. Maud gave the young private her best smile.

"Lead the way, sir."

She had barely started off, before she realized the

advantages of not having Randall by her side. It was difficult to look at the faces of all the military men she passed since there were so many, but she only missed a few. She searched among them for the familiar lean face with the strong chin and the deeply set eyes that sparkled wickedly from under arched brows. She looked, too, for Jeremy's round pale face and sea gray eyes, hoping a glimpse would reunite her once again with the two men most dear to her in all the world. But as she followed the grenadier's tall fur hat up and down several narrow, dirty streets, she began to lose hope that she would stumble across them. And if she did not, how was she to let them know she was here, short of going right into the camp itself? General Wilkes was sure to hear of that, and might rescind his invitation to take her along on the march.

Over the head of the orderly, she spied a faded wooden sign bearing the outline of an Indian woman. Maud sighed, resigned to settling in her room and then trying to figure out the best way to make discreet inquiries on how to locate two soldiers in this sea of an army. The tavern was only four doors away, when she glanced across the street and her eyes locked on the startled gaze of Alan Desmond.

He had stopped on the walkway, and was staring at her as though she was a spectre and not a real woman at all.

Maud caught her breath, struck still where she was standing, afraid and unable to move. With a whoop, he was across the street, dodging a careening horse and wagon that nearly overran him, threading between a herd of sheep to reach for her and grab her up, swinging her around.

"I don't believe it! Egod, is it really you!" he cried, laughing and kissing her all at once.

Maud clung to him. "Alan, oh, Alan. Oh, it's so good to see you. You feel so wonderful . . . oh, I've missed you so . . ."

When they could stop trying to speak and hug and kiss each other at the same time, he stepped back, still gripping her shoulders, holding her at arm's length.

"I still cannot believe it's actually you! How did you get here? When did you arrive? God's blood, it's a miracle!"

Maud looked quickly away. "I'll tell you all about it, but not here on the street. Look, everyone is staring."

Alan laughed and drew her arm through his. "They're envious because I just kissed the prettiest girl in the town. Come on. We'll find a quiet table somewhere, and drink a toast to being together again."

A few minutes later, they were seated at a small plank table in one of the smaller rooms of the Belle Sauvage with a squat amber bottle of claret and two glasses. They leaned toward each other and spoke softly, even though the room was nearly empty. Alan impulsively leaned closer and kissed her lips.

"I've missed you, Maud. I did not realize how much until this moment when you're here with me."

"And I missed you," she said, running her fingers lightly down his long cheek. "So much."

"Is that why you came to Albany?"

"Yes . . . and no. I couldn't bear the thought of you going off to fight in a war; I might never know what happened to you. I wanted to follow you, yet I didn't see how I could go into an unknown country all by myself. Then providence stepped in."

He nuzzled her cheek. "What kind of providence?"

Maud hesitated. Yet he had to know sometime. "General Wilkes. He came backstage and offered to take me with him on the march. So, I came."

Alan sat back in his chair. "You what!"

"Now don't shout. Everyone will look at us."

"I don't care if everyone *is* looking! My God, Maud, what have you done? Have you sold yourself to that lecherous old goat, just so you could see if I made it through a war?"

Maud glanced around the room and smiled weakly at three men sitting at a table near the door, who were watching them with curious eyes. "Please, keep your voice down . . ." she muttered through her clenched smile.

Alan dropped his voice, but none of the intensity. "Don't you know that when he offered to take you with him he meant as his *mistress?* You can't be so naive as to think he would bring you along just for the pleasure of your conversation!"

"No. I know exactly what he wanted. But that does not mean I intend for him to have it."

"How do you propose to get out of it? You'll be under his protection."

"I don't know. But I'll think of something. After all, I've managed to stay out of his bed so far, haven't I? And it hasn't cooled his ardor in the least. Besides, I can always tell him I have the French pox."

Alan shook his head and poured himself a large glass of claret. "Maud, my love, you do manage to get yourself in the damndest situations." He lifted his glass to her. "I look forward to seeing how you get out of this one."

"Are you still glad I came?" Maud said meekly.

He took a long draught of the wine, then bent forward, and kissed her lips again. She could taste the claret. "Yes, of course, I am. Only, I warn you. If I find you in Wilkes's army cot, I'll take my sword to both of you!"

"Tell me about your life here," Maud said quickly,

to change the subject. "How is Jeremy? Do you think you can get away from the army?"

"Not at present. This is the most amazing gathering of military might I have ever seen. Three British battalions, plus two Continental forces, and, I'm told, a contingent of friendly Indians who are expected to arrive momentarily. We have infantry, grenadiers, bateaumen, cannon, muskets, howitzers, and grenades—in short, it is such a force as to astound the eyes and the mind. Jeremy is not quite as impressed as I, but he agrees with me that we'd like to see how this great machine is put to the test."

"General Wilkes does not strike me as the kind of officer who should be in charge of such a great army."

"He's not in charge; he's only one of the major generals who direct the battalions. Yet the commander in chief is an even greater bungler than Wilkes! His name is Abercromby, but he is such an old woman that the men call him Nabbycromby behind his back."

"Then how—?"

"His second in command is a fine officer—Major General Howe. He is actually the one who will run this campaign, and I do believe most of this army would follow him into hell itself, if he asked them. Old Nabby is content to sit back and let him, too."

Maud noted how Alan's eyes brightened as he talked about the service. Obviously he had found something here he had never expected, something that struck a chord. "I don't understand," she said, "how it is that Wilkes expects to take me along? Am I to be secretly hidden in one of the wagons? Won't the other generals object if they find out?"

Alan laughed. "Hardly, when they themselves bring along their own paramours. Oh, not Howe, perhaps, but surely Nabby has his little comfort, riding on one of the eighteen wagons that carry his private effects."

"Eighteen wagons!"

"Well, you can't expect a gentleman to go to war without his privileges. I'd wager Wilkes has at least ten wagons of his own. And I'm certain he intends you to be ensconced in one of them."

"Oh dear."

Reaching forward, Alan took both her hands in his and bent close to her face. "You look so vulnerable, and so beautiful. Egod, Maud, I can't tell you how glad I am to see you again. Or how much I want you . . ."

She looked deep into his eyes. All the wanting and the caring was in them, and her heart swelled with love for him, with happiness at being with him again. "Oh, Alan," she sighed as their lips met. Her hands slipped up his arms to enfold him and pull him closer. His fingers wound into her hair, drawing her to him across the table. The kiss deepened and lingered, and Maud forgot about the others in the room. Had she remembered, she would not have cared.

"Ahem!"

The angry exclamation broke slowly upon them, thrusting them apart. The magical spell shattered, as out of the corner of her eye she caught a glimpse of bright scarlet close to her face. Maud turned her head and found herself looking up into the angry, purple face of Ambrose Wilkes.

Chapter Seventeen

"Apparently I am interrupting!"

Maud sprang quickly back, but Alan only smiled up at the General. "As a matter of fact . . ." he started.

"No! Not at all," Maud said hurriedly. "We were just . . . saying hello . . ."

"A rather fond hello, I think. A bit too fond for a young lady who has just been brought to this town at my expense and under my protection. Private, stand at attention when in the presence of your general!"

Alan glared at Wilkes and dragged himself reluctantly to his feet. "Your servant, sir," he said in a mockery of a salute.

"Why, you miserable cur. A private is the lowest form of life on earth. I could order you a thousand lashes for this insolence."

"Please don't," Maud said emphatically. "Not if you want me to stay." She glanced at Alan, and her heart sank at the fury on his face. His hands, clenched at his sides, told her how close he was to throwing army discipline to the wind. That would be disastrous for them both.

"Get back to your post," Wilkes snapped. "And I don't want to see you anywhere in my vicinity again. Is that clear?"

Alan's taut lips twisted into an insolent, tight smile. "Please, Alan," Maud said, rising from the table and pleading with him with her eyes. "Please go." *Don't throw caution away,* she added silently. *Let me handle this. Don't make it impossible for both of us.*

He knew what she was thinking. With massive self-control, he snapped a salute and stalked to the door, stopping only long enough to give her a brief glance. When he was gone, Maud motioned to the chair he had left.

"Won't you join me for a glass of claret, General?"

He didn't move from his rigid stance. She could see how angry he was by the heightened color of his face, the lips drawn in a straight line, the accusing little eyes in their pudding of flesh. In all the time she had known him, he had never been this angry with her. It was a little frightening, yet perhaps it was inevitable as well.

"Madam," he said stiffly. "I hurried over here because I was told you had arrived. I neglected my affairs at camp in order to make you welcome. And I find you in the arms of that . . . that *actor!*"

"Alan Desmond is my friend."

"That was a bit close even for friendship. You have treated me shabbily, Madam. After I brought you here. Brought you to the Colonies."

Maud took a deep breath. "General, I realize I owe you a great deal, but I think it is time to be honest with you. I love Alan deeply. I have loved him for a long time. That is why I could never return your interest in me. I never tried to encourage you—"

"You agreed to come on this march with me!"

"Yes. I apologize for that. I wanted so much to come."

"You wanted to follow this actor."

Maud said down in the chair. "Yes."

Wilkes gave an exasperated exclamation and stalked around the table to face her. "I see it all now. You were using me."

She glared up at him. "Didn't you intend to use me? You can't pretend you have any real affection for me."

"That is not the same thing at all! This is what I get for becoming involved with play actors. Very well, Madam. Since I have already hired a room for you here, you may stay the night. After that, you must make your own way. I wash my hands of you."

She called after him as he stalked toward the door. "I remind you that you received back every penny that I owed you. Surely our accounts are squared."

Stopping just inside the door, Wilkes glared back at her. "And I remind you that our bargain was for more than money alone. And for that I intend to collect . . . and in more ways than one! It will be such a misfortune when Private Desmond is ordered into the first ranks under fire. I believe old King David was the first to eliminate a rival in that expedient fashion. You can be assured I will do him one better. If Alan Desmond fails to be killed in battle, I may even shoot him myself. Good day to you, Madam Makejoy."

After he was gone she sat back down, filled her glass, and downed it in one long gulp. The three men still sitting at the far side of the room were watching enthralled, as if it had all been part of a play. Now they were eyeing her in a leering kind of way, and the room she had to cross to leave began to take on the aura of a battleground . . . Just a little more wine, and she would have the courage to start.

"Are you all right?"

Maud looked up to see Alan slip back into the chair across the table.

"What are you doing here," she exclaimed, relieved and anxious at the same time. "He'll have you flogged, if he sees you!"

"He didn't see me. I watched him leave and waited

until I could slip back inside. What did he say to you?"

"He was very angry. He's washed his hands of me, so I suppose I won't be riding one of his wagons after all."

"Good. That solves that problem."

"He said he would shoot you himself, if you weren't killed in the war."

"Not if I can shoot him first."

"He told me I could stay here for tonight, then I will have to make my own way back to New York. Oh, Alan. I've made such a muddle of everything."

"It's not a muddle at all. Come on. Get your things. I'll take you to the women."

"What women?"

"The women who follow the army. Most of them are wives of the soldiers. You can pretend to be mine."

"But—is that allowed?"

"Of course, it is. You won't travel in style, as you would have with Wilkes, but neither will you have to pretend to have the French Pox. And you can sleep with me. Hurry, let's go before he changes his mind and comes back here."

He grabbed her arm and pulled her from the room, stopping only long enough at the door to collect her box. Then, with it tucked under his arm and Maud hurrying by his side, they left the Belle Sauvage and started toward the long hill beyond the town. Covered in a sea of white tents, from a distance it had looked like washing strung out across the terrain. But once Maud entered the long, orderly rows, she quickly lost track of where she was. They all seemed the same—small, pointed squares with flags on stakes in front. There were soldiers everywhere, as well as, she was surprised to see, many women and not a few children. The soldiers sat in groups, many polishing their muskets, some playing card games, mumblety-peg, or dice. Some sat and smoked long clay pipes, while their women worked over a low cookstove with a child or two tugging at their skirts. It all appeared so tranquil and domestic that Maud found it difficult to believe this was a group of men preparing to go to war.

They hurried past a group of officers' marquees, larger and more elaborate tents with tables in the front, where officers in silver lace worked through stacks of papers.

"Does one of those belong to General Wilkes?" Maud whispered, looking furtively around.

"No. He has his headquarters in town, along with Howe and Abercromby. We turn here," Alan added, guiding her arm.

It seemed as though they walked another mile, before they reached the outskirts of the camp. Several women were sitting in front of the last group of tents, sewing and spinning out threads on a distaff. One of them rose when Maud and Alan approached.

"Have you brought us your wife, then, Private Desmond," she said cheerfully. The wicked mirth in her eyes told Maud she was certain this was no wife.

"I have indeed, Molly. I trust you'll take good care of her." Alan laid Maud's box on the ground near the woman's feet. "Maud, this is Molly Cunningham. She's the major general of the women's corps."

Molly had a round face liberally sprinkled with freckles. She was middle-aged, and wore her hair pulled severely back and tied in a knot at the base of her neck, which made her appear even older. Her eyes were pale blue and etched with laugh lines. She extended a hefty arm and gripped Maud's hand firmly.

"Maudie, is it? Well, you're welcome, my dear. We travel light and we're not so fancy, but if you pull your weight, you'll find us good company."

"Maud's only just arrived in Albany," Alan said. "She'll be going along on the march."

Molly gave Alan a sly glance. "Well, now, and you never said a thing about how you was wed. No matter. Come along, my girl, and I'll find ye a bed."

With an easy grace, Molly lifted Maud's box and started toward the nearest tent. Maud glanced up at Alan, who tipped her chin and kissed her lightly. "I'll see you this evening, as soon as I can get away," he whispered, and sent her after the older woman.

She reminds me of Cook, Maud thought, as she started toward the open flaps. If Molly turned out to be half the friend Cook was, perhaps following the army would not be so bad after all.

She barely had time to get used to her new surroundings, before camp was struck and the march to the north began. Alan had not been able to come back the night before, but Jeremy had, giving her such a warm welcome that she felt sure there would be no more constraint between them. He had filled the evening with his lively conversation, sharing all he had experienced up to that point about Army life. He could tell her little about the women, but by the time the march began the next day, she had learned most of what there was to know, much of it from Molly.

"I been traipsin' along on one march or another ever since I was sixteen," Molly said, as the two of them tied up bundles of clothing that morning. "I like to be there for 'im, to wash his linen and cook his meals. Ben and me, we never had youngins, and that helped. Otherwise I'd of stayed home in Dorset. 'Course, there's many a one here with two and three and even four little kids, but I never thought that was much of a life for a little one."

"I'd always heard that women who followed the camps were . . . well, of a different sort."

"You mean the fancy skirts," Molly said, laughing. "Oh, they're here all right, but they don't bother much with the likes of us. Nor we with them. Besides, it's been my experience that the closer we get to where the fightin' is, the more they drop by the way.

Maud sat one large bundle on the ground and picked another stack to wrap up in a linen bed sheet. "I also heard that some of the officers brought their mistresses along," she said, trying to sound casual.

"That's true enough, but they mostly ride in the wagons belongin' to their man." She gave Maud a long sideways glance. "To tell the truth, not to be nosy or anythin', it strikes me that Private Desmond and yourself—well, I mean, he's obviously a gentleman and you're obviously a lady—and I just wonder what either of you is doin' here around the likes of us."

Maud smiled to herself, thinking of her very unladylike station at Thornwood. She wondered what Molly would think if she knew that most of her ladylike demeanor had been learned on the stage.

Before she could frame an answer to Molly's question, they were interrupted by the arrival of their wagon, and Molly turned her attention to other matters. By that afternoon they were bringing up the rear of the long, serpentine column of red-coated soldiers that wound around the base of the hill and north toward the river in the distance, farther than the eye could see.

Maud had already met most of the women in the wagons around her. Two of them she had taken to instantly—Molly and Georgette, who was also from Suffolk, though not near Thornwood. One she liked—Charlotte, a very quiet young woman from

Kent, who had one youngster at her skirt and another at her breast, and one she did not care for at all—Livia, a loud, lewd, bawdy wench, who had taken on much of the persona of her loud, lewd, bawdy husband, a private with twenty years in the military. The others were mostly still just unidentified faces.

She quickly began to see why Alan had been so impressed with Abercromby's army. Altogether there were over three thousand regulars, marching in neat rows like a flowing scarlet ribbon along the roadway. Behind them came the Royals, the Continental regiments in their blue coats and with long muskets over their shoulders. Their ranks were not nearly so formal nor so disciplined as the regulars, but they appeared to be enjoying themselves more. There was a long stream of wagons, more than she had ever seen in one place before. Many were open, but some were covered with colored cloths, like huge mobcaps over their wagonbeds. There were bateaumen hauling long boats tied to wagons, oxen dragging flatbeds with cannon lashed to them, and smart groups of musicians fluting, drumming, and bagpiping the soldiers northward. It seemed to Maud that one look at this mighty force should be enough to send the French running for cover.

She rode beside Molly on the careening wagonseat, clutching the sides for support, and commented on the small number of women compared to those whom she had seen in the camp.

"Most of them stayed behind," Molly said dryly. "The General didn't want any along, and most were content to obey him and keep their comforts. But there's a few like me who don't intend to sit and twiddle their thumbs whilst their man is facing danger. I'm thinking you feel the same."

"You've done this before?"

"Oh, a number of times. Once—in Germany it was—I even took up a musket myself, and fired it, too. It was that or be killed along with Ben. But mostly, I get as close as I can to the fighting, so I can tend to him if he gets hurt. Besides, I can't stand the waitin' and wonderin' that comes with being left in the camps."

"That's how I feel," Maud said quietly. "How close do you think we will be able to get?"

"Don't know yet. Ben told me there's a camp called Fort Lyman at the end of the river. Likely we'll have to wait there."

The train was so long that they made little time that day. In the evening a camp was made near the fork where the river divided. To Maud's delight, Jeremy and Alan came looking for her, and the three of them cooked supper over an open fire. The day had been sweltering, and the evening was little better. Maud was stirring the pot when a shadow fell over her and she glanced up, straight into the painted face of a very large, very fierce-looking Indian. Crooked red and black streaks slashed across a face that might have been carved in stone.

She gasped, dropped the ladle, and ran to stand behind Alan.

"He just wants to see what you're cooking . . . I think," Alan said, lifting his musket just in case.

"Judas!" Jeremy exclaimed. "I've never been this close to one. Makes your blood run cold, doesn't it?"

Maud peered around Alan's shoulder at the Indian, who stood watching them with a face that betrayed nothing of what he was thinking. Fierce was not the word to describe him, she thought. He was tall and broad, with a lithesome physique. He wore a blanket over one shoulder, that barely covered the paintings and necklaces that decorated his bare chest, long-fringed leggings, and beaded moccasins. His head was shaved, except for one knot at the back that trailed a long black and white feather. There was a hatchet thrust through his belt, and a beaded knife holder dangling from his waist. One hand clutched a long musket, while the other lay impassively at his waist, poised to draw the hatchet or the knife, Maud was sure. She had an impression of broad, high cheekbones, hard eyes, and an overpoweringly unpleasant odor that permeated the air around him, all of which added to her fear.

"Do you think he's friendly?" Alan whispered to Jeremy.

"Well, he hasn't tried to scalp us yet. But I wouldn't move too quickly."

As they spoke, several more Indians came down the pathway between the tents, accompanied by a white officer in a blue coat faced with red and wearing a white brigadier wig. He was chatting with one of the Indians in some incomprehensible language, and he did not seem to be aware that one of the group had stepped over to glance into Maud's cooking pot.

"I think they're our allies," Alan commented, as the group swelled to even more savages. The one who had been staring at them gave the pot a last contemptuous glance, and went loping off to join the others walking toward the officer's marquees.

"If those are our allies, I fear to see our enemies," Jeremy quipped as he laid his gun down.

"What was that terrible odor?" Maud asked, sitting down to ease the trembling in her legs.

"I'm told they like to smear themselves with bear grease. And wash their hair in urine."

"Ugh! There's no accounting for people's taste, is there?"

"Beauty is in the eye of the beholder, my love," Alan said, laying his musket on the ground and stretching out beside it. "And the smell is no worse than London's Fleet Street on a windless night or the tide flats of the Thames. It's all in what you're accustomed to."

"All the same, I hope I don't come that close to any savages again."

"Did you recognize the tribe, Jeremy? I'd guess one of the Iroquois. Mohawk or Onondaga?"

"You've been talking to the Continentals. I haven't seen enough of them yet to identify one from another. They all look pretty grim to me."

"Yes, I have had several conversations with some of the Royals, and they tell me these Indians have some rather grim practices. Some of the French Indians like to eat their captives. They've been known to force their white prisoners to partake as well. It's something to do with absorbing the strength of their enemies. As for torture, no one can surpass them in barbarity. It's almost an art form with them."

"It sounds as though it might be better to be killed than captured."

"I agree. Maud, you look terribly pale." He reached out and squeezed her arm. "What are you thinking?"

She gave him a forced smile. "I'm thinking that perhaps I should have stayed in New York!"

Although it was no great distance to Fort Lyman, it took the English nearly two weeks to move the staggering number of troops and equipment that made up their army. They followed the river north, traveling mostly along the road that had been carved out along the bank over the years. The farther they journeyed into this unsettled country, the more they were surrounded by woods so thick and untamed that Maud thought they must have looked this way since Eden. By the time they reached Fort Lyman, she was beginning to see the forest as a living thing—moody, mysterious, frightening, beautiful, frustrating in the way it made every movement difficult, entrancing in its untouched, centuries-old mystery. The small fort seemed like a little piece of civilization, shaking its fist defiantly at the encroaching wilderness.

Two years before, a road had been gouged out of the land between Fort Lyman and the southern tip of Lake George. The next leg of their march was along this road—if, Maud thought, you could call a narrow path riddled with tree stumps a road. Though only a dozen miles separated Fort Lyman from the southern tip of Lake George, it would take so long for the huge number of men and military supplies to gather there, that Maud and Molly, who were bringing up the rear of the train, knew it would be at least a week before they could move on. And then it would only be by luck and conniving.

"If Lord Howe knew you were here at Fort Lyman, much less planning to go on, he'd send you packing back to Albany before you knew what was happening," Alan said on one of the occasions when he was able to visit her in her tent.

"Lord Howe! That's all I hear from you these days. You're mightily impressed with him, aren't you?"

"He's the best soldier in the army, maybe in the whole British military. I never thought I would admire any British officer, but I have come to value his sound reasoning and respect for his men."

"Is he the reason you insist that I cut off your hair?"

"Yes. He says it will make it easier for us to move about in the forest. And also give the Indians less of a souvenir."

Maud gave a shudder and went on wielding the scissors against Alan's shoulder-length hair. He had always worn it pulled back in a queue and tied with a ribbon, and now, with it shorn nearly to the base of his skull, she felt he had lost one of his most attractive attributes.

"You can use those scissors next on my coat," Alan went on. "Lord Howe wants us to wear our tunics short, like the Rangers do. It should make the fighting that much easier."

"It sounds to me as though he means to get all of you killed!"

"On the contrary, he's trying to save our lives. He's the only officer I know who learned from Braddock's fiasco at Fort Duquesne in '55. He knows that if you want to fight in these woods, you have to give up formal formations and stay behind trees, as the Indians do. The Colonists know it, too. He's made us scale down our provisions, our ammunition, our uniforms, everything that might hinder wilderness warfare. He's a genius."

Maud lifted the last long lock of Alan's hair and trimmed it by six inches. "But I thought General Abercromby was in charge of this army."

"He is. Lord Howe is his brigadier. But old Nabby is quite content to let Howe run things, while he sits in his tent and nurses his bad stomach. It's an arrangement that suits everybody."

"There. I've finished. And you look very strange."

"It'll grow back," Alan said, rising from the barrel on which he had been sitting and removing his scarlet tunic. He ran his fingers through his shortened hair. "It feels very peculiar, but I suppose I'll grow accustomed to it."

"Do you want me to do your coat now?"

She held up the tunic to examine it, but he took it from her hand. "Later. We've better things to do first."

His arms slipped around her, and he pulled her to him and bent to kiss her lips. Maud let the coat drop to the dirt floor. Her arms enclosed his hard body, and she gave herself over to the lovely, warm feel of his lips on her mouth.

"I've missed you," he said breathily, sliding his lips away from her mouth to course her cheek. With one hand he lifted her hair and caught her earlobe lightly in his teeth, sending warm thrills of delight down her body.

Maud arched against him and gave a long sweet shudder. "Losing your hair hasn't changed anything else about you," she whispered with a chuckle.

"That's because you didn't cut off what really matters," he whispered back.

She laughed and broke away, intending to tease him a little. "We shouldn't. Molly might come back at any moment."

Alan stepped up behind her and enclosed her in his arms. "No, she won't," he murmured, his lips coursing her neck. "I told her to stay away."

"Alan. You didn't! Why, she'll think . . ."

"Then she'll think the truth. Tomorrow, we'll give her some time with her little gunner. Why do you think I allowed you along this far, my love, if it wasn't for this?"

Maud fought against the rising swells of desire his hands and lips awoke in her. "You didn't *allow* me. I chose to come," she said with a gasp, as his fingers found the point of her breast and rubbed against it.

"For the same reason," he murmured, as his fingers began to unfasten the buttons on the front of her simple dress. Maud arched against him as he opened her bodice and reached over her shoulder to plunge his hand deep inside and cup her breast. She turned in his arms and worked at the buttons on his breeches. She could feel the swell within them hard against her.

Because the day threatened rain, they had closed

the tent flap earlier, making a small, steamy cocoon that enclosed them in its warmth and privacy. Standing beside the cot, Alan slowly undressed her, until she stood before him, her creamy skin lustrous in the dim light. She worked at removing his uniform—the leather stock, the white linen shirt and breeches—until he stood clasping her to his lean, unclothed body. She loved the feel of him, the muscled shoulders, the broad chest with its soft, dark river of hair, the hips with their hard bones, the flat stomach, the dark tuff that gave way to the elongated, swelling length of his maleness, thrust now toward her and seeking entry between her thighs.

As his ardor rose, she expected him to lay her on the cot. Instead, and to her surprise, he moved her against the center tent pole, lifting her lightly to stand on a low wooden box. Pressing against her, he forced her legs apart and thrust deeply upward, lifting her even higher. Her arms closed around his shoulders, and his head bent against her breasts, as with increasing need he plunged deeper, driving with growing desire.

Maud caught back the cries she wanted to make. Her back arched even more, thrusting out her breasts to his eager mouth. His lips sought her breasts, turning from one to the other to catch the taut nipple in his teeth and suckle them wildly. Her body was a flame, a soaring heat that swelled with every new thrust, until she could bear it no longer. With a cry, he emptied himself into her, clasping her tightly to him and resting there.

His back was damp with the sticky heat of the tent. Drops of perspiration ran down his face, as she reached around him and lifted his lips to her gentle kiss.

He swung her off the box and lifted her easily in his arms to lay her on the cot. They lay entwined, as their bodies slowed and cooled and began to be touched with the tiny sadness that always followed such heightened ecstasy.

For a long time neither spoke. Alan smoothed her cheek and drew her head down to nestle in the hollow of his neck.

"So this is the reason you 'allowed' me to come with you," Maud said, half in jest.

"Well . . . not the only reason. But you have to admit, it's a good one."

"And I suppose it's the reason you'll allow me to go on?"

All at once Alan broke away from her and sat up, cradling his knees with his arms. "As a matter of fact, I wonder if you should. So far we've been fairly safe, but there might be a lot more danger involved as we get closer to Fort Carillon. It might be wiser for you to stay here at Lyman. I know Lord Howe would insist on it, if he knew."

"Then we won't tell him, will we?"

Alan looked down at her and laughed. "I have a feeling that no matter what I allow, you're going to follow me to Lake George."

She ran her fingernails lightly up his back. "Your feeling is correct. You can allow or not as you wish, but I intend to go on."

Alan turned quickly, caught her hand, and pulled her around under his long body. His face was very near to hers, and his smile was one of grim determination.

"Headstrong woman! Did your mother never teach you that a wife's duty is to obey her husband without question or argument?"

Maud laughed. "You're not my husband. And even if you were, I think you know I would not be a namby-pamby kind of wife, who meekly accepts orders."

He edged her arm behind her, forcing her to arch her body up against him. The hard nubs of her nipples burned into his bare chest. "No, you would be the kind who needed a good beating every week to teach you to behave."

Maud gave a throaty chuckle. "I'd like to see you try to give me one!"

Alan clamped his mouth on hers, hard and insistent. Maud pursed her lips against him for a moment, before the forceful magic of his tongue began working on her. Her lips parted to receive him, her body went warm and limp in his arms. Her freed hand crept up his back to grasp his hair, entwining it in her fingers as she pulled him down to her.

Alan lifted his lips from her mouth and ran them down her cheek. "I don't have to beat you. I can love you into submission," he said, laughing.

"You are a scoundrel, sir," Maud said, lightly pelting him with her fist. Silently she admitted there was some truth in what he said. Lying in his arms, being one with him in making love together, was the most she wanted out of life. How could she make him understand that for that very reason, she was unable to let him march away to war without her? How could she go on living, if she had no idea where he was or what was happening to him? Nothing or no one, not Lord Howe or Alan himself, was going to make her endure that.

He kissed her again, more easily this time, and they settled in each other's arms. Alan smoothed the hair away from her forehead, and nestled his head against it. The riotous racket of the creatures in the surrounding woods was almost deafening. Crickets and tree frogs, the occasional cry of a predator, followed by the screech of its prey, and once, far off, the eerie, primordial howl of a wolf, all gave evidence of the teeming life going on around them. Maud's soft breathing soon told him she had drifted into sleep. He pulled her close, reveling in the clean smell of her hair against his cheek.

He had only been half-joking about forcing her to stay at Fort Lyman. The truth was, he wanted her there because then he could feel that she was safe, even though he wasn't. It might be a rag-tag kind of fort, but it had better defenses than a tent camp on the banks of a lake. Suppose the French attacked the British at their rear, in order to deflect the huge assault on Fort Carillon? Or, worse still, what if the Indians used the absence of the English army as an excuse to destroy their camp? He had heard about the horrors of the massacre at Fort William two years before. The thought of that happening to Maud . . .

Alan gave a shudder and wrapped his arms tighter around her. She gave a contented sigh, as she nestled her head in the crook of his neck. Her shallow breath was warm on his throat.

This battle would probably offer the best opportunity he would ever have to finally confront General Wilkes, and it would be easier to concentrate on that if he felt Maud was secure and safe at Fort Lyman. Yet he knew without a doubt, that nothing he could say was going to keep her here. Stubborn woman! He should have married her long ago. As her husband he would have the right to make her do as he said.

Married her . . .

The thought gave him a jolt. He pulled away and looked down at Maud sleeping quietly, the cloud of her hair dim in the darkness around her face. Her long lashes rested in dark crescents on her cheek, and her beautifully shaped lips were slightly parted in her slow breathing. He ran his finger lightly down the oval of her face. He had never seriously considered marrying anyone, during all these years when revenge was the goal of his life. Marriage with its conflicting loyalties and concerns would only interfere with what he had to do. Until this moment, he had never thought of Maud as a wife, dear as she was to him.

How had it happened that she had become all the things he had sought to avoid by not having a wife? There was no other woman in the world he cared to be with, but her. Her safety and happiness mattered more to him than his own life. He even had to admit that at times during these last few weeks, she had managed to edge aside his goal of revenge against Wilkes, and put in its place the simple joy of just being with her.

What foolishness! Was he going to allow his love for Maud — for surely he did love her — to dim the image of his murdered family? No. He would avenge his brother and mother, and only then would he seriously think of marriage.

He settled back, drawing her head against his chest. Yet he would have preferred to leave her behind as his wife. That way she would have been both provided for and respectable. Perhaps he should examine the idea further.

It was a long time before he finally left her, still sleeping in the tent.

Chapter Eighteen

After leaving a small force at Fort Lyman, the main body of the expedition set out for the ruins of Fort William Henry on the shores of Lake George. It was slow going. Though the army had been scaled down to the bare essentials, there were still so many men, wagons, artillery, and supplies, that it took several days for them all to assemble. Maud was one of the last to arrive. The horrible state of the road made for a bumpy trip, but all that was forgotten once the forest opened up on to one of the most picturesque lakes she had ever seen. The blue water sparkled in the late afternoon sun, as if diamonds were scattered on the surface. On either side, hills dense with pine, maple, and oak flanked the shimmering lake, closing it in on the northern end to form a narrow stream.

There was much to be done before the army set off down the lake the following morning, and Maud, who was trying to keep out of sight, suspected that she would not see Alan before he left. She was wrong. He slipped away and found her late that evening. Those who could, were taking the time to rest before the momentous events of the next day.

"Shh," he whispered, touching her shoulder as she lay fitfully on the camp cot. "Come outside."

Moving carefully so as not to wake Molly, Maud threw a shawl over her shift and followed Alan outside. He took her hand and led her away from the tents to a more private stretch of shoreline, where they sat hidden by the shadows. Sitting on the ground, he pulled her down beside him, into the circle of his arms.

"I hoped you would come," Maud said quietly. "I didn't want you to leave tomorrow without . . ."

"Without one last goodbye? Don't worry, my love. I'm not one for risking my neck in the interest of honor or bravery. I'll be careful. I want you to promise me that you won't go any further down the lake. You simply must wait here until this thing is over. One way or another, I'll come back to you."

"I've already decided to wait here. Frankly, I don't see how I could go with you without being noticed, and from what you've told me of Lord Howe, he'd probably throw me overboard and leave me to drown."

Alan smiled. "Yes, he might at that. You know, I'm rather glad I've had the opportunity to get to know Brigadier General Augustus Howe. It's taken away some of my hatred and contempt for British officers."

"You mean General Wilkes, don't you? But why, Alan? Why do you dislike him so much? I've never understood that."

Abruptly Alan stood up and walked to the water's edge, staring out over the moonlit lake without answering. Maud waited for a time, then rose and went to him, slipping her arms around his waist. "You don't have to speak about it, if you don't want to," she said lightly. "I won't mention it again."

He caught her hands at his waist. "No, perhaps it's time I did. I've kept it to myself for too long." He laid his arm around her shoulder and walked with her along the shore.

"A long time ago, in Scotland, my family was involved in the rising, when Prince Charles Stuart raised his standard against the English Crown."

She looked up in surprise. "You're a Scot? But you don't sound like one!"

"I've had a long time to lose my accent. And I learned early on, that if I wanted to succeed on the stage, I'd better sound like an Englishman."

He stopped, picked up a small stone, and sent it skipping out over the water, rippling the silver surface. "Wilkes was one of the officers who led a party sent by the Duke of Cumberland, to punish the highlanders after the battle of Culloden Moor. He was a major then, and for a fat, stupid, lethargic man, he was surprisingly ruthless in carrying out his orders. He swooped down on my family home, burned the houses, barns, and outbuildings, stole the cattle, and scattered the tenants."

Alan stopped, staring out at the water. It was more difficult than he had imagined to say these words, much as he longed to share them with Maud. The images, with all their power to hurt, constricted his throat.

"My mother, my brother Neil, and I had to watch it all. I was a boy then, and Neil was two years older. He was a bonny lad, handsome, intelligent, and brave. I admired him more than anyone in the world. We both wanted to follow our father to serve the Prince, but my father would not hear of it. He made us promise we would stay and care for our mother and our home, and the homes of our people. It was a solemn promise, and one we held sacred.

"One of the farmers who had gone with my father brought us word of the disaster at Culloden Moor. He told us how my father died. He warned us that the Duke's men had set about teaching the Highlands a lesson by ravaging the countryside, and he begged us to hide. Of course, Neil would have none of that.

He was the Laird now, and he was going to care for everything just as our father had done."

Alan's voice faltered. Maud watched him, sensing how difficult it was for him to tell her about his family and his past. She wanted to put her arms around him, to tell him how honored she was that he would share this part of himself with her. Yet something told her to keep that small distance between them.

"They came a month later," Alan went on. "A whole platoon of soldiers, and one fat, sneering, arrogant officer who sat on his fine horse and watched almost in boredom, while his men carried out his orders. They herded us together outside. When my mother had realized they intended to burn the house, she grabbed up a few things from the parlor—a chest of letters, a silver bowl, a few other odds and ends. One of the soldiers tried to grab them from her, and Neil went to her defense. He knocked the man down, then went for his dirk. The officer barked an order and five men grabbed Neil, pinning his arms. Before we knew what was happening, one of them had a bayonet against Neil's chest. The soldier hesitated one second, glanced up at the officer, who nodded permission, then thrust it through my brother's heart."

"Oh, Alan," Maud breathed and laid her hand on his arm. For the first time since he had begun speaking, he looked down at her, laying his hand over hers, glad of the comfort of her touch. "Did they hurt you, too?" Maud asked.

"Not physically. I wanted to flail out at them, let them kill me along with Neil, but my mother cried out at me not to. For her sake I held back, watching Major Wilkes in all his smugness, and swearing that someday I would make him pay for my brother's life. We stayed on, living in that burned-out shell of a house another year before my mother died. If people really do die of broken hearts, then surely she was one of them."

He laid his arm around Maud's shoulder and pulled her close. Resting her head against his shoulder, she slipped her arm around his waist, hoping that all the love that overflowed her heart could ease the pain of these terrible memories.

"I never realized the General was such a cruel man," she said quietly.

"Yes. It's difficult to believe that such a foolish creature as he is today, could have been responsible for so much evil years ago. But he was, and I swore that someday I would see that he deeply regretted it. I've kept a watch on him all these years, waiting for the right moment. If he had gone to India, I would have found a way to follow him there. The Colonies seemed a godsend."

In the bronzed light, his face was stark and grim. Maud tightened her grip on his waist. "But you might have killed him at any time in London. Why now? And after so many years?"

"I was never concerned about how much time it took. I've had ample opportunities. But I didn't want to be hanged for murder, and I do want him to remember who I am. I never felt I had the right chance until now."

Her fingers dug into his tunic. "But how is it that he never recognized you? Why hasn't he tried to protect himself?"

"Because he's never known my real name." He looked down at her, lifting up her chin with his hand. "That's one reason I decided to tell you about this. If I am killed tomorrow, I want my actual name recorded. Alan Randall Desmond Sinclair. Promise me you'll do that."

"Alan, you don't intend to use this battle as a

means of killing General Wilkes, do you? Tell me you won't!"

He shrugged. "Perhaps I won't have to. Anything can happen in battle, although with thirteen thousand Englishmen facing three thousand Frenchmen, this one doesn't promise to be too severe. Do I have your promise?"

Maud threw her arms around him and hugged him tightly. "Oh, Alan, don't talk of being killed, or of killing. Just come back to me. I love you, and I don't want to lose you. If you should die tomorrow, part of me would die as well."

Her words moved him as he had never been moved before. Perhaps it was because he knew he might soon be staring death in the face. He had long ago determined that once he got even with Wilkes, the rest of his life was not going to be all that important. Yet now he suddenly found that he wanted very much to live. She was so alive in his arms, her eyes were filled with so much love and concern for him, her face bathed in moonlight was so beautiful; for the first time since that awful day years before, Alan realized how precious life could be.

He bent to kiss her and they clung together, not in the throes of passion as so often before, but in the desperate attempt to hold tight to each other before it all became too late and lost forever. A marvelous relief swept over Alan. Sharing his secret with Maud had lifted some of the weight of hate and revenge, which had filled the dark places of his soul for so long. The veneer of humor and lighthearted enjoyment of life he had so carefully cultivated was, he began to realize, a deeply rooted part of his true self. The love he felt for Maud, and the comfort and healing of her love for him, had allowed him to become the man he was meant to be. He was overcome with gratitude and love for her.

"Marry me, Maud," he breathed against her hair. "Tonight, before I have to leave you tomorrow."

She gasped and pulled away from his arms. "Marry!"

"Yes. I can rouse Lord Howe. I know he would marry us. I love you, Maud. And I know you love me."

Maud turned from him, fighting the swell of confusion his words created. "I cannot marry you, Alan. Not tonight." Not ever, she added silently to herself.

"Why not?" he cried, coming behind her to slip his arms around her waist and hold her close. "I hate the thought of leaving you here unprotected. I want to give you everything I can, while I'm still able."

She steeled herself against his loving words and the feel of his lips on her neck. "And would I be any more protected as your widow than as your grieving mistress? No, you have already given me everything I want in life."

She turned in his arms to rest her head against his chest, reveling in the feel of his hard body. There were no words to tell him all she was feeling. That she could never marry him now. She was a milkmaid, a serving wench, and he was a wealthy Scottish aristocrat. He needed a wife who had money and was well bred, who could help him to rebuild his home, his fortune, and his status in life. Marrying her would only drag him down.

She closed her eyes against the tears that burned there. She was so grateful he had shared his past with her. Now she understood why she had never come first in his life, why he never seemed to lack for money, why he had thrust her at Wilkes without ever really wanting her to become involved with him. Her heart longed to say "Yes, I'll marry you gladly," and take his hand to go search out Lord Howe. But she would not do that to him. She would not ruin his future for the sake of a few blissful moments and a ring on her finger.

Alan tipped up her face to reflect the bronze glow of the moonlight. "I love you, Maud. And I want you to be my wife."

"And I love you. But I don't think decisions about marriage are best made on the eve of a battle. Promise me you'll come back to me. That is all I want or need."

"All right. I'll bow to your wishes now. But afterward—"

"Alan!"

Jeremy's furtive whisper came from the dark shadows of the trees. "Alan, come on. We've got to get back."

"Jeremy!" Maud cried. Breaking away from Alan, she went running toward Jeremy as he stepped from the forest and into the moonlight on the beach. "Oh, I'm so glad you came," she said, clasping him tightly. "I'm so thankful you didn't go away without saying goodbye."

Jeremy gave her an awkward hug. "Oh, stop now," he said, trying to laugh. "It's not like we'll be going into any real danger. There's too many of us for that."

Maud gripped his arms. "Promise me that neither of you will take any crazy chances. And don't let Alan get anywhere near General Wilkes."

He glanced up at Alan. "You told her?"

"Yes. I thought she should know."

"Don't you worry about either of us, Maudie. We'll be right as rain. You just keep safe here, until it's over. If we don't both get back to our tents right now, we'll spend tomorrow in the guardhouse instead of on the march."

Alan reached down to kiss her once more, then stepped into the shadows along with Jeremy, where they were lost to her view. She stood for a moment looking after them, wondering how she was going to get through the next two days, then started slowly back to camp.

Never before had there been such a sight on Lake George. Maud spent the entire morning with the other women, watching as the flotilla bearing Abercromby's army moved slowly up the lake. It stretched out for a distance of six miles, a thousand boats bearing men and provisions, artillery and ammunition, moving toward the narrows that flowed around Fort Carillon and into Lake Champlain.

She tried to keep the bateau in which Alan and Jeremy were seated in sight, but it was soon eclipsed by all the others that followed. The army was moving in three divisions, with the regulars in the center and the Continental provincials on either flank. The varicolored uniforms, the regimental flags snapping in the light breeze, the music from the military bands of each regiment, gave the procession a festive air. The first group on the lake that morning was the Royals under Thomas Gage, accompanied by Major Rogers and his Rangers. They were followed by the boatmen and the regulars under Lord Howe, seven regiments in all, led by the 42nd Highlanders. To the right and left of them, in their blue uniforms, were the provincial regiments from Massachusetts, Rhode Island, Connecticut, New York, and New Jersey. Bringing up the rear were the artillery flatboats, to which were lashed dozens of cannon, howitzers, swivels, and mortars. Last of all came the rear guard of provincials.

Four hundred Iroquois—persuaded by Sir William Johnson to support this mighty army against their traditional enemies, the French—arrived too late to go by bateau, and instead took to the woods alongside the lake, hoping they would not arrive after the Fort fell to the English.

The magnificent sight did little to comfort Maud, for all she could think of was the possible danger involved. She thought she was hiding her concern pretty well, until Molly stepped up to lay a hand on her shoulder.

"Don't fret, dearie. He'll do fine. I never saw such a splendid army in all my years of following my Ben to the wars. Why, the Frenchies—if they got any sense at all—will turn tail and run all the way to Montreal, when they see this comin'."

Appreciating the thought, even if she did not agree, Maud smiled and wiped a treacherous tear from her eye. Molly did not look too concerned, and she knew much more about what to expect from this enterprise than Maud. It was a comforting thought.

Alan sat in the bateau, wedged tightly between Jeremy and a private from Cornwall, and tried to concentrate on the beauty of the hills beyond the lake. The crowded boat was unusually silent, and the lapping of the oars sliding through the still waters seemed strangely peaceful. So peaceful that he was startled when Jeremy leaned his head close, and whispered: "Has it occurred to you that what we are about to do may turn out to be just a little bit dangerous?"

Alan shrugged and adjusted the long musket that stood on end between his knees. "What will be, will be."

There was not a man in the bateau, Alan knew, who was not thinking with some trepidation of what lay ahead. Even he, for all his indifference, had made a point of revealing his true name to Maud the night before.

Jeremy went on: "Is that what you thought, when you let Lord Howe talk you into joining one of his scouting parties?"

"It made me a corporal, didn't it?" he said, pointing to the white shoulder-cords on his tunic. " Besides, if I have to fight this war, I'd as soon stay close to Lord Howe."

"I don't know. He's enjoying all this a bit too much for me. Just watch out that you shoot Frenchmen, not Englishmen."

Alan gave him a sharp glance. "Wilkes's regiment is at least two miles behind us."

"Just a word of caution. Look, we don't know what's up ahead, so now is as good a time as any to say it. Thanks for coming along."

It was the first time Jeremy had given any indication that he appreciated Alan's joining him in the military, and Alan found that he was moved by it. He clapped a hand on Jeremy's shoulder. "I'll watch out for myself. You do the same."

Jeremy nodded and Alan went back to studying the hills, which seemed to grow taller as the lake narrowed. Because he had been selected by Lord Howe to join the scouting party, Alan had learned a little about what lay ahead, and there was only a little to learn. Without the Indians to act as scouts, it was impossible to learn exactly how the fort was situated on the stretch of narrows that connected Lake George with Lake Champlain. They knew the river was treacherous with rapids there and unnavigable. They had a sense that it continued straight north, before looping to the east and around the spit of land on which the fort was situated. There was a sawmill somewhere on the eastern shore, which the French had built, and also a portage road. Both were heavily used by the French troops so Lord Howe had decided to strike out along the western shore of the narrows, in a wide circle that would eventually bring them out in front of the fort itself.

It seemed like a sound plan, Alan thought, yet he wished they had been able to learn the lay of the land more exactly. The French had only a fifth the number of men in Abercromby's army, but they were ably led by a General named Montcalm, who was also expecting a sizeable number of reinforcements from Montreal at any time. Alan glanced back over his shoulder at the huge flotilla of boats that almost entirely covered the surface of the lake, and was reassured. Perhaps when Montcalm realized the size of the army he was facing, he might give up without a prolonged fight. He hoped that wasn't just wishful thinking.

It took most of the day for the army to assemble on the west bank of the narrows. They came ashore at a place called Sabbath Day Point, twenty-five miles down the lake, and here they waited for the baggage, artillery, and rear guard to catch up. They were off again in the dark at about eleven, and by daybreak had entered the head of the narrows. Alan and Jeremy had slept fitfully, sitting upright and crammed together with thirty other men in an uncomfortable bateau. By noon the entire army had disembarked on the western side of the narrows, and the first plan of assault was ready to begin.

They had not arrived unnoticed. Montcalm had withdrawn his forces into Fort Carillon, but he sent out an advanced party of three hundred and fifty men, who watched the landing from a high rock. When the French party headed back through the woods to carry the word to General Montcalm, they were quickly swallowed by the forest.

Brigadier General Howe took only enough time to lay out his plan. Since the French occupied the sawmill and the portage road on the eastern shore of the narrows, it was decided that the army would march in four columns—preceded by a detachment under Major Rogers—around the mountains rimming the western shore of the narrows and coming out in front of the fort to attack by land. The long open fields facing the bastions of the fort would provide the perfect approach for a large well-equipped force.

Rogers set out at the head of two provincial regiments. Lord Howe and Major Israel Putnam, a Continental officer, followed, leading two hundred rangers. Behind them came three other advance columns.

Alan was to go with the small group of regulars accompanying Lord Howe, and thus he marched out before Jeremy. He hoisted his musket and threw his friend a parting smile, as he followed the column along a narrow path that was soon swallowed by tangled thickets. They turned out to be only an indication of worse to come. As the column pushed deeper into the forest, Alan had his first doubts about the wisdom of Lord Howe's plan.

Never had he seen such woods! So thick that they blotted out all sunlight, and grew darker and more mysterious with every mile. Heavy undergrowth pulled at his boots or gave way to a matted slough of wet leaves. The noise was earsplitting: eerie cries and caws of birds and the rattle of insects, stirred to hysteria by the trampling of men fighting their way through the walls of vines and thickets. Thorns pulled at his uniform and scratched his face. Grasping fingers of vines clutched at his cap and the long nozzle of his musket. The broken, rocky terrain made marching impossible, and once he nearly slipped and twisted his ankle trying to keep up with the officers ahead.

In half an hour's time, he knew he was hopelessly lost and could only hope that the others were not.

That hope faded, as hour after hour they thrashed about with no sense of direction at all, hoping they were headed toward the east.

He sensed that the afternoon was waning without really seeing the light clearly. Perhaps Lord Howe would call a halt soon and they might make camp, though he could not imagine what kind it would be in these impossible woods.

He stopped as he heard a loud thrashing up ahead. In the dense gloom he could see nothing, not even his own officers, but it was obvious something was happening.

A voice rang out: *"Qui vive?"*

My God! A French patrol.

"Français!"

He recognized Major Putnam's voice, trying to make them believe they had stumbled onto a party of Frenchmen. In a breathless moment of silence, he almost began to believe it had worked.

And then came the crashing blast of musket fire.

It started with a few popping noises, then quickly erupted into a barrage of earsplitting blasts. Where Alan stood, the woods were so thick and dark he could see nothing. He dove to the ground and scrambled through the leaves on his stomach, wondering if the whole of Montcalm's army was bearing down on them. Bursts of red shafts of fire, and smoke spreading like a fog through the trees, gave the woods the aura of hell itself. He reached a small clearing, where he could see a group of English soldiers, some of them sprawled on the ground, others bending in the underbrush and firing into the trees. Behind him he could hear the cries of the Rangers, trying to steady the panic-stricken regulars. Rising to all fours, he scrambled across the clearing to the group on the other side.

Within the circle of the troops, were several

sprawled bodies, bloody and still. With a sinking heart, Alan recognized the uniform of Brigadier General Lord Howe.

"Oh no . . ." he moaned, and reached to turn the General over onto his back. Lifeless eyes peered upward into the smoky trees.

"He was struck in the first fusillade," one of the nearby soldiers said in a strangled voice. The man's face was stricken, even as he continued to load his musket and fire into the woods. Alan looked around. They were all in pain.

In a burst of insane anger, Alan rose to his feet and fired at the dark thicket of trees, not seeing any enemy, but simply hoping to hit one. One of Major Roger's Rangers standing nearby, grabbed his arm and pulled him down.

"Hold your fire," he ordered. "They've gone. I think it was only a patrol."

"God damn it! Why!"

"He shouldn't have been up here in the van. He should of stayed back in camp."

One of the young soldiers had tears streaming down his cheeks. The shock of Lord Howe's death had not yet given way to the terrible grief that Alan knew would come. He kept it at bay by keeping busy.

"We'll have to take him back. Here, help me get his sash off."

As the gunfire died away and the troops behind them reassembled, the small group around the General's body laid out his sash and lashed it to a stretcher made of interlaced branches. With a sense of stunned disbelief, the men bedded down to get through the long night. At dawn, carrying the body between them, they set out to retrace the path they had taken from the landing place, a path now well defined by the trampling it had taken.

Alan knew that as long as he lived, he would never

forget the sight of General Abercromby's face when Lord Howe's body was carried into camp. It was not grief that was etched there, not regret, not disbelief. It was fear. Plain, unvarnished fear of the awesome responsibility that had fallen on his unwilling shoulders. It was common knowledge that General Abercromby had been content to allow General Howe to be the real leader of his army, while he himself filled the post of Commander in Chief, a post he had earned by many years of dogged service to his King and country. He did not want to lead this army against a formidable enemy. Nor had he prepared to do so. Now, suddenly, he was forced into that leadership, and he found the whole idea ghastly.

To his credit, the old man gathered his officers around him and began to attempt to figure out the best way to proceed. Over the morning several things became plain. The French ambush they had stumbled on in the woods was only a small column from Fort Carillon, who had been attempting to take the same western route back to the fort which the English were attempting. The two had accidentally crossed each other's paths in the dense wilderness, and in that first skirmish, a shot had ripped through General Howe's heart, killing him instantly. Major Rogers, hearing the firing, had turned back to aid Howe's column and trapped the French between them. The French had fought their way back to the fort with terrible losses. Only fifty had escaped. One hundred and fifty-two were killed in the fighting, or drowned trying to cross the rapids. One hundred and forty-eight had been captured.

It might have been considered a victory, except that the cost had been so terrible that there was no joy in it.

Since the terrain on the western side of the narrows was impossible, General Abercromby turned his attention to the eastern side, and sent a detachment to take possession of the portage road and the sawmill, both of them abandoned by the French. They quickly determined that Montcalm had withdrawn inside the fort, after having burned the bridge across the treacherous narrows.

Abercromby started the army moving, and by late afternoon everything except artillery and baggage had reached the encampment. The General took up headquarters in the sawmill, while reports poured in concerning the number of the French inside the fort and the nature of its defenses.

Alan was on one of the patrols who scouted out those defenses. Later he stood near the General's table and told what he had seen.

"There's a wide plain facing three sides of the fort, with the lake on the other. The fort itself is square with bastions at four points and two demi-lunes on the north and the west."

The General grimaced and gripped his stomach, which bothered him now more than ever. "That's the customary design."

"Yes, sir. But the Marquis has made it more impregnable by throwing up a breastwork fully across the plain. They must have cut down every tree in sight, and piled them up to make a log wall eight or nine feet high. It appears very strong, though I don't think it could stand up to cannon fire for long. There's also an abitis, a tangle of branches and trees some distance ahead of this wall, to make it an even more difficult approach. And immediately in front of the breastwork, they've laid a line of sharpened branches."

"Montcalm's been busy." He rubbed his wide chin. "Very well, Corporal. Thank you."

The night saw two new groups arriving, reinforcements for the French inside the fort—bringing their total number of defenders to thirty-six hundred—and four hundred Iroquois with Sir William Johnson, who took up a position on top of a high hill where they could see the battle and join in the expected massacre. The English now had a force of nearly fifteen thousand men. How could they lose? That thought was Alan's only comfort.

Alan and Jeremy sat for a long time near the lake's edge, quietly talking about which of several plans Abercromby might follow the following morning.

"I say he'll bring up the cannon and blast that abatis and breastwork to tinder. Then we'd have the whole plain free."

"I don't think so," Alan said thoughtfully. "The walls of that fort are going to cost us dearly. I say secure the supply road, position a few cannon where they would do the most good, then starve them out. They can't last long without supplies, and eventually they'll surrender,. That way we'd not lose a man."

Molly's husband, Ben, who had been quietly listening to their conversation, leaned forward to jab a stick at the low flames of the campfire. "I say you're both wrong. The usual approach is to send a part of your regiments against the breastwork, while the rest move in a flanking maneuver to take the fort from the low ground, catching the Froggies in the middle. I've seen it done before, and I'll wager he'll use it. Old Nabby's been in the army too long to try anything different."

"You're probably right about that," Alan muttered, feeling a familiar pang as he remembered the cold corpse of Lord Howe left back at the landing place. "If only Howe hadn't died!"

"It was meant to be," Ben commented dryly. He had lived through too many sudden deaths to be much moved by this one.

Jeremy leaned back on his elbows on the damp

ground. "That's as good a way as any to look at it. If I can believe that I'm meant to live or die, perhaps I won't worry so much about tomorrow. It's when you think that if only you'd moved a little to the right or left, or maybe made this choice or that choice differently, that you go crazy with worry."

Alan snapped a twig in half and threw the pieces on the fire. "I'd like to think that all this must have some purpose, or we wouldn't be here. I want to believe that what will be will be."

"You've followed this army life for a long time, Ben," Jeremy said. "What do you think about the night before a battle?"

Ben sat back, resting his arms on his knees and staring into the embers. "Well, I try not to think too much about it at all. I don't worry much about dying. I've had a good life. The thing that bothers me the most is the hurt it'll give my old girl. She's been a good soldier all these years, and I'd hate to see her left with nobody and nothing. But I guess that's the risk she takes, alongside o' me taking my risks."

Jeremy yawned and rose stiffly to his feet. "Well, if all of us don't stop thinking and start getting some rest, we won't be worth shooting tomorrow. I'm turning in."

"Me, too, I suppose," Ben said, shuffling to his feet.

Alan looked up at them. "I think I'll stay awhile longer. I don't feel sleepy yet."

He watched as the two men were swallowed by the darkness outside the fire's glow. The truth was, he had too much on his mind to sleep. Ben's comments about his wife brought images of Maud all too vividly to his mind. He had not done enough to leave her well cared for, if he was killed in the fighting. He should have told her about Joseph Menzies, given her an address. Perhaps before he turned in, he would write a letter to Menzies himself, asking him to see that Maud received enough from the estate for her care.

Impatiently he kicked at the fire. This was not the time to be thinking about such things. The camp was quiet now, and most of the men were asleep. He had been deliberately waiting for this dark stillness, and now that it was here, it was time to act, not sit around worrying. Getting to his feet, he stamped at the embers of the fire, wrapped a dark cloak around his scarlet tunic, pulled his hat down over his forehead, and slipped into the darkness.

It took him nearly half an hour to reach General Wilkes's marquee. A few of the officers in the nearby tents were still up, and occasional voices broke the silence. From the sound of it, they were spending their last night before the fight in games and gaiety, probably at cards. He only hoped Wilkes hadn't joined them.

The sleepy sentry standing guard before the General's marquee suggested he was inside, and the dim reflection of a light through the tent indicated he was still awake. Alan stood hidden in the trees nearby, and waited for the sentry to be distracted. It came, sooner than he had hoped, when one of the men guarding the noisy marquee called the man over. Alan waited only long enough to see that the space in front of the tent was empty, then silently slipped through the flaps.

A single guttering candle threw out a circle of dim light that did not reach much beyond the table on which it sat. General Wilkes was sitting at the table, nodding over a stack of papers. A quill had fallen from his hand, to lay haphazardly across a silver inkwell and sander. Alan hesitated only long enough to familiarize himself with the rest of the tent, then sidled silently around the edge. Stepping quickly up behind the General, he grabbed him around the neck with one arm, holding him in a choking vise, while forcing the blade of his knife against the exposed throat with his other hand.

Wilkes gave a strangled start of surprise. His eyes flew open, bulging with shock.

"Don't make a sound or I'll cut you ear to ear," Alan hissed. He felt the General's body stiffen, as he yanked the man's head farther back. His voice was an intense whisper. Though he could not see Wilkes's face, he knew the beady little eyes were flitting around desperately, and he pushed the blade of the knife even deeper.

"I don't intend to kill you *now*, and if you keep still, I won't have to," he whispered in the General's ear. "I simply want you to listen to what I have to say."

A gurgling noise escaped Wilkes's throat as Alan tightened his grip. "You remember me, don't you, Wilkes? Alan Desmond? Only the name is not Desmond. It's Alan Sinclair, of Donnamuir. Do you recall Donnamuir, General? You should. Or perhaps you burned so many places in Scotland, and ruined so many people, they've all become a blur in your memory."

He had Wilkes's attention now. He felt the General's body give a little. "I want you to remember Donnamuir, Wilkes. You were only Major Wilkes then, out to make your way in the army by teaching the highlanders a lesson. You came with your little party of bloodthirsty men, and destroyed my home."

Wilkes gave a series of gurgles which Alan cut off with an even tighter grip on his neck. He turned the knife slightly, so that the razor edge bit into the flesh of the General's throat. "Only following orders, were you? That's the excuse men like you always make.

But you had no orders to kill my brother, that young man who was only trying to protect his mother and his home. Remember that, Wilkes? You gave your soldier permission to thrust a bayonet into my brother's heart. You killed him for no other reason than that you felt like it that particular day.

"I've followed you for years, Major Wilkes, to remind you of what you did at Donnamuir. I want justice and I want revenge, and I intend to have it. Oh, not here, not in your tent, where I could so easily cut your throat. But tomorrow, in the fight with the French, keep a watch on your rear and your sides, Major. I'll be there. You won't see me, but you'll know my eyes are on you, and sometime during the day, when I feel the time is ripe, I'll avenge the blood of my brother, Neil Sinclair."

The whisper Alan had been using close to Wilkes's ear grew in intensity. He leaned even closer, his breath hot on the General's face.

"Remember me tomorrow, Major Wilkes!" With a quick flick of his wrist, he drove the knife far enough into the General's neck to raise a long, thin red welt. Then, in one motion, he blew out the candle, shoved the General in his chair to the floor, and darted through the flaps. Pausing only long enough to make sure the sentry had not returned, Alan was through the door and into the darkness of the woods before the General, thumping around on the floor, made it to his feet. He waited, hidden in the distance, wanting to see what Wilkes would do. As he expected, the General was close behind him, thrusting aside the flaps and stepping outside, holding his handkerchief to his throat while he scanned the darkened woods. The sentry came running up, making excuses for his absence and asking if something was wrong. Alan fully expected an alarm to be sounded and a search party sent out for him, though with the number of men in the camp and the huge length of ground the cantonment covered, he was not too concerned that they would find him.

He was surprised to see Wilkes stand quietly, pressing the handkerchief to his throat, while his eyes darted back and forth across the black curtain of the woods. He heard him ask the sentry if the man had seen anyone running from his marquee, then scathingly dressed him down for leaving his post. But he set no alarm going, and ordered no search party.

Alan wondered about that all the way back to his campsite. Perhaps Wilkes had realized how useless it would be to try to find one man among this huge army, or perhaps his pride kept him from admitting he had been ambushed in his own marquee. Maybe he was having trouble separating that one experience at Donnamuir from all his other crimes.

When Alan reached the campsite, there was nothing left of the fire but a few glowing embers. He wrapped his cloak around himself and stretched out on the ground, to try to get a little rest before dawn. A tiny smile hovered at the corners of his lips, as he wondered whether General Wilkes was going to get any sleep this night.

Chapter Nineteen

It carried like the crackling of thunder in the distance, traveling across the mirror-still lake like the dim warning of a coming storm. Maud lifted her head and looked up into a cloudless, empty sky, as blue as the feathers of the jay squawking at her from the branches of a nearby pine.

Surely this was no storm. A horrible suspicion brought her to her feet, and sent her hurrying to the edge of the lake to look out over the silver water. It was coming from the direction Alan and Jeremy had sailed only two days before. The air, which had been hot and sticky all day, grew even heavier and pushed its hot breath down on her. Her chest was so constricted, she could barely breathe.

Maud gripped her hands across her waist and began to pray.

Alan had not been among the group of engineers who met early that morning in General Abercromby's tent to advise him of the best way to proceed. But he was one of the first to hear the General's decision.

"A frontal attack!" he exclaimed, when Sergeant Stacey told him the Captain's orders. "Well, I don't suppose that will be too bad, if the artillery prepares the way."

"He's not going to wait for the artillery. He knows about the French reinforcements, and he's crazy to get this done before he has to face a larger army."

"But that's not what the prisoners told us. Surely Montcalm has no more than three or four thousand men, against our fifteen thousand. What is there to worry about?"

Stacey shrugged. "Who can explain generals? Tell the line to form."

The word spread along the ranks—a frontal attack against a tangled wall of trees and a log barricade, with no cannon to back up the line. It sounded insane, but it just might succeed. If the French did not fight any better than they were reputed to, it might carry the day.

Alan and Jeremy were not in the first wave of troops. They watched as a line fanned out across the plain like a streak of blood, flags flying, drums beating. A wave of red swept toward the tangled trees, as the first fusillade from the troops behind the wall filled the air with flame and smoke. At the abatis the wave broke as men fought their way through.

Alan and Jeremy watched, as the first blast from the French shattered the English line marching across the open field. The noise from the continuing barrage blasted their ears, as they waited with the reserves behind the trees. The acrid smoke choked their lungs and left a bitter residue in their mouths.

The first line stumbled and wavered as holes formed in its ranks. Men lay on the ground or were caught in the tangle of trees, while those who had struggled through huddled to move forward. Many of those who did were cut down before they could reach the log wall.

Alan grew more and more appalled, until a wave of anger swept away any feeling except the need to go out there and help save the day. When the order came, he rushed on to the field beside Jeremy, running toward the abatis. The first wave of men had forced several holes in the abatis, and Alan and Jeremy made for the first one, ignoring the bodies of two men grotesquely pinned there. Once on the other side, they were abruptly halted by a wall of flame and smoke from the log wall, half the length of the plain in front of them. Both of them dove to the ground and crawled forward. Over the blasts of the muskets, they could hear the officers screaming orders that were echoed by the frantic tattoo of the drummers. Alan noted with amazement that the majority of men around him attempted to follow the firing positions that had been drilled into them: moving in a line, dropping to their knees as one, raising their muskets to their shoulders, firing, dropping back for the line behind them to rush ahead and fire, moving forward all the time to the staccato of the drums. With men falling around him, he was overcome with a desperate sense of trying to survive. Alan crawled on his stomach, trying to fire from as low a position as possible. He had a dim realization that there was blood everywhere; he was slipping on it. Shattered bodies, men with no arms or legs, holes in their chests, sightless eyes staring at him in surprise where there was still a face, and always behind it, the pattern of the drum carrying orders to the ranks. When he heard the pattern change to retreat, he turned without thinking to slog his way back toward the ruined abatis. He stopped near it, hearing the thin cry of a soldier calling for help. The man was pinned beneath the heavy corpse of a Continental officer, his face a mask of blood.

Alan threw his musket to Jeremy, who had rushed to his side, and reached down to drag the American off.

"Can you walk?"

The man nodded his head weakly. As Alan dragged the man to his feet, he saw that one leg was shattered and bent in a grotesque angle. Half-dragging him, he made it to the abatis and pulled them both through to the other side, where another soldier stepped up to help Alan drag him back to the safety of the trees. By the time they got there, the wounded trooper had fainted dead away. They laid him on the ground, and Alan, suddenly breathless, collapsed beside him. He could not believe he was still alive. He looked down at his own body, wondering that it was whole and unscathed when so many others . . .

The survivors regrouped among the trees, looking with dazed eyes at each other.

"Why doesn't he bring up the cannon?" one of the soldiers muttered.

"It would take too long," Alan answered sarcastically. "And it would be too sensible, seeing as how the enemy is so well entrenched."

"Surely, the General won't be insane enough to try a frontal attack again."

"I wouldn't place any bets on that," Alan answered, his voice thick with bitterness. He glanced over to see Jeremy sitting nearby, with blood running down the side of his face like paint on an Indian.

"You're hurt," Alan said, scrambling toward him.

"Not so bad. It probably looks worse than it is. A ball grazed my head coming through that damned abatis."

Alan tore off a strip of his shirttail, and wound it around Jeremy's head to stem the flow of blood. It quickly oozed a spreading scarlet spot. "Are you certain you're all right?"

"Just a little dizzy."

An officer walking the line bent to look at Jeremy's wound. "You'd better go back to the sawmill, and have the surgeon look at that. Can you walk?"

Jeremy nodded and dragged himself to his feet. He took two steps and fell as his knees gave way. Alan jumped up to catch him.

"Help him," the officer said, and moved on before Alan could protest.

"Come along then, old friend," Alan said, throwing one of Jeremy's arms over his shoulder and gripping him around the waist. "I think this afternoon's performance has earned us both a small intermission."

She sat by the lake all afternoon. The first distant rumble of gunfire seemed to go on forever. Maud gripped her hands together and prayed that it was over, and Alan and Jeremy were safe. She had risen to go back to her chores, when it began again, louder than before. Molly came up beside her, followed by two of the other women, all of them staring out across the still expanse of water, as if by looking hard enough they would be granted the sight of what was happening.

After leaving Jeremy with the surgeon at the sawmill, Alan was sent to headquarters to act as a courier. There he learned that Abercromby had ordered a second frontal assault on the French lines. He spent the next several hours running back and forth between the front lines in the trees that faced the abatis, the marquees where the brigade officers waited for instructions, and General Abercromby's headquarters near the portage road. There he heard Abercromby direct that orders be sent to General Wilkes's brigade to make another assault.

Alan quickly stepped forward and offered to take the orders. He was handed them with barely a glance by the harassed adjutant, and told where to find

General Wilkes's brigade. Half an hour later he was handing the orders to Wilkes himself.

Without looking at the messenger, the General tore open his dispatch and read the order. Alan waited, noticing with some satisfaction how the General paled slightly as he read what he was asked to do.

"God's eyebrows! Another frontal attack! It's suicide," Wilkes muttered. Noticing that the corporal was still waiting, he barked, "Nothing to return. Tell General Abercromby we'll carry out his command."

Only then did the General glance up and recognize Alan. He jumped to his feet, staring at him, his pudgy mouth hanging open.

"Very well, sir," Alan said, smiling, and slipped outside before Wilkes could cry out for his arrest. He had no intention of returning to headquarters. Instead, he grabbed up a musket and fell in among the men assembling for the march toward the field in front of the Fort. The lines were so confused, and the men so anguished over making what seemed like another hopeless and useless attack, that no one paid him much mind. He was glad Jeremy was back at the field hospital, for his friend would certainly have tried to argue him out of what he was going to do. Some small part of him cried that this was not the way to get his revenge, that an honorable challenge would be more in keeping with his character. But he refused to listen to that part of his conscience. He would never have a better opportunity to get Ambrose Wilkes than right now, and he was determined to take advantage of it. He wanted Wilkes to make this attack while having to watch for him in every direction. He wanted him to feel the fear of a trapped animal with no place to hide. He only hoped the man was not such a coward as to stay far from the action, for that would make it more difficult to make it look as though he had been shot by a French bullet. Alan pursed his lips in a determined line. He would find a way to kill the General, no matter where the man positioned himself to watch this assault.

The woods facing Fort Carillon were a madhouse. Wounded men lay everywhere on the ground, many crying out for help. The remnants of the last futile assault, those who could still walk, were staggering in a daze among the trees, wondering where to go. Others had slumped on the ground, their backs against the trees, thanking God that they were still alive, and trying to wipe the memory of those moments on the field from their minds. Their officers moved among them attempting to regroup and fall back, to allow room for the next wave of troops.

That fresh brigade crowded its way toward the edge of the trees, Alan at the front. He stopped in the shelter of a group of pines, and stared at the open ground just ahead. It had been a horror following the first attack. Now, after the fourth, he could not believe what he saw.

The ground was littered with bodies. It was impossible to say how many were dead, for the ground undulated with the slow movements of those still alive and unable to rise. The grass, where it could be seen, was trampled into a morass of mud and gore, vividly red with the blood of the finest army in the world. The abatis, which had to be crossed before reaching the first French entrenchment, was mangled and broken, and thick with bodies hanging grotesquely from its tangled branches. Smoke from the last onslaught of firing hovered over the field, just above the littered ground. The smell was overpowering, a sickening mixture of saltpeter, sulphur, blood, and death. And this was the ground that the next battalion of troops had to cross in order to overrun the French line.

Alan got a grip on himself. He was not here to fight the French, he said silently, and immediately turned his attention to spotting Wilkes. He came upon the General almost at once, sitting on a huge white charger, staring out at the horrible field with a face even paler than when he had read his orders. Wilkes gave a shudder, then turned his horse back under the trees, and began issuing commands to bring up the line. Immediately his troops ran to take up their positions. A first long line of troops was followed by three others at intervals. Alan dropped back to the third line, convinced that by the time they moved up, things would be so disastrous and confused that Wilkes would be an easy target at the edge of the woods.

All the officers were busy maneuvering their men into position. Wilkes and his immediate aides moved among them, riding back and forth to clarify orders and direct the men. When Alan saw the General's white horse approaching the row of troops where he waited, he deliberately maneuvered himself to the front. Wilkes pulled up not ten feet away, issuing commands to a captain standing there. Something in Alan's gaze caught his attention, and he turned to look straight at him.

For a long moment Alan's burning, mocking eyes held the General's knowing, flat gaze. Though not a word was spoken, understanding passed between them. *I'm here and I intend to follow you until I kill you,* Alan's said. *I know who you are and I dare you to,* the General's answered.

One of the officers called to Wilkes, and he turned away. Pulling his horse around, he gave Alan one more glance, then cantered back toward the edge of the trees.

The rattle of the drums began up and down the line. The first row of the assault had still not moved, when a stirring deep within Alan told him something was wrong. He had fully expected that fat figure on the white horse to gallop to the rear where he could safely oversee the attack. Instead, Wilkes was cantering back to the first line of troops, which had begun moving slowly toward the edge of the trees.

Alan broke from his position and began to run, ignoring the outraged barks of a sergeant behind him. He broke through the second line and was nearly to the first, when he saw Wilkes galloping up in front of the wavering line of troops. The General had pulled out his sword and was raising it over his head, encouraging the men to break from the shelter of the trees and out onto that terrible field. Even as the first roar of musket fire erupted from the French entrenchment, Wilkes was flying onto the field ahead of his men. A ragged cheer went up, as the troops resolutely flowed out onto the field, inspired by the action of their General.

Alan stopped, staring, as the long wave of men was cut down. Acrid smoke was everywhere, but through it he could make out the flowing motions of that white horse and the man on its back, his scarlet tunic glowing through the thick fog. He saw the horse rear and Wilkes arch his body and then slump over the saddle. He saw the horse go down, crashing on the troops around it, while its rider was thrown several feet away.

In an instant Alan was out on the field. He groped his way through the smoke, keeping low to the ground, crawling and dodging his way to where Wilkes had fallen. When he reached him, he scrambled forward on his belly to yank him over on his back. The General's tiny eyes were open in a startled, sightless gaze. A thin line of blood, already congealing, ran from his open mouth and down his chin. There was a hole in his chest the size of a man's fist.

Alan was seized with a cold fury. Outrage—that after all this time his quarry had been stolen from him—consumed him in a frenzy that set his head pounding. With a cry of rage, he grabbed up his gun. Paying no heed to the musket balls and grapeshot zinging the air around him, he rose straight up on his feet and began to race toward the French lines.

They sat there for hours, listening as the sound rose and fell; sometimes the noise was so faint it could barely be heard, and at others, rumbling in waves like distant thunder. There were pauses in between, some of them so long that the women looked at each other, their silent glances speaking the thought they dared not put into words—that it was finally all over. Then it would come again, that soft, ominous, long, crackling roll.

Evening came late on these long summer days, and the light was still strong when they first were able to make out the boats on the lake, rowing toward them. Maud's eyes were sharper than the others', and she was the first of the women able to distinguish the boats from the wavering lines of heat on the water's surface. By the time the first bateau drew close enough for the women to make out the hats of the soldiers sitting inside, they could clearly see the other boats, spreading out across the lake like the gaudy flotilla that had sailed away only a few days before.

"Why are so many of them coming back?" Molly's voice was soft, as though speaking to herself. Maud looked at her questioningly. "I mean, I'd think they would leave a good part of the army up there to hold the fort," she went on.

"Maybe they're bringing back French prisoners?"

"Aye. That must be it."

By the time the first bateau drew near to the shore, it was obvious to the waiting women that they were not filled with French prisoners. Maud recognized some of the faces of the men who dragged wearily ashore. Alan and Jeremy were not among them, but so many boats were still coming, that she was filled with hope. Then the word spread quickly, brought by the returning regulars.

"A retreat! I don't believe it," Molly cried. "How could it be?"

"That's what one of them told me," Maud answered. "I don't understand it, but he said the whole army is running back here, and we'd best get out of their way. You haven't seen Alan, have you?"

"No. Have you see Ben?"

"No, not yet."

"I don't think their regiment's got back yet. A retreat! It's not possible with such a fine army. What could have happened?"

At this point Maud cared less for what had happened than for finding Alan and Jeremy. Yet as the twilight gave way to darkness, and she continued to run among the crowds of men who waded ashore from each new arriving bateau, without finding either one of them, her anxiety grew like a spreading sickness within her. She began to pay particular attention to the boats carrying the wounded, who were being laid out on the grass near the water's edge. She moved among them, bending to lift a bandage or turn a face toward her, and always without success. When it grew too dark to make out their features, she went back to her tent at the edge of the camp, weary and desolate.

She scratched at a tinder and lit her one small candle. She sat it on an upturned barrel on one side of the oiled canvas, then turned to sink down on the narrow cot opposite. She could not keep the unbearable thought at bay. Neither man had returned with their regiment, and tomorrow she would have to walk among the others, asking if anyone had seen them fall. She sank her head into her hands, as the image of their torn bodies lying on some mountain road before the walls of Fort Carillon forced itself upon her mind. The tears rolled down her cheek, and she fought back long, raking sobs. It was another hour before she blew out the candle and fell into a fitful sleep without even bothering to remove her dress.

"Maud!"

The whisper was so soft, that it was its intensity more than its sound that awakened her. At first she thought she must have dreamed hearing his voice. And then it came again.

"Maud. Wake up!"

Instantly she was awake. Throwing her legs over the side of the cot, she peered into the darkness, trying to make out his form. But there was no one there.

"Maud!"

It seemed to be coming from the outside of the tent near her bed. Maud threw herself back on the cot close to the wall. "Alan?"

"Yes. Shh. Keep quiet and come outside."

Throwing back the tent flap, she ran into the night and around the side of the tent, stumbling on a tree root in the dark. Before she could make out his dark body, his arms were around her, pressing her tightly to him. She threw her arms around his neck, clasping him to her, searching his lips and finding them, covering his face with her kisses.

"Alan! Oh, I was so afraid. I thought you were—"

He stopped her cries with his lips, then bent to whisper into her ear. "Be quiet, my love. I don't want to attract attention."

"What's the matter?" Her fingers searched his face, enclosing it between her palms, as though he might disappear if she did not hold him.

"I'll tell you in a moment. You're still dressed. Good. Go back inside, and get your coat and a blanket, then come with me."

"But—"

"Hurry. We haven't much time." Gently he wiped the tears off her cheek with his thumb, and pushed her back toward the tent. Reluctantly, mystified, Maud ran back inside and grabbed her heavy shawl and the blanket on her bed, bundling them under her arm. Outside, Alan grabbed her hand and led her away from the tent and into the blackness of the forest, weaving his way as though he could see a path that was invisible to her.

"Where are we going?" she whispered.

Without answering, he pulled her along. They pushed through the dense undergrowth for nearly an hour, before finally emerging into a small clearing surrounded by high rocks. The moon had risen by now, and it fell on a man who rose wobbly to his feet as they came out of the brush.

"Jeremy!" Maud cried and ran to hug him. He clung to her as never before, and it was a moment before she realized why. "You've been hurt!"

"Only a little. Got a frightful headache, but it should be right as rain in a day or two."

Maud dabbed at the bandage around his head. Only a thin strip of white cloth was left, but it gleamed in the moonlight. "How terrible! You might have been killed. Both of you might have been killed! I thought you had been, when I couldn't find you earlier today."

Jeremy sank back down on a nearby boulder, while Maud turned to Alan. "Just what is going on here? I don't understand it at all."

Alan sank to the ground to lean back against a rock, and pulled out a pewter canteen. "Have a dram of brandy, my love? It'll give you strength for what's ahead."

"No, I don't want any spirits. What do you mean, what's ahead? I won't go another step with you, unless you explain what you're doing."

Alan jammed the stopper back in the neck of the canteen. "We're leaving the army. We were pressed into it—at least, Jeremy was—and now we're taking advantage of the panic and confusion following our glorious retreat, to take our leave."

Maud stood without moving as his words sank in. Then she knelt beside him. "But, is that wise? You could be hanged for desertion!"

Alan reached out and drew her into the circle of his arms. "Yes, we could, possibly. But I'm betting they'll assume we're two of those thousand corpses lying back on the plains in front of Fort Carillon, and they'll declare us dead. And in fact, Corporal Alan Desmond is one of those corpses. Alan Sinclair will now resume his life."

"Corpses?"

"Oh yes. More dead bodies than I've ever seen in one place before. Thousands of them."

"How could that be? It was such a . . . fine army."

Jeremy leaned back and closed his eyes. "I'm not certain I understand it yet."

"It's simple. Lord Howe was killed almost the moment we arrived, and the plan of battle fell on General Abercromby's shoulders. The General allowed himself to be convinced that the fort could be taken with a frontal assault without the help of cannon. When the first wave of troops accomplished nothing except to litter the ground with English dead, his brilliant answer was to launch another. And another

355

and another."

"Six in all," Jeremy muttered.

Alan seemed to be speaking to himself more than to her. "Six times the lines were ordered to sweep away a well-entrenched enemy by marching straight into their line of fire. Jeremy and I were lucky. We were in the first assault and escaped with our lives. By the sixth attack, the men were advancing over the bodies of their comrades."

"The 42nd Scots was in that sixth line," Jeremy said quietly. "They were cut to ribbons."

"The Black Watch. I recognized some of them, though I never let them know who I was. Not many survived."

Maud could not miss the desolation in Alan's voice, even though he tried to sound merely cynical. She had never known him to be so deeply affected by anything. "How many men did we lose?"

"I heard one officer estimate over sixteen hundred men killed. The French probably lost four hundred or so. And all because we had no leadership. General Abercromby's idea of fighting a battle consisted of ordering a new attack after he heard that the last one had failed. It was more than I could stomach. When we were finally ordered to retreat, reason told me this would be the perfect time to leave what had become a lost cause."

"And you, Jeremy? Did you agree or did he drag you along?"

"You forget, Maudie, I was forced into this in the first place. Besides, I prefer to confine my dramatics to the stage. Real life is a bit too intense."

Alan sighed and pulled her closer. "It was the most honorable, brave, and utterly stupid exhibition I have ever witnessed."

Maud nestled close against him, and thought over all that he had told her. She was not surprised that both men would want to leave the army, and considering the confusion that must be taking place back in the camp, and the fact that so many men had died, perhaps this *was* the best time to get away. Unless . . .

Abruptly she sat up. "Alan, you are telling me the truth, aren't you? You're not running away because you challenged General Wilkes?"

Alan pulled the stopper out of the brandy canteen. "I didn't have to. He was shot down in one of those futile charges."

"Oh." She looked quickly away, suddenly overwhelmed with such mixed feelings that they were difficult to sort out. Her first regret over a life lost gave way to great relief. Wilkes had seemed such a pompous, shallow man at times, and his threat back in Albany was no idle one. Yet he had helped her to be reunited with Alan. She could not be glad that he was dead, but she was thankful that he could not follow them now.

Beside her, Alan took a long swig from the canteen and wiped at his mouth with his sleeve. He had still not come to terms with all that had happened. He had hated Wilkes for so long, had thought of him as an evil, conniving villain for so many years, that it was hard to reconcile that image with the courageous man who had led the charge out onto that terrible field. Why had he done it? Simply to cheat Alan of the chance to stalk and kill him? Surely there had been other ways to get rid of that threat. And the truth was, Wilkes had tried none of them. He had never sent a search party out to track him down and jail or execute him — something Alan had fully expected him to do.

Was it possible that guilt over his actions so long ago had driven Wilkes to ride first into that line of fire? Had the man felt remorse over his past? Alan wiped at his eyes with his hand. If that was true, he had never given Wilkes the chance to express it. He had never *wanted* to give him that chance. He had only wanted a cold, merciless revenge.

He shivered, as if to throw off these useless thoughts. Wilkes was probably reacting in the only way a King's officer could react—by rushing into battle. At any rate, he was dead now, and Alan's long mission was over. Now it was time to think of the future. He reached his arm around Maud's shoulders and hugged her. What mattered now more than anything else, was getting her safely through these woods and back to civilization.

Maud had a sudden image of Molly, standing by the lake, staring out at the boats as they drew toward the shore. "And Ben? Do you know if he got safely back?"

"He made it through the first attack alongside Jeremy and me."

Jeremy lifted his head. "I was told he went back in one of the later ones, and was cut down at the abatis."

"Oh, poor Molly," Maud cried, burying her head in Alan's shoulder. All at once she was so happy to be here with Alan and Jeremy, and so glad to be away from armies and battles and war, that her joy constricted her chest, making her breathing difficult. The pain she felt for Molly only made more clear what she might be going through had Alan been killed.

Alan's arm tightened around her. "It's over now, and time to put it behind us. We've got a long way to go yet, before we can be sure that we're not being followed."

"Do you know where we're headed?" Maud asked, looking up at him.

"Yes. I learned something about this country when

we were at Albany. The Mohawk River cuts westward from the Hudson. If we strike west and then south, we should cross it somewhere close to Sir William Johnson's plantation. From there—after a suitable time to let things die down—we can make our way east to Boston."

It seemed a sensible plan. And it did not surprise Maud that Alan had thought it out so carefully. She looked over at Jeremy, who was sitting in a pool of moonlight with his arms resting on his legs and his head drooping. "Do you agree, Jeremy?"

He looked up and tried to give her his old, jaunty smile. "Oh, I'm agreeable to anything, as long as it gets me out of the army."

Alan handed the canteen to Jeremy. "Here, take a little of this. You look as though you still need it." He watched his friend, realizing that for him, Jeremy's safety was second only to Maud's. Indeed, it was more because of Jeremy than his own disillusionment that he felt it imperative that they escape from the army. Both Jeremy and Maud were now dependent on him, and he must, at all costs, bring them through these woods to a place where they could be cared for and safe.

"We'll rest here until daylight, and then take to the woods again. Jeremy and I brought along a few provisions from the camp, and we ought to be able to find food in the forest. I've never before seen such plentiful game anywhere."

Jeremy pulled up his haversack. "And I've a few turnips and an onion, to make what we catch palatable."

"You can't keep carrying that haversack," Alan said. "It will slow you down. Keep what you can and leave the rest."

"I've got a pocket under my skirt, Jeremy," Maud added. "I can carry some of the lighter things."

"All right, and I can put the rest in the tails of my tunic. It *will* make walking easier."

"Good," Alan said, getting to his feet. "Now, I think we should bed down for the rest of the night. A fire would be too risky, so we'll simply have to wrap ourselves in our army issue blankets. Thank God, it is not too cool. Do you think you can manage sleeping on the ground?" he asked, smiling down into Maud's upturned face, luminous in the golden moonlight.

Maud was beginning to catch their infectious sense of adventure. She laid her arm around Alan's waist, holding him tightly. "I'm so happy you're both alive and safe, that nothing else matters."

They started off the following morning, as soon as there was enough light to see their way. Even so, they soon found that once back under the thick canopy of the forest, it might as well have been midnight. Once the sun was up and the light stronger, it was still twilight under the trees. When, after an hour of walking, a flock of passenger pigeons flew overhead, the light was almost completely blocked by their thick numbers, and the trio had to wait until they had flown off before they could go on.

The forest was intimidating, but it had a mysterious beauty, Maud thought. Tangles of brush and young trees made them fight for every step. Trees that looked as though they had stood since the millennium wove their branches over them, and reached long tendrils to clutch at them as they passed. The floor was a matted tangle of leaves and dead branches, that dragged at their boots or at times created sudden bogs into which they slipped ankle deep.

Yet there was a wild joy in the riotous birds that were everywhere. They spotted a deer and her fawn frozen in place as they slipped by. Rabbits, chipmunks, raccoons, and numerous other small animals could be heard scampering through the underbrush at their approach. And occasionally the mournful howl of larger predators in the distance carried through the trees.

They stopped after an hour to eat a cold meal from the provisions Alan and Jeremy had brought along, washing it down with water from a wide, clear stream nearby. It was so lovely they lingered there awhile to rest, and to watch the busy life that centered around the water. By being very quiet and still, they could observe two beavers a little farther down building their high nest over the water. Otters scampered and played nearby. The fish were so thick, one could almost reach down and pluck them from the water. They were tempted to catch and eat some, but Alan felt they should not take the time to build a fire.

"I had no idea a forest could be so old and so rich in wildlife," Maud said quietly, as Alan shifted the haversack to his back again. "It's almost magical."

"It's a wondrous country, isn't it? Untouched for thousands of years," Jeremy said, dragging himself to his feet.

"It's certainly rich," Alan said. "Once people know just how rich, it won't stay this way long."

Maud picked up Jeremy's bandage, which she had rinsed and spread on the rock to dry. "I disagree. It's too rocky and full of trees to ever farm. No one would want it. I hope it stays wild like this forever." She moved to wrap the cloth around Jeremy's head, but he folded and shoved it into his haversack, which he had decided to keep.

"I don't need it anymore. The wound has long since stopped bleeding."

They moved back under the dark canopy of the

pines, going in single file with Alan in the lead. The terrain grew more difficult than ever, and Alan had to stop frequently to pull out his battered compass and try to determine whether they were still going west. At times Maud felt they must be dragging fifty pounds up the mountain, the ground rose so steeply. While it made it easier going down the other side, there was always another rise to climb again, and she began to grow very tired. She was relieved when she spotted a small clearing ahead over Alan's shoulder. Perhaps they could stop and rest . . .

A wild screaming erupted around them. Maud looked up quickly as a face materialized from the forest—a horrible face smeared with ochre, soot, and white paste. She had an impression of a wide, red mouth screaming at her, as a hatchet was raised over her head and her hair grabbed and twisted behind her. With a scream of sheer fright, she threw up her hands, which were gripped in an iron vise as she was shoved to her knees. She caught a glimpse of Alan ahead, first struggling and then overwhelmed by painted bodies jumping and yowling over him.

Indians! My God, how could they have forgotten . . .

Her head was shoved to the ground and her hands pinned behind her. "Dear Lord—" she cried, expecting the knife to slash at her scalp any second. Grimacing, her face thrust into the rotting leaves, her body tensed, she prayed, waiting for death.

Chapter Twenty

The screaming subsided into a wild babbling, issuing from the mouths of the dancing figures surrounding her. With her body tensed for the expected blow, Maud longed to cover her ears, but her hands were held fast. Then, suddenly, she was jerked to her feet, her arms thrown outward and lashed tightly to a long, curved wooden stick.

She glanced up to see Alan being dragged up in front of her, his outspread arms similarly bound. A tall, muscular Indian grabbed her hair and pulled her face around. He stared down at her with eyes blazing with hatred. Here was none of the vacant curiosity of the Iroquois, who had wandered into the camp at Fort Lyman. This face was contorted with malice and dark with anger. Her blood froze, as once again she waited for the expected blow.

The Indian released her hair and shoved her to stumble ahead of him across the clearing. He was obviously in command of the others, who, although they argued in their incomprehensible language with him, deferred to his decision. Otherwise, Maud suspected that they would be lying dead among the trees by now.

She stumbled along, still too frightened to realize how uncomfortable and strained were the bonds on her wrists. The long, awkward bow made it difficult to keep her balance, while the span of her arms drove her hands through the heavy brush on either side, where they were lacerated by thorns. The Indians moved in quick loping strides that she could not begin to match. Before they had traveled half an hour, she was not so much walking under her own power as she was being pushed and dragged. Yet there was no rest, as the savages did not ever seem to tire. At one point Alan tried to turn and speak some word of encouragement to her, but he was viciously clubbed by one of the braves and nearly fell. After that none of them tried to speak, but simply focused on keeping one foot in front of the other, until they were too numb and too weary to think. Maud was as conscious of Jeremy slogging behind her as she was of Alan in front, until she became too obsessed with trying simply to stay upright to notice.

They walked all the rest of that day, heading west, she thought. Her body was one long ache, when at last they pushed through the trees and into a wide expanse of open clearing bordering a stream. The clearing was filled with squat log houses, some of them quite long. They had rounded thatched roofs, and there were poles like scaffolds in front of them and circles of stones that framed a campfire. Maud's eyes were blurred with weariness and the quickly falling twilight, but she could make out women hurrying toward them, and children scurrying about. Smoke rose from the fires, and there was a smell of something delicious that hovered around the edges of other, oppressive odors.

Women, naked to their waists, surrounded them, poking at their chests and faces, howling with glee as they shoved the three of them toward one of the huts. The big Indian who had been the leader of the group that captured them spoke some angry words, and the women, still howling, shoved them inside and threw them on the ground. The bow that held her cramped arms made it impossible to lie down, so Maud struggled to a sitting position and sank back against one of the poles that supported the roof. It was a long time before she could open her eyes to see the two exhausted men nearby.

Alan was cursing quietly to himself. "How could I have thought we would walk these woods safely? I should have known better!" He glanced over at Maud, trying to focus her eyes on him, and his heart turned over. She looked so tired and so pitiful, and it was all his fault. He had wanted to take her where she would be safe, and instead he had landed them in this terrible, frightening situation, where they were all likely to be killed. He pulled at the tight ropes that bound his wrists to the bow, but they would not give way. He could not even comfort her, he thought bitterly.

Jeremy groaned and shifted position. "Isn't this Mohawk territory? I thought they were the friends of the English."

"They are the friends of Sir William Johnson. Not all the Iroquois tribes agree with their sachems. Many waver between the French and English. This could be a rebel group. Or, after that debacle at Fort Carillon, this could mean the Mohawk have switched their loyalty to New France. What *is* obvious is that they don't like us!"

"What will they do to us?" Maud said quietly. She really wasn't anxious to know, yet perhaps, she thought, if she was prepared, she would be better able to handle it.

"I don't know," Alan answered. He had a pretty good idea, but he did not want to share it with Maud. When they had been dragged into the village, one of the first things he noticed were the two stakes at the end of the long row of huts. He knew how they were used, from the stories the soldiers had told back at camp. Burning at those stakes would be preferable to being boiled alive, or, even worse, forced to watch and then eat the flesh of the others. He had been told that was the custom among these savages.

A shudder went through his body. No, he would never let that happen to Maud. He would kill her himself, before he would let them touch her.

"I'm so thirsty," Maud moaned. Her head drooped and fell on her breast as she lost consciousness. Alan was glad to see it. It was likely to be the only peace she would have during the next hours. He shuffled along on the ground until he was near her, and touched her leg with his. He had never loved her so much, or felt so helpless to care for her. His anger at himself was overwhelming. She was going to die, and it was all because of his shortsightedness!

Yet his anger gave him renewed strength. There must be something he could do to save her. That had to be some way to get them out of this.

He looked over to see Jeremy staring at the ground in utter dejection. When he glanced up to catch Alan watching him, he tried to smile. "This may be the end of the road, old friend," Jeremy said quietly. "I'm sorry it had to be this way. Especially for Maud."

"Don't give up so easily," Alan snapped back. "There must be something we can do. Think, think!"

Jeremy looked toward the door of the hut; the howling outside had increased. Through the open door he could see the natives streaming by, heading toward the far end of the village. "I'm afraid they hold all the cards."

Alan yanked harder at the thongs binding his wrists. "Perhaps so, but we're smarter. We've got to think of a way out of this."

Jeremy's head drooped from exhaustion. The long walk—on top of the wound he had suffered at Fort Carillon—had drained him of all strength. "Right now, I think it is time for a *deus ex machina*," he said with a sigh.

Alan gave a bitter laugh. "I'm afraid it is only in plays that God intervenes to make everything right. Too bad you're not a real magician, though."

"Yes. We could use a little magic right now." Jeremy's head slumped forward as he, too, lost consciousness.

Alan leaned his head back and closed his eyes, wishing he could be granted the blessing of sleep. But he was too worried and angry with himself for that. For the first time in many years, he began to pray.

Whether it was due to the intervention of the gods, or to simple good luck, Alan never knew, but shortly afterward two Indian women appeared at the door of the hut. One bent to cut the thongs at their wrists, while the other laid a bowl of some kind of corn mush and a jug of water on the ground near the door.

Alan watched them warily, until they moved back outside the hut and sat down in front of the opening, peering inside. Then, after rubbing his numb wrists, he scrambled closer to Maud and cradled her in his arms.

"Maud, love . . . are you all right? Wake up. Here, take a little sip of water." It might be poisoned for all he knew, but he suspected it was not. They would not want to be deprived of their fun. Already he could hear the drums beginning and the howling increasing near those dreadful posts. He smoothed the long strands of hair from her forehead, and dribbled some of the water on her lips. Choking, she awoke, saw what it was, and drank greedily.

"That's better. Not too much at once, though."

Maud moved her cramped arms tentatively. Relief that she was no longer tied to the bow swept over her, and she turned to bury her face against Alan's chest. His aching arms closed tightly around her, and she clung to him. The thought flitted through her brain that perhaps they were already dead, but she quickly realized by the sound of the drums in the distance that the worst was still to come.

"My love," Alan murmured against her hair. "I'm so sorry I got you into this."

She smiled and reached up to lay her palm against his cheek. "As long as I'm with you, I can bear anything," she murmured.

Alan kissed her damp forehead. "They've brought food. Can you take a little?"

Across from them Jeremy stirred as consciousness returned. "Food?" he muttered. "Did you really say food?"

"Yes." Alan pushed the bowl toward him. "It doesn't look very palatable, but take some anyway. It will help give you back your strength."

"But why?" Maud asked quietly. "Why feed us, if they intend to kill us?"

"I don't know." Perhaps they want to fatten us up, he thought to himself. "Just be glad."

As he drank some of the water, he noticed the women had moved away from the door of their hut. On all fours he began to make a circle of the place, and quickly determined that there was no way of escaping without being seen. The door opened onto the main alleyway down the middle of the village, and to get out any other side meant they would have to dig underneath the logs. No wonder the Indians had released their bounds.

He worked his way back to Maud, who was looking a little livelier. "If only they hadn't taken our coats," he said more to himself than the others. "We have no supplies and no weapons. Nothing to work with."

Jeremy looked up from the bowl of mush he was

scooping out with his hands. "Wait a moment. Maud, do you still have your pocket?"

"The one underneath my skirt. Yes. They didn't know it was there."

She reached up underneath her skirt to touch the tape that was tied around her waist. Attached to it was a large linen pouch. "It still has the things you put inside."

Alan's eyes flared with the first signs of hope since they were captured. "Let's see it," he said eagerly.

She opened the pouch and spread the contents on the ground. Alan could barely hide his disappointment. "There's not much to work with here. Ecod, Jeremy, what did you save all this useless stuff for?"

Jeremy handed the bowl to Maud and limped over to run his fingers over the few items on the ground. "I'd rather go without my clothes than the bits and pieces of my trade," he murmured absently.

There was half an onion, several threadbare handkerchiefs, a small black cloth wrapped tightly and tied with a string, a large silver half-joe and four smaller brass coins, a set of cups that nested inside each other, three cork balls, and a loop of thin strands of hair. A twist of thin rope and a long piece of ribbon completed the collection.

When Alan heard the soft swish of moccasins outside the door, he spoke a warning to Jeremy, who quickly grabbed up the contents of the bag and thrust them inside his boots. By the time the Indian women bent to enter the hut, both men were leaning over the bowl of mush, eating with relish.

The antagonism of the women could almost be felt. Grabbing up the bowl and jug of water, they hurried out, obviously delighted to leave them still hungry. Maud was so tired, she hardly cared. As long as she could rest in Alan's comforting arms, she could bear the hunger and thirst. The fear was more difficult, but even that was eased by having him nearby.

All the same, it promised to be a terrible night. The noise of the pounding drums grew louder, and the howling of the Indians more frenzied as the long hours wore on. It was made even worse by the fact that they could not see what was happening outside. Every time they ventured near the door, a painted face would glare back.

The three of them stayed close together during the night, wondering what the morning would bring, and why they had not yet been hauled out to the stakes. They talked quietly and slept fitfully during the long darkness, trying to think of a way to escape, trying to give each other courage to face the morning, trying to say goodbye.

"I think I could bear anything, if I didn't know it was my fault that you both have to suffer," Alan said over and over.

"You did not drag us here, you know," Maud tried to comfort him. "I came willingly, and so did Jeremy. Besides, what is past, is past. We have to help and support each other now."

At last the morning came, bringing with it a blessed quieting of the drums. Just after dawn, a bowl of corn mush was thrust at them, and afterwards Maud finally fell into a deep sleep. She was wakened from it by rough hands hauling her to her feet.

Judging from the light outside the door, it had to be nearly noon. There were no women this time. Instead, several young men, wearing painted swatches of color on their chests, streamed inside the hut, yanking the three of them to their feet and pinning their arms behind their backs.

Maud looked fearfully over her shoulder at Alan. He held her eyes with his forceful gaze, trying to calm the terror he saw there with his own strength. "Courage, love," he murmured, as he was shoved toward the door.

Maud and Jeremy were thrust after him to stand outside, blinking in the strong light. Maud looked down the long open space between the log huts to the end, where the blackened stakes jutted up from the earth. With a sinking heart, she saw that bunches of jagged branches, tied in bundles, had been piled around them. Fear rose like bile in her throat, but she choked it down. She would not give these savages the satisfaction of hearing her cry out.

The women appeared. One of them jerked Maud's arms in front of her and tied her wrists tightly with a thong, leaving a dangling length of about four feet. Maud focused on Alan's hard gaze. "I love you," she said quietly, thinking that if those were to be her last words, they were the most she would want to say.

Another woman stepped up to grab the end of the rope, and began pulling Maud down the empty row. She stumbled as she was yanked forward, and it was a moment before she realized that they were leading her away from the stakes and toward the forest. She twisted around, looking back over her shoulder, and saw that Alan and Jeremy were being shoved in the opposite direction, toward those terrible posts.

"No!" she screamed. She had steeled herself to face death beside Alan, but the thought that one of them might die without the other, drove her to desperation. She tried to dig her heels in the soft dirt, struggling against the rope and making the women tug at it harder. "Alan, I want to die with you! Don't let them take me away—"

"Maud!" he cried, sickened as he realized she was being led away from him. He struggled against the tight bonds, trying to dodge around the Indians to run back. The men only bore down harder, striking him with a long stick and twisting the thongs around his arms. He had a glimpse of Jeremy's white face against their dark skin, as he struggled to look back over his shoulder. Maud's screams grew louder and more desperate. Alan was filled with utter desolation. She needed him, and there was nothing he could do to help her. This was the end result of his arrogance in leaving the camp and taking her with him. He and Jeremy would die horribly, and Maud—God knows what kind of a life she would face. Slavery, forced to become the concubine of some primitive savage, beaten and abused by the Indian women . . . all the stories he had ever heard about captive white women came roaring back.

Her cries rent the pristine morning air. Tears burned behind his eyes, too, as he was shoved again and went stumbling toward the other end of the village.

"Maud . . . I love you! Never forget!" he shouted, twisting around. "Never forget!"

He hoped she could hear him. He had no other comfort to give her.

Alan had lost all sense that he was being prodded toward the stake, until he was thrown against it and his hands were tied behind the back. The Indian women began energetically piling more bundles of loosely tied branches in a wide circle around him, carefully leaving a narrow path through the center. He looked frantically around for Jeremy, and saw that he was standing to one side with his feet fastened by a length of rope to a slim tree.

The rawhide thongs that tied his hands bit into Alan's wrists, as he struggled against them. They felt damp, and he knew that once they began to dry they would shrink, drawing them even tighter. He had no doubts that these savages intended to make his death as slow and painful as possible.

One of the Indians came striding toward him to stand with his arms crossed over his chest, looking him up and down. There was utter contempt on his otherwise impassive face, and Alan was debating whether or not to spit into it, when Jeremy's voice warned him not to do anything rash. Not yet at least.

The Indian poked at Alan's chest with a long brown finger. "English!" he said.

"Scot!" Alan snapped back.

The Indian jabbed his finger at his own bare, painted chest. "Straight Arrow."

"The chief," Jeremy said in a stage whisper just loud enough for Alan to hear. "Try to be impressed."

Fighting down his anger, Alan noted the strong face, deeply set, hostile eyes, and long nose. Straight Arrow was impressive all right. He stood over six feet and was ramrod straight. He looked hard as flint, but his eyes suggested a shrewd intelligence.

"Any chance he can change their minds about burning me?" he said in an aside to Jeremy.

"Probably not, but it's worth a try."

Alan looked directly into the chief's impassive face. "Straight Arrow is a great chief. His fame is spoken for many miles."

There was just the slightest glimmer of a smile on those frozen lips. Thank God he knows some English, Alan thought.

"You English," the chief said again, poking his finger toward Alan's chest. "You die."

"Not English. Scot! Straight Arrow's friend!" God, what a foolish way to talk, he thought to himself. He had seen enough plays about savages to know that this was the way they were supposed to speak, and it was amazing to find that they really did.

Straight Arrow's eyes narrowed. "You fight with

English at Ticonderoga. You enemy."

"Ticonderoga is the Indian name for Fort Carillon," Jeremy whispered from the side.

"Yes, but the English not fight very well. I leave."

Straight Arrow appeared to think this over. "You fight with Great Father in France now?"

"Oh God, Jeremy, do I have to answer that?"

"Tell him yes."

Alan nodded. "I fight with Great Father in France."

The chief looked at him for a long moment. In the silence, Alan began to hope that perhaps there might be the slightest chance for a reprieve. Then all at once another Indian came bounding up, leaping around the chief. He wore a bear's head on top of his own, with the open mouth stretched wide to reveal sharp teeth. There were birds' wings stretching from the back of his head to either side. The mask had dried and shriveled, and the face below it appeared the same. The old Indian shook a long club wrapped with a dried rattlesnake in one hand, thrusting it at Alan's face.

"The shaman," Jeremy cried. "He isn't going to let you get off so easily."

The witch doctor jumped around the stake, shouting and babbling. Behind him the drums took up the rhythm, as the rest of the tribe began chanting and pounding their feet on the earth.

Bounding back to the outer circle, the shaman grabbed a large basket cage made of woven branches, and rushed back to thrust it at Alan's face. Alan was almost afraid to look at what lay inside, until he saw that it was a large black crow, its blue-black feathers glistening in the light. As the drumming and the chanting began to swell, he looked frantically over at Jeremy, then back at Straight Arrow who had not moved from in front of him.

"My death will anger the spirits against you," he

shouted into the chief's face. The Indian thought for a moment, then raised his hand. Immediately the noise stopped.

In the silence Alan spoke quickly. "I have the ear of the Spirits. Anger them and you will pay dearly."

It was difficult to tell if the man could even understand him. Yet the dead quiet was in Alan's favor. Now, if only Jeremy would take advantage of it!

The crow flapped its wings in the cage and began to speak.

"Caw . . . caw . . . aw . . . Straight Arrow . . . caw . . . caw. *Na'e!* Listen to Scot. Great magic."

There was a stir among the Indians. The shaman looked at the cage, then bent to peer closer.

"Speak, great bird," Alan said in as firm a voice as he could muster. "Tell this great chief of my power." And pray Jeremy has learned a little Mohawk!

Jeremy had learned just enough to throw in a few key Indian words, as the bird flapped and cawed and spoke to the chief. After a moment it began to have an effect. Straight Arrow glanced anxiously at his shaman and stepped back. On the far side of the circle, the others began a low moan of awe and terror.

The shaman was not impressed. He peered around, trying to see where the sound was coming from, then shook his rattlesnake at the cage and gave several angry incantations over it.

Take advantage of the chief's incredulity, Alan thought, and spoke directly to Straight Arrow: "My magic is very great. I make this great bird speak. I can make the forest speak as well."

A hushed silence fell over the crowd as a thin, wailing cry seemed to come out of the trees behind Jeremy. *"Ne sga't* Hawennio, the Great Spirit speaks. Listen to Scot . . ."

Never had Alan been so thankful for Jeremy's talent in throwing his voice. The eerie sounds seemed to float on the wind out of the darkened forest, rising and falling in such a way as to make the hairs on the back of his neck stand up. It was even beginning to effect Straight Arrow, who looked around with growing apprehension.

"Hawennio is God," Jeremy whispered to Alan.

"Na'e, na'e . . ." screamed the shaman. "Otgon . . ."

Straight Arrow looked from his shaman back to Alan. "Otgon . . . the evil one."

The witch doctor glared at Alan from beneath the shriveled mask, shaking his feathers as he danced angrily up and down. He knew there was a trick involved, but he could not yet figure out what it was or who was doing it. He began to rattle off incantations at the Chief, who had backed away from the stake to stand outside the bundles of faggots. Straight Arrow was trying hard not to be impressed, but finding it difficult.

"Sioto, my shaman, say your magic evil," he exclaimed, once the witch doctor had calmed down.

"Sioto lies," Alan replied, as the shaman again began shaking his stick.

"Sioto say his magic greater than Scot magic."

"The Great Spirit has given me much wisdom. Sioto's magic is of Otgon, the evil one." And pray he got the name right.

The shaman leaped up and down, howling his protest until Straight Arrow lifted his hand and brought him to a stop. Wise as he was and brave as he was, the chief was obviously wary of dealing carelessly with powerful spirits. He mulled the matter over a moment, then made his decision, gesturing toward the women who began keening their high-pitched cries as they piled more bundles of faggots around the stake.

"A challenge!" Alan yelled over the women's eager cries. The chief heard and raised his hand for silence again.

"I make Sioto a challenge. His magic against Scot magic. We shall see who has been given the power of Hawennio!"

Although Straight Arrow hesitated, this was just the kind of game he loved. It would be an amusing diversion, and if the Scot lost, his people would still have the pleasure of flaying and burning him. On the other hand, old Sioto had grown almost too arrogant of late, and it would be very satisfying to see him humiliated. He glared at the shaman. "You agree?" he asked in his own language.

The old man gave his grimace of a smile. "I will strip away their feeble powers and destroy them," he answered.

Straight Arrow looked at Alan and nodded. Two of the women rushed to untie Alan's hands, but he called to the chief to stop them.

"I do not need my hands for my magic," he announced. "Bring my friend to me. I shall convey all my power through him."

Jeremy opened his mouth to protest, until he saw that the chief was impressed. The women loosened the ropes on his ankles, and he hurried over to stand next to Alan.

"I hope you know what you're doing," he muttered.

"I'll be in a trance. They love that. And you'd better use every sleight of hand trick you've ever learned!"

"Wouldn't it be better to be untied, so we could make a run for it if we got the chance?"

"We'd never make it. Our only hope lies in your talents, my friend."

Jeremy's eyes glinted with growing enthusiasm at the challenge. "It will be a pleasure to get the best of that old horror of a shaman. We'll use the coins first."

Alan threw back his head and began to mutter, quietly at first, then raising his voice to a roar: *Hocus-pocus, ledgermain, Pinetti Sciatorium, Palingensia.*" When he ran out of familiar magician's terms, he began adding every nonsense word he had learned in his years of acting. After he worked himself up sufficiently, his head lolled to one side, his eyes closed, and his body grew rigid. "Now," he whispered. Jeremy stepped toward the chief and drew a coin from his ear, then from under his moccasins and out of his nose. He made the silver half-joe appear and disappear, until he had every eye focused avidly on him. He finished by having the crow chirp off several more sentences, then pour a stream of coins from its beak. Afterward he calmly walked back to stand beside Alan, who slowly roused himself from his trance.

"How did we do?" he whispered.

"They loved me! Look at Sioto's face."

It was the shaman's turn now. He began leaping about and shaking a new rattle made from a turtle shell. With great aplomb, he stopped, pulled out a long arrow, took careful aim, and threw it at the naked chest of a young man standing ten feet away. A long streak of red seeped out from underneath the arrow, which was clutched in the young man's hands. He pulled it away, laughed, and brandished it above his head.

"The old trick arrow," Jeremy muttered. "It slides within itself. I didn't think Indians knew about it."

"What's next?" Alan muttered.

"Let's try the rope."

As Sioto beamed and crowed, Alan threw himself back into his trance, drawing it out even longer and keeping everyone's gaze on him, while Jeremy drew the long piece of rope Maud had carried from his sleeve. He took it in his dextrous hands, had the Chief chop it in two with his knife, then astounded the crowd by making it whole again. The success of this trick, which had been used by street performers since the fifteenth century, sent old Sioto into paroxysms of rage. Calling forward another of his assistants, the shaman danced around him, displaying a stone as big as a man's fist. Moving several feet away, he made a great sweep of his arm and threw the stone at his assistant's face. The man fell to the ground and groveled in agony, until Sioto came running up to him with a basin, into which the man coughed out four small stones.

The crowd laughed and stomped their moccasins in approval.

"This old goat could play Drury Lane," Jeremy muttered under his breath.

Alan felt a stirring of despair. He thought of Maud being led away, and his heart turned over. How would he ever be able to save her, if he and Jeremy could not save themselves?

"He's better than I thought he would be. What's next?"

"Go back in your trance," Jeremy said, with a defiant grin on his lips. Alan threw himself into another series of babbling, jerked his body against the stake, then allowed his head to loll forward. Opening his eyes just enough to see, he watched as Jeremy pulled apart a handkerchief, then put it back together; laid out the three cups and moved them around so quickly they appeared to be fifty; threw a cork ball into the woods and then found it again under Sioto's arm. When he had the wide-eyed crowd sufficiently dazzled, he took three sticks, ordered that they be thrust into the fire but quickly extinguished. Then, using the powder impregnated in a strand of the rope, he magically fired them again, and proceeded to juggle the flaming tapers for a full minute. Even Alan was impressed.

Alan came out of his trance, as Jeremy moved back to his side. "That was worthy of the great

Piretti," he murmured.

"Sioto is about to have a stroke. Look at the way he's babbling at the Chief."

"I don't trust either one of them. We're not out of this yet, my friend. Do you have any wonders left?"

Jeremy gave him his old jaunty grin. "Why, Mister Desmond, after all these years, you must know me better than that. What do you think I was doing last night, while you were comforting Maud?" He waved one of the cork balls in his lithe fingers, and it disappeared up his sleeve. "Why, I'm just getting started!"

Maud had no idea how long they had been traveling. Time seemed to have stopped forever for her. Hour after hour she continued to force one foot in front of the other, not even aware of how tired she was, because of the weight of sorrow that lay on her heart. She pushed the thought of what Alan and Jeremy must be enduring from her mind. She tried not to dwell on the future, and the hopelessness of it. What were the stories she had heard about white women, who had become captives of savage tribes? Forced to become little more than slaves; made to marry or become the mistresses of savages and even bear their half-breed children; never accepted by the Indians and forever alone!

And with no hope of rescue. Who even knew she was gone? Who would care? Perhaps General Wilkes might have been concerned, but he was dead. Without Alan or Jeremy, she was utterly lost and abandoned.

It was dark by the time they reached another village. They had walked all day with only brief stops. Twice she had been allowed to drink from a creek when they stopped to rest, but she had been given no food. She was light-headed from hunger, and too tired to care.

The village seemed much like the one she had left that morning—a long row of log huts with thatched, cone-shaped roofs and a wide, open space dotted with campfires and low wooden frames. From the acrid smell, she decided the objects dangling from the frames must be hunks of meat.

They led her to the longest of the huts and left her outside to be eyed curiously by several naked children, while her captors bent to enter the door. She was swaying on her feet, when they reappeared, grabbed her arms, and dragged her through the low opening.

The small fire burning in the center of the hut made a tiny circle of light surrounded by deep darkness. The room was stifling hot, and heavy with offensive odors of grease and human sweat. Several figures sat in a semicircle around the fire, their faces lost in the dim light.

Maud's eyes blurred as she looked around at them. With a kind of detached indifference, she watched as one of the figures rose, separated itself from the circle, and moved toward her. She caught her breath, waiting for only God knew what.

A familiar voice, melodious and low, spoke her name. She looked up into a face bending toward her, smiling.

"Good evening, Mademoiselle Maud. We meet again. Did I not promise you we would?"

Maud blinked her eyes, trying to clear them to make out the familiar features on the long face before her. Her knees gave way and her eyes closed, as she fainted dead away into the arms of the Chevalier Hippolyte de Prevaloir.

Chapter Twenty-one

When she opened her eyes, there was no one else in the hut except the Frenchman, who was cradling her head in his arms and attempting to put a wooden cup to her lips.

"Drink a little of this, Mademoiselle. You look exhausted."

Maud pushed his hand away. "What is it?"

"It's only a little wine. I carry it with me. Not even the water is safe to drink in these savage villages."

She struggled to sit up. "I don't understand. Why are you here? How did you get here? Nothing makes any sense."

Prevaloir sat back, resting his elbows on his knees and lacing his long fingers together. "It has been a shock for you, no? Yet it is not so strange. I am the most amazed for seeing you here. When I heard a white woman with golden hair and traveling with two English had been captured, I never dared to hope it was you. When I heard the two men were with the army, my hopes perhaps rose a little. But when you walked into this hut, *mon dieu*, I was overcome."

Maud pushed a long strand of hair away from her forehead, and turned away from Prevaloir. Her mind was a jumble of conflicting thoughts. She was relieved to be with one of her own kind and out of the clutches of the Indians, yet she remembered all too well the last time she had been with this man. It did not reassure her. "My friends . . . ?"

"I am afraid there is no hope for them. You would have shared their fate, but for the fact that I learned of your capture and wished to rescue you."

"What will they do to them?"

Prevaloir flicked at the wide cuff on his sleeve. "In the end they will be burned alive. Before that, they will endure as much agony as can be inflicted without actually causing death. It is the way of the Indian."

The tears began to run down Maud's cheeks. "So cruel . . ." she said, choking as she tried to brush them away.

"To us, perhaps. You must remember the Indian sees endurance of pain as an act of great bravery. The more one can endure without crying out, the braver one is considered. They expect such trials when they are the victim, and naturally they enjoy putting other victims to the same test."

"Alan . . ." It was barely a whisper.

"I think perhaps you had better forget about Monsieur Desmond. Think instead of the fact that you are now here under my protection. Without me, you surely would have become the slave of one of these Mohawk warriors, and I can assure you, you would probably never see civilization again."

His voice was testy, as though she did not appreciate her good fortune. Maud looked at him warily. "And with you?"

One eyebrow climbed upward. He, too, was remembering that scene in the garden in Bristol. "I am not a savage, Mademoiselle. I have made no secret of the fact that I have a *tendré* for you. But you have been through a great ordeal, and need time to recover. My friends and I are about to leave these forests for the pleasures of Montreal. You shall accompany me and . . . well, we shall see . . . Now, you must drink some of this wine and take a little food for the journey. It will not be an easy one."

Maud took the cup he offered her and raised it to her lips. She could feel the searing wine all the way down as she drank, yet it did seem to revive her strength. She was going to need that strength, she knew, not only to make the trip out of the wilderness, but also to figure out what kind of a future, if any, lay ahead for her in New France.

At least she would not have to worry about Prevaloir for a few days.

That night she was left alone to fall into a heavy sleep, from which she was awakened before dawn. To her relief she was given a horse to ride alongside Prevaloir and another Frenchman. For the first time she realized that Hippolyte was wearing a uniform, as was his companion. There were two other men along, rough fellows in fringed leather leggings and shirts and fur caps, and two Indians. The trappers, she learned, were *coureurs de bois,* French Canadian woodsmen, while the Indians were traveling to the nearest trading post to bring back goods for the tribe.

They reached the trading post before evening and spent the night there, before embarking in canoes the next day for the long journey by water to Montreal. It took several days to make the trip, stopping at night at various small trading posts and forts along the way. She was relieved that the men treated her generally with respect, and even Prevaloir — except for the long, hungry looks he gave her — left her alone with her thoughts.

Those thoughts were terrible in their grief and misery. By now the terrible suffering Alan and Jeremy had been forced to endure must be over, though that was little comfort when she thought about never seeing them again. She tried to push such thoughts from her mind, and retain a numbness that would keep grief at bay. For the most part, she succeded.

However, she could not refrain from scathingly pointing out the Chevalier's uniform.

"You never mentioned you were in the French Army back in England. Did you conveniently forget?"

"I did not think that information would be well received."

"You mean, it would have kept you from mixing among people who trusted you. What wonderful information you must have picked up from those you duped, like General Wilkes."

"Bah. He was an idiot. But there were many others who casually mentioned significant information. You English are very open, you know. And gullible. It was easy."

"Perhaps we expect people to show a little more honor in their dealings. You were nothing but a common spy!"

"I do not consider myself common, Mademoiselle. I served my King in as useful a fashion as possible. When that usefulness was over, I sailed to New France to serve in another way."

"What happened? Were they beginning to recognize your little game?"

He shrugged. "A spy's usefulness is always temporary. I grew tired of the game."

His cavalier manner only made her distrust him all the more, even if he had rescued her from the Mohawks. When, at last, the great, flat mountain looming over Montreal finally came into view, she could not be exactly happy, but she was relieved to think she would finally be leaving the boats. And perhaps, when she was living in a real town, she would find it easier to see less of Monsieur de Prevaloir.

* * *

To her great disappointment, she soon learned that she was not going to be allowed to go into the town of Montreal. Instead she was taken straight to a small scow berthed on the river below the town, and locked in a tiny cabin. For the first time she began to feel like a prisoner of the French, and especially of Prevaloir, who made no secret of the fact that this shabby treatment was by his direct order.

She sat on the narrow plank that served as a cabin bed, and thought fearfully that if he came after her in this small, confined space, she would find some way to kill herself, if not him. The pain of Alan's death was still so strong that at times she felt as though she did not want to live anyway. She was looking around the cabin for something she could use as a weapon, when she felt the boat begin to move. She rushed to the one small window where she could see the green forested shore opposite the town slipping by. But where could they be going? As far as she knew, there was nothing to the north but more wilderness.

With nightfall the cabin grew very dark, since she had no candle. She lay down on the cot and finally slept, lulled by the motion of the boat, the creak of the timbers, and the quiet of her little room. She woke to sunlight streaming through the window, laying silver patterns on the floor. The quiet motion of the cabin told her that the boat was moored once again.

Maud splashed some water on her face, tried to smooth her dress and rebraid her long hair. When she heard a key in the door, she stood with her back to the wall, almost afraid to see who would enter.

A boyish sailor with a long greased pigtail down his back walked inside. *"Bon jour,* Mademoiselle," he said, dragging off his cap. "I bring you some breakfast, *oui?*"

"*Oui*," Maud muttered. He reached through the doorway to lift a small tray and place it on the table.

"You eat, then I take mademoiselle ashore."

"Ashore? Where?"

"To ze town."

Maud moved to the table and reached for a cup of steaming broth, lifting it to her lips. "What town? I did not think there were any other towns in New France except Montreal."

The boy smiled at her naivete. "Quebec, Mademoiselle. Ze town is Quebec."

Quebec. She vaguely remembered hearing the name mentioned by the soldiers on the long trek to Lake George. At least he had called it a town. That was encouraging. She gulped down her food while the sailor waited, then climbed the ladder to the upper deck, her jailor right behind her.

Quebec appeared to be a huge rock. From a small collection of houses at its base, a great cliff wall rose upward, with more spires and roofs at its summit. Along the wharf there were warehouses flanking the river, and many ships of various shapes and sizes moored as far as she could see in either direction. It was a town, but it was also a fortress.

Eagerly she climbed down the rope ladder to a waiting longboat. In a few minutes of rowing, she was brought to a stone quay, helped up a short flight of steps, and deposited on a jetty flanking the wharf. Her hopes that she would be allowed to roam free were quickly dashed, when two soldiers wearing the white uniforms of the French army stepped up beside her.

"Mademoiselle Makejoy. Come with us, please," one of them said in perfect English while taking her elbow.

387

Maud tried to pull away. "Where are you taking me? Let me go!"

"The Chevalier de Prevaloir has ordered us to escort you to a safe lodging. You will come without making a scene. It would be better for everyone."

Maud glared at the man, but could see no way out. And since she knew nothing of this strange town, perhaps it would be wiser to do as he said until she could see for herself if there was going to be any possibility of escape.

She expected to be taken to the top of the cliff, but instead was led through a maze of narrow streets at its base. This section, which the ensign told her was the older part of the town, was larger than it looked from the river. The streets near the river were lined with large warehouses, but farther in, they were fronted by rows of neat houses, three and four flights tall, whose windows gave glimpses of elegant rooms within.

They quickly reached a small square, fronted on one end with a plain church whose spire Maud had seen from the deck of the scow. There were a few stalls around the edges which suggested this was a popular marketplace. More prominent, however, was a very large pillory, much stained by the remains of garbage thrown at its hapless victims. To Maud's relief it was empty.

At the opposite end of the square, facing the church, stood a stone building with a *Pension* sign over the door. Maud remembered enough French from the plays in which she had performed to recognize that it was a hotel, a very shabby one judging from the plain, deteriorating entranceway into which she was led.

An old man in a linen smock and a grizzled wig came bustling out of a door behind the counter, and exchanged several sentences in French with the ensign who still gripped her elbow. The old man then led them up a narrow flight of stairs to an upper floor, and along a dark corridor to a room at the end. Taking out a ring of very large keys, he opened the door while the ensign stood back and motioned her to enter.

Maud pulled back, outraged at being little more than a prisoner, and growing more frightened by the moment.

"Mademoiselle will please to enter," the soldier said, propelling her forward by her arm.

"This is outrageous! I am an English citizen. You have no right—"

The door was slammed on her protests. She heard the ominous metal ring of the key turning, even as she grabbed for the handle, pushing and pulling on it.

"Open this door!" Maud yelled. "You can't do this to me! I am a citizen of the British empire—"

"Tell your King George," came the muffled voice on the other side of the door.

She could hear the tramp of the soldier's boots as they walked back down the corridor, and the soft chuckling of the landlord. She kicked wildly at the door, but only succeeded in bruising her toe, then began searching around the room for any possible means of escape.

It was a small room and very clean. The bed was little more than a straw mattress over tightly laced ropes on a frame, but it was covered with a spotless white coverlet. There was a woven mat on the floor, and a stand with a bowl and pitcher against one wall. Its best asset was a large window that looked out on to the square, and was framed with blue linen curtains which could be pulled across for privacy. Maud knelt on the wide wooden seat below the sash, and began inspecting the window. If she lifted the sash higher, she might just be able to squeeze through, she thought, but when she began tugging at the sash she realized it had been fastened tightly. It was also high off the ground, and one glance below revealed a French soldier standing guard near the door to the hotel. She slumped on the window seat, as she realized how difficult it was going to be to escape from this place. Of course, a lot depended on how long they intended to hold her here, and she had no way of knowing that.

The day dragged on. Maud kept her fear at bay and herself somewhat amused by watching the activity on the square. As the morning wore on, it filled with people coming and going. There were often little sideshows, as when a juggler set up on one corner and a musician with a monkey on a chain on the opposite one. The pillory was in use for nearly two hours, much to the amusement of the housewives in their aprons and caps, and the children who threw stones and rotten food at its hapless occupant.

There were so many people moving about the square, that at times she almost forgot her own predicament. Mostly they appeared to be farmers and their wives. Yet among them wandered priests in their long black cassocks, nuns in flaring white hoods, uniformed soldiers, woodsmen in fringed leather shirts, an occasional Indian with feathers tied to his scalp lock, and, now and then, an elegant lady in a satin dress with wide hoops and a lace shawl over her tall wig, fussed over by pages and footmen and with a demure maid following behind.

At noon the old man brought her a tray of food, opening the door just long enough to reveal another soldier standing outside. The French military must not have much to do with fighting this war, Maud thought, if they could detail two men to prevent her escape. Yet she was disappointed, for she had decided her best hope of getting out would be when someone opened the door to bring her a meal.

Late in the afternoon she heard a commotion in the corridor outside her room. The key turned in the lock, and Hippolyte de Prevaloir walked inside, closing the door firmly behind him. Maud rose from the window seat and glared at him across the room.

"How dare you keep me a prisoner here!"

His thin lips lifted in a humorless smile. "Have you been mistreated?"

"I am locked in this room, guarded by soldiers! It's an outrage. I am a free citizen of Great Britain. How dare you treat me this way!"

Prevaloir made a clucking noise with his tongue and drew out a handkerchief from the cuff of his sleeve, flipping it and touching it to the jutting, knifelike point of his nose and the thin line of his moustache.

"I remind you, Mademoiselle Maud, you are not in England now. You are in New France, and our two countries are at war with one another. That makes you my prisoner, no?"

"I came to you in good faith—"

"You were sent to me by Chief Straight Arrow at my request, and with great reluctance since he wished you to be given to one of his warriors as a reward. Must I remind you again, that your circumstances would be very different right now had that happened?"

Maud looked away, somewhat shamed to remember the awful fate from which this man had delivered her. Yet that did not justify her being held a prisoner. "It seems I exchanged one jailer for another," she said bitterly.

Prevaloir walked across the room to stand near her. Casually he reached up to pull the curtains across the window. "The term jailer wounds me deeply. It is my dearest hope that we can be friends."

Maud moved around to the other side of the bed. "Friendship is not forced. Friends do not lock one another up."

With the drapes across the window, the room took on a twilight dimness. The Frenchman turned back to her, casually following her across the room to take her hand and raise her fingers to his lips. "Perhaps friend was too vague a word. What I wish from you, my dear Maud, involves a good deal more than friendship."

Maud looked frantically around the small room. There was nowhere to go, no place to run. She was trapped alone with this man, whom, she knew, was there to take her, willingly or by force. She yanked her hand away and tried to slip around him, but he pushed her back against the wall, pressing her against it with his hard body. Fear welled up within her, choking her throat. "I've told you, Monsieur, I do not want this—"

He dropped his head to nuzzle her neck with his wet lips. Cringing, she shrank from him and tried to shove him away. Gripping one of her wrists, he pressed her arm against the wall. His other hand wove its way up her waist to fondle her breast.

"Let me go!" Maud cried, struggling against him.

"Don't fight me, my little Maud," Prevaloir murmured against her neck. "Relax and be easy. I can be a very persuasive lover, if you will only allow me."

"I don't want a lover, and especially not you! I love someone else."

He lifted his head, and for the first time his cold, hard eyes took on the frost of agate. "There is nothing left of that lover of yours, but a few charred bones which the vultures would not even bother with.

You are holding on to a fantasy. Forget Alan Desmond. I love you, I want you, and I am here."

"And I am your prisoner! This is nothing but rape, pure and simple," she cried, trying to fight down her increasing panic.

Prevaloir laughed, showing pointed, narrow teeth. "Ah, but there is a place for rape between lovers. It heightens the passion . . ."

Her panic was swelling into a flood. "Damn you! Leave me alone!" she cried, but her rising fear only seemed to inflame him more. He forced his lips against hers, thrusting open her mouth with his tongue, invading, searching, exploring every part of her mouth. She could feel his rising hardness through her dress, his swelling excitement. She struggled against him, twisting her body, trying to lift her knee to shove him away, but it was hopeless. He was too strong. His lean body, which at times had seemed so effeminate, was as tough as a whip, and Maud's puny strength was no match for his determination. Though she knew ultimately he would force her, she made up her mind she would make it as difficult and unpleasant for him as possible. Yanking away her hand, she raked her nails along his cheek, grimly satisfied to see the red welt she left.

With a cry he lifted his head and swung his hand against her face. The slap left her reeling, and she slumped against the wall, just enough for him to grab her around the waist and sling her over onto the bed.

She scrambled upward before he threw himself on top of her, knocking her head against the wall. Thrusting up her skirt, he dove underneath, grabbing at her flesh.

"You . . . are a . . . savage . . ." he said breathlessly, tearing away her bodice and clutching at her freed breast. Her head slammed against the wall, over and over, thump . . . thump . . . as her body sank beneath him . . .

It was not the wall. It was not even her head. De Prevaloir froze above her, his hands stilled, his head lifted, listening. Maud realized then that the thumping was coming from the hall. Someone was pounding on the door.

There were loud voices on the other side, a soldier protesting, a woman shrieking in raging streams of French.

The Chevalier's face drained to a pale shadow of the rudiness it had shown only a moment before. *"Mon dieu,"* he muttered, and scrambled off the bed to begin fastening his clothes. As the pounding and the screaming grew louder, Maud slipped off the other side of the bed to the floor, pulling together her dress, poised there, ready to fight him if he came after her again.

Prevaloir straightened his coat and smoothed his hair, in an attempt to regain his dignity. Throwing Maude a venomous glance, he walked across the room and pulled a large brass key from his pocket, then opened the door just enough to slip through. She heard the door close and the key turn, as she slumped back against the wall, relieved to be safe at least for the moment. Outside in the hallway she could hear loud, angry exchanges in rapid French, the woman's voice high-pitched and emotional, Prevaloir's answers smooth and quiet. As they faded away down the corridor, Maud pulled herself to the bed and straightened her dress. She had no hope of being left alone for long, but, she thought, looking anxiously around the room, even a little time would allow her an opportunity to find something she could use as a weapon. Of one thing she was certain. That Frenchman was not going to come back and try again to rape her without paying dearly for it.

Yet as the evening hours slipped away, she began to believe that he was not going to return. It was nearly dark outside when she heard steps in the hall, and the same young ensign who had brought her here stood at her door, demanding that she follow him. Maud stepped out into the hall, wondering what was going to happen next. As she followed the soldier down three flights of darkened stairs into a series of stone corridors below the pension, the possibility that Prevaloir might have decided to release her began to fade rapidly.

The long stone hallways were damp and cold. She could see doorways on either side leading to large rooms steeped in blackness and thick with a miasma of odors. She identified one of them closely enough to realize furs must have been stored there. Other rooms held stacks of huge kegs, no doubt filled with wine. It was a storehouse of some kind, that began underneath the hotel and continued nearly the length of the block.

When the ensign stopped in front of a door covered with iron grillwork, she realized at once why he had brought her here. Inside there was a small cell, damp and dark, with a cot on one wall and a plank table in the center, flanked with one chair. A pierced tin lantern sat on the uneven surface of the table. When the candle inside was lit, luminous lights like the twinkling of tiny stars fell on the green slime along the walls.

Maud's heart sank. This was the worst yet. "I'm not going in there," she protested. "You cannot do this. I demand to see a judge or a lawyer."

The ensign's young face showed some sign of distress, but it was obvious he was not going to allow that to get in the way of obeying orders.

"I apologize, mam'zelle, but the Chevalier has commanded it." He gripped her arm and pulled her into the cell.

"I won't go," Maud yelled, digging her heels into the uneven stone floor and raking her nails at his sleeve. He whipped an arm around her waist and carried her, flaying heels and all, across the room, where he dumped her on the cot. Before she could get back on her feet, he was out the door and locking the grill.

She ran to the door, shaking the grill with her fists and screaming at the soldier who ran rapidly back down the corridor. Once she realized she was alone, she went back to the chair and sat down, as close to tears of despair as she had been when she was first captured by the Mohawks.

She would never escape from this place. It was too strong and too well fortified. No one would hear her screams down here. She would be forgotten forever in this dungeon, and no one would care. She would be absolutely in Prevaloir's power.

The candle had burned halfway down when the little old man appeared at her door, bringing her a tray of supper. She barely looked up, as he sat it down on the table and stood watching her.

"Madam," he said in halting English, "I bring you ziz." Maud glanced up to see that he was handing her a small brown object. Hesitantly she reached out for it.

A book. And in English. Her desperate eyes were like two round globes in her white face as she looked up at him.

"To amuse you," the old man said with a shrug. "Ziz place . . . not even a window . . ."

"Thank you," Maud murmured. It was some small comfort to know that others were ashamed of the Chevalier's shabby treatment of her, but she wished their guilt extended to bringing her a weapon.

The old man reached into his pocket and pulled

out the stub of a candle, which he laid on the table beside the lamp. Though he did not explain, Maud had already heard the faint scratching noises that signified the presence of rats in these dark corridors, and she was grateful to be able to keep a light burning through the coming night. Her eyes filled, and the treacherous tears began to roll down her cheek.

The old man turned quickly away, muttering to himself in French. He might have been cursing his superiors for all Maud knew, yet he still shut the grilled door and locked it before shuffling back down the hall. She pulled the thin blanket off the cot and around her shoulders, and sat at the table, trying to read the pages of the little book through the blur of tears in her eyes. Though she soon lost track of the hours, she stayed at the table until she fell asleep from sheer weariness. Once during the night she woke long enough to drag the cot away from the wall and out into the center of the room, close to the dim light that still emanated from the stub of a candle on the table.

When she woke again, the candle had burned itself out, and the cell was filled with the shadows of daylight. Maud sat up, groaning with soreness from sleeping on the uncomfortable bed, and realized that steps in the corridor had wakened her. In an instant she was alert. Of course, it would be de Prevaloir, come to take advantage of her isolation and helplessness. And she still had nothing she could use as a weapon.

Scrambling to the back of the cell, she pressed against the damp wall, as she saw the ensign step up to open the grill. The door swung open. Perhaps it would only be the little man bringing her breakfast . . .

Chapter Twenty-two

Maud's eyes grew round as a figure swept into the room, a woman wearing a green satin gown with hoops so wide she had to step sideways to get through the door. She stood glaring at Maud with eyes black as coals in a face white with lead paste. Her lips were painted vivid scarlet, and her brows were penciled into high arches. Above her forehead a pale green wig rose in curls and puffs, with a ruffled, flat straw hat perched on top.

Her dress shimmered in the dim light, and Maud wondered if she was not perhaps still asleep and dreaming this apparition. Then the woman spoke.

"*Mon dieu*, you are a sad sight!"

She swept across the room to stand before Maud, looking her up and down with obvious disgust. "A frightened little guttersnipe. Sink me, but what can Hippolyte be thinking of!"

Though laced with a French accent, her English was clear enough for Maud to take offense at being called a guttersnipe. Before she could open her mouth to object, the woman reached out and pulled her away from the wall to turn her around. Her grip was strong and not gentle.

"Disgusting! Dirty, starved, and this hair—" she said, reaching out to take a long strand in her painted fingers. "Sink me, I don't know if I can do anything with this or not."

"Just a moment . . ." Maud said, jerking away. "Who are you—?"

"Ah, well," the woman said, ignoring Maud. "I have no choice. We must work with what we have. Take her away, Anatole."

The soldier stepped up and gripped Maud's arm. "Just a moment . . ." Maud cried, trying to pull away. "I insist on an explanation."

Yet when the soldier pulled her toward the door, she stopped objecting. If this insulting woman was going to take her out of this dark cell, that was all that mattered.

The ensign stepped back at the doorway long enough to allow the woman to sweep out ahead of him. Her wooden pattens made a loud noise on the cobbles as she hurried down the corridor, still clucking her tongue and rattling off a stream of French that suggested her opinion of the cellars. Without loosening his grip on her arm, the soldier pulled Maud down the corridor to the stairs and up into the small entranceway of the hotel. She was so glad to leave that she willingly followed him, and when they went out into the daylight of the square, her hopes rose even though she told herself not to expect too much. After all, she had had nothing but disappointment since falling into Prevaloir's hands, and perhaps this was just another of his ruses.

In front of the hotel, the woman stopped before a burgundy carriage long enough to give a string of orders to the soldier. Then she climbed aboard, and the driver, dressed in satin livery, called to the sleek bay and rolled off.

Maud looked a question at the soldier, but he only gripped her arm tighter and shoved her off down the street. After walking through several narrow roadways, they came to a stairway that led up the high cliff. He motioned Maud ahead of him.

"Where are we going?" she asked, though he had not bothered to answer any of her questions so far.

"To Madam Claudan's," he said brusquely. "Be glad you are out of those cellars."

He gave her a little shove to start up the stairs. "But who is she—?"

Evidently he had explained all he was going to. Still wondering if she was being delivered or about to face something worse, Maud made her slow way up the steps, pausing frequently to rest from the long, difficult climb. At the top she realized that they had entered the upper town, newer, more spacious, and cleaner than the one below. The ensign led her down several broad streets to a house that sat behind broad stone gates surrounded by greenery. He pulled on the bell and was immediately answered by a house servant, again in green satin livery, who let them inside. They walked through a small garden to the steps of the house, where the door was opened by a round-faced maid in a high starched cap and dark blue gown.

"This is the girl?" she asked the soldier. When he nodded she took Maud's arm and pulled her inside. "Very good. I will take over now. Thank you, Ensign."

Maud stood in the hallway, looking around with wondering eyes. She had not seen such elegance since leaving England. Silver sconces on the wall, flocked paper, tile floors, molded ceilings . . . she felt as though she could still be dreaming. But the little housemaid was all too real. She clucked her tongue just as the woman had done, looking Maud over with obvious horror.

"First you must have the bath, Madam. Then perhaps we will know if there is any hope . . ."

"Bath! A real bath! Maud still had no idea what lay ahead, but it couldn't be too terrible, if she was going to be allowed to bathe first.

And bathe she did. Her skin was scrubbed raw and her hair washed thoroughly. Afterward, it was brushed until it shone, she was powdered and scented and dressed in a plain, clean dress of sprigged muslin, and given a pair of kid slippers and stockings embroidered with tiny red roses. Heaven itself could not be any better, she thought, even though by this time she was beginning to wonder if this house was only a more elegant version of the one Eliza Finchley had run back in London.

Her curiosity was not satisfied until that afternoon, when, after a light luncheon, she was led into a room draped with silk hangings on the windows, where the woman she had seen earlier that morning lay stretched on a chaise lounge, wearing a ruffled banian and nibbling at a plate of fruit.

"Well, Mademoiselle," the woman said, sitting up on the chair as Maud entered. "I must say, you look a sight better. I am impressed. This morning I would not have thought there was so much hope for you."

She rose to walk around Maud, looking her up and down as she had done in the cell.

"Really . . ." Maud protested. "I am not a prize horse, Madam. Though I am grateful to you for the bath and the clean clothes, I would prefer an explanation. Why have you brought me here?"

"You are impertinent! I would expect a little more gratitude, considering the circumstances you were in when I found you this morning."

"I am grateful to you for taking me out of that dreadful place. But I would like to know why you did it. And why you have been so kind to me."

"It is not kindness. Come here," she said, motioning Maud to a gilt chair near the lounge. "Sit by me."

Maud sat gingerly on the edge of the chair, as the woman draped her long body back on the chaise. "We have not been introduced. I am Madam Claudette Claudan."

"Maud Mellingham. I am also known by my stage name of Maud Makejoy."

"You are an actress?"

"Yes. I have appeared on the stage both in England and in the Colonies."

Claudette tapped a finger on the arm of her chair. "You do not look like an actress. They are usually . . . what do you say . . . *prostituée*."

"I think you mean whores. Some are, but not all. Some are artists."

"And you are the *artiste*, no doubt. *Bien*, you have too much elegance to be a whore. I am relieved to see it."

"Really, Madam Claudan—"

"Do not excite yourself. I have brought you here not because of anything *you* are, but because of someone else. In short, you are here with me in order to prevent you from being with the Chevalier de Prevaloir."

"You know him?"

She gave a bitter laugh. "I know him very well. He is my paramour, my life, my only reason for being. And I will not see him fall into the clutches of an English . . . *actrice*."

Maud leaned forward eagerly. "But madam, I don't want the Chevalier. On the contrary, I have begged him to leave me alone. He has treated me shabbily. Oh yes, he did save me from the Mohawks, but since then I have been virtually his prisoner. He has tried to force himself on me . . ."

"Ah, I know. If what you say is true, you can thank me for saving you in the *pension* yesterday."

"That was you outside in the hall?"

"But of course. He thought I would stay in Montreal, but I followed, once I knew he had brought a beautiful woman back with him. I heard he had brought the woman to that place, and I was determined he would not have her. Of course, when he moved you to the cellars, I was almost fooled. But I have as many informants in this town as the Chevalier. I discovered where you were, and I determined that the only way to keep you from him was to have you here, under my wing, as you English say."

"That was kind of you," Maud murmured.

"No, kindness is not involved. Jealousy is involved."

Maud looked into those slanted eyes, cold as winter ice on the St. Charles River. "If you really wish to keep me from him, you will help me escape this place."

The black eyes looked through her. "I think not. Once you were gone, he would be after you in an instant. No, I have the better plan. You shall be my protegé. I shall introduce you to the ton, help you further your career, even assist you in finding the proper paramour. As long as you are near me, you are safe from him, and he will certainly be safe from you."

Maud's heart sank, and her hopes of getting back to the Colonies with it. "Madam, I am not ungrateful, for, as I told you, I have no feelings for Monsieur de Prevaloir at all. But I long to return to my own people. As for a paramour, I assure you that is the last thing I am interested in right now. The man I love was killed by the Indians, and I don't think I shall ever get over it."

"Poof," Claudette said with a wave of her hand, ignoring the tears that sprang to Maud's eyes. "A woman is nothing without a man, and there are many fine ones here in Quebec. Once you are introduced into society you will lose your heart, I guarantee it, and the sooner, the better. Nothing helps one forget a lost love as well as a new love."

Maud turned away to stare out the window. While she did not for a moment agree with Madam Claudan, she could not help but feel that she might be better off if she could accept someone new. Perhaps in the end it was better to flit lightly from one love to another, rather than fasten your whole heart on one person who, when he was gone, took part of your very being with him.

"Now," Claudette went on, majestically unaware of or interested in anything Maud might be feeling, "I am rather tired. Mimi will show you to your room — a small guest room on the floor above — and help you settle in. Tonight I am having a few guests for supper, and I wish you to impress them. I will tell you more about it later."

She lifted a small glass bell which summoned the maid Maud had met earlier. Dismissed, Maud followed Mimi from the room and up the stairs to a tiny but neat little bedroom. A gown was lying on the bed, shimmering gold in the soft light from the curtained window.

"What is this?" Maud said, running her hand over the shining fabric.

"It is the gown Madam wants you to wear this evening. If Mademoiselle would try it on, I shall have the seamstress fit it for you. Madam Claudan has declared it must look perfection."

"Madam thinks of everything."

Suddenly discouraged, Maud turned away to look out of the window at a deep garden below. She was as much a prisoner here as she had been since leaving Montreal, she mused. The circumstances were certainly better, but it was still captivity. And she could see no way out.

"Mam'zelle does not like the dress?" Mimi said hesitantly.

"Oh . . . yes, it is lovely. Send for the dressmaker. I'll try it on."

Her lack of enthusiasm was obvious. "It is very beautiful," Mimi said in an effort to cheer her up. "And the color shall go so well with the gold of Mam'zelle's hair."

Maud thought wryly how this little maid would probably sell her soul to wear such a gorgeous gown. Once she might have, too. "Yes, you are right. It is as lovely as any dress I've ever worn." She picked it up and held it to her. It shimmered in the light like cascading gold dust. "Have you been with Madam Claudan long, Mimi?"

The girl's round face took on a softness when she smiled. "Oh yes. My Maman was her lady's maid in France. When the Madam came to New France, she brought me, since the journey would have been so difficult for my Maman."

"Do you like it here in New France?"

Mimi fussed with arranging the folds of the dress. "*Oui*, Mam'zelle. Once I got accustomed to seeing those terrible savages on the streets and those rough *coureurs de bois*. The men of the army make all the difference."

"I suppose you have a beau of your own among them?"

"No, Mam'zelle. There was one . . . Andre. But he went off to Fort Carillon and was killed there."

"Oh. I am sorry. Was he killed by the English?" she added hesitantly.

"No, Mam'zelle. It was one of those savages. Iroquois, I think. Since then, I try not to lose my heart so easily."

Maud laid the gown back on the bed. "You are a wise girl, Mimi. I think you and I will get along very well."

By the time Maud was decked out in all her finery for the evening's soiree, she had actually begun to enjoy herself. It was a long time since she had worn such elegant clothes, or been so pampered and fussed over. Once she was completely dressed, she stood looking at herself in the long gilt-edged mirror in Madam Claudan's bedroom, and thought, well, all that trudging through the wilderness at least had not diminished her looks.

The dress had a startlingly low decolletage, a long-pointed stomacher, and an overskirt of gold paduasoy with an underskirt of softly striped satin. She had insisted her hair would not be powdered, but had allowed Mimi to sweep it up over poufs and curls to make it high in the front with long tendrils of golden curls down the back and over her shoulder. She had a gossamer fan of fine chicken skin — so thin you could read a book through it, and dusted with golden sequins — which she wielded with all the archness learned from her days on the stage. The barest touch of powder on her face, a discreet satin patch near one eye, rouge on her cheeks and lips, and darkening of her naturally arched brows set off her features to perfection. Madam Claudette was very pleased, enough so to add dangling diamond earrings and a gold necklace from her own jewelry case.

"Sink me, you shall be the sensation!" she said, standing back to look Maud over. "For tonight only, you shall outshine me. After tonight, never again!"

Yet Maud wondered if that were true, for when Claudette joined her to go downstairs she had decked herself in the perfect counterpart to Maud's golden elegance, in a shimmering black dress with a black sequined gauze scarf draped provocatively over her shoulders. As different as night and day, and equally impressive, Maud thought. And while she knew she had the advantage of youth, Madam Claudan displayed elegance, experience, and assurance in every bone. It should be an interesting evening, she thought, smiling to herself.

And it was. The "small" company turned out to be nearly fifty people, most of them officers of the French army stationed outside the town. There were women there as well, most of them paramours of the officers, and none as striking in appearance as she herself or Claudette. She only had the briefest of introductions to the women, for from the moment the men walked in the room, they swarmed around her, openly flirting and attempting to entice her interest.

She was interested to meet several of the men whose names she had heard bandied about while moving north with the English, the most notable, the Marquis De Montcalm himself. He was a small man with very bright, intelligent eyes, and she enjoyed talking with him, the more so because he was known to be fiercely faithful to his beloved wife back in France.

Her worst moment came when Prevaloir walked into the room and stood motionless, staring at her as though she were a ghost. She had wondered if Claudette had told him about her, and she knew from the shock on his face that she hadn't. Nor did Claudette give him time to ask about it. She was by his side in an instant, laughingly introducing Madam Makejoy, and luring him away to the punch bowl before he could reply. Maud did not miss the fury in his eyes, directed both at her and at Claudette, but since it did not seem to bother his mistress in the east, she decided she would not let it bother her either. For the first time, she felt truly grateful to Claudette.

It was Madam Claudan who, later in the evening, informed the group that they had a performer among them. Once they knew Maud had been on the stage, nothing would do but she must recite something for them. And if there was a song to go with it, so much the better.

While she was not certain why Claudette would want her to be identified as an actress, Maud decided to go along. She chose a lively epilogue from one of Master Ciber's plays, which was usually followed by a song. It was in English, of course, but no one seemed to mind, and by the time she finished, she was being hailed as the best thing to grace Quebec since the last ship from Le Havre arrived.

The party lasted until well into the morning hours, when groups of the officers went tipsily wending their way down the streets singing snatches of her song. Claudette and her Chevalier had disappeared by that time, and Maud gratefully made her way alone up the two flights of stairs to her room, where Mimi helped her undress. She fell into bed weary, but, for the first time in weeks, feeling almost happy.

She was awakened the following morning by Claudette, who swept into the room and perched on the edge of her bed.

"Well, my little prisoner. How did you enjoy your punishment?"

Maud wiped at her eyes and struggled to sit up. "It was . . . very nice . . ."

"Very nice, she says when she was the toast of France's finest gentlemen! Sink me, what would it take to make you exclaim with delight? No matter, you did very well last evening. I was afraid at first the performance would not come off, but you handled it beautifully. You must have been very popular in England."

"I had my share of acclaim."

"What did you think of the gentlemen? Did no one interest you?"

"They were all very pleasant, but I told you, Madam, I am not looking for a lover."

"Nonsense. There was not one who would not have gladly taken you under his protection . . . well, perhaps one, but the Marquis is a very special person indeed. All the rest are dying for love of you. Take my advice and claim one of them right away. You will be safer and infinitely more comfortable."

"Does that mean I cannot stay here?"

She thought a moment. "No. You can stay here for the moment anyway. Of course, Hippolyte was furious with me. It will take some time to soften his resentment. But now that you have half the officers of France at your feet, his plans for you are *passée*. And as long as you are not someone's *amie*, then you must stay close by me. However, it will be better for us both if you find a protector, and soon."

Maud shifted to sit up against the headboard and gathered her courage.

"I have another idea. It came to me last night after I went to bed. Suppose you help me set up a theater here, where I can perform. Officers love having a playhouse in a garrison town. And that way I could repay you for all you've given me, and earn a reputation as an actress rather than as another available woman."

Claudette pursed her thin lips and thought a moment. "These men would have little patience for English drama."

"Then I shall learn French parts. Perhaps Mimi could help me. She seems an intelligent girl. We could keep it informal, and perhaps even some of the officers themselves might take some of the roles. They might like that."

Claudette rose from the bed to walk the room, silently pondering Maud's suggestion. At the door she stopped and turned back. "It might work. Certainly it would be a diversion for men who are often idle, and who have too much time on their hands for their own good. Let me think about it."

Maud felt a surge of excitement at the thought of getting back to work. She pulled up her legs under the sheet and clasped her arms around them. "Oh, I would love to do some of my favorite roles again—"

"I would not wish you to be too available. I do not trust Hippolyte. Given the opportunity, he might try to snatch you away once more."

"Believe me, Madam Claudan, that is the last thing I want!"

"Very well then. I shall think about it and . . . we shall see . . ."

The door closed behind her. "Well," Maud said out loud to herself, "at least she didn't say no!"

In the end, Madam Claudan did agree, partly to keep Maud as much in the company of the officers as possible, and partly to keep her busy. "Of course, we shall have to get the approval of the Church, but that should not be too difficult. Catholics tend to be somewhat tolerant of the theater."

Unlike Quakers and Presbyterians, Maud mused, remembering Philadelphia.

The young French officers were predictably enthusiastic about the project, and with their help, a little used stable was quickly transformed into a theater, with a low stage, makeshift boxes around the sides, and two small dressing rooms at the rear. There was no machinery, but Maud had no doubt that it would be improvised as the needs required.

She soon found herself so occupied with the playhouse, that she almost forgot she was actually being kept in Quebec against her will. Madam Claudan still insisted that she live in her "palace," as the finer homes in Quebec were called, and that she accompany her on frequent social occasions. Yet Maud eagerly took advantage of every free moment to walk the narrow streets to the theater to plan, to paint, to practice—all the activities that putting on a production required.

As she got to know the city better, she found those walks very pleasant. The town was small enough for her to begin to recognize some of the people along the route—pleasant-faced shop owners, priests in their solemn gowns, scholars from the seminary, nuns from the Ursuline convent, and always, soldiers. By now she could separate the white-coated French regulars from the Quebec militia and the Colonial Marines. All three had nothing but contempt for each other, an attitude she remembered well from those days with the English and American forces in Albany. There was much about human nature that remained the same, no matter whose flag they fought under.

It was pleasant to be recognized by the elite of the town: Governor Vandreuil doffed his plume hat to her as he passed in his carriage emblazoned with a coat of arms, as did Intendant Bigot, the business and finance manager of the Colony. Both men had made illegal fortunes from their positions, Claudette had told her, but that was not unknown in England either.

Maud soon became a familiar sight, walking along the narrow streets with the maid, Mimi, a few steps behind. More and more Mimi was given over to her use, to the relief of both women. It had happened almost by accident, when the girl brought Maud's chocolate one morning trying to keep her face turned to hide a long red welt across her cheek. When Maud questioned her about it, she admitted that she had carelessly dropped Madam Claudan's silver spoon on the rug and the madam had struck her. This seemed so unfair, that Maud made up her mind then and there that she would ask for Mimi's services. When Claudette agreed, she began taking her along to the playhouse, where her help was invaluable and nobody cared if she dropped anything.

The first play, a comedy by Monsieur Voltaire, was to be presented two months after the playhouse was first proposed. The second, a week later, was to be an original by one of the officers, also a comedy, that poked fun at the native residents of New France. It had the usual amount of bumbling fools, mistaken identities, lovelorn chevaliers, pratfalls, and foolish props that were the staples of a comedy everywhere. Maud worked hard with Mimi to learn her lines in French, and only hoped that the Governor and others of local descent would not be offended by its broad satire.

The first performance was received with great enthusiasm. Two days later, Claudette insisted that Maud accompany her to one of Intendant Bigot's entertainments, in his great stone chateau by the St. Charles River outside town. These were popular affairs, but Maud had found them tiresome and would have preferred to stay home and practice her lines for the second play. Claudette would not hear of that, so she decked herself out in the gold dress once again, and rolled off in Madam Claudan's coach for the trip to the woods of Charlesbourg.

She had just finished a game of loo and risen to leave the gaming room, when she felt her arm gripped and looked up to see Hippolyte de Prevaloir at her side.

"I've been trying to get you alone all evening," he murmured, steering her toward the open terrace doors. "Walk with me a moment."

"I don't think Claudette would approve," Maud replied archly, moving out of his grasp.

"But it's warm in here. Look at your heightened color. A moment of air is the sensible answer."

There were so many other people around, that Maud felt she could not afford to make a scene, and so she let him lead her to the terrace. After all, it was safe enough. They would never be out of sight of the room, and it *was* very warm.

She stood by the stone railing, fanning herself, feeling his eyes burning into her. Now that they were outside, she realized the evening was not as hot as it had seemed inside the crowded room. In fact, there was a decided coolness to the air, the first indication of change in the seasons.

De Prevaloir seemed to read her mind. "You'd never guess from this pleasant evening, how terrible the winters are in this place," he said lightly.

"Are they very hard?"

He gave a short, bitter laugh. "That is an understatement. I'm told there are eight months of ice and snow, and cold that seems as though it will never end. It is the most difficult thing about living in this place, and probably the reason my country has never been able to entice the numbers of settlers to come here that are found in the English colonies. But then," he added dryly, "I did not bring you out here to talk about weather or politics."

She looked straight at him. "Why did you bring me out here?"

He leaned against the stone rail and crossed his arms over his chest. "You two women think you are very clever, don't you? Claudette has thwarted me at every turn. But you will not succeed in the end."

"I don't know what you are talking about."

"Oh, I think you do. Have your little fun with your starry eyed officers and their ridiculous theatrics. Enjoy society while you can. In the end, I intend to have you to myself and myself alone, and someplace where no one will be able to step in and interfere. I do not give up easily, madam. I do not give up at all."

Maud turned back to the door. "If you've quite finished, I think we should return to the others."

He didn't move. "Do not forget what I say, Madam Makejoy. Someday when you least expect it, when you are so sure you are safe that you forget to watch, then I shall be there to have my way with you."

"That is one thing I am not likely to ever forget, Monsieur de Chevalier," she said lightly snapping her fan and walking back inside the chateau. The room which had seemed so warm a few moments before, now seemed very cold indeed. Or was it simply a reflection of the chill his words had stirred in her heart?

Those words haunted her the following days, as the second play was readied for its grand preview. The author, a young, gangly captain from Provence was as excited and nervous as if his little play was being presented at the *Comédie Française*. He scurried around trying to see to everything and succeeding only in getting in everyone's way, until Maud felt herself catching some of his incipient panic. That, added to the anxiety de Prevaloir's words had evoked, was enough to bring on her old despondency; yet she fought down depression in a determined effort to put on a good performance.

On opening night, she got through the first two acts very well, and if the boisterous laughter coming from the pit was any indication, the play was going to be a great success. By the third act, which was the funniest of them all, she began to forget her own feelings and enjoy romping through the play. Her only fear was that the author, who was playing the part of a bumbling, stupid *coureur de bois*, would let his nervousness interfere with carrying off his part. When he appeared on stage at the end of the act she began to relax a little.

Until she began to notice strange discrepancies in his performance. Between her lines she took covert glances at the tall, gangly figure mumbling his lines in rustic new world French. Surely Captain Laurent was not that tall or that broad-chested? Nor was his voice the right timbre. It was far deeper than at rehearsal. And the fake beard was not long or as tangled as it had been before. A terrible intuition began to constrict her chest, which she tried to ignore as she cavorted around the stage.

Her role did not allow her to get near the woodsman until the end of the play, when, with a cry, she was to faint into his arms. Maneuvering around the stage, Maud managed to edge closer. Her lines faltered as she looked and looked again, not believing what her eyes told her was true, and yet not able to step out of character long enough to discover for sure if she was right.

"Maurice, appel le Docteur," she said, struggling to remember her lines as she stared up into a pair of wicked, twinkling green eyes.

The woodsman stepped closer and smiled down into her face.

"Je suis le docteur. Votre amant d'un autre temps, Jacques," said a voice that struck like a knife through her chest.

"Alan . . . ?" she whispered, staring up at him, straining to see beyond the thick hair that covered half his face. "Is it . . . can it be . . . ?"

"Say your line!" he whispered.

" . . . *Vous?*" she managed to get out before falling into his arms in a dead faint.

Chapter Twenty-three

Gradually Maud realized that she was lying on a cot in one of the small dressing rooms. The woodsman from the play was bent over her. Beyond him she could glimpse Mimi's white face, and the bearded, anxious face of a second *coureur de bois*.

Her eyes grew round, and she scrambled back up the wall and away from the man staring into her face.

"I'm not a ghost," Alan said, laughing. "Look, see," he said taking both her hands and raising them to his lips. "I'm real flesh and blood."

Maud stared at him, still not able to believe it was true. "But . . . I thought . . . the Indians . . . you were dead . . ."

"Of course, you did. And we probably should be dead. But we're not. We escaped and came here to find you. Oh, my darling girl, you can't know how glad I am to see you again!"

He pulled her to him, clasping her against his hard body. For the first time, Maud's heart began to swell with joy, the utter, beautiful joy of having him near, alive and close. Her arms tightened around him, and the tears cascaded down her cheeks as she laughed and cried all at the same time.

"Alan . . . oh, Alan . . . I never expected to see you again . . ."

They clung together until a soft cough behind reminded them that they were not alone. Maud let go of Alan long enough to throw her arms around Jeremy's neck and hug tightly. "And Jeremy, my dear friend! I still can't believe that you're both really here!"

"To tell the truth, I still can't quite believe it myself." He gave her a quick squeeze, then stepped back while Alan moved to sit beside her on the bed, clasping her hands.

"But how did you do it!" Maud exclaimed, looking at them both as if they were phantoms rather than living men.

"I'll tell you all about it, but first, Jeremy, would you keep watch outside? I don't think we're ready for the world to know we're here yet."

"You look exactly like those French woodsmen who come into Quebec from the wilderness," Maud said, touching Alan's thick beard. "But the Chevalier de Prevaloir is here, you remember him? He might recognize you."

"I know. That's why we must be cautious."

Jeremy gave her a wink. "I think I'll just go along. If you're wise Alan, you will, too." As he moved away he bumped into Mimi, who was still staring at the three of them, trying to sort out what was going on. "Can this girl be trusted?" he asked Maud.

"Well, sir!" Mimi said, in French tinged with outrage. "I resent that. I don't tattle, and certainly not on my mistress here, who has been very good to me!"

"She's fine," Maud answered. "These are two of my dearest friends," she said to the girl. "They are English, and no one must know they are here."

Mimi, who had already deduced that Alan was more than a dear friend, smiled at her. "Your secret is safe, mam'selle."

As Jeremy slipped from the room, Mimi went to stand discreetly by the door, listening for footsteps.

Actually, Maud did not care if the maid was watching. She clasped Alan in her arms and held him tightly, reveling in the sensation of his hard body against her own, his warm hands moving sinuously against her back, his lips teasing her cheek and the hollow of her neck. Her heart threatened to burst through her chest with joy.

"I'd better not begin to enjoy this too much, or I won't be able to leave," Alan whispered in her ear, as his tongue traced its rounded edges. "Egad, but you feel good. There were times when I never thought I'd hold you like this again."

Maud pulled away to look into his tanned face. "I had given up hope. I was so sure you were dead. How in the world—"

She was interrupted by Mimi, who whispered loudly, "Someone is coming, Mam'zelle." Before the maid finished speaking, there was a brisk knocking on the door, followed by Claudette's voice:

"Maud, *cherie*, are you all right? We are most concerned . . ."

"Mimi, hold them off," Maud whispered, shoving Alan toward a large wooden armoire standing against the wall. It was jammed with costumes, but he was able to climb inside and scrunch down behind them. Maud scrambled back to the bed, as Mimi opened the door just wide enough to peer through.

"Mademoiselle is resting," she managed to say, before Claudette shoved her aside and sailed into the room, followed by Prevaloir.

"What is wrong with you girl, fainting like that on stage? Why, when you didn't take your calls, we were worried sick!"

"I . . . I was so nervous, I hadn't eaten anything all day, and I suppose it caught up with me." She put a white hand languidly to her head, but sat up when she saw de Prevaloir looking around the room, scowling with suspicion. "I'm much better now, truly," she added, swinging her legs over the side of the bed. "Why don't we go now? It's the Governor, isn't it, who's arranged the party after the play?"

Claudette bent to put a hand to Maud's forehead. "Nonsense. You do seem peaked. And it is the Comte de Bouganville, who is entertaining tonight. He will understand if you are a little late. I shall send my carriage back for you once we are there."

Maud held her breath, while de Prevaloir opened the door to the armoire and gave the interior a cursory glance. When he closed it again, she said brightly: "That is most considerate of you. I'm sure I shall be fine by then."

"Mimi shall stay with you," Claudette said, wielding her painted silk fan.

"I will also leave two of my men outside," Prevaloir added. "They will escort you to the party."

"You are too kind," Maud muttered. But she was vastly relieved when the two of them left the room.

"I shall wait outside, mam'zelle," Mimi whispered and followed them, closing the door behind her. Maud rushed to the armoire and helped Alan disengage himself from the tulles, gauzes, sequined satins, masks, wigs, and various other paraphernalia that had been collected for the company.

"I'd forgotten the smell of the theater," he said, pulling off a long gauze scarf that had wrapped itself around his chest. "That was close. I certainly don't want the Chevalier de Prevaloir to know I'm in Quebec yet. Not until I figure out how we're going to get you off this rock."

"Oh, my love, do you think you can?" she said, taking his arms and pulling him back to the bed. "We're right in the middle of the French army, and so far away from the Colonies!"

"I'll think of something. After all, we got this far.

When we left Straight Arrow's village, I thought we'd never find you. I was sure you had been sent off to be the slave of some Indian chief across the mountains. It was Straight Arrow who told me where you had gone."

"But why? And how on earth did you ever get on such friendly terms with that savage?"

Alan laughed. "It was amazing. We had a contest of magic with his witch doctor, Sioto. Of course, it was Jeremy who performed the magic. I only stood there and pretended I was mentally ordering him about. That old faker, Sioto, tried every trick he knew, but he couldn't fool Jeremy. Once they got past the simple things, he went on to pull out every elaborate trick in his bag. He hurled a stone at one of the braves who was obviously working with him, who shrieked and moaned and rolled on the ground, then spat out four smaller stones. That one is as old as Methuselah.

"He levitated objects using the thinnest hairs, he made tents shake, and—for his grand finale—he made himself disappear from inside a hut. But Jeremy had figured out that there was a tunnel under the floor, and he simply appeared in the old man's place. By the time it was over, the Indians were convinced we were gods. Of course, Straight Arrow knew better, but he was glad to see his old medicine man get his comeuppance, so it worked out all right. He spirited us quietly out of the village a little later, then told his people we had returned to the Great Spirit in the sky."

"And he knew I had gone with Prevaloir?"

"Oh yes. He sent you to him at the Chevalier's request. At the trading station we learned he had taken a woman with him to New France, and about the *coureurs de bois*. We figured out the best way to follow you was to pretend we were one of them. So far it has worked beautifully."

"But where are you staying? There cannot be many safe places."

"In one of the taverns in the lower town, though we can't be there much longer, or we might begin to seem suspicious. My love, have you had a hard time here? You look tired, drained . . ."

She clasped him to her. "No, no. It's just the shock of seeing you again. Oh, Alan, I had given up hope of ever getting away from Quebec. They watch me all the time, and though Claudette has been able to keep Prevaloir away from me, he as much as told me that he was only biding his time."

He ran his fingers through her hair, reveling in the clean smell of its golden strands. "The bastard! I'll kill him first."

"You mustn't do that. You must be careful," Maud said, laying her palms on either side of his face and drawing his lips to hers. "I couldn't stand to lose you again!"

"You won't. Now, I must go, before I risk your life, too."

She forced her hands away. "When shall I see you again?"

"Send Mimi to the Coq D'Or tavern on the rue Champlain tomorrow morning, when the market opens. We'll have something worked out by then."

"Oh, Alan," she cried as he pulled his hands from her fingers. "I love you . . ."

He threw her a kiss and slipped outside, closing the door behind him. Only then did Maud realize that she was still wearing her dress from the play, and would have to change to be ready for the party. She jumped up and began tearing at the laces.

As it turned out, Mimi made the trip to the grubby tavern on the rue Champlain two mornings in a row, while Maud waited enviously in Claudette's chateau, wishing she could be the one to see Alan and Jeremy. She was not completely certain Mimi could be trusted, even though the girl had been very kind and friendly to her. The little Frenchwoman threw herself eagerly into the secret intrigue of these meetings, and, as far as Maud could tell, had proved to be a clever accomplice. When she told Maud that the two men would be ready to leave the city the following night, she seemed to almost regret their intrigue would be ending.

"Jeremy, he says there is to be another soiree, this time at the Bigot palace near the Côte de la Montagne. He says that at ten o'clock *exactement*, you are to pretend to be ill and insist on taking the carriage back home. Monsieur Alan will be there to spirit you away."

"Oh dear, that sounds as though there will be all kinds of possibilities for disaster."

"Once you are away from the palace, you will disappear, poof! down the Sillery Road. No one will know where you have gone."

"The Sillery Road? How far does he think we will get by roadway? Even if we make it through one of the gates, it won't be difficult for our carriage to be overtaken. Are you sure he said this, Mimi?"

"*Oui*, mam'zelle. It was his exact words." Mimi absently picked up a corner of her overskirt and twirled it around her fingers. She did not seem to want to look at Maud directly.

"Well, I suppose there is nothing else to do but try to follow his directions. Do you know if anyone has suspected they are not what they seem?"

"I did not sense it. I do not think they spend much time in that tavern."

"That is wise of them." Maud realized she was twisting her hands in her lap. She would be so grateful when all this was over with, and she could be free and with Alan again. *If* it worked out that way. It must work out that way! She heard Mimi give a soft cough, and looked up to see her still standing, watching her.

"Mam'zelle . . ." the girl said hesitantly. "I have the favor to ask of you. I would like you to allow me to come with you and Monsieur Alan and Monsieur Jeremy."

Maud was amazed. "You want to leave Quebec? But why? You're French, and this is your home."

"Yes, but . . . Mam'zelle has seen that Madam Claudan is not so nice a person to work for. After my Andre was killed, I thought I should never be happy again. Yet in these two days, I have learned to feel. I am in suspense. I must be careful to put on the performance, so no one will suspect what I am really doing. And I laugh. Monsieur Jeremy makes me laugh very much."

Maud gave her a wry smile. "It sounds as though you've been doing more than just listening for instructions in these meetings."

"*Oui*. Somewhat more. It was hard not to with such engaging company. Please, Mam'zelle Maud. Say you will take me with you! You are the kindest person I have ever known, the only one who did not treat me as just a little housemaid."

"That's probably because I was once a housemaid myself, and I know what it is like."

Mimi's eyes widened with surprise. "You! But you are a great lady!"

"I've learned to be a lady, but I was not born to it. In fact, I was a kitchen maid before I became a housemaid. So, you see, I was even lower on the scale than you. And I had a mistress who makes Madam Claudan look like Father Christmas."

Mimi's smile lit up her round face. "Perhaps that is

why we seem a little like friends."

"Yes. Friends." She studied the girl for a minute, still wondering if she was blindly walking into some kind of trap. "Very well, Mimi. If we are going to escape from New France, we will all of us need to be as clever as possible and depend on each other. If you really want to go, I won't object."

"Oh, *merci*, Mam'zelle. I will help you all I can."

"Perhaps if I tell her I'm going to bring you home with me tomorrow night, Claudette will let me go that much more easily," she said lightly. All the same, she would watch her little maid very closely until then.

The following evening Maud carefully chose the simplest dress out of the several that Claudette had fitted out for her. During the day she made a point of complaining of a mild headache, laying the groundwork for what was to come that evening.

"Perhaps we should not attend Intendant Bigot's soiree this evening," Claudette suggested, eyeing Maud suspiciously.

"No, I refuse to allow a little headache to interfere with my pleasure. Or yours either, for that matter."

Since Claudette had half-expected Maud to say she wanted to remain at home while she went off to the party, her suspicions were eased by the girl's reply. They set off that evening in Claudette's French carriage, called a *cleche*, each with their maid in attendance, and Claudette smiling with satisfaction because she would be able to watch Maud the entire evening.

Bigot's town palace was older than his chateau in the St. Charles Woods, but it was splendidly outfitted with the best that stolen money could import from France. Lights glittered from candelabra in every room. A sumptuous supper was laid, wine flowed freely, and a small orchestra offered dancing from formal minuets to country reels in one of the larger drawing rooms. Maud moved among the rooms, flirting with the French officers and appearing to enjoy herself, except for the frequent times she raised a hand to her head and closed her eyes in a sudden spasm of pain. After making certain everyone around her was concerned, she made light of it and continued on.

As the clock neared ten she fought down her nervousness and went to seek out Claudette, who was involved in an energetic game of piquet. Luck was with her, for Claudette, who had been gambling some high stakes, was winning at the moment. Maud was glad to see it, for it meant she would not be anxious to leave the table.

"I fear that my head has grown worse," she said, tapping Claudette on the shoulder. "I really would like to go home to bed. Would you be willing to leave?"

Claudette barely looked up from the pile of coins on the table. "Leave! La, girl, can't you see I'm winning? It would not be sporting to pick up now."

Maud looked up to see Prevaloir's cold eyes on her from across the table, where he was standing behind the Comte de Bouganville's chair. "You do look a trifle pale, my child. I will be happy to escort you back to the house," he added casually.

Claudette tore her gaze from the cards and eyed them both. "That will not be necessary, Hippolyte. Mimi can accompany our Maud. But really, girl, why don't you wait awhile, and we can all leave together?"

Maud wavered on her feet, gripping the table to keep from falling. "I really don't think I can. I hope I'm not coming down with something . . ."

"Merciful heavens, Claudette," the sympathetic Comte exclaimed. "Let the poor girl retire to her bed. We can't have our favorite chanteuse getting sick, can we?"

Claudette laid her cards on the table. "Perhaps I should go . . ."

There was a loud chorus of nos from the other players, who were determined to win back some of what they had lost.

"Oh, very well," Claudette said with a sigh. "Send two of your men with her, Hippolyte. They can escort Maud home."

"I'll get your cloak," the Frenchman said in clipped tones.

"Thank you," Maud murmured, turning away. At the door, he draped the warm velvet around her shoulders. She was relieved to see Claudette's coach pull up in front of the portico, but noticed that Prevaloir stood there, watching her as she made her way to it. A footman ran to open the door and let down the step, offering her his hand as she climbed up. She glanced up at him and caught her breath, as she recognized Jeremy's round face beneath a white wig and a tricorn hat. Quickly looking up at the box, she saw Alan sitting there, looking straight ahead, swathed in a great coat and holding the reins lightly in his gloved hands. Quickly she climbed into the comforting darkness of the cab, while Mimi took the seat opposite her. As the *cleche* rolled over the cobbles toward the corner where the Côte de la Montagne wound up the cliff, she allowed herself a tiny sigh of relief.

They had just started up the hill, when there was a cry and the coach pulled to a halt. Maud jumped to the window as she heard the Chevalier de Prevaloir's voice dismissing the guard. To her horror the door was jerked open and he climbed inside, sitting beside her, his cloak wrapped tightly around him.

"I thought this moment would never come," he said softly, reaching for her and pulling her tightly to him. "This was the perfect opportunity."

"What are you doing here? Let me go!"

He released her long enough to lean out the window and shout to the driver to take them to the citadel. Then his arms were around her again, pulling her to him. She struggled to get away, but his hands went around her throat, tipping up her chin. His breath was hot on her cheek, and his eyes glinted in the darkness.

"I told you I would bide my time. It was just a matter of waiting for the right opportunity, and you gave it to me tonight."

"Get away from me! How dare you! Madam Claudette will have your head for this!"

"Claudette will never see you again. I won't make that mistake. This time I'm going to put you, where she'll never find you."

A cold fear touched her heart and spread through her chest. "This is an outrage," she cried, fighting against him. He pulled her face to his and kissed her, smearing her lips with his. Across from them Mimi stared wide-eyed, then reached to pull his arms away.

"Monsieur, this is not proper!" she said, and followed it with a long stream of ever-increasing French invective. Prevaloir shook her off as though she were a bothersome insect, then shouted to the driver to stop the coach. Once it had rattled to a halt, he opened the door and shoved Mimi through it onto the street.

"You cannot do this! Madam Claudette—"

"Find your way home, girl," Prevaloir snapped and with a "drive on," slammed the door, throwing himself back inside long enough to grab Maud, who was trying to open the other side and climb out. Clapping one hand over her mouth, he forced her back, half-laying across the seat with his body over hers. She felt the coach moving again, rattling swiftly over the cobbles. Inside she struggled with Prevaloir, until it occurred to her that perhaps it would be better to let him be distracted while Alan took them wherever he wanted. With her eyes round and fearful, she sank back as though the struggle had wearied her.

"That's better," the Frenchman muttered, busying himself with kissing her throat. "How I've longed for this . . ." he murmured, as his free hand pushed away her gown and his mouth moved over her shoulders and slid down to the dark valley between her breasts. "All the time . . . watching you on the stage while other men ogled you and desired you . . . knowing that you were going to be mine . . ."

Maud gritted her teeth and tried limply to push him away. The coach was going now at such a pace, that they were jostled on the leather seat, at times nearly falling to the floor. With his lips he pushed away the edge of her gown to grasp the exposed nipple of her breast, suckling it with delight. She fought down her revulsion by reminding herself that the longer he was distracted, the more chance they would have of getting away. When she felt the coach slowing to a stop, she deftly moved her leg so as to draw up the hem of her skirt. Prevaloir's free hand went instantly to her knee and slid up her thigh, as she heard a brief exchange of voices. She knew they must be at the St. Louis gate. If she could only keep the Frenchman occupied until they got through . . .

The coach rolled on, quickening its pace. Maud made up her mind that she would submit to his avid exploration until they were well away from the town, even if it meant letting him take her in the bouncing, rolling cab. They had only gone a mile or two further, however, when they hit a large rock in the road, and both of them were thrown on the floor of the coach. Prevaloir's hand fell from her mouth, and his attention was suddenly restored as he realized this was a dirt road and not a cobbled one.

Immediately he was at the window, throwing down the sash and leaning out to shout to the driver to stop. Maud shrank away and reached for the other door, ready to jump out as soon as the coach slowed. As the coach rolled to a stop, the Chevalier threw open the door and jumped out, looking angrily around at the dark field that stretched on either side of the road.

He stopped and looked up at the driver, his quick mind taking in the fact that all of a sudden nothing was what it should be. Surely these were not Claudette's servants.

On the other side of the coach, Maud saw Alan fasten the reins and climb down to face the Frenchman. "Well, well," Alan said, pushing back his cloak and throwing his hat up on the seat. "This is a fish I had not expected to net."

Maud walked around the back of the coach and stood watching the two men. When she felt a hand on her shoulder, she looked around to see Mimi standing beside her.

"Monsieur Jeremy took me up beside him," the girl whispered. Jeremy himself had stepped up near Alan, ready to help when needed.

For the first time Maud realized that Alan had shaved off his beard. Prevaloir, peering into his face, gave a sigh. "Desmond!" he spat out the word. "I might have known."

"The same," Alan answered, stepping close enough to the Frenchman to ball up his fist and knock him square in the mouth. De Prevaloir fell backward on the ground, struggled to sit up, and rubbed at his chin.

"That was for your despicable treatment of Maud," Alan snapped.

Prevaloir gave him a thin smile. "Fisticuffs. Just the kind of common weapon I would expect from a low-life actor!"

Alan thrust away his cloak, revealing a longsword at his side. Pulling the blade from its scabbard, he said: "Oh, I can fence, Monsieur, if you prefer the weapon of a gentleman."

Scrambling to his feet, Prevaloir drew his own sword with an easy flourish. "The word gentleman is highly inappropriate, yet it will give me great pleasure to kill you. You have interfered with my life enough."

"The interference has been all of your making, Monsieur. *En garde!*"

Alan lunged as the metal blades crossed with a loud clang. Maud shrank back against the coach, peering through the darkness to make out the dark forms of the men as they circled and lunged, circled and lunged. Then, in a series of clanging parries and attacks, they went at each other. Mimi hid her face in Maud's shoulder, while Jeremy reached down to pick up a stone and slip closer, ready to help in a very ungentlemanly way, if it looked as though Alan might lose.

The two men grunted with exertion as they flailed at each other. They were evenly matched, much to Prevaloir's surprise. With a series of circling motions, the two swords were forced points upward, as Alan pinned the Frenchman against the coach.

"Your stage fencing taught you well," Prevaloir hissed. "But you'll find this is not playacting."

"I learned to fence at the Royal Edinburgh School, Monsieur, not on a stage. And it is you who will feel the point of my blade."

"Bah!" the Chevalier exclaimed and shoved Alan

backward, whirling his blade at him. Nearly losing his footing, Alan stumbled, but managed to parry the flashing blade with his sword. Moving forward in a series of driving lunges, he forced Prevaloir backward, then drove the Frenchman's weapon away from his body, just long enough to thrust his own blade deep into an exposed shoulder.

With a grunt Prevaloir staggered backward, lowering his sword and gripping his shoulder, where blood oozed through his fingers. He sank to his knees on the ground, as Alan, still breathing heavily, calmly walked over to Mimi. "Give me one of your petticoats, girl," he snapped.

Mimi tore away the garment as Maud stared at the Frenchman. "Is he killed?" she breathed.

"No. Just wounded." Alan walked over to where Prevaloir had swooned, and began wrapping the petticoat tightly around the wound. Blood was everywhere, and it required a tight bandage to stem it.

Alan turned the Chevalier over, while Jeremy felt for a pulse in his throat. "He'll live," Alan said, throwing the Frenchman's cloak over his body. "He can walk back to the St. Louis gate and get help, once he's awake. By that time we should be halfway to Montreal."

He hurried the two women back into the coach, while he and Jeremy climbed to the driver's seat and started the horse off again. Maud barely noticed where they were going until she felt the carriage slow; opening a window, she saw that they were riding through a tiny, darkened village. Once it was behind, they followed a winding road that descended a long hill before leveling off beside the silver sheen of the river. Near a clump of trees, Alan stopped and helped the two women out, then, with a slap on the rump, sent the horse back up the road to the village, dragging the empty coach.

"The residents of Sillery can return Claudette's *cleche*," he muttered, as he led the two women to the water's edge, where Jeremy had already begun pulling a small skiff from underneath its hiding place of branches and dead limbs. The four of them climbed aboard and pushed off into the water.

"We caught the tide just right," Alan said, laying a hand on Maud's shoulder. "That was why we timed this as we did. I was afraid Prevaloir's unexpected presence might have delayed us."

They rowed for nearly a quarter of an hour, before drawing up beside a fishing boat moored in the middle of the river. As they climbed up a rope ladder to the deck, a young man in a fishing smock took Maud's hand to help her up.

"This is Pierre," Jeremy explained, as the young man pulled off his slouch hat and gave the women a short bow. "He's agreed to take us out of here."

"Merci, Pierre," Maud said, giving the young man her hand. Embarrassed, he bowed several more times.

"Je vous en prie, Madam."

"The pleasantries can wait," Alan said, as he hurriedly tied up the skiff. "We had better get underway, or we won't have the advantage of darkness when we pass Quebec."

"Quebec? But I thought we were going to Montreal."

Alan smiled at her over his shoulder, as he began helping Pierre and Jeremy with the halyards. "That was for Prevaloir's benefit, in case he was only pretending to be unconscious. No, if we can get safely by the French cannon on the Beauport shore, we'll be heading for the St. Lawrence Gulf."

The sail flapped open to the breeze, as Jeremy pulled up the anchor and the boat dipped leisurely with the tide, skimming along the silver river. Alan came to stand by Maud, his arm around her as they watched the dark shoreline slip by.

"I assumed we would be taking the river all the way down to the Hudson," she said, smiling up at him.

"No, I prefer the dangers of the open sea to running a gauntlet of Frenchmen. Besides, I have no longing ever to face Indians again. I might not be so lucky the next time."

"But how far can we get on the ocean, in a small boat like this?"

"Pierre has agreed to take us to Louisburg where, with any luck, we can get a ship for the Colonies. We're not out of the woods yet, though. Those cannons could blow us out of the water, if the Chevalier has raised the alarm."

It was soon apparent to Maud that Pierre knew the river like the back of his hand. He deftly maneuvered the fishing craft along the channel, moving leisurely below the dim lights of Quebec—which glimmered ominously in the darkness—passing under the noses of the French cantonment along the bluffs, and gliding on below the dark shadow of the Isle of Orleans . . .

She refused to leave the rail, watching and holding her breath as the little boat slipped along on the tide toward the northern reaches, taking on more sail as the wind increased. She hoped it looked like an innocent vessel making its way on the night tide toward a fishing excursion in the Gulf. However, if the Chevalier had made his way back to town, the soldiers on the bluff might be watching for any boat trying to leave Quebec . . .

She breathed a little easier when they slipped along without incident; soon they left Quebec with all its dangers far behind them. "Let's go below," Alan whispered breathily in her ear.

"Don't they need you here?"

"No. Jeremy and Pierre can handle the boat. I'd like a few moments alone with you."

She needed no further persuasion. Jeremy and Mimi sat close together in the bow, dark silhouettes against the night as they watched the shoreline slip by. Pierre was at the tiller, concentrating on the river. None of them noticed as Alan and Maud disappeared down the hatchway to a tiny cabin below. It was cluttered and smelled strongly of fish, yet neither one minded. The little room offered them their first moments of privacy since being reunited, and that was all that mattered.

Alan sank on the small bunk and pulled her down next to him. With his palms on either side of her face he kissed her long and lovingly, their tongues tasting each other's depths. Maud's arms went around him as they stretched out on the bunk, entwined together. She ran her hands along his cheek and neck, rejoicing in the feel of him, explored his chest, and down his waist. Her fingers traced the swelling mound below, the curve of his hip, his muscular thigh, and she rejoiced in the familiar feel.

Alan felt the curves and molds of her body in the same way, hardly able to believe she was really in his arms again. He threw back her cloak and loosened her gown, to lift her breast to his teasing lips. His hands sought her ankle and moved upward to the delicious curve of her legs, and then to cup her where he longed to go. With his finger he explored the moist depths, massaging and teasing until her whole body was a taut bowstring crying out for fulfillment. Only then did he turn to stretch above her, thrusting inside and muffling both their cries by burying his head against hers.

Afterwards Maud's pounding heart eased as she

clung to him, feeling that she had never known such complete joy.

Catching his fingers in her hair, Alan kissed the soft, sweet hollow of her neck.

"I never want to lose you again," he breathed. "We'll be married the moment we reach Louisburg."

Her body went stiff as a shadow fell across her happiness. She could never marry him. That decision, reached so long ago on the night he had revealed his true identity to her, was as relevant now as before. He needed a wife who was as wellborn and rich as he himself was; who came from the same class. It would only drag him down to marry someone like her.

"As long as we're together, that's all that matters," she said, not wanting to raise the spectre of an argument, when they were so happy to be with each other again.

Alan soon fell asleep in her arms. She held him, stroking his hair away from his brow, and watching as the light of dawn gradually began to seep through the chinks in the planking of the boat. It was not until the light had turned to bright day, that she acknowledged with a joyful heart that they were really free.

Chapter Twenty-four

A cold wind off the East River cut like a knife through the thin fabric of Maud's cloak. She pulled the hood close around her face against the biting wind, and slowed her steps so as not to allow her patterns to slip in the dirty slush of the walkway. This was her first winter in the Colonies, and already she knew it was not going to be like those she had known in England. The crisp air of autumn had turned the leaves to vivid colors, red, golds, greens, vermillions, like none she had seen before. Everything was more intense. A snowstorm in early December was mostly melted by now, except for the muddy stains along the walkways and hedges, but the cold had not diminished. It was more penetrating and longer-lasting than any English winter. At times she felt she would never be warm again.

But then, everything in this young, vibrant country was more intense. It was like a gangly youth, poised on the edge of bright adventure, full of bounce and energy, loud, boisterous, unsure of its destiny; one minute charming you with its humor and liveliness, the next, making you want to throw up your hands in despair. She loved it!

Seeing a break in the traffic of wagons and carts, she dashed across Dock Street to the other side, where the Cross and Crown Booksellers store beckoned. She stood looking through the panes at a display of goods fresh off the ship from London.

Charlotte Lennox's latest novel, bound in burgundy leather with gold edges, drew her like a magnet. There was a new history of the Roman empire, and a beautifully bound collection of new maps of North America. That should be interesting, she thought, having now traveled over so much of New England and New France herself.

For a moment she was transported back to the silver sweep of the St. Lawrence Gulf and the desolate town of Louisburg. The French stronghold had only recently fallen to the British, and its shattered buildings and blackened ruins gave mute evidence of the terrible bombardment and siege it had endured. She was not sorry when they found a ship bound for New York so quickly. Now she felt as though she had been around the world, even though she knew she had not.

The novel was tempting, until she looked inside her reticule and resigned herself to holding on to the coins she had. Their lives were too unsettled as yet to be spending money on anything but the basic necessities. Alan had insisted that they must be frugal, until he received a draft from his agent in Scotland. He only hoped that after all this time, he would not have to go back there to clear up his accounts and obtain the money that he knew was waiting.

The rooms they had rented in Frau Quaddman's house on Maiden Lane were comfortable but very plain, and only the fact that newlyweds, Jeremy and Mimi, lived across the hall made them bearable. Yet they would have to do, until Mister Bennett could organize a new theater and they could begin making a living again.

She pulled the cloak tighter around herself and smiled. What did she care for a few privations, when she had Alan so close? After believing him lost forever, it was heaven itself to walk into a room and see him look up from his chair, smiling at her, reaching out his arms to draw her into his lap. To lie in his arms on the corn-husk mattress was ecstasy, to feel his lips coursing her face, her breasts, her body . . . how could she ask for anything more? Marriage, perhaps, but that she still refused to consider. When Jeremy had insisted that he and Mimi be married by the ship's captain on the way to New York, Alan had begged her to make it a double wedding. Yet she still could not rid herself of the fear that by marrying her, he would someday rob himself of the chance to find a highborn, wealthy wife, who could give him boundless security and opportunities. She loved him too much to stand in the way of his advancement. Even though he argued that her reasons were absurd, she refused to give in.

The deep drone of a bell from Trinity steeple reminded her that she was late, and Alan would be wondering where she had gone. She yanked the strings of her purse shut and wrapped the cloak tighter, hurrying down the street. It might be cold, but her happiness made her warm within.

With her head bent against the wind, she did not see the man coming straight at her as she rounded the corner until she collided against him, knocking his thin, black-suited figure back against the wall.

"Oh, my dear sir . . . I'm so sorry . . ." she said, reaching to help him regain his footing on the muddy walkway.

"That's . . . perfectly all right . . . no bother . . ." the man muttered, straightening his hat and knocking the snow from his shoulders. He looked up to catch her eyes staring at him.

Maud gave a gasp. She felt the blood drain from her face, and her eyes grew round as she peered at the man, stepping back toward the street.

Both of them froze, their eyes locked. "Why, bless

my soul—" the man muttered.

"No!" Maud gasped and stumbled backward, nearly losing her footing. "No . . ."

She turned, darting into the street, heedless of the drays and shouting drivers, the startled horses that pulled up in their traces as she darted around them. Blindly she ran, hearing the cries of the man calling behind her to wait, not seeing or caring where she went, only that she melt away into the crowd. Down the street she darted, cutting through an alley and along another road, until she felt certain she was lost among the traffic and pedestrians. The wind and the cold were forgotten. Nothing else mattered but escape.

An hour later she finally made her way to the King's Arms Tavern, where she hoped Alan would still be waiting. The darkened tavern was warm inside, heavy with smoke and the rich, tempting odors of food and frothy beer.

She was relieved when she spotted Alan sitting in one of the booths, smoking a clay pipe and calmly reading a broadside by the light of a two-pronged candelabra. Slipping in opposite him, Maud tried to stop the shivering of her body, which she knew was not entirely from the cold.

He looked up from his paper, his eyes narrowing in concern. "Where have you been? I was beginning to think something had happened to you."

"Something has!"

"My dear," he said, reaching for her hands and rubbing them in his fingers. "You're frozen. And so pale you might have seen a ghost."

Maud gave him a thin smile. "I have seen a ghost. Oh, Alan . . ."

Her eyes filled with tears. He bent closer, speaking

low: "Not the Chevalier de Prevaloir?"

"No," she said, shaking her head. "Not him. Someone worse. Lawyer Ramsey!"

Alan laughed with relief. "You must be mistaken. Lawyer Ramsey, here in New York? It's impossible."

"It was him. He even recognized me. Oh, Alan, I know he's followed me here to take me back to Newgate Prison. That terrible brooch! I was never able to return it, and Lady Julia is just the kind of person who would pursue a vendetta to the ends of the earth. I just know she's sent him after me!"

"Calm down," he said, lifting her fingers to his lips. "That seems very unlikely."

"Could he do that? Could he arrest me here in America for something I'd done in England?"

Alan frowned. "Well, possibly he could. Living in the Colonies is almost the same as living in England. But I can hardly believe . . ."

"It's true. I know it's true."

"Here," he said, pushing his tankard of warm cider toward her. "Drink a little of this. It will help to calm you down, while we think of some way out of this."

"I want to go back to Frau Quaddman's. It's the only place I'll feel safe."

He forced her to take a few sips of the cider, then agreed that perhaps it would be best to go back to their rooms.

With a comforting arm around Maud's shoulders, Alan steered her to the entrance, where, behind a large oak bar with the cage raised, the barkeep waited to collect their payment. While Alan dealt with him, Maud stood near the door, hardly noticing when it opened and several people entered, stomping their boots on the sandy floor. Then she glanced up and gave a gasp.

"What the—" Alan exclaimed, as she darted behind him, trying to shield herself with his body.

"Maud Mellingham!" Lawyer Ramsey cried, running after her. "At last!"

"Alan . . . Help!" Maud said, cringing behind Alan's big body. He realized at once what was happening and stepped in front of the thin lawyer, blocking his way.

"Miss Mellingham has done nothing wrong. You have no right to badger her." He reached up to shove the man backward. "Leave her alone!"

"Badger her—" Ramsey said, stepping out of the way of Alan's long arm. "Leave her alone?"

"You can't arrest me," Maud cried, still keeping behind Alan. "I never took that brooch. Someone put it in my purse, and I had to sell it because I needed the money. But I never stole it, and you can't arrest me for it!"

"Arrest you? Why would I want to do that?"

"I didn't steal it . . ." Maud said, her voice rising in despair.

"Wait a moment," Alan said, taking her by the shoulders. "Just calm down, and we'll get this all straightened out." He turned to the lawyer, who had a comical look of disbelief on his narrow face. "You haven't followed Maud to New York to arrest her?"

"Dear me, no. Why would I do that? I've come to bring her something."

Alan looked from Ramsey to Maud and back again. "I think we had better sit down," he said at last.

The table near the window was more inviting than the dark booth had been. Light filtered through the beveled glass and was tinted pale green, like the sea on a bright day. It fell on the polished pine surface and gleamed there like burnished gold.

Maud took a seat across the table from Lawyer Ramsey. She was still not convinced that he was not going to arrest her, and carry her back to England as a felon in the hold of a ship. In fact, she half-believed his protestations of innocence were a trick, meant to get her off her guard. The man had been so thick with Squire Bexley and his horrible wife, that she did not see how anything else could have brought him so far or caused him to follow her so tenaciously.

"Now," Alan said, all businesslike. "What is this all about?"

Ramsey pulled out a sheaf of very legal-looking papers sealed with a huge blob of pale wax. "These are yours, Miss Mellingham. And a good deal of trouble I've gone to get them to you! You were not easy to find."

Maud stared at them as though they were a monster metamorphosing before her eyes. "I don't want them."

Reaching for the papers, Alan broke the seal and scanned the top one, then the others. "But—"

"Exactly," Ramsey said, sitting back in his chair and pulling on the tabs of his brown worsted waistcoat. "Lord Bambridge was most insistent. With his last breath, he made me swear that I would find Miss Mellingham no matter how long it took, or what means I must go to. He was so anxious, you see, to right the injustice he had done you."

"Lord Bambridge is dead?" Maud said, forgetting herself for the moment. "I'm so sorry," she murmured, remembering the old man's warm smile and sympathetic eyes. "But what injustice had he ever done me? He was always very kind to me."

"I think you'll find the answer here, my love," Alan said, looking at her strangely. "According to this document, he was your father!"

She stared at him. "My father? But that's impossible!"

"Not at all, my dear Maud," Ramsey broke in, in

his best legal voice. "Lord Bambridge was indeed your father. Of course, he was married at the time he lost his heart to the little governess his wife had hired to teach his daughters. She died when you were born and, to save any harm a scandal might cause his sickly wife, he had the Mellinghams bring you up. He made certain you were well cared for all the years you were growing up, but it was only as he was dying that his conscience overcame his scruples, and he charged me with telling you the truth."

"My father . . ." Maud whispered, calling up in her mind the image of the stocky, dignified old gentleman, who had always given her a kind word. And her mother, whom she had never known, was a governess, an educated lady. No wonder she had always had a more inquiring mind than the other servants.

"That's not all," Alan said with a smug smile. "It appears Lord Bambridge's conscience required him to leave you a legacy."

"That is correct," Ramsey broke in again, afraid Alan would break the news before he could. "Three hundred pounds per annum. That should go a long way toward mending any damage he might have done you."

Maud stared openmouthed. "Three hundred pounds! Why, that's a fortune! Alan, we're rich!"

Alan laughed. "Not rich, exactly, but certainly comfortable. I can't believe it. I've captured an heiress!"

Ramsey sat back in his chair and pulled a second envelope from his pocket. "I have the draft for the first year's legacy with me. Once it's delivered, I can return to England in peace. And none too soon, I confess. This traipsing around the world is too wearying for a man who prefers the quiet and contemplation of the Suffolk countryside."

Maud finally found her voice. "Not yet. Not before

I take a portion of that money and buy the finest brooch in all New York, for you to take back to Lady Julia!"

"To Maud Mellingham Makejoy, actress, heiress, and hostess *extraordinaire!*"

Alan lifted his glass in the air, while around the table Jeremy and Mimi rose to join him. Maud beamed at them. They were her best friends in all the world, and their toast was so sincere and loving it brought a lump to her throat.

"Thank you," she said, swallowing. "Thank you so much."

"It is we who should thank you for this excellent dinner," Jeremy said, as he resumed his seat. They were grouped around a circular oak table in the rose chamber of the King's Arms, enjoying their most sumptuous feast since leaving England. Maud had arranged it as a celebration for her good fortune, and had insisted that everything be first class, from the oysters and turtle soup that began the ten courses, to the custards and sweetmeats that ended them. The four different wines that accompanied the meal had also been chosen with care, and with no regard to expense. The food and drink were excellent, but the real pleasure was in the bountiful joy they all took in sharing Maud's sudden reversal of fortune. It warmed her heart, and more than once that evening, she said a silent prayer of thanks for having found such dear people. They were her family now, the family she had never had before.

"Of course," Alan said dryly, "after this meal, Maud may no longer be an heiress. It must have cost the earth."

"No matter," Maud said with a careless wave of her hand. "I shall probably never make so light with my purse again, but I felt it was appropriate this one time, considering all we've been through."

"What will you do next, Mam'zelle?" Mimi asked. Her round cheeks were pink from the wine, and her hand had seldom left her husband's during the meal. "Will you purchase a house here in New York, or go back to England?"

Maud smiled at Alan. "Oh, I think we'll stay in New York, don't you? England seemed inviting, until I realized that Lady Julia is actually my half-sister. The thought was horrible to me, but I imagine it would be even more horrible to her!"

Alan laid his arm around her shoulder and pulled her closer. "Before you even think of buying houses or gowns or anything else, there is something much more important which must be done first. Now that you are a rich, wellborn heiress, you no longer have any objection to marrying me. I would like the ceremony to be tomorrow morning."

Maud looked deeply into his eyes, struggling for the last time with her own demons. "Perhaps it is time," she said quietly. "Perhaps this is the best gift my father has given me." And it was true. Lord Bambridge had made it possible for her to bring more than her own poverty to Alan: a name, even if it was not legitimate, the heritage of a fine family, and a dowry. Little did Lord Bambridge realize when he dictated that letter, all he was giving her.

Alan reached over and kissed her lips, still as warm and inviting to him as they had been that first day in his London rooms. " *'And I yield my body as your prisoner,'* " he murmured, and felt the shudder course through her slim body.

She laid the palm of her hand on his long cheek. "That's Congreve," she said lightly. *"Love for Love.* And I never got to play Angelica!"

"You will. When I build my permanent theater here in New York, you shall play all the great roles."

"Oh, I don't think so," she said lightly. "I think I would prefer to stay at home, entertain the De Lanceys and the Clintons and the other society ladies of New York, and raise six plump, beautiful, happy children."

Alan's cheeks paled. "Six! My God, woman, you aren't that rich!"

"Wealth does not always mean material possessions."

"Ahem," Jeremy said, coughing discreetly. "Come, Mimi, my little French dove. I think perhaps it is time to leave these two alone. Besides," he added, draping an arm around the girl's shoulders and smiling down into her adoring face. "We've been too long from our own pleasures. Good night, my friends. Thank you for the wonderful dinner."

Maud and Alan were barely aware that they had gone. She leaned to meet his embrace, and kissed him with all the fervor of her overflowing heart. When it was over, he ran his finger lightly down her cheek. "I love you, Maud Mellingham Makejoy, soon-to-be Sinclair," Alan whispered.

"Just Maud Sinclair," she whispered back against his cheek. "I think we shall return Maud Makejoy to King Edward's account books, with my heartfelt thanks. That's no name for a respectable married lady."

Alan smiled into her warm, glowing eyes. "As long as Mrs. Sinclair can still be Maud Makejoy for me on those occasions when I need her."

Maud gave a low, sultry laugh and yielded to his enfolding arms. "Always, my love. Always!"

WAITING FOR A WONDERFUL ROMANCE?
READ ZEBRA'S
WANDA OWEN!

DECEPTIVE DESIRES (2887, $4.50/$5.50)
Exquisite Tiffany Renaud loved her life as the only daughter of a wealthy Parisian industrialist. The last thing she wanted was to cross the ocean on a cramped and stuffy ship just to visit the uncivilized wilds of America. Then she shared a kiss with shipping magnate Chad Morrow that made the sails billow and the deck spin. . .

KISS OF FIRE (3091, $4.50/$5.50)
Born and raised in backwoods Virginia, Tawny Blair knew that her dream of being swept off her feet by a handsome nobleman would never come true. But when she met Lord Bart, Tawny saw at once that reality could far surpass her fantasies. And when he took her in his strong arms, she thrilled to the desire in his searing caresses . . .

SAVAGE FURY (2676, $3.95/$4.95)
Lovely Gillian Browne was secure in her quiet world on a remote ranch in Arizona, yet she longed for romance and excitement. Her girlish fantasies did not prepare her for the strange new feelings that assaulted her when dashing Irish sea captain Steve Lafferty entered her life . . .

TEMPTING TEXAS TREASURE (3312, $4.50/$5.50)
Mexican beauty Karita Montera aroused a fever of desire in every redblooded man in the wild Texas Blacklands. But the sensuous señorita had eyes only for Vincent Navarro, the wealthy cattle rancher she'd adored since childhood—and her family's sworn enemy! His first searing caress ignited her white-hot need and soon Karita burned to surrender to her own wanton passion . . .

Available wherever paperbacks are sold, or order direct from the Publisher. Send cover price plus 50¢ per copy for mailing and handling to Zebra Books, Dept. 4155, 475 Park Avenue South, New York, N.Y. 10016. Residents of New York and Tennessee must include sales tax. DO NOT SEND CASH. For a free Zebra/Pinnacle catalog please write to the above address.

PASSIONATE NIGHTS FROM
PENELOPE NERI

DESERT CAPTIVE (2447, $3.95/$4.95)
Kidnapped from her French Foreign Legion escort, indignant Alexandria had every reason to despise her nomad prince captor. But as they traveled to his isolated mountain kingdom, she found her hate melting into desire . . .

FOREVER AND BEYOND (3115, $4.95/$5.95)
Haunted by dreams of an Indian warrior, Kelly found his touch more than intimate — it was oddly familiar. He seemed to be calling her back to another time, to a place where they would find love again . . .

FOREVER IN HIS ARMS (3385, $4.95/$5.95)
Whispers of war between the North and South were riding the wind the summer Jenny Delaney fell in love with Tyler Mackenzie. Time was fast running out for secret trysts and lovers' dreams, and she would have to choose between the life she held so dear and the man whose passion made her burn as brightly as the evening star . . .

MIDNIGHT CAPTIVE (2593, $3.95/$4.95)
After a poor, ragged girlhood with her gypsy kinfolk, Krissoula knew that all she wanted from life was her share of riches. There was only one way for the penniless temptress to earn a cent: fake interest in a man, drug him, and pocket everything he had! Then the seductress met dashing Esteban and unquenchable passion seared her soul . . .

SEA JEWEL (3013, $4.50/$5.50)
Hot-tempered Alaric had long planned the humiliation of Freya, the daughter of the most hated foe. He'd make the wench from across the ocean his lowly bedchamber slave — but he never suspected she would become the mistress of his heart, his treasured sea jewel . . .

Available wherever paperbacks are sold, or order direct from the Publisher. Send cover price plus 50¢ per copy for mailing and handling to Zebra Books, Dept. 4155, 475 Park Avenue South, New York, N.Y. 10016. Residents of New York and Tennessee must include sales tax. DO NOT SEND CASH. For a free Zebra/ Pinnacle catalog please write to the above address.